SEARCH ANGEL

ALSO BY MARK NYKANEN:

Hush
The Bone Parade

SEARCH ANGEL

—— A NOVEL ——

Mark Nykanen

HYPERION NEW YORK

To the memory of my grandmother, Lillian Coyne

Copyright © 2005 Mark Nykanen

Library of Congress Cataloging-in-Publication Data

Nykanen, Mark.
  Search angel : a novel / Mark Nykanen.—1st ed.
    p.   cm.
  ISBN 1-4013-0019-7
    1. Adoptees—Crimes against—Fiction.   2. Birthmothers—Crimes against—Fiction.   3.
  Women detectives—Fiction.   4. Psychopaths—Fiction.   5. Psychological fiction. lcsh   I. Title.

PS3564.Y52S43 2005
813'.54—dc22

                                                                                        2004059773

Hyperion books are available for special promotions and premiums. For details contact Michael Rentas, Assistant Director, Inventory Operations, Hyperion, 77 West 66th Street, 11th Floor, New York, New York 10023, or call 212-456-0133.

FIRST EDITION

10 9 8 7 6 5 4 3 2 1

PROLOGUE

PAUL SIMON'S SONG is in my head. The one about the mother and child reunion. Nothing new in that. I could probably sing it in my sleep. In fact, I probably have.

It's a beautiful day. They were calling for rain, but there's not a cloud in the sky. There'll be plenty of rain soon enough. It's already October. I tracked Katie down in August, but it took me a while to work all this out. When I first came up here, the lawns and trees were green. Now I'm looking at leaves as big as my hands all over the sidewalk.

She lives on a pretty street. It could have come straight out of a Frank Capra film. There's actually a white picket fence on my left. Not hers, but it's nice anyway, and I can't help running my hand over it.

In some ways I feel I already know Katie Wilkins. I've seen her from a distance, and even photographed her with a telephoto lens. I'm good at the sneaky shot. And she's a great subject, really cute. Everything about her is cute: her hair, figure, clothes. She's cute like Katie Couric's cute. The same kind of look. It's easy to see why this Katie got "in trouble" in her teens. Why she could still get in trouble.

I've done my homework on her. She's single, no kids, lives alone. It's better this way, for her and for me. There's not going to be some husband standing there all bug-eyed, or kids asking a bunch of stupid questions.

When I spot the house, the one I've driven past nine times, it's all I can do to keep from running up and pounding on the door. That's what anticipation does to you. It builds and builds and builds until it's ready to explode.

But I'm not going to make a spectacle of myself. The neighborhood's too quiet. I've walked three blocks from my car and hardly seen anyone. Not a single kid. She sure hasn't surrounded herself with what she never wanted.

I can't help wondering if she's going to see herself when she sees me. The same nose, maybe? Or mouth, eyes? Her own reflection in my features? It's not unusual for birth mothers to notice this stuff right away.

Three steps up and I'm on the porch. The doorbell sounds unfriendly, shrill, as if it can't decide if it's a bell or a buzzer.

She opens the door. This is the moment, the one I've been waiting for.

"Hi, Mom." I let those two words linger as her brow knits a thousand questions. Then, with her lips quivering and threatening to slice the silence, I say, "I'm your son."

"I don't have a son."

Her immediate denial makes her look ugly. A better man, a less bitter one, might feel devastated; but I've searched and planned and rehearsed this over and over, and I'm not going to be denied.

I force a smile, and my words come more easily than I might have imagined.

"Yes, you do. You had me thirty-two years ago at St. Vincent's in Cincinnati."

She all but doubles over, her hands gripping her gut. It's as if the memory of labor is ripping her apart. She knows she's not lying her way out of this one.

I've got the details. She may have lied to lovers, to the husband she had for three years, but she can't lie to me.

"Look, I know it's a shock, but I had to see you. I had to. It's nothing to be ashamed of, and I haven't told anyone anything about you. If you want, I'll go away and never come back. You'll never have to see me again."

She shakes her head, a little less uncertain.

"No, come in. Come in."

She closes the door behind me and raises a hand as fluttery as the notes of a flute. It takes me a second to see that she's gesturing to a sofa where she wants me to sit. But I don't want to sit down. She's the one who sits, flattening her pants with her palms as if she's straightening the memory of a skirt.

"I knew this would happen one day. How did you find me?"

"I followed my heart," I tell her, "and it led me here."

She starts to cry. I hear the word *sorry*, then "I'm so sorry." She says something else, too, but I can't make it out.

I use the breakdown to put my arms around her and raise her to her feet. She reaches up to be hugged, comforted. I indulge her for a few seconds before I begin to lead her to the back of the house.

We take only three short steps before she freezes.

"What are you doing?" That look is back, the one she gave me when she tried to deny her own motherhood.

"I'm taking you back there so you can lie down."

"I don't want to lie down." Her eyes narrow and dart to the front door, and I wonder if she's going to try to run.

"Sure you do. It's okay. Relax a little."

I reach into my jacket and show her the knife. I let her see it up close. I tell her not to say a word, not even to think about screaming. Or running. The blade speaks, too. Volumes. It has the shape of a wiggling snake. It's like a dagger out of *The Arabian Nights*. Form does follow function, especially in matters of the flesh.

I nick one of her belt loops. Just that quick it's in two, the ends sprouting loose threads. I nick another one. Her eyes are plenty wide now. She backs against the wall. Here comes the best part. I bring the blade down the front of her blouse, popping buttons off like grapes. They clatter on the tile. They sound loud to me, but I bet they sound even louder to her.

She's trembling. "Who are you?"

I shake my head. "You tried to deny me once before, Mom. Don't do it again. That hurts."

I point my blade down the hall. She backs along the wall, afraid to look away. That's okay, I like the eye contact when I remind her of the details: "St. Vincent's, the fifteenth of May. Ten-twenty in the morning. Eight and a half hours of labor."

She begins to sob. She's a slave to memory. Aren't we all?

The first door opens to her bedroom. I herd her inside and tell her to take off her clothes. When she starts to say no, I slice open the front of her pants. I can see her white underpants, white like her skin, the secret skin that hides her womb. Then I see a little button of blood. I've nicked her. Didn't mean to, but the effect, if nothing else, is undeniable. She disrobes, defeated. She discards her clothes as if they no longer belong to her.

I take mine off, too, but fold them carefully and lay them on a dressing table. You could look at her clothes and mine, and they'd tell you the whole story. They'd even tell you the ending.

She weeps and shakes and tries to pull her hand away, but I'm very persuasive, and I've had lots of practice. Lots of mothers. I adopt a new one whenever I feel the urge. And I'm feeling it right now. I've felt it for months, ever since I saw Katie's name on the registry of birth mothers. Katie Wilkins: Does a name get any more American than that? Then I saw her picture, and I knew she'd like nothing more than to meet me. They always want to meet their son.

Sometimes my moms shower me with kisses. Sometimes they deny that

I ever existed. And sometimes they cry. But they always end up doing exactly what I want them to do. Just like Katie.

She's getting better at taking instructions, even in this, the most intimate of arts.

I whisper in her ear. I tell her I've missed her, missed her more than she'll ever know. But she doesn't respond, and I realize she can't talk. She is, to put it simply, insane in these her final moments. It's like nothing belongs to her.

Nothing does. Not anymore. Not even her son.

1

A BED OF NETTLES, this business of telling secrets, and Suzanne found herself tossing and turning on it as they began their approach to Chicago. The landing gear lowered, and she realized the shudder that radiated from the wings to her window seat could just as easily have arisen from her body: She was on the verge of making the most painful confession of her life to the biggest and most important audience she was ever likely to face.

She spotted the blue-capped, blank-faced chauffeur with the "Suzanne Trayle" sign standing just outside the security checkpoint and had to fight an impulse to walk right past him to the nearest ticket counter for a return flight home to Oregon. She'd come to Chi-town to give the keynote address to the annual conference of the American Adoption Congress, but after reviewing her speech for the umpteenth time on the plane, she felt as keyed up as a long-suffering understudy about to take the stage for her first real performance.

The convention organizer had told her that they wanted her to speak about opening adoption records. Suzanne had been so flattered—and had agreed so quickly—that the personal implications hadn't been immediately apparent: How can you talk about opening adoption records if you're not willing to be open yourself?

So she'd resolved to come out of adoption's darkest closet, a decision that had been much easier to reach when she was still about two thousand miles from the podium. As she wound down the Chicago lakefront, peering through the smoky windows of a limousine at the whitecaps surging to the shore, her uneasiness prompted assurances that by nine o'clock it would all be over; but then she recalled how many times she'd used this tired—and ineffective— gambit to try to weasel her way through a pending crisis.

And it's not going to be *over*. Don't kid yourself. It'll just be starting.

Red, white, and blue pennants snapped in the breeze as they pulled up to the City Center Complex, an unimaginative name for an uninspired-looking convention hall and hotel.

The driver hustled around the stretch to get her door, and she managed a smile as she remembered a famous photographer saying that the outdoors was what you had to pass through to get from your cab to your hotel. But these were tonier times for Suzanne, and the cab had turned into a limo.

Before she made it to the reception desk, a short man with freckles all over his bald head intercepted her.

"I'm Douglas Jenks, and I'm *so* glad to see you." His smile burned as bright as those spots on his polished pate.

"It's good to meet you, too."

The convention organizer. She shook his hand, as cool and limp as raw salmon—and so at odds with his animated face—and thanked him for the invitation.

"No, don't thank me. Do *not* thank us for one second. We want to thank *you* for coming. This is so great having you here. And the timing with that story in *People*? It couldn't have been better. Like you planned it. The—"

"I didn't, really."

He went on undeterred. "... ballroom is absolutely packed. We're sold out, *and* we've had to clear out some chairs in the back so we can make room for the overflow. Lots of TV, too," he added with even more delight.

Suzanne barely had time to consider the gratifying—and intimidating— size of the audience before he was reminding her of his invitation to join him for dinner.

"I'm so sorry," she said. "I can't. I have to beg off. I really need some time to get ready." The truth? She didn't think she could hold down dinner.

"Okay," he said slowly, drawing out both syllables skeptically. "Well, we do want you at your best. You're feeling all right, aren't you?" He frowned, and in an instant fleshy cornrows traveled up his brow and the front half of his spotted scalp.

"I'm fine. Don't worry." Suzanne touched his arm reassuringly. "I just need to get settled from the plane ride."

She edged toward the reception desk and handed a credit card to the young man waiting to check her in. The Congress was hosting her, but there were always incidentals to pay for.

"All right. Come down when you're ready. We'll be waiting. Ciao-ciao."

As he turned away she had to stifle a laugh because with that silly goodbye, and his orange spots, he suddenly reminded her of Morris the cat in those old commercials.

She just managed to bite her lip—pain the moment's preferred antidote— when he executed a spirited and surprisingly graceful spin to wheel back around.

"Sorry, almost forgot." He dug through a three-ring binder and pulled out a note. "A distinguished-looking man with silver hair gave me this earlier and asked me to give it to you."

One glimpse at the crisp penmanship confirmed that it was, indeed, from Burton. But distinguished-looking? Silver hair? She'd always thought of it as gray. He'd made her husband sound like a Supreme Court Justice, which he definitely wasn't. Not yet anyway. Try administrative law judge for the Oregon Construction Contractors Board. He'd applied for a circuit court judge pro tem position, but was still waiting for the governor to promote him to the bench. Despite his steroidal ambition with the gavel—or maybe, now that she thought of it, *because* of it—His Honor had suffered a serious lapse in judgment in following her here. Hardly the first such lapse, and far from the worst, but can't an estranged husband stay estranged? At least for a while?

The note proved blessedly brief: "Good luck, sweetheart. I'm with you."

But not brief enough to keep her from seeing that he could have chosen his words more carefully, too, made them less susceptible to sarcasm. *I'm with you.* Where were you a few months ago? And where are you now?

A quick, furtive look around the lobby assured her that he wasn't haunting its remote corners. Thank God for small favors.

She took the key card from the receptionist and handed it to the bellman.

They stepped off the elevator on the sixteenth floor, and she trailed him to a plummy suite with a large bedroom. Nice. The Congress was treating her well.

She heard the bellman opening the drapes and turned to take in a view of Lake Michigan as wide as the horizon itself.

Two weeks ago clocks were set back an hour, and though it was still early evening, the blackening sky, with its gray filaments of cloud, looked like an eerie reflection of the dark, windswept water.

A chill prickled her arms, and as she rubbed them, the bellman, more alert than most, pointed out the thermostat. He turned it up, and as he left she handed him a five.

She unzipped her laptop case and reviewed her speech, double-checking the most painfully revealing lines.

The words she'd written over the past few weeks left her stomach feeling as if she'd never left the elevator, and more glad than ever that she'd declined the invitation to dinner. Hardly tempted in any case by the morel-stuffed mahi-mahi that was, at this very moment, taking its final bow on terra firma.

The bellman had hung her garment bag in a closet with a full-length mirror on the door. After slipping on a cerulean blue dress that highlighted her eyes, she gave herself a once-over, fluffed her honey-colored hair, which promptly deflated in palpable protest, and called it good.

Not quite. In deference to the harsh lights that seemed to bear down on every podium she'd ever commanded, she reluctantly applied mascara, lip gloss, and enough blush to enliven her pallid Portland complexion. About as much as she'd concede to the dogs of demeanor. But she'd learned the hard way that when you went before your public, you really did ignore your appearance at your own peril. That hideous photograph of her in *People*? Taken at a speech she'd given in Orlando two months ago. All the proof—and impetus— she'd ever need to primp.

She returned to her laptop, checking the time on the screen. Fifteen minutes and counting. One more look at the speech, even though she'd committed every last pause to memory.

Second thoughts? "Try third and fourth ones, too," she murmured. *But you're not turning back now.*

The title sounded simple enough, "Opening Records in the Era of Open Adoption," but simplicity in all guises is pure deception—ask any magician worth his wand—and this surely proved true in the scroll of words her eyes now scanned.

Minutes later she made the trip back down the elevator and glanced in the ballroom as she headed to the backstage entrance. Packed! Camera crews choked the aisles, including one from *60 Minutes* and another from *Dateline NBC*. Both shows had been hounding her for interviews. Ed Bradley himself had called, not some assistant to the assistant producer. She'd liked his manner on the phone, very smooth, yet chummy, but supposed that every reporter had learned to give good phone, a skill as necessary to their success as it was to the practitioners of another, more bluntly seductive art. He was so good she'd almost asked him what he was wearing.

All the attention was a sign, she supposed, that she was truly emerging into national prominence and mainstream interest, coming as it did only three weeks after that cover story in *People*. The headline? "The Orphans' Private Eye," a gussied-up way of overstating the humdrum nature of her work, which typically entailed hours of web searches and visits to the dustiest removes of distant libraries. She had allowed to the reporter that occasionally she did the work of an actual gumshoe—surveillance, interviews, impersonation—and evidently that had been enough to earn her the colorful sobriquet. But danger, the kind often associated with PIs? Not a bit. Her world was no more noirish than a cheese blintz.

The initial blip of publicity had occurred two years ago right here in Chicago when she'd appeared on *Oprah*; but she'd shared that hour with birth mothers and their children and had been featured only briefly, which had been fine with her. But *60 Minutes, People, Dateline NBC*? This was a whole new level of fame, and she wasn't sure it was good for the open adoption movement to be wedded so closely to one person, even if that person happened to be her.

"Like I said, SRO," the conference organizer startled her as she sat backstage. "They're standing all the way clear to the back of the ballroom."

"Great." But her stomach swirled even more over the great number of ears that would soon be listening.

She parted the curtain to take a peek and picked out Burton in less than five seconds. Sitting erect, as if still in his hearing room. Red regimental tie. Bold for Burton. (Never "Burt," unless she wanted to goad him. Sometimes "Burty-boy" in bed, but that seemed like a long time ago.)

At the table right behind him sat Ami, French for dear friend, which surely she was, in addition to having become her trusted assistant.

The spry young woman had knocked on Suzanne's door when she was nineteen and in need of help searching for her mother. She'd been a student with no money, save the dribble of student loans on which she subsisted. But she'd insisted on paying for the search by helping out in the office.

They'd found her mother seven months later, homeless and strung out on meth near the docks of Port Angeles, Washington. Bunny was one of the lucky ones—the meth had broken her spirit, but not her mind. Not yet. Still one day at a time for her. Always would be. She huddled next to her daughter, their shoulders almost touching as they finished dinner.

Ami had never stopped helping out in the office. She now had her master's in social work and had become indispensable and irreplaceable to Suzanne, which was a whole lot more than could be said for Administrative Law Judge Burton Trayle.

The chandeliers dimmed, and even the clatter of plates and utensils softened, as if the light switch controlled the ambient noise level, too.

"We have with us this evening as our keynote speaker a woman all of you know."

The curtain had opened, and the conference chair, an older woman as elegant and sparkling as a formal gown, was speaking from the podium.

"Many of you have met Suzanne Trayle in person. Some of you owe your reunions to her perseverance, and all of you have seen her on television and read the wonderful stories that have been written about her . . ."

Applause interrupted the chair, and she stepped back to let it build.

"Thank you. I'm sure Suzanne appreciates that. No one has done more to bring the emotionally charged issues of adoption into the mainstream of American attention, because Suzanne is not just a first-rate search angel, she's a powerful advocate for opening adoption records."

Amid the cheers, Suzanne heard Burton's telltale whistle, odd in a man otherwise so mannered. It was an ear-splitting screech that would have startled even the stream of scam artists and miscreants who flowed through his courtroom, had he ever been taken with an uncontrollable urge to issue it in such a staid setting.

"As many of you know," the chair said in a clear voice that rose above the fading clamor, "Suzanne's searches have resulted in more than a thousand reunions between birth mothers and adoptees, and she found all of them in the past decade alone."

This too brought expected applause, though thankfully not another of Burton's whistles.

"Tonight we're here to listen to Suzanne's wise words, but first let's honor her great success by giving this most amazing search angel the reception she so richly deserves."

They rose to their feet as Suzanne approached the podium. She received the light embrace of the chairwoman, and placed her laptop on a table to her right. Tonight it would prove more prop than tool.

She looked up with a smile that granted breadth to her oval face, crinkling her high forehead and cracking, as genuine smiles will, the shell that people wear.

Suzanne gestured for them to sit, saying, "Please, you're embarrassing me. Down—down."

When they were seated she looked at them slyly, arched her eyebrows, and said, "Aren't we the lucky ones? As adoptees, we can't get arrested for marrying our first cousins. We can't even get arrested for marrying our sister or brother, for that matter."

The audience hooted. They understood, as a casual observer might not, that Suzanne was playing to the fear that so many of them had suffered when they'd selected a mate: Was their intended related? Was a blood link hiding in the secrecy of conception?

She recognized the generosity of the laughter and was a savvy enough speaker to not let it linger. She was in performance mode, and even the concerns she'd had over the most revealing parts of her speech had receded, as tides often do before a flood.

"The other day I read that the biggest problem with being an adoptee is that it's like showing up for a mystery movie five minutes late."

More knowing laughter.

"But it's getting easier to figure out the beginning of each of our movies, isn't it? Not easy, mind you, but eas*ier*. County and state records are going on-line. The same is true for newspapers. Hospitals are getting better about responding to e-mail," she said as she removed a disk from her laptop. "It's not like the old days when we'd have to write them and plead and wait . . . and wait. Remember that?"

A collective groan assured her that they did.

"We can go online and do a lot of our work with the help of a simple disk. Not sexy. Not a lot of sizzle, but it works." She held up the one she'd just taken out of her computer. "This contains most of my records. I leave a backup at home and work on the road. Every one of you can do the same thing. I urge you to attend my workshop tomorrow, 'Seeking Love, Finding the Link,' because that's what it's all about. I urge you to put me out of business because . . ."—and here she paused long enough to hear a single utensil slip to a plate—"when I'm no longer in business, that'll mean the closed adoption system, with all its secret records, has closed down for good. That'll mean it's dead, which is the destiny it deserves."

This line was intended to rouse them, and it didn't disappoint. When the wave of approbation finally broke, Suzanne placed the disk aside and offered updates on the states that had moved toward opening adoption records, where adult adoptees could determine the identity of their birth parents. But she pointedly reminded her audience that it was still far simpler to list the few states where records were open and available to them than it was to run down all the states that continued to stonewall adoptees, treating them as wards who had to be protected from the most basic of all truths—their birth.

She paused to take a sip of water, then looked out at the crowd.

"But tonight I want to talk to you about a deeply personal matter that I've avoided for a long time. It's a subject I couldn't bring myself to talk about until recently."

Her eyes took in Burton, who sat forward, looking worried, and Ami, who nodded at her with a wariness Suzanne had never before seen in her assistant.

"As many of you know, I'm an adoptee. I was left on the steps of a firehouse in Los Angeles on January 16, 1958. I was only a few hours old. No note. No apologies. No clues. Only a thin white blanket and the cardboard box I was left in.

"The State of California assumed custody of me, and I lived in a state-run orphanage for the next five months until I was adopted by my absolutely wonderful parents. I'm as indebted to them as I am to life itself.

"These facts are all public, but my life hasn't been the open book I've pretended it to be. I've kept one chapter tightly sealed for all these years: I'm not just an adoptee, I'm also a birth mother."

Ami looked up, no longer wary but startled; Burton raised his hand to his chin. He knew this, of course, and all the facts that followed.

"At age fourteen—yes, fourteen—I became pregnant with my son. Like so many other young women adoptees, I'd sought the only connection I could to my lost and presumably 'loose' birth mother. It wasn't a conscious decision— nothing of that nature is ever conscious at that age—but the desire for a connection to my birth mother was real, and no matter how pathetic it seems now, it resulted in the beautiful baby boy I had thirty-two years ago when I was still a child myself.

"I gave my son to the closed adoption system, and in one way or another I've been searching for him ever since."

Her throat thickened, and she heard a chair move, bodies shift positions, and noticed how intently her audience was staring at her.

"I gave up my son because I was told that having a baby out of wedlock would violate every sense of common decency. In other words, I was shamed into giving up my son. Shamed. I was told, in effect, that I could keep my baby and raise him in shame, or I could give him up and give us both a good life.

"Giving up my baby to the closed adoption system did not give me a good life. It's given me countless hours of agony; and as an adoptee who's never known her own mother, I can't believe my son is better off for not knowing me."

She gripped the sides of the podium.

" 'Give up your baby, or live in shame.' Up until about twenty years ago, when the open adoption movement began to take hold, that's what most birth mothers were forced to hear. And let's not overlook the unpleasant but very real fact that in spite of these gains, it still goes on: Every year thousands of young women in this country sign over their babies to the closed adoption system. But great progress *has* been made: More than half of all adoptions in the United States are now open, so those children will always know who their birth parents are, and their birth parents will always know who's raising them. This is a healthy and critical development, but what about the millions of birth mothers who gave up their babies in the 1950s, 1960s, and 1970s? And what about their children, now in their thirties, forties, and fifties?

"These are the adult adoptees who are still denied access to their birth records in most states; and not a single state permits a birth parent to see her child's amended birth certificate, which contains the names of the adoptive parents. They're completely shut out by a system that thrives on secrecy and lies."

She took another sip of water and noticed her hand trembling as she placed the glass back on the podium.

"These people are desperate. I see this every day: middle-aged adoptees trying to find medical information about their birth parents because of a health crisis in their own lives or in the lives of their children. I see birth mothers fighting terminal cancer *and* an insidious system that won't let them see their son or daughter before they die.

"People ask me all the time why I do this kind of work. That's why. I want basic human rights for *all* adoptees and birth parents, not just for those lucky enough to have experienced open adoption in the past twenty years."

She took a deep, deep breath.

"The birth mothers, frankly, tear my heart out. After listening to literally thousands of their stories, I'm convinced that most of them were coerced into giving up their children. They were treated like social lepers, removed from their towns and cities and placed in homes for unwed mothers. Their mail and visitor lists were closely monitored to leave little chance that a prospective father would propose marriage—and deprive one of these money mills of a profitable baby.

"Many of these birth mothers signed adoption papers while heavily drugged, or during the most grueling moments of labor. Can you imagine that? Signing adoption papers during *labor*? It happened time and again.

"Others were threatened that if they changed their mind and wanted to keep their baby they'd have to pay all the hospital costs, doctors' bills, lawyers' fees, even their room and board at the 'homes' where they were held as virtual prisoners.

"I know. I endured some of that abuse myself and lived in shame for many years."

Her head shook slightly, anger and anguish mingled as sand, and then she paused—she had to for fear of breaking into tears—and was stunned by the absence of any response other than those intently staring eyes. She was an experienced speaker and could usually read a crowd, but now she sensed nothing. It was as if the walls themselves had absorbed every emotion in the room save hers. Then she wondered if what she really felt was the crowd's barely subdued anger: Did they feel betrayed by her many years of silence, by finding out that she wasn't the woman she'd claimed to be?

Turning from the microphone, she tried to clear her throat discreetly; but discretion's not possible when the attention of a crowd is pinned on you as unblinkingly as a spotlight.

"This is very difficult for me, as you can probably tell, but it's important to address this issue. Even though the hour is late for my saying this, we must choose to live openly. But to live openly we must open all birth records to adoptees and their birth parents, as they did long ago in England, Scotland, Germany, Israel, Mexico, and in many other countries as well.

"But not here. Not in America. We may even be regressing. There's now an attempt to criminalize the work I do, and the work that all of you do when you search for your child or birth parents. This abominable legislation would seal birth records for ninety-nine years, and if we violated its most dreadful provisions, we could go to prison.

"I'm going to vow to you right now that I *will* go to prison before I'll stop searching on behalf of adoptees. And I'll go to prison before I'll stop searching on behalf of birth mothers. I'll go to prison before I'll ever bow to a system still determined to shame so many women who gave up their babies for the lie of a good life."

Though her resolve made her appear calmer, she felt shaky, very shaky, and told herself that in another minute it would all be over. She was now willing to believe any bromide that would help her survive this speech; her stomach was swirling, and her palms were as cold and damp as dead leaves.

She leaned closer to the microphone and spoke her last words clearly: "We must end the secrecy, the scars, and all the shame. We must demand not only open adoption, but the opening of all birth records to adoptees and birth parents. And we must demand this . . . *now!*"

Silence followed her like a shadow as she stepped away from the podium. Not a single clap. A camera light blinked off. Then another, darkness as disappointment. She felt a gathering anger creeping closer. They must feel betrayed, that had to be it. But shouldn't they understand? Then a hand struck a hand, and another pair joined in, and the applause built in seconds into an explosion of sound that rocked the room, and finally drained the grief that had been hiding in her eyes for years.

2

I DON'T LIKE PUNS. As amusements go, I'd rank them just above a deep incision and two degrees south of a family dinner. But I couldn't help thinking that I'd hit the mother lode the night I saw Suzanne Trayle speak.

There she was, the most celebrated search angel of all, pulling a disk out of her laptop and telling us she had all her records right on that disk.

I realized right away that if I could get my hands on it I'd have the names, addresses, and maybe even the most intimate details of hundreds of birth mothers. I'd be able to pick and choose my moms without having to bother with the tedious research. I'd know who was married, who had kids, and most important of all, who lived alone (in all that shame Ms. Trayle was so worked up about).

So right from the start I knew what I'd do: I'd copy the disk and return it to her. And then, when the timing was absolutely perfect, I'd let her know that someone had it. Telling her would be the heart of my plan.

But to get the disk, I'd have to get into her room. I've gotten into hotel rooms before, but never in a place with electronic locks. But there's always a weakness in a system. It's true of people, and it's true of hotels. I started looking where I always look first, at the bottom of the food chain. At the City Center Complex, that was the housekeeping staff. You can count on any hotel to provide two things: a bed, and maids who are paid next to nothing.

The next morning, the second day of the conference, I was haunting the hallway when María Alvarez pushed her cleaning cart up to Room 1633 and knocked. No answer. I didn't think there would be because Ms. Trayle had gone to breakfast, and I could still see her at a table down in the atrium talking to some of the other people attending the conference. When María used her passkey, I made my move.

I had no hope of finding Ms. Trayle's laptop in her room. She had it with her. But that wasn't my purpose in slipping in behind the maid. I wanted to compromise her, and I've studied human nature long enough to know that you've got to do this in steps. The first one cost me a hundred dollars, all twenties, all for María. I'd come prepared.

"I just want to look around," I said. "That's all. Police business."

She looked scared, but she took the money. I don't think she believed me for one second, but she believed in the currency of Los Estados Unidos and stuffed it into her pocket.

I did look around, but, again, this wasn't my purpose. I wouldn't have taken a thing with María standing there.

After checking the drawers and under the bed, I turned back to her and held out five hundred dollars in fifties. Five hundred dollars for a hotel maid from Mexico isn't chump change.

"For me?" she managed in her broken English.

"Si," I replied. "Para la llave maestra." For the passkey. I've lived most of my life in Arizona and spoke her language well enough to know that, strictly speaking, "llave maestra" means "teacher key." But that's what they call a passkey, and I liked the twist in meaning because *la llave maestra* would definitely teach Ms. Trayle a lesson.

But first I had to get María to take the money. She was hesitating, so I placed the bills in her hand and said, "Para ti," as gently as I could. For *you*.

She handed over the passkey and walked out of that room, and probably kept on going right out the service entrance of the City Center Complex.

I wheeled her cleaning cart back out to the hall and closed the door.

Now that I had the passkey, I starting thinking about when I'd go into Ms. Trayle's room. While she slept? That might work, but only if she didn't use the chain lock. They're such teasers, the way they can taunt you with a vertical slice of a terrified face. There's always that single eye staring out and some woman going, "What do you want?"

Every room also had a dead bolt and a horizontally mounted steel latch that was V-shaped, like a woman's groin, and slipped over a ball-headed bolt. As a psychologist, I couldn't help noticing that the very image of sexual penetration might actually prevent me from entering her room. But I'd also found that when you have all these gadgets hanging off a door, people often don't bother with any of them. It's too much trouble, and at some level they think that if they start with one of them they've got to use them all. So why bother, especially with those hefty electronic locks to keep them safe.

If nothing else, when Suzanne left to do her workshop, I could come and go as I pleased. She'd probably leave something behind.

She did. Her most intimate apparel, and her toiletries with their uniquely female uses. I left none of it untouched, unexamined, but after I returned to my room I realized that my needs had not been satisfied. Not at all. Going through her possessions made me want the disk even more. Then I looked in the mirror and forced myself to be honest. Yes, I wanted that disk, but I also wanted the risk. I craved it. Roaming around her room and going through her stuff had been titillating. The adrenaline rush had awakened my desire for violation, which never sleeps for long. So it was probably predictable that I then asked myself a question that led me to take my biggest risk ever: *Why* not *try getting into her room tonight, after she settled down for the evening?* Maybe she'll come back tired and just close the door and call it good, put her faith in that electronically coded lock.

I had nothing to lose. If the door only opened an inch before the chain tightened, I could leave. I could always visit her house or office in the weeks to come. But if those extra locks were just hanging there, I could copy the disk and plan my future visits right away.

Was the disk really worth the risk? What would *you* say to the satisfaction of your greatest pleasure? Think about it for a second or two. Is it young boys? I've seen that in my practice a time or two. What if you were to be given the secret hiding place of every young boy who could be cowed into silence by your most urgent impulses? Boys who would whimper less and less as you satisfied yourself more and more? Boys who would look up from their shallow graves with eyes that still longed for all that you had brought them, who could make you believe in this lie even as the chill settled over their skin, and made yours snappy with desire?

You would do what I did. At least you'd try. The worst that could happen is she'd wake up and scream, and I'd run. But the payoff? The payoff would be unimaginable.

It was a little past two-thirty in the morning when I used the passkey again. I'd watched Ms. Trayle all evening, seen her drink wine with dinner and retire to the lounge with several others, including her husband, who was some kind of judge. I'd read plenty about him. They'd even mentioned him in the *People* story, said the Trayles had a "challenging" marriage without saying why. But anyone who knew his history would know that he had "poor impulse control," as we say in my field.

He looked dapper enough in a gray suit, but he had a nervous habit of adjusting his tie, like Rodney Dangerfield used to do. And then I noticed that he did this every time he was about to touch his wife, put his hand on her shoulder or arm. No wonder he was nervous; she kept brushing him off. She did it smoothly, the way some women do, but it was clear to me that she didn't want him touching her. But was he discouraged? No more than a dog going after a bone.

After adjusting his tie one more time, he put his hand on her thigh, which she did not take to at all. She leaned toward him and spit out some words. He said something back and left her with her appalled acquaintances.

I'd say a good hour and two more glasses of wine passed before she seemed to relax. All that time her laptop was on the seat beside her. It looked as much a part of her as the skirt I saw clinging to her bottom when she walked over to the table. I'll admit I thought about taking my pleasure with her, but I told myself that this would be a huge mistake, that the disk held the promise of a thousand reunions just as sweet. But as I slipped the passkey into the slot and turned the handle, I wasn't sure I'd be able to control myself.

What man could have claimed otherwise? Not the ones I've treated. They're almost always driven by their basest impulses.

I opened the door slowly, and actually nodded with pleasure when I saw that she hadn't used the extra locks. She'd gone to bed without any fear. But then I remembered her in the lounge and understood that she'd bought her tipsy bravado with the wine that had soothed her nerves, the ones upset by her husband.

Her long body lay stretched out under the covers, her blonde hair fanned across the pillow. It was tinged green by the clock on the nightstand, like she lived in envy of the world that had taken her son. The way she announced that she was a birth mother surprised me. Not the news itself, but the brazen way she told everyone. I've actually known about her son for more than a year. If there's one thing I've studied closely, it's birth mothers; and if there's one birth mother I've studied more than all the others combined, it's Suzanne Trayle. A long time ago I started asking myself why she was so interested in finding birth mothers and their miserable offspring. She always said in interviews that it was because she was an adoptee, but I never bought it. There are lots of search angels out there who are adoptees, and a few who are birth mothers, but none of them are as possessed as Suzanne Trayle. Or have near her numbers. She's like a search angel on steroids, way too invested in *The Search*. That's what they call it, capital letters and all. I remember when it first hit me.

I was watching her on *Oprah*, and I thought, *She's burning from both ends. I'll bet she's got one of her own somewhere.* She wouldn't have been the first, as she owned up to in her speech, that whole "like mother like slut" syndrome. So after seeing her on national TV, I started my own search. I had an advantage and used it to the max. When I found her kid, I can't say I was the least bit surprised; but I was completely floored when I found out who he was, even more shocked than I was to hear her talking openly about her very own bastard. Maybe she thought the publicity would help her find him, bring in some hot tips, but if that's the case she's in for another big disappointment: I made sure his trail's covered up a whole lot better than her body was on that bed.

I looked at the outline of her legs, and the rise of her chest with every soft breath. Not sexy? Not a lot of sizzle? Isn't that what she'd said a few hours ago? I beg to differ. I stood there feeling nothing but sex and sizzle and knew it would be very hard to restrain myself. My breath was short and shallow, and I could feel myself coming alive with desire. The strain in my pants was exquisite—I love that kind of pain—and for many minutes I just stared down at her. She was completely appealing. She might have been in her mid-forties, but she looked soft and sumptuous and so willing to please. Sleeping there, she even looked kind, like a woman who'd never hurt you. Yet she'd hurt her own son very badly. SHE GAVE HIM AWAY! She must have been a real sex machine back then. Maybe she still was.

No, I told myself, *don't* do it.

I swallowed, and with that simple act I turned my eyes to her laptop. It opened easily, quietly, and there was the disk, the one she'd held up to the crowd the night before.

In minutes I made it back to my room and fired it up. You can't imagine the thrill when I saw that she hadn't lied. These were her records, her birth mothers. This, as I said at the start, was the mother lode; and even though I hate a cliché for the way it robs anything new of meaning and emotion, I used it right then like I'm using it now. I would mine that mother lode forever, and there'd be no way for her to stop me. Why? That was a secret I'd share with Ms. Trayle at just the right time. For now, I was content to take a few moments to stare at the names and addresses and biographical notes of all these birth mothers. I now had the means to lead me to all the moms a man could ever want.

It was easy to return the computer and disk, but much harder to leave. I stood by the foot of her bed again with my body urging me on, while my mind told me to get out of there. *Now!* It was at this moment, while I was teetering on the edge of indecision, that I smelled the wine, the undercurrent of alcohol alive in the room. A moment later an interesting thought occurred to me. I'll never know if it was related to the sour notes playing in my nose, but I realized that with the help of a tiny hyphen, the word *therapist* turns into *the-rapist*.

The disk, lying safely in its own bed, was the least of Suzanne Trayle's concerns.

3

S UZANNE'S LIPS MOVED, and she heard herself clearly enough:
He was singing in my ear the whole time. The same line over and over.

But when she looked up Cara didn't nod, didn't offer a comforting "uh-huh," didn't do or say anything, and that's when Suzanne realized with a start that she hadn't spoken at all.

She swallowed just to feel her throat, then broke the silence.

"The whole time he was singing in my ear."

"What was he singing?"

Song lyrics like a wraith, a specter so haunting that her voice froze up again, the ghost of an icy puddle after a boot has cracked its pale face. But she'd been in therapy long enough to know that resistance this strong pointed a direct arrow to where she needed to go. To what she needed to say.

Cara sat across from her on an auburn couch, leather like the lounger whose cool surface always surprised Suzanne at the start of every session. The blinds had been opened on a window over Cara's shoulder, but this was November in Portland—gray skies and drizzle—and the backlight was too weary to keep Suzanne from seeing her narrow face, or the short gray-streaked hair as stubbornly impervious to style as her clothes were to fashion; Cara favored loose cotton tops and baggy slacks that obscured all but the briefest hints of her lean limbs and tight torso.

She looked at Suzanne expectantly, waiting for her to say what needed to be said, whatever that was. Only Suzanne could know.

The first sounds to climb out of her strangled throat were not words at all: She was humming.

Cara had to know the song. She'd come of age in the sixties. So had Paul Simon. *In one way or another, so have we all,* thought Suzanne. But Cara wouldn't make it easy for her by offering the name of the song, much less the lyrics, because that would only make it harder for Suzanne to heal. They both knew the rules of engagement: Cara the experienced therapist, Suzanne the experienced client.

"'Mother and Child Reunion,'" Suzanne said. "That one."

Cara leaned forward, spoke softly. "It's a beautiful song."

"It *was* a beautiful song. He kept singing it over and over while he was pushing himself into me really hard."

Cara nodded, eyes unblinking as an actress.

"My head kept hitting the headboard. I know this sounds weird, but at first I didn't notice the song because of what he was doing."

"Doing?"

"His penis. Raping me." Suzanne still couldn't put those words into a single sentence. "But then it was like I was suddenly hearing a voice from far away, only it was my head—the sound of it hitting the headboard—and it hurt so much. There was all this blood."

Her hand rose to the bandage on her brow, right by her hairline, so blonde it blurred into her scalp. Before dropping back to her lap, her fingers paused under her left eye, tenderly exploring the puffiness that had not yet receded from the purple crescents.

Cara watched, said nothing, silence the great talker in this room.

"He had a knife." Suzanne's voice seized up again, reminding her that feelings have memories, too, even the ones we can't remember. She coughed, but speaking still made her feel like she was slogging through wet sand.

"One of those things that's shaped like a snake. I saw it reflected on the clock face. I kept looking at the clock, telling myself that in five minutes it would be over, at three-ten he'll be gone. And then it was three-fifteen. But he didn't hurry. Everything I've ever heard, they're supposed to rush to get it over with, but not him. And that song, he never stopped."

She grabbed another tissue from the glass table that squatted between them, and wiped her eyes and nose. Nothing dainty about the gesture. She didn't feel she had enough dignity left to sit there and dab.

"Even now I keep thinking, what's an hour? I watched the clock for a whole goddamn hour with him behind me, hurting me, banging me around. I kept trying to see his reflection, but all I saw was that knife. And I felt it. With each . . . thrust . . . he'd press it against my neck."

Never a hint of his features, just the knife and the face of the clock, and her watch lying on its side, the weak certitude of the second hand sweeping around and around. She'd prayed for its collapse, as if the stoppage of time could freeze him, too.

It didn't make sense that his hour had lasted to this moment, and threatened to last forever, while the few hours she'd spent with her baby thirty-two years ago had fled almost instantly.

Odd thoughts, odder feelings, and they'd begun to infect other moments as well. When she woke up this morning she'd looked at all the everyday objects—her books, bureau, the door opening to the bath—and found a shading of strangeness in each of them, the fusing of the familiar to the foreign to form the utterly eerie.

She'd swung her legs out of bed, as if to flee the day's first surge of anxiety, but before her feet hit the cool hardwood floor, she'd been hobbled by the idea that she could multiply the homeliest seconds into infinity, or take their sharpest splinters and reduce them to final decimals, and they'd all send back the same stark message: that time, so set and determined to the rest of the world, had become so incontinent, so indeterminate to her. Like the invisible strings of the universe itself. Nothing steady, nothing to hold on to. Forty-eight hours ago she'd felt strong enough to finally reveal her most closely guarded secret to a packed ballroom. Now violence had claimed her and shattered every means by which she measured normalcy.

"Suzanne, what are you thinking?"

Suzanne shook her head. Icy beads of perspiration dripped down the insides of her arms.

"No, tell me."

"I was thinking about how he messed up time for me. I can't even look at a clock without . . . *feeling* . . . him. He took his time, and now it feels like he's taking all of mine." She flattened her arms against her sides, crushing the icy drops.

"Is there anything you can do about this?"

"Throw away my clocks?"

Her stab at humor made Cara smile—pleased, apparently, to see that some playfulness had survived in her client—but did little more than shadow the laugh lines in Suzanne's own face.

"I remember you once saying that when you painted you sometimes lost track of time. Maybe you should paint."

Suzanne nodded.

"The weird thing?"

"Yes?"

"Was that I was glad Burton was there."

"There's nothing weird about that at all. He's—"

"But I hated the fact that he showed up in Chicago. That was so Burton of him, to think he could make some big gesture like that and I'd just come around. But after . . . it was over, I called him. I called him first. I wanted him there."

Cara sipped from an earthenware mug before speaking. "He was safe. And he's someone who loves you."

"Cara, come on! He's the reason I'm seeing you."

"I know, but when we're really scared we turn to the people who love us. And even though he hurt you, you know he loves you and wants to get back together."

Suzanne began to weep over the whole messy mix of good Burton and bad Burton: his betrayal, but also for his comforting of her in the hotel room; and for calling the police, and fending off the night manager, who'd had the indecency to worry aloud that she'd tell the news media about the attack, as if she'd want that kind of attention.

Burton, Burton, Burton . . . He'd never left her side during all those wrenching hours, not when she'd needed him to endure the brusque questions of a shockingly indifferent detective, and not during the considerably more sensitive, though infinitely more repugnant rape exam at Cook County Hospital. He'd taken her hand at the start of the procedure and then cradled her slumping head as the East Indian physician removed evidence of the rape from the most private—and most violated—part of her body.

Seconds after the long white curtains had fallen closed behind the doctor, they swished open for a nurse who drew blood.

"What's that for?" Suzanne had asked in a voice so feeble she could scarcely believe she'd given a speech hours ago.

"I'm sorry," the woman said softly, "but we need to run a blood test to check for any previous exposures. But you should definitely get tested again in three months, and at six months too, because a lot of these guys have been in prison, and the infection rate for HIV is . . ."

Raising his hand, Burton had brought silence to that emergency room cubicle with the same unspoken authority that he commanded in his hearing room. The nurse had meant well but had left Suzanne with a festering worry.

Burton had flown home with her, and they'd spent yesterday cuddling on the antique velvet couch, the one they'd picked up years ago at an estate sale.

But even the warmest thoughts of Burton were quickly subverted by the memory of what he'd done with another woman. Solace slipped away so easily now, and Suzanne found herself right back where she'd been minutes ago: thinking about her attacker.

"Oh, God," she moaned.

"What?" Cara said.

"He's an adoptee. That's why he was singing that song. And he must have known who I was."

Cara nodded. Was it to keep her talking, or had she suspected this from the start?

"Of course he's an adoptee. The 'Mother and Child Reunion.' Why else would he choose that song? What do I do? Reunions. Mother and child re-unions. I don't think this was random at all. I think he picked me out."

Chilling, and probably why she'd resisted seeing this till now. All resistance, she realized, is mired in mayhem.

"Great." Suzanne threw the balled-up tissue into a wicker wastebasket. "That sure narrows it down." To what, she wondered? Two, three million male adoptees? Where were they that night?

She thought of her birth mother, as she often did when confronted by questions with no easy answers, and the only picture she had of her: a faded black-and-white snapshot of a tall, willowy woman with light hair in a dark skirt leaning against the doorway of a tract home in Orange County, California, shading her eyes with a hand that held a cigarette, the smoke rising above her brow; her other fingers steepled provocatively on the curve of her hip.

Her busy blouse—geometric shapes in no discernible pattern—had been full, and open to the third button. This was the single detail Suzanne had always seized upon, as if the key to understanding the mother she'd never known—and by all reason would never understand—could be divined by the way she'd bared her neckline.

Only the picture, never the woman herself. Dead at forty-three, prophetically—or so it might have seemed from the photograph—of lung cancer.

Suzanne had found her grave no more than ten miles from where the picture had been taken, a headstone not much bigger than a shoe box. *This isn't my mother,* she'd said to herself as she squinted at the barely familiar name, the date of birth, and the date of death. *This is a monument to muteness.*

Her own silence was gently prodded by Cara:

"Have you talked to Burton about this?"

"About what?"

"About your theory that the rapist was an adoptee."

"No, it just occurred to me."

"Maybe you should. No one knows more about what you've been through."

Not true, Suzanne thought. *You know more, Cara.* But she could see that her therapist was trying to help her set up a support system, and Burton, flawed as a cracked coffee cup, was a good part of hers.

He'd certainly known her in every possible way for thirty-two years now. He was the father of her son, conceived in the cliché of a backseat wrangle.

She still wasn't sure how much he'd taken, and how much she'd given; but she was certain, three decades on, that he'd been plenty pushy, and she'd been very young. Her protests had been lost in the muddle of their struggle, like the button he'd torn from the top of her fly. She'd gone home with the flaps of her waistband peeled apart, as if in surrender to all that he'd desired.

He'd made promises to her almost immediately. Burton was good with promises, he just had trouble keeping them. He'd turned eighteen only days before, and within weeks he joined the army. Within months he was in Vietnam.

He repeated his promises in most every letter he'd sent her. She'd saved them, yellowed pages with splotches from his sweat and her own tears, inky blooms that still spoke clearly of the tumultuous year when she had given birth, and he had taken lives.

Burton came home decorated. She left home in disgrace. Years after she'd graduated from college, and had broken her engagement to a promising young medical student, Burton had reappeared and said, "I'm here to marry you. I said I would, and I will."

She'd stared at him in disbelief. But Burton, she was surprised to learn, had suffered his own regrets.

Commiseration was their common ground, and it proved far more compelling than she would have guessed when he first appeared at her door. They did marry a year later, ten years to the day since she'd given birth. She had gained a husband, and lost a son, oddly linked developments that most brides did not have to try to reconcile on their wedding day.

She drew her eyes away from the table, the tissues, to the ever patient Cara.

"I was afraid to call Burton."

"You mean in the hotel?"

Suzanne nodded.

"Why?"

"Because I was afraid that man wasn't gone. I was this pathetic creature curled up on the bed bleeding and going, 'Are you still here? I don't want to see you, so please tell me if you're still here.' I was so afraid he'd kill me if I saw his face."

Nothing but the whir of the heating unit had answered. She twisted inside, remembering how she'd kept her eyes sealed as she fumbled for the phone, as if to say to his undying presence—the pain she still felt most acutely between her legs—that she wasn't looking. *Promise. Promise.*

"Suzanne, you were not pathetic. You'd survived one of the worst ordeals a woman can experience, and you were making sure he'd left. Those were rational choices in the face of irrational forces. You should commend yourself. I do."

But Suzanne didn't feel commendations were in order. Not for her. Not for Burton. Not for the mustering of basic decency in the face of such brutal defilement. Surely she could ask more of herself, of him, of the world at large.

She settled in her tiny silver hybrid car and hit the electronic locks. They snapped into place with a sharp click that sent a shudder down her spine. It felt the way an empty tank sounds when it's struck. She experienced a similar sensation after every session, as if she had been drained, too.

The trees were almost bare. Cara's office nestled on one of Portland's shadiest streets, but most of the leaves had been raked away, and those that had fallen to the pavement had been crushed and trampled and formed a muddy carpet of dying colors for all the passing cars.

The drive home took less than ten minutes. Once in the door of her butter-colored cottage, she reset the alarm system, brewed ginger tea, and hurried into the bedroom she'd converted into an artist's studio years ago.

If Cara thought painting would help her feel better, she'd take her medicine immediately.

She'd minored in art as an undergrad (majoring in psychology) but had painted only in spurts over the years, output almost always associated with stress of one sort or another.

When Burton had taken up openly with Gabriella eight months ago, her need for diversion drove her to enroll in an evening class in pastels. A new medium, and a persuasive one: After the first hour she put aside all thought of oils and acrylics in favor of pastels, which she thought of as crayons for adults. They looked like child's play, but the colors were richer and applied much more evenly.

More than a hundred of them spanning the entire splintered spectrum lay on a table to her side. She slipped into paint-spattered overalls, which she preferred to a smock, and picked up a crimson pastel.

She looked out a broad window sectioned by white mullions and studied a slender Japanese maple that stood alone in her tiny backyard, its few surviving leaves fluttering in the late autumn air, as if reveling before their final rest.

A gesture line quickly appeared on the paper. Like the first sentence of a story, it would shape all that followed. Then she drew more lines, and the spindly trunk began to appear.

Her hand paused long enough to pull a box cutter out of the pocket of her overalls. She extruded the blade with a practiced flick of her thumb and raked it over the rag paper. A light touch. She wanted to disturb the surface, not destroy it. Not a widely used technique, her instructor had said, but useful for adding texture to the work. The exposed fiber would now absorb more pigment, deepening the colors she applied. The paper's response to the razor would always remain, like old scars that never wear away, no matter how many layers of skin live and die above them.

She tried to lose herself in image and form, but this time the distraction didn't work. She kept asking herself, *What if? What if Burton hadn't taken up with Gabriella, that minx of an accountant who'd straightened out his books, and then gone right to work on his body?*

If he'd been faithful, he would have been in the hotel room with her. No rapist in his right mind would have chosen to taken him on, too. Even if Burton had gone soft in middle age, he was still six-two and weighed just over two hundred pounds.

The phone rang, and she assumed it was he. She walked over to check caller ID, not wanting to hear his voice right now. But it was Ami, who plowed right through the pleasantries to tell her to get down to the office as fast as she could.

"Why? What's wrong? Are you okay?"

"I'm fine. Look, please just come right now."

"Is it Burton? Is he all right?"

"Burton? It's not about him. Please don't make me tell you about this on the phone. Just come."

Suzanne shed her overalls and washed the pastel oils off her hands and was out the door in less than three minutes, spurred by the fear she'd heard in Ami's voice, but consoled by the certainty that all that could truly go wrong had already taken place in a hotel room in Chicago two days ago.

As Suzanne headed up the exterior stairs to her second-story office, Ami threw open the door and used both hands to usher her inside. She locked it behind them and reset the security system with the same alacrity that Suzanne had marshaled at home. This worried her: She knew why she now lived in fear, but Ami?

"What's going on?"

"It's Karen Sephs."

"What about her?"

Ami bit her lip as a child might, and Suzanne recalled that whenever her assistant was terribly upset she looked half her age. Her dimpled cuteness, while alluring to all manner of men, didn't help. Neither did her size; she was barely five feet tall with a boyish body. And while she'd been blessed with a smooth complexion, she'd always rued the profusion of freckles that spotted her cheeks and brow and speckled the ridge of her perfectly straight nose. To avail herself of adulthood, and the perquisites it provided, she wore her thick sienna hair long, and never in braids, and her skirts short and often snug.

But Ami's game attempts to appear twenty-four were quickly undermined by her lip biting and the terror Suzanne saw in the young woman's eyes.

"She was murdered and . . . raped."

Ami added that last loathsome word in a voice so hushed it could hardly be heard, as if a softer tone could ease the painful reminder. She handed Suzanne a printout of an online news story. Dateline Denver.

Suzanne felt clubbed by the headline: "Brutal Rape, Murder in Home."

Karen had been grotesquely attacked, a "macabre murder," according to the unusually literate detective quoted in the news account. A hot iron had been used, and the preliminary evidence suggested that it had been the means of death, necessarily slow, necessarily grisly.

"We're looking at revenge," the detective was quoted. "This is much too personal."

The story noted that Karen's six-year-old daughter had been at a sleepover the night of the killing.

Thank God. Suzanne remembered a picture of Darlene and Karen.

"Would you get me the file?"

Ironically enough, Suzanne felt her anxiety ease as she moved into motion and wondered if she was at all unusual, or if everyone worked not only to live but also to survive themselves.

Ami dug out the file and handed it to her.

They'd helped Karen search for her son for almost a year. The boy had been fifteen minutes old when she'd last seen him. She'd never held him. It's better this way, the sisters at the home for unwed mothers had told Karen. As if they could have known.

When Suzanne opened the folder, the picture of Karen and Darlene slid onto her lap. It had been taken at an alpine lake last summer. That poor kid, Suzanne thought. Now another orphan, a ward of the state. No grandparents. No aunts. Only a deadbeat uncle who'd abandoned his own children, if she remembered right.

Darlene was a cutie. A pixie with white blonde hair pulled back for a day of play. And the bluest eyes. What had those eyes seen? Surely not her mother in death. Please.

Ami's hands were shaking. Suzanne looked up and saw her face crumpling, the freckles folding into one another.

She rose and hugged her, holding Ami as she had only once before, on the day they'd found her mother. A joyous burst of tears then. Now she let the girl grieve. At times like this Ami really did look so very young; but then she'd find herself faced with a challenge, and her sudden resolve could add years to her real age. Suzanne had witnessed this transformation a number of times, but this was not one of those moments. Ami's slight body shook, and she sputtered when she spoke.

"I was talking to Karen just last week. She was so happy."

"I know, I know."

"We found him. She was going to see her son for the first time."

And that's when Suzanne realized she'd have to tell him, break the news that the mother he'd never known had died, become lost to him forever.

Only a few months ago Karen had been sitting on the couch in this office crying with joy. Suzanne and Ami had learned that her son lived in Fort Lauderdale, Florida, with a wife and a child of his own. He was a real estate broker and a volunteer soccer coach.

"He's got a *great* life," Suzanne had told her.

Karen's relief had been palpable, as it was for most birth mothers when they found that their children had survived without them, had not been mortally harmed by the most critical decision they would ever make. Relief that Suzanne hoped someday to share.

She guided Ami to the same couch.

"Can I get you anything? Something to drink?"

"No, nothing," Ami said, her eyes redder than her hair. "Is there anything I can do?"

Suzanne shook her head. "Just sit there. I'm going to get you some water."

Ami protested as Suzanne swept out the door to the bathroom down the hall.

She needed cold water herself, to splash her face and feel a sensation greater than grief, if only fleetingly; but when she stepped into the lavatory, she felt so weak she had to grip the porcelain basin. Her eyes rose slowly to the mirror.

She looked awful. The purple crescents below her eye had darkened. So had the bandage on her brow. Time to change it. The rest of her face appeared as gray as the Portland sky.

The weakness ebbed, and she felt strong enough to retrieve a washcloth from the cabinet below the sink. She soaked it and pressed it gratefully to her hot face before wringing it out. A step from the door, she remembered to fill one of the mint green pitchers they kept on a shelf next to the mirror.

She eased her way back into the office, where she found that Ami had propped the photo of Karen and Darlene against her computer monitor and was staring at columns of numbers. She filled Ami's glass and handed her the washcloth.

"It'll make you feel better. It did me."

Ami opened the cool damp cloth and covered her face with it, unusually unmindful of her makeup.

"I'm going to Fort Lauderdale," Suzanne announced.

Ami unveiled herself. "What are you thinking?" A question she often posed to Suzanne.

"I've got to tell her son in person. I can't do it on the phone. As far as I know, we're the only ones who knew about him."

"Did she ever contact him?"

"I seriously doubt it. She said she'd let me know how it went once she worked up the nerve to call him."

"But she said she was going to."

"They all say they're going to, you know that. And then a lot of them can't bring themselves to do it for months on end, sometimes years."

Ami stared at her and nodded, looking much older than she had a few moments ago, the hidden age that grief lays bare.

"I wonder if he'd want to go to the funeral."

"I'm wondering about that myself," Suzanne said.

Call him up and tell him his birth mother's been murdered? A woman who in all probability he's never even met. And that there's a funeral? Throw his whole life and the life of his family upside down?

Suzanne looked away. *She* couldn't do it, not to another adoptee; she remembered all too clearly the pain of never knowing more than her birth mother's headstone. The loss of the funeral itself had hardly mattered, but the loss of the life they might have known together she grieved still.

"I can't believe Karen would want him to find out about all this with a telephone call."

Her eyes had been drawn back to the news account still lying on her desk. Then she heard a sharp clicking sound, and looked up to see Ami tapping the screen with her finger.

"I'm going to try to get her phone records."

"Good idea. And could you find out about the funeral arrangements? I'm assuming they'll be in Denver."

"You going to go?"

"I think so, and then book me on to Florida."

"Do you want me to come?"

"No, I want you to hold down the fort, and stop by my house and water my plants while I'm gone."

"All the really important stuff." But Ami worked up a smile before turning back to her monitor. Suzanne saw the girl's reflection on the screen as clearly as she'd seen the reflection of the knife on the bedside clock. Ami was biting her lip again, and starting to cry silently, as Suzanne had when he'd pressed that blade against her neck. Karen had undoubtedly cried, too, but Suzanne couldn't imagine that her tears had fallen in silence. Not in the grip of such murderous madness.

4

I JUST FINISHED DEVELOPING Karen's pictures, and I'm sure she's never looked better. After such a successful session in the darkroom, I'm ready for a run. It's a great time of year to be living in the Valley of the Sun, temperatures in the seventies and eighties. I just wish the air wasn't so filthy.

Right outside my door an old Dodge truck is sitting at the stoplight pumping out clouds of smoke, big blue pillows of poison. It's not unusual to see that, either. Traffic literally comes with the territory. I've got a corner lot on two busy streets. People drive by all the time, but the thing is, they never take a second look at my place. I've watched them carefully, and I know it's true. They drive by talking on the phone, or smoking, or picking their nose, but they never take a good long look at my house. Just another tan, two-story stucco, as anonymous as sand. Nothing you'd ever notice, but upstairs I've got my enlarger, photo paper, and all my chemicals in my darkroom.

Right now Karen's pictures are drying on the lines I have strung across the room. All I have to do is think of them and it puts me in a fine frame of mind.

My neighbors are just as clueless as the people passing by. All they know is that I'm a psychologist who likes to run. That's all they're ever going to know. And the fact that on most days I head out early, before the traffic gets this thick.

It's nothing for me to knock off five, six miles before work, but this morning I'm only going to run up to the university mall to see the grad students' annual photography show. It opened last week, but I was out of town taking my own pictures; and since my return I've been developing and printing them, and burning in the details that mean the most to me.

Within minutes I'm passing Frank Lloyd Wright's contribution to local architecture, a pink birthday cake of a building known as Grady Gammage Memorial Auditorium. When it was designed, one of the administrators described Wright as "dour"; but I think he had a wild sense of humor and used it to the great expense of the locals, and everyone else who paid for this abortion.

The student union isn't any better. Huge, with all the outward charm of a modern-day mausoleum. I pop upstairs to look at the work of the grad students and see even less to admire. Look at this, a series of photographs of smooth round rocks that bear an obvious resemblance to mammaries. Mother earth drivel. And this one, of a cue ball at the instant it cracks apart its racked target, titled "Random Element."

Nudes too, but nothing edgy. Nothing remotely daring. Nothing at all like the photographs of Karen. I painted red arrowheads all over her body with that steam iron. By the time I finished they pointed every which way. I felt like Cupid with my own *brand* of love. Tough love. The toughest, for mothers who need it the most.

I started taking photography seriously when I was twelve. My first portraits were of "Mother," who claimed to have saved me from a "brutish" life. She modeled for me and was also the subject of my earliest surveillance photos.

At thirteen I had my debut in a group show at my middle school. *Portraits of Mom.* A biting title for the series of twelve photographs that were, I want to say, much more daring than anything I'm looking at here. There might have been a *Portraits of Dad,* too, if he hadn't wised up and left the lush.

Mother was impressed—*honored* was the word she used—and said she'd come to the show. I'm sure she saw my work as a tribute and worthy commemoration to all that she'd done to "rescue" me, as she'd often reported to the nearest ear. It made me sound like a stray at the pound and was more appropriate than she ever realized.

I used the grainiest print stock I could find and mounted each black-and-white photo on black cardboard.

She'd willingly posed for so many pictures that she had no reason to suspect my real artistic aims; and my teacher, for all her good intentions and talk of free expression, had no idea of the risk she took when she agreed to display a few "family" photos.

It makes me laugh even now to consider what I did on that day, perhaps the most pivotal of my life.

I paired each formal portrait of Mother with a surveillance shot. The first showed her smiling on the sofa, the perfect Mom photo (title: "Say Cheese"). Its mate showed her in roughly the same position, but with her head thrown back, her mouth open, her tongue a headless sea creature poking out from the shell of her lips. The neck of her nightgown gaped open to her belly, suggestively shadowing the inside curve of one of her breasts.

The next photo was even more shocking. First, there was the shot of her waving from the front door (title: "Have Fun at School, Hon"), juxtaposed with an eight-by-ten of her lying on her bed in the same casual summer dress, but in such a state of disarray that I had to crop the bottom of the picture to avoid showing her lack of underpants. But the wantonness was present on her face, her lips as smeared from sex as the ones I'd been forced to crop.

I had seen a lot of Mom, more than I ever wanted, but there was nothing obscene in any of the twelve photographs. Disturbing? I won't argue that, but not obscene. Not even close.

When Ms. Asher actually saw them, she stepped back, clearly surprised by their content. The other students were exhibiting clay figures of swans and ducks, mosaics of clowns shaped with tiny blocks of sponge, and the standard psychic download of obsessively rendered horses and dogs favored by girls of that age who are too frightened of their sexuality to express it in any other way. Oils mostly, with some charcoal. Standard fare, except for my offering.

"Are you sure your mother doesn't mind?" Ms. Asher asked.

"I'm sure," I said. "She understands the demands of art."

It was precisely what Ms. Asher needed to hear, she the great believer in free expression.

For the first time in my life I waited with a rich, raw sense of anticipation. I would experience it many times again in the future, and for reasons not entirely divorced from what happened next.

When Mom arrived, she didn't disappoint. I smelled the booze when she was a good five feet away, and I watched with intense pleasure as she focused on my photographs.

"You little rat," she said. "You goddamn ingrate."

She'd never made me so happy, and based on her history it was only going to get better. I expected her to take a swing at me. Banked on it, because I saw this as a prime opportunity to have Children and Family Services, the Post Adoption Division, give her a good comeuppance; but instead she took her bag and created a six-foot swath through my exhibition, which wiped out about half of my photos and knocked over a house made of meticulously painted matchsticks on an adjoining table.

Fearing the worst, fearing that she wouldn't turn her anger on me, which would have been a first, I walked up and said, "But, Mother, you said I could."

That's when she hit me. Not with an open hand, either, but with her fist, a detail duly noted in the CFS report.

I took the punch and the one that followed without faltering. I tried to give her my most insolent look, even as tears spilled from my eyes (a surprising though welcome response brought on by a blow to that extremely sensitive area between the upper lip and nose).

Ms. Asher screamed for help and tried to intervene. I felt sorry for her. I probably should have warned her about my mother's proprietary interest in beating me. I was hers, and nobody could say otherwise. Hadn't she told me over and over to never tell anyone anything about what went on in our house? And here was Ms. Asher trying to stop her from beating her boy. The poor woman took an elbow to the chest that I later learned had bruised her breast so severely that she'd received medical care, and a fist to the face that snapped her wire rims and cut her just below the left eye (a single stitch, which I managed to capture on film a few days later. Title: "TKO").

Six months passed before my mother regained custody of me.

Our relationship was never the same. She knew I had her by the short hairs and that she could never afford another "episode," as CFS put it in their report. I used that edge to my considerable advantage through the rest of my teens. I got what I wanted when I wanted it, and only in her most hateful moment did she let her animus show. That came on the summer afternoon after my junior year in high school when I walked into the house and found her sitting in front of the fireplace in a string bikini, her flaccid flesh on rude display.

The fact that she'd cooked up a roaring fire made no sense at all, and she was in no rush to explain it, either.

"Good day at school?"

She was full of false cheer and too drunk to remember that school had been out for three days. I'd been at a friend's house checking out his new laptop. They were still a novelty then.

But she didn't really care about my day; she rushed on without waiting for an answer. Her real agenda was in her hand.

"Know what this is, *son*? Your Decree of Adoption." She waved it in the air. "And you know what's on it? You want to know the mistake they made when they gave it to me?"

I felt my insides lurch. She had it—my birth mother's name. Nothing else could have given her so much leverage, or made her so happy.

She confirmed my suspicion with the biggest smile she'd ever given me.

"Mommy's name, Harold. Your *real* mommy, as you always like to say."

I winced. When she smiled again, I knew she'd seen my pain. She relished knowing that she had what I wanted most. It was the one essential she could deny me. Not love, because it had never been there. Not food and shelter, because once she signed the adoption papers she'd had no choice about providing them. Only this, a name. *The* name. I started toward her.

"Stop!" she shouted. "Or I swear I'll throw it in there."

She eyed the flames. They looked huge and hungry. That's how she held me at bay. I still had hope that she wouldn't burn it.

"You could find *Mommy* with this. You know that?"

She wouldn't have known any of this if I hadn't shared the progress of my search over the past few years. I'd been sure to tell her every step because each one made her crazy with jealousy. We had that kind of home: We tortured each other. Her turn:

"Without this, it's a hopeless search."

Not true, not even then, but true enough that I wanted to rip her stinking heart out.

"You thought you were pretty smart, didn't you? Showing off those pictures of me."

"What? That was four years ago." I couldn't believe she was still fuming over some middle-school art show.

"You think I can forget about that? The humiliation? You think that goes away? No." She shook her head like it was an infected wound. "That never goes away. You might as well have put my picture up on a billboard with the words 'Unfit mother!'"

The heat from the fireplace, those hungry flames, continued to melt my every impulse to move. A smile cracked her heavily made-up face.

"So I thought and I thought about what would hurt you the most. What would make you think about what you did to me for the rest of your life? And then I remembered this." She waved the decree again. "There's only one thing I could do. I could take her name away forever. Me?" She pointed to herself. In her near nakedness, it was a disturbingly coquettish gesture. "I looked at it once, but what do I care about her? I don't even remember the birth bitch's name. Don't even know it. And you know what, *son*? You're never going to, either."

Right then she tossed it into the fire. I ran toward it, willing to stick my hand into the flames to retrieve it, but she blocked my way.

Her eyes were as red as coals, and she stank of sweat and gin, tonic and lime, and the rancid halo of her greasy hair. I tried to push her out of the way, but she was slippery with sweat, like she'd been in a sauna, and all I succeeded in doing was pulling her top off, two cups no bigger than coasters.

She laughed when I stumbled, and stepped aside without making any effort to cover up.

"Be my guest, son." She put her hands under her breasts and fluffed them lewdly. It was as crude a gesture as I've ever seen; and later, when I had time to think, it left me wondering what she'd really intended with her invitation.

The page had curled and blackened and looked like a shadow. When I reached in and tried to grab it, the decree disintegrated.

Only the burns healed.

Conveniently enough, she died two days after my eighteenth birthday and left me with a substantial sum of money. I can't say I was surprised by her death or the windfall; my photos weren't the only surveillance I'd conducted in that house, and the art show wasn't the only plan I'd ever had for her. I knew her net worth and made sure that her will remained unaltered, which wasn't a difficult task, considering the state she was in most of the time.

Was I grateful to her for the money? No more than I was to the U.S. Treasury for printing the bills. I didn't even bother to attend her funeral. I'd put her to rest years ago. She was only catching up.

My generous inheritance paid for my undergraduate and graduate degrees and sustained me as I started my counseling career. I still draw on those funds to support my research and travel. The cost of the former has been greatly reduced, thanks to Ms. Trayle's disk. I now have it saved on one of my own. Whenever I'm lonely I pop it in, and then I watch what comes up. The possibilities are endless, as she'll soon see.

I can't bear any more of this "art" photography. In moments I'm running back past the Frank Lloyd Wright birthday cake building, then down the road that leads directly to my house, to the pictures of Karen before her final surrender. Right now I'd be willing to wager that Suzanne Trayle considers Karen's death a lone tragedy, and by no means part of a larger plan. The big picture hasn't become apparent yet, but it will.

I run up the sidewalk to the house, and I'm in the door and up the stairs in seconds. The pictures have been hanging on the line that I've strung across the room, like the Tibetan prayer flags popular with the peaceniks at the university who still think they're living in 1972. The entire collection is here, from the photos I took before she knew I was in her neighborhood, to the last ones of her alive, when I'd invaded every last centimeter of her space.

I've never moved so quickly on a birth mother. Never could. But after I sent everything on that disk to my home computer, I downloaded it back on to my own laptop. An hour later I sat in my hotel room with Ms. Trayle's scent still clinging to me, staring at the files. I was erect over every prospect. It was as if even my body were pointing to the screen saying, *Yes, her, her.* There were so many "hers."

But I wanted a mother I could have on my way home from Chicago. I found two in Phoenix, but didn't want to dirty my own nest. And then I saw Karen pop up. *Do it,* I said to myself, and without even realizing it I had the phone in my hand. "What time are your flights to Denver?" were the next words out of my mouth.

For some reason Ms. Trayle's disk didn't mention Karen's daughter. An oversight on the great searcher's part? Maybe. I never would have gone after Karen if I'd known. I don't like to share my mothers. I didn't even know about the kid until afterward, when I found a barely decipherable note lying on the kitchen table. Kid's handwriting saying something about missing "Mommy" at a sleepover. *You're going to miss her for a lot longer than that,* I thought.

But she was one lucky kid. Lucky for me, too. I hate dealing with them.

There was also an initial surprise. When Karen met me at the door and I told her I was her son, she shook her head no. This wasn't the abject denial I'm so used to from these birth mothers, who refuse to acknowledge who they are, *what* they are. This was absolute certainty, and she offered it with a degree of sincerity that I found very off-putting.

"No, you've really made a mistake," she said with so much assurance that I had the unpleasant suspicion that she knew what she was talking about.

When I tried the biographical details I'd lifted from the files, she told me I was right about the specifics, but wrong about her.

"*My* son," she said with transparent pride, "lives down in Fort Lauderdale, Florida." She looked me in the eyes and touched my arm gently. "You must be terribly disappointed."

She had no idea.

"But I have the name of a search angel who could probably track down your mother, too. Come in."

So the net of opportunity caught me just as I was about to fall.

Flesh of my flesh, bone of my bone. Isn't that right, Karen? After such an un-pleasant start, I still claimed the birthright you denied your own boy, the home you pushed him away from. Didn't I? And then I gave you a bed to lie in. The bed *you* made.

She knew it, too. Just like all the others. That's the remarkable thing. All of them really do know it. I see it in their eyes as soon as they realize their death is a fait accompli. They're almost relieved. They're finally getting to pay for what they've done. Wretches. They know they deserve it, and they accept their penance, as the Catholics call it (and a lot of them are Catholics, or *were*, for all the obvious reasons). Or you could say their lives finally have closure, as we say in my profession.

I whispered a few more words to Karen. I wanted to make sure they were the last words she'd ever hear. They weren't true, but that made them all the more satisfying to say.

With her eyes rolling, her skin on . . . fire . . . I brought up her beloved son, the child she'd tried to trump me with, the one she'd shared so many tantalizing details about, like his name, where he worked.

"I'm going after him, too," I told her. "I'm going down to Florida right after I finish with you."

Flesh of my flesh, bone of my bone.

I treasure these pictures, but even with the final photo of Karen in my free hand, it's the entirely innocent memory of Suzanne Trayle that lengthens and thickens me and forces my rubbery legs to the darkroom floor.

As I kneel, I see Ms. Trayle stretched out on the bed, blonde hair on her pillow, and I feel all over again the way my body hungered for hers. Then I remember waking her up and everything else that happened in her hotel room.

That's what sears *my* mind at the moment I come.

Fascination? Obsession? I don't know what you'd call it, but Suzanne Trayle fills more of my thoughts every day.

I shower and hurry back to my desk. It's time to keep a closer eye on Ms. Trayle—with the help of my private eye. He's an ex-cop who works for a flat fee tracking credit card purchases and the like. This isn't work I could easily do, and it's not work I'd want to do. And besides, his retainer is reasonable enough. I never have to see him, I've never even met him, and I never use him to track the mothers I plan to make mine. That would be stupid. But I do have a powerful need to know all I can about Ms. Trayle, and as I start up the floppy with all the bios of all those moms, I feel the need even more strongly. We are linked, aren't we, Suzy, by a growing range of intimacy: yours, mine, and the birth mothers who now belong to both of us.

I look at the names.

5

ON THE DAY of Karen's funeral, the rain poured down in a rage. It was as if all the leaky seams in the Denver sky had finally exploded.

Suzanne hurried into the vestibule of Our Lady of Angels Church, shaking fat drops from her black umbrella onto a white marble floor already slick and shiny from the mourners who had arrived before her.

Her umbrella and coat had done little to shield her calves, and her damp hose clung to her skin and chilled her.

She noticed a musty smell as she joined the line waiting to sign the guest book. Next to it stood a picture of Karen and Darlene, taken when the six-year-old was in preschool. Fitting, Suzanne thought, that Karen as a mother should greet the mourners first. It was the identity that had proved most troubling for her, and most rewarding.

The two of them had been smiling, Darlene on her mother's lap, inseparable, as most mothers and young daughters are. The challenges come later, in adolescence. Poor Darlene would never know the ache of rebellion, nor the ambrosia of reconciliation that usually follows in young adulthood.

Karen had been frozen in her maternal moment before a sky blue backdrop, preserved for all of time in her budding middle age.

She's only going to look younger as we get older, Suzanne thought. If we see this picture in twenty years, that's what we'll say: She was so young when she died. Deny the future and you freeze the past. It's always that way. You can't move the past forward or back. It stands alone and anomalous and never ages. The poignant, whispery power of the past is as unending as it is unbidden: in photographs and memory, in graveyards and hearts.

Suzanne signed the guest book and asked herself if Darlene would ever study the signatures to try to find people who could help her make sense of her mother's murder. As if sense can ever be made of such despair.

It had been years since Suzanne had been to church, but as she settled in a pew she remembered the rituals and the haunting images that appeared everywhere she looked, in the figure of Christ long crucified, in the stained-glass saints that stared down from the vaulted windows, in all the symbols—chalice, cross, and thorny crown—that promised salvation from the endless trials of eternity.

She spotted the back of Darlene's diminutive head in the first row, her hair beautifully braided and pinned across the top of her head to form a blonde tiara. She wondered who had done it. Surely not her uncle, whom she assumed was the hulking man sitting to the girl's side, whose own lengths of gray hair fell down his back in unruly ringlets.

He had his arm around his niece's shoulders as casually as he might have embraced one of his drinking buddies in a bar; but Darlene sat erect, as if unwilling to concede his presence or the scant comfort it seemed to offer her, and kept her gaze on the simple wooden casket in front of the altar.

A Father Pacheco held mass, and Suzanne carried herself through the motions as mechanically as the Catholic schoolgirl she'd once been.

In his homily, the priest avoided any direct reference to the violence that had claimed Karen, but her closest friend proved far less restrained.

Kathy Gaines was stout and had to use the handrails to help herself up to the pulpit. When she spoke, her anger and sorrow made her stammer, and Suzanne found herself nodding, urging the woman on. Someone has to speak out. Someone did. Kathy Gaines decried the cruelty of Karen's murder and demanded justice.

"Not in the afterlife, whatever that is," she said defiantly as her wet eyes swept the dank church, "but here. Now!"

She spoke for five more minutes before she was smothered by a flood of emotion. Two men helped her to her seat.

Father Pacheco named Karen's survivors: brother Curt and daughter Darlene. Only then did the girl react, slumping forward, burying her face in her hands, and issuing a howl so singularly primal that tears flushed down Suzanne's face.

She listened to Darlene's cries soften to a heartrending mewl, which did not cease for the remainder of the mass.

When Father Pacheco said, "The souls of the just are in the hands of God," she snapped to herself that it was the souls of the unjust who should be so neatly dispatched.

At last the priest raised his hands above his head, "I say to all of you, go in peace. Do not carry vengeance in your hearts. Take with you the glory of God."

Suzanne resented how easily he spoke those words, a man of the cloth who would slip off his robe, slip back into the rectory, and know nothing of the demons that would haunt Darlene for the rest of her life.

Do not carry vengeance.

She thought he might as well have told them to grow wings and fly home for all the understanding of human nature contained in that smug admonition.

As the pallbearers wheeled Karen's casket down the aisle, Suzanne witnessed the single most painful moment of this agonizing morning. Darlene, still whimpering, suddenly broke away from her feckless uncle, who reached out to grab her, and succeeded only in yanking her beautiful braids loose, spilling them from atop her head.

The girl ran after the procession, threw her arms around the casket, and screamed, "No, Mommy. No! Mommy, *please!*" with an urgency that shattered the frail standing of Suzanne's heart.

Kathy Gaines, whose own face glistened with grief, bundled Darlene in her arms.

Suzanne merged in the center aisle with the other mourners and eased past the thick wooden doors of the church entrance. She raised her umbrella to the Rocky Mountain rain and heard the drops chattering on the dark fabric as sharply as teeth, as if even the chilly sky had begun to shiver.

Five hours later she caught her first glimpse of Fort Lauderdale as her plane banked to the left. Three hundred miles of waterway made the city the "Venice of Florida," according to the airline magazine she'd been reduced to reading in a vain attempt to put aside the piercing memory of Karen's funeral.

Fort Lauderdale evidently derived much of its identity by association to grander locales. She'd also read that the big shopping strip, Los Olas Boulevard, was the "Rodeo Drive of Florida," and promptly wondered how an identity could possibly be real if it was constantly grounded in the experience of others. Twitching over her own transparency, she realized this was exactly what an adoptee would think. Who else would trouble herself over such trifles?

But were they really trifles? she asked as their descent steepened. Adoptees were constantly wrestling with identity. How could they avoid it? They'd grown up with people they didn't resemble physically, emotionally, or in any other way, and they frequently found themselves at odds over the most quotidian concerns, matters as simple as musical preferences: loving Brahms or heavy metal while their adoptive parents listened to Charlie Mingus or Loretta Lynn.

The vast majority of adoptees might have found shelter, but never their own true homes.

She could think of nothing that spoke more painfully to adoptees than the issue of authenticity: Who am I? Where did I come from? Do I have a history, or is it all made up for me? Did my adoptive parents really "choose" me, or did they take what they could get?

As the plane touched down she remembered that in the 2000 presidential election, this part of Florida—Broward County—had raised serious questions about the authenticity of American politics and the legitimacy of political lineage.

It fits, doesn't it, she said to herself, *that I'm coming here to tell an adoptee that his birth mother's been murdered, and I don't even know if he ever met her.*

She smelled the salty sea air the second she stepped off the plane, and she recalled the palm-shaded beaches ballyhooed in the tourist brochures, the same seductive stretches of sand that still lured so many thousands of college students for spring break and had become the setting for that tacky sixties movie *Where the Boys Are.*

It didn't take Suzanne a full second to find herself startled by yet another odd link to Fort Lauderdale, and to wonder if she'd ever stop refracting the world through the prism of pain: Connie Francis, who'd starred in the film, had also been raped in a hotel room. This was Suzanne's first trip after surviving her own assault, and she felt caged by her fears.

She tried to distract herself by eavesdropping on the conversations of the retirees who surrounded her at baggage claim, gabbing about their grandchildren or the cruises they themselves were about to embark upon (apparently, Fort Lauderdale was a home port for much of the cruise industry).

At least half of the passengers appeared to be in their seventies or older, the Shame Generation, as she had come to think of them. The mothers who had relinquished their children in the 1940s and early 1950s were generally resistant to reunions when their daughters and sons came calling. Their unrelenting guilt, and the profound obstacles it created for their offspring, had long bothered her.

Many of these moms still feared the reactions of their own siblings or the children they'd reared later, still feared besmirching the reputations of long-dead parents. They were much different from the women like Karen who'd given up their babies in later decades. These moms were usually in their forties, fifties, sometimes their sixties, and often eager to meet their children, deeply guilty not over the act of love or passion that had led to conception, but for picking up the pen that had led to adoption.

She drove the rental to a posh hotel in downtown Fort Lauderdale, willing to spend a considerable sum because it actually had bothered to highlight security features on its website.

But as Suzanne pulled up to the entrance and handed her keys to the valet, the locks and guards and cameras did little to quell her concerns; the hotel in Chicago supposedly had been safe, too.

By the time she got to her room, the sun had set. She tipped the bellman and threw the bolt lock and latched the chain. Then she tested the door handle. Locked down, but she still didn't feel safe.

Her fears, and the deepening darkness outside, made her dinner decision easy: room service.

After eating, and having the cart removed, she threw *all* the locks again, checked the windows (even though she was on the eleventh floor), and pulled the shades.

She lay in bed trying to decide whether to call Burton. Better, he'll worry otherwise.

The call was over so quickly that she wondered if he was alone and if she cared.

Maybe she was too tired to care, to have Burton's affair with Gabriella, that libidinous, number-crunching body snatcher, register on her fading consciousness.

The day had begun in Portland with a six-thirty flight to Denver, and here it was sixteen hours later ending in a hotel room on the other side of the country. Tomorrow she'd face a more daunting task: introducing herself to Jack Smithers, Karen's son, and telling him the most horrible news he was ever likely to hear.

For the next hour she lay in bed trying to imagine how she'd do this, reviewing everything she and Ami had learned about him, before realizing that a deeper unease had permeated her mood, a free-floating fear that finally forced her to sit up in bed and turn on the light.

Disgusted, she made her way into the bathroom and took a dose of NyQuil. Sleep was proving as elusive as a sense of safety.

Jack Smithers worked at Wind and Sea Realty. Suzanne had nabbed his plate number off the Net, along with the make and model of his car—a 2004 green Ford Explorer, which seemed like overkill for the flatlands of Florida, though maybe you needed a four-wheel-drive SUV when you were selling swampland and sand.

She promptly chided herself for subscribing to the worst stereotype of a Florida real estate agent. Maybe he's helping low-income people into fixer-uppers. Or young couples into starter homes.

The message line at Smithers's office said they opened at nine, giving Suzanne ample time to have breakfast at an outdoor café across the street. A wonderful Florida day: sunshine, blue sky, light breeze—bright enough to justify the big sunglasses that hid the last of her bruises.

She felt far more comfortable out here than in her hotel room. Even after taking the NyQuil she'd awakened two hours later, a weary pattern of fitful sleep that had plagued her since the rape.

Despite her preparedness, the Explorer still startled her when it turned into the realty lot at 8:40. She watched Karen's son climb out of the vehicle and saw that he looked a lot like his mother. They shared the same round face and short build, though he was a tad more rotund than Karen had been. This could have been the effect of his pale blue suit, which would have made even a tall man appear shorter and wider. His hair was lighter than his mom's, but he was younger, of course, and lived under the strong Florida sun.

He's the picture of normalcy, Suzanne thought, and all that's going to change as soon as—

And then it hit her—the reason for last night's deep unease: What if he'd murdered his own mother? What if Karen *had* contacted him, and he'd killed her? Weren't experts in parricide reporting that adoptees were murdering their parents at rates notably higher than nonadoptees?

But Karen was his birth *mother, not the mother who raised him,* she insisted sharply to herself. An important distinction. But it provided only flickering relief because she also knew that adoption literature had long been marred by sporadic stories of violent reunions. A man meets his mother at long last, imagines a madonna but finds a mere mortal instead. All the rage, all the abandonment issues explode, and at the end of the search there's no longer a hapless woman with her own regrets, but the lifeless remains of a battered body.

No. Suzanne shook her head as she put down her coffee cup. How could a man rape and torture his mother to death, and then throw on a suit and go to work? He was probably slogging through new listings at the moment she was murdered.

God, I hope I'm right. She offered the little she could of a prayer and checked her watch. Time enough to call the police. And then what? Offer some far-fetched theory that would have him as a *remotely* possible suspect in a distant murder? Thoroughly defame the poor guy *and* have him find out about his birth mother's cruel death by having a detective show up at his door? That's assuming she could even find a detective dim-witted enough to follow up on a "lead" this thin. *That's not why you flew all the way out here. Get a grip. He's going to need help, not harassment.*

"Finding Homes for People Like You" greeted her in tall red letters in the lobby of the realty office, along with a large photograph of the quintessential American family standing with their shaggy dog by a white picket fence, house in the background.

How many times had Jack Smithers walked past this photo and wondered about *his* perfect American family? Suzanne knew she would have.

She introduced herself to the receptionist, who buzzed Smithers. He appeared within seconds, bearing a big smile and a firm handshake.

He led her back to his office, offering the standard issue chitchat about the weather ("another perfect day in paradise") before smoothly segueing into questions about the type of home she was interested in.

She eyed him closely as she sat down by his desk. "I'm not actually looking for a house, Mr. Smithers. I'm—"

"Jack's fine. Are you thinking of a condo, or a—"

"To be honest, what I've been looking for is you. I've been at it for some time now."

This made him sit back, and he sounded no less alarmed when he spoke.

"Are we . . . related in some way?"

As he spoke she saw him taking in the color of her hair and eyes, similar to his own, ignoring the fading evidence of her injuries.

Suzanne disabused him of this quickly. "But I do have something to talk to you—"

"Is it about my birth mother? Have you found her? Is that what this is all about?"

He sounded panicky, a reaction Suzanne had seen often. He sensed a revelation, and while some adoptees are relieved by the prospect of finding a parent, most know that their world is about to be shaken to its foundation. For Jack Smithers, even the foundation was about to crumble.

"Yes, that's what this is about. Did your birth mother ever contact you?"

Smithers said she hadn't. "I didn't even know she was looking for me. Are you saying she is?"

"That's . . . right. She searched for about a year. I helped her. That's what I do."

"I know you!" His voice rose. "I thought you looked familiar. You're that search angel."

"I'm no angel, but I take it that you know who I am and what I do."

"Oh, sure. My wife and I had a boy last year, and ever since I've been thinking about getting a hold of a searcher and finding my mother. But now I don't have to because you're saying she found me."

For the first time he sounded cheered. This was horrible, having to break the news to him.

"That's right. She found you. Her name . . ." A pause for the tense: Was? Is? Then just a pause: ". . . Karen Sephs. I gave her your work number and home number, and your address. I also gave her pictures of you from your Florida license and high school yearbook."

"Boy, you really do your homework."

"So I want you to know, because it's important for you to hear this, that she knew what you looked like. And she knew about her grandson, and the life . . . the really good life you've made for yourself."

"What do you mean, she *knew*. What's wrong? What happened? Did something happen to her?"

Suzanne resisted the impulse to look away when she spoke.

"Your birth mom passed away a few days ago."

He swore and buried his face in his hands.

"I'm so sorry to have to tell you this."

He swung his chair to the side, his eyes pooling as he stared at the street.

She noticed photographs of his wife and child on his desk, the baby photos, and pulled several pictures of Karen out of her shoulder bag.

"You'll want to keep these."

He turned back, reached for the photos, and studied them.

"Your mom was very happy for you."

"Was she sick, or was it sudden?"

"Sudden . . ." Suzanne stopped, unwilling to go on. He must have sensed this.

"How?"

"How?"

"How did she die. Was it an accident? A car—"

"She was killed . . . by someone." She didn't know any other way to tell him. She had no experience to fall back on, and no reason to think she'd ever have to do this again.

"Murdered?" he said. "You mean she was murdered?"

This time Suzanne had to look away.

"A man entered her home, police still aren't sure—"

"Wait. This isn't some sick game you're playing?"

"No, not at all." She handed him her card. "I'm exactly who I say I am. You said you'd heard about me. You can go online right now and check me out. You'll find stories about me. I understand your grief, I really do. Your mom was more than just a client to me."

He put up his hand in apology. "I'm sorry. I just . . . I just can't believe this. Just the other night I was saying to Monica, that's my wife, that I really needed to do the search. There might be medical issues we'd need to know about for our boy—"

"We can get all of that for you."

"You see, once we had him I had this feeling that I needed to know more about who I am. And now I'm finding out my mother was murdered. Do they know who did it?"

"No, they don't know. But I have the name of the detective who's heading up the investigation."

He'd been all over the news when she was in Denver. She'd seen him twice on TV briefing reporters, full of himself, reveling in all the attention, impressions reinforced by his brash answers, and the callousness with which he discussed the condition of Karen's body.

She'd taken him for the kind of cop who'd stolen all of his behavioral cues from the big screen. But Karen's son might want to talk to him, so she'd made note of his name.

Only now she imagined how he'd casually, maybe even brutally, disclose the means of murder. Her stomach knotted over the immediate implication: If she wanted Jack Smithers to find out as gently as possible, she'd have to tell him herself.

As if to give her an opening, he said, "How? How was she murdered? Was it quick?"

Suzanne shook her head. Easier in that moment than saying the word *no*; but a gesture could never spell out what she needed to say, what he needed to hear.

She leaned forward and spoke as kindly as she could: "He sexually assaulted her, and then he killed her."

"What do you mean he killed her? How did he do it?"

There was no way to do this kindly.

"He killed her with an iron."

"A golf club?"

"The other kind, for clothes."

"For clothes?" he said.

"Yes."

"Did he . . . beat her with it?"

"He burned her with it."

"Burned her to death? With an iron?"

"That's what the medical examiner concluded."

Jack Smithers stared out the window again. A seagull defied death to nibble the crust of a roll in the street. The gulls reminded Suzanne of the crows back home, always scavenging.

"I can't tell you how sorry I am to have to tell you this."

He nodded, still not taking his eyes from the window. The tears that had dampened his face had dried, and he looked less like a man in the obvious throes of grief than one in the first stages of shock. He sounded it, too, speaking in a monotone.

"When? What day?"

"The fourteenth. Sunday."

He groaned loudly and raked his hair with his fingers. "I don't believe it. I don't believe it."

He tore open his Day-Timer, as if to double-check the most recent of memories.

"That was Simon's birthday. His first birthday. That was one of the happiest days of my life." His voice broke, but he talked through his tears. "The weird thing is, I kept wondering about my birth mother that day. I couldn't stop thinking of her."

"She was probably thinking of you, too."

"Did she ever have any other children?"

Suzanne brightened over the opportunity to deliver good news. "Yes, she did. You have a six-year-old half sister, Darlene."

"Is she okay?"

"She's really shook up. She's staying with her uncle right now. Your mother's brother." The deadbeat who'd abandoned his own kids, but she spared him this.

Jack was hungry for everything she could tell him, and she spent the next two hours filling him in on Karen's life.

She brought out more photos, gave him all she could of Karen's personal history, everything that she and Ami had pieced together.

He was still in pain, still grieving, but grateful.

She eked out sufficient details about his son's birthday party—who had been there, the gifts the boy had received—to jettison even her smallest doubts about Jack Smithers: Like the overwhelming majority of adoptees, he was innocent of any crime.

But this conclusion, so pleasing in the presence of Karen's son, left her hounded by the intractable question of guilt as she drove back to the hotel: Who the hell's still out there, roaming around? The answer was brief and bereft of all comfort: a man who would wield a hot iron on a bound woman, who would set her skin on fire and mug her screams.

These corrosive images burned holes in her thoughts as she rode the elevator up to her room. She reminded herself that she'd found a hotel with a reputation for security, and that she was safe. *No need to worry, you're okay.*

But she still looked up and down the hallway before opening the door, and when she entered her room she threw all the locks quickly, checking the handle again when she was done.

Her eyes darted from the bed to the bathroom so intently that she almost stepped on a pale yellow envelope. Even after spotting the hotel logo, the fluid line quality of the cursive letters, she felt chilled by its presence. It had arrived in her absence, uninvited, an *invader*. Her fear had driven her to see such an innocuous-looking envelope as evil, as a malevolent creature possessed of its own power, its own volition, because it had entered her personal space without permission. Though she recognized the irrationality of her response, she could not shed her initial apprehension as she pulled out the message form.

It had been taken by a hotel operator, whose handwriting was Catholic-school clean. For all of a second the familiar check marks and boxes proved reassuring, but then Suzanne read the message itself: "Are you using the chain this time? I'm only a motion away."

She crushed the form with her fist and whirled on the door. Yes, she'd used the chain, she'd used all the locks, but none of them could make her feel safe.

The damp, balled-up form slipped from her hand as his breath coated the back of her neck, memory as cruel as any killer.

She tossed her suitcase onto the crisply made bed and packed in under a minute, toiletries and laundry and neatly pressed slacks all a jumble.

Shaking horribly, she called hotel security for an escort. She wasn't leaving this room alone.

6

I WISH I COULD have stared into her eyes when she read my message. Did they widen? Did she squeeze them shut? Did she stop breathing when she realized that *my* eyes are always on her?

The answers depend on the kind of woman she is. The kind who runs to the door to see if it's double locked, or the kind who's so scared she wants to jump out a window?

Flight or fight?

We'll find out soon. Perhaps.

I'm teasing, but why not? Teasing is such sweet torture.

I have a cancellation. It happens at least two or three times a week. They still have to pay. I don't care about their maudlin excuses. Not that I ever let the time go to waste. Not when there's so much of my personal work to do, which I must admit forces me to cancel *them* on occasion.

It's still a thrill to unlock this cabinet. It's on the wall behind me. It's the first thing my clients see when they look away from me. I've watched their eyes settle on the doors, and I've noticed a couple of them focusing on the little chrome lock. If they only knew, do you think they'd sit there for long? No, they'd run screaming from my office into the streets and they'd never stop. Especially these clients.

It tickles me to consider their response to the photos. Once I develop them, I keep them here in my office, and for good reason: To all appearances, they're patient files, *confidential* files. In reality (not to put too fine a point on it), they're an archive of agony. I've heard about those creeps who take a snippet of skin or hair, or the underwear of the women they've indulged themselves in, but I find all of that deeply objectionable. What I take from my mothers is never missing, because I take pictures of them. It's as if I've stolen the air itself, but you can't steal what can't be sold. Anything that's ineffable falls into the same category: love, hate, horror.

I'm quite methodical in my approach. First, I snap the surveillance photos as they go about their lives. At this point they're blissfully unaware of what awaits them. Then, and I shudder even now as I recall this particular step, I take pictures of them bound and, if need be, gagged. The latter depends wholly on the proximity of friends, family, lovers, even strangers, anyone whose conscience could be pricked by a scream, though I love to let my moms cut loose. Some of them have shrieked so loud that I've had birds stop their mating calls, and cicadas still the madness of their belly membranes.

Finally, and to think of this gives me a renegade erection, I photograph them in their death throes with the lens only inches away.

You could think of it as a simple series of shots, wide, medium, tight, or you could see it as I do, as incremental intimacy until there's nothing left to hide, until the heart lies bare in its naked desire for one more beat.

At first, the camera's eye gives them hope. I've seen this time and again. That's because it occurs to them that *this* is my purpose, to take pictures of them, not to actually *kill* them.

And so what I see as I go through the archive now is the genuine hint of hopefulness that initially appears on their faces. The pleading, too, though that never leaves their eyes. Eyes plead more readily than any other part of a person, much more persuasively than the mouth with its meaningless blather. That's how I judge an actor or an actress, how I determine if they've known real emptiness, whether it's been caused by their family or an enemy of long standing, though often they are one and the same.

Since poaching from Ms. Trayle's disk, I've introduced some new . . . twists . . . you might say. A kink or two to amuse me, and to bedevil the great searcher herself. But nothing so obvious as to constitute a "signature," as the profilers at the FBI like to call it, an MO so distinct in its delivery that the poor fools who employ it practically call out, "Arrest me!"

There's a myth—you see it in movies and read about it in books—that deep in our heart all of us really want to be stopped from what we're doing. I'm willing to grant that there may be some practitioners who feel a perverse need to get caught, but I'm not among them. Why would I want that to happen? It's the catching that's fun. Ask a fisherman if he'd prefer to be gargling on a hook at the end of his line, and see what he says. Frankly, if I wanted to die, I'd do it myself.

Look at this picture, for instance. Would I want *that* to happen to me? No way. No sane person would ever want that to happen to them. That's what makes poaching from her list so delicious. I not only get to photograph the death throes, their every scar and shudder, but I get to share the results, although indirectly, with the woman who supplied me with my mothers. The news, when it hits her, is my own personalized thank-you note.

The outer door opens. My ten o'clock has arrived. Patsy, one of my favorite clients. She never cancels. She's far too invested in our therapeutic relationship to ever miss an appointment.

She's eight years older than I am, and sexy in a chubby, peaches-and-cream sort of way. You don't need to look twice at Patsy to know that you wouldn't need an iron to make her skin sizzle. The Arizona sun would do the job just fine. She'd bake and blister in hours.

But I don't think it's her potential that I find so appealing. It's her history that seduces me. I love to hear about her secret needs and fears. That's why I specialize in this field. That's why virtually all of my clients are now birth mothers.

Plus, Patsy and I conspire together. We have since I found out she works for Catholic Social Services. Working there is her penance. She actually *confessed* this to me during our first session more than three years ago. Her "duties," as she called them, offer her the opportunity to petition her Lord not with prayer, but with "good acts" to atone for the child she had out of wedlock and gave up for adoption.

Her good acts have continued under my guidance. She pulled records for me, secret records that only an adoption agency like Catholic Social Services or the state Adoption Division have access to. I told her the truth, that I was searching, too. I didn't say for whom. I didn't have to. She said she understood. "We all need our mothers," she added in her most understanding voice.

She waits for me. I can feel her presence on the other side of the door. "Patient Patsy." Another pun, much less amusing than "mother lode," but few words have ever moved me as much as that one.

I lock up the cabinet—I won't keep her waiting any longer—but the images will sustain me for much of the day. If my birth moms bore me too much with their whining and carping about how *they've* been wronged, I'll let the pictures superimpose themselves on their faces. My very own montage, the melding of the past with the present, the dead with the living, those who scream with those who weep.

The imagination is so powerful, and it wanders where it will. But I can't let it go too far, not if I really do want to avoid dirtying my own nest.

I hear a great deal from Patsy about guilt. She says she's haunted by her "relinquishment" of her daughter. That's the word they all use now. Not abandonment. No, that's too brutal. Too honest. Relinquishment, like they gave up their place in line at the liquor store.

At times like this I'm tempted, dearly so, to put Patsy's grief to rest for her. I could do it so easily. She trusts me implicitly, would do whatever I ask. Recognizing this is like springing a gate for a greyhound: Every part of me wants to move, to chase down the rabbit of her lovely hide, to gnaw on it at my leisure.

Instead, I maintain my professional demeanor and listen to poor Patsy, while the memory of Karen forms a mask over her face, and every freckle on Patsy's cheeks and nose and brow smolders silently. It's as if I can sniff the death that's already there.

I'm disturbed by my reaction because I know what a mistake it would be to poach from my own practice. So I try to contain myself, to take pleasure in the impulse alone. I keep my hands by my side. I don't even take notes. I'm a study in concentration, but inside my head there's a constant hissing, a message riding my tightest wire:

"Patsy leave. Patsy leave. Leave, you stupid bitch. *Leave!*"

But the hissing that would spare her life succumbs to the jabbering images that demand it, that see in every one of her freckles a red spot that quickly pools and runs down her face.

The whole time she cries, and I see that these red streaks are tears. She tells me she's searching for her daughter, but so far with no success. I hear this as a seaman hears the currents below, in the rock and straddle of his body. I also hear the taut wire strummed by the gale ripping through me, the hissing-hissing-hissing "Patsyleave-Patsyleave-Patsyleave . . ."

My hands rise to my desk, where they are content not with the handle of my letter opener, but with the thumbing of its blade.

She says a military family might have adopted her baby, and I manage, "A military family?" with the practiced empathy of the well-trained counselor.

Yes, she says, full of despair, a military family, and they're so hard to trace. I nod again. I know. I've been there myself. Ten, twelve states in a childhood. Foreign countries. (*Sprechen sie Deutsch? Italiano? Español?*) Try plowing through all those birth indexes, and hospital, county, state, and school records. Could take a lifetime, despite what those rip-off artists on the Net say about finding "Anyone, Anywhere, Anytime."

I tell Patsy to grieve, that I understand the pain, and with this she looks at me knowingly, oblivious to the trace of my fingers still warming the edge of the opener.

Then she cries some more, and I find myself leaning forward. A voice speaks to me. It speaks to me as clearly as I am speaking now. It says, "Kill her. Kill her."

I tell myself I'm not without feeling for this woman, but this is an academic exercise, as much a production as my display of empathy, my gentle coaxing and urging of her emotions. I hear the words "I wish you the best of luck in your search" and don't hear the words "even if you did abandon your baby when she was only a few hours old. Even if you do deserve to die."

When I stand I see that I'm performing my functions adequately, that my jockstrap has restrained my erection. I have done nothing more than amuse myself, as I often do, with the possibilities that present themselves with these creatures. Once again, I have successfully walked the fine line between temptation and titillation. I will not soil my own nest.

She apologizes for her emotional displays. Most of them do, and I reassure her that it's quite all right to grieve openly. Even necessary and normal. This draws her grateful thanks.

We schedule another appointment, and I give her a few minutes to drive away.

I walk outside. It's a glorious November day. The smog of our beastly summer has been finally swept away by the breezes that clean the Valley this time of year. At the height of summer it's all palms and pavement and ghostly mirages, endless streams of heat radiating upward until the air itself looks roasted and warped.

But today I can see the mountains. It's a terrible time of year to leave, but I must. I've picked out a new birth mom from Ms. Trayle's disk. This time I made a point of double-checking for kids. And guess what I found? I was the one who made the mistake with Karen. Not Ms. Trayle. In my eagerness, I overlooked a category and failed to click on a key link. Never again. But learning this gave me new faith in Ms. Trayle's list, made me treasure it as I did on that very first night. The accuracy of the list is critical because I don't want any mistakes with the next one. We're about to move up the scale of terror. Cortisol levels are going to spike. Why? Because Ms. Trayle will see a pattern emerging with my new mom. She'll see it because I'll point it out to her. And she'll understand the depth of her dilemma for the first time.

Flight or fight? Neither will be an option. She'll be forced to sit absolutely still while I have my fun, a delicate, frozen flower waiting to be shattered.

My new mom. I like the way I'm already thinking of Jesse Bonham as "Mom." And you know what? Before I'm through, Jesse will think of me as her son. She won't want to, but she will. They almost always do.

7

THE MOST DAUNTING Monday in memory. Suzanne had all she could do to force herself to step into the garage, the first time in the three days since her return that she'd dared to venture outside her home.

She'd flown back to Portland Friday night in the same panic in which she'd fled her hotel room in Fort Lauderdale. After drawing the shades and checking her cottage to make sure every window and door was still wired to the security system, she'd reached Burton. He'd been good enough to stay with her, sleeping on the couch without complaint.

They'd called the police on Saturday morning, but the detective who'd shown up several hours later had said there wasn't much he could do. After easing his ample frame onto their recliner and sighing annoyingly, he added that without substantial leads in Chicago, they didn't have much to work with.

"That's where this case'll be solved. Not with this." He held up the wrinkled message form.

"But what about the phone records at the hotel?" Burton asked.

The detective shook his head. "Those records won't tell us much. Stalkers don't go making calls from their home phone. And he probably used a blocking device."

At Burton's insistence the detective finally agreed to try to get the phone records, but he as much as said that her case, with its origins and evidence thousands of miles away, would have a low priority in his underfunded, overworked department.

It was a struggle to return to work. Suzanne tried unsuccessfully to put aside her fears as she drove through the heart of Portland's damp downtown, dodging buses and airport shuttles, light rail cars and hulking SUVs, and the pedestrians who braved them all by bolting from street corners at the first blink of red.

But at her office the routine felt reassuringly normal, until the jaunty UPS guy appeared an hour later. He flirted with Ami as she signed for the big envelope. Nothing unusual in that, nor in Ami's interest in him; she delayed his departure with chitchat about the rain, which in Portland was dragging the lake of conversation for the stiffest of bodies.

Ami was still smiling as she closed the door and spun around playfully on her heel, raising the hem of her short pleated skirt, a teasing twirl prompted by the young man who had just taken his leave. She found the tab on the upper edge of the envelope and filled the office with the familiar scratching sound of it opening.

In the midst of Ami's sprightliness, Suzanne had been refreshing herself with the facts of a new case, a Miami birth mother in her late sixties. The woman had kidney cancer and was desperate to find the daughter she'd given up for adoption forty-six years ago.

It's likely that Suzanne wouldn't have given the UPS envelope another thought—several arrived every day, and Ami handled all routine matters—if her assistant hadn't gasped and dropped a letter on her desk.

Suzanne spotted her name in the formal salutation.

Dear Ms. Trayle:

By the time you read this, the police will have found the body of Jesse Bonham. I had a lot of fun with Jesse, as I did with Karen, and I'm going to have a whole lot more fun because I'm poaching birth mothers from your list of clients.

"Ami, get me the phone."

Startled out of her stricken state, Ami reached for the receiver and handed it over. Suzanne dialed 911 as she read on.

Does that make you angry? Does it make you scared? Does it make you want to run to the police? I'm betting it does, but I'm also betting you won't do it. Want to know why?

Right then Suzanne heard the 911 operator, and in the next few seconds read the following words:

Because I know where your son is. Yes, your son, the one you abandoned thirty-two years ago. The one you can't find. And I'm delighted to tell you that if you breathe so much as a word of this to the police, the FBI, or anyone else, I'll kill him.

She stared at the phone. The operator, undoubtedly attuned to the challenges of such calls, kept asking if she could help until Suzanne hung up. Her eyes returned reluctantly to the letter.

Do you have any idea what that means, Ms. Trayle? Think about how Sephs died. By all means, find out what I did to Jesse Bonham. Then think about how creative I could be with your own flesh and blood, and I use that term with the utmost regard.

Here's something else you won't do, under penalty of your son's most painful death. You will not warn your birth mothers about the pleasures they'll soon give me. Not a word, because that would spoil all my fun. I love posing as their son, because I am a son, and choosing's the best part. And you'll make sure little Ami behaves, too, because if either of you violates this agreement I'll go to work on your boy.

Should you doubt me, and you should never doubt me, Ms. Trayle, I'm going to tell you something about your son, something no one else knows, no one important to you or me anyway. Your son has a birthmark on his lower back. It extends from below his waist. I saw it poking out from his swimming trunks this summer. Look closely at the picture, and you'll see what I mean.

What picture?

"Can I have that?" She indicated the envelope still in Ami's hand.

Ami started to speak, but Suzanne hushed her and hurriedly opened the envelope wide. Wedged into the corner was a photo of a man holding a woman's hand at a swimming pool. In her other hand she held a newborn in an infant carrier, the kind that snaps into a baby's car seat. They were facing away from the camera. The only clear feature on them was the birthmark on the man's lower back. It protruded from the waistband of his trunks, as it had once protruded from his diaper.

Her stomach twisted as she read the final paragraph.

If you do go to the police, guess what I'll do? I'll rip that birthmark right off his back, and then I'll send it to you. That's when you'll find out everything you never wanted to know about your son, your granddaughter, and your daughter-in-law. You'll also find out where they lived when you see the return address on the package. But I promise that you won't want to see any of them then.

"That's what I was trying to say." Ami pointed to Jesse Bonham's return address on the envelope. "That's what he did with this one."

Suzanne nodded numbly, and her eyes fell to the letter's closing:

> Best wishes,
> The Searcher

She laid it on her lap. "The Searcher," mocking her with his moniker, but that wasn't the worst part, not even close.

"I'm going to call her house first," Ami said, edging over to her desk.

Another numb nod from Suzanne as she silently implored Jesse to be there. Make a mockery of *him*. But the fact that he'd known Jesse's address in Las Vegas gave her little hope that they'd find her alive.

Suzanne stared at the photograph, unable to look away. To see even this much of her son after all these years was a staggering experience. And he has his own daughter, my granddaughter. And a wife. But her eyes kept returning to her boy. She'd known he'd grow up, but she could hardly believe that such a tiny baby had become a man. A strong back, narrow waist. He looks fit. Like Burton in his prime. Burton's going to want to see this. And the letter? Should she show him that, too? She'd have to give that a lot of thought. Burton wouldn't hesitate about going to the police. He was an authority figure. He believed in other authority figures. Maybe she should go to the police. Instead, she sat there staring at the photo, feeling sharply indulgent with Jesse's life in question.

But there are clues here, she told herself: the pool, the angle of the sun, a bench to the side, and the leaves on a tree limb in the background (a maple, but might it be a regional species?). And what about the baby carrier? Is there a name on it? Most parents label their children's belongings if they go to child care.

She pulled her magnifying glass out of her top desk drawer and pored over the picture. No name. In the same spirit, she reread the letter. Sadly, the words she found most alarming—"I'll rip that birthmark right off his back"—clued only her connection to the young father in the photo, and frightened her as much as Jesse's return address: The son of a bitch also knew where her son and his family lived, had crawled close enough to photograph them.

She laid the letter and picture on her desk with care, as if they needed tending, not she.

More than three decades since the birth of her son, and she still felt flattened by the gravity of her grief.

Labor had been the most painful experience of her life. Her baby had been positioned sideways, and she'd struggled for twenty-eight hours to have him. The doctors and nurses were coldly indifferent to her screams. They knew she was from St. Mary's, the home for unwed mothers, and their lack of concern made their condemnation clear. No anesthetics, not till the final thirty minutes when they put her under. They might just as well have called her a whore. Back then it would have hurt no less.

"There's no answer at Jesse's."

Ami caught her eye before continuing.

"I'm checking the AP wire for Las Vegas, and I'll try her at work."

"Good idea," but Suzanne said no more because hearing Jesse's name finally triggered a single vexing question that had been percolating since she'd read that he was "poaching"—what a god-awful word—birth mothers from her list of clients: How did this creature get the list? Was he a hacker who'd worked his way into her computer files? Or—and this possibility forced her to close her eyes in anguish—had he somehow slipped into her office or home?

Her body swirled with the memory of the rape. Even sitting she could feel her legs turn to jelly. It was as if her blood and bones were reaching a conclusion too dreadful for a simple dawning in her mind: that her rapist was the same man who stole the list and murdered Karen, and now Jesse (if she was to believe him, and she feared above all else that his credibility and cruelty were not in question).

Wait, wait, wait, she said to herself. *Do you really think he took a break before raping you to make a copy of a disk? Come on, a rapist rapes. He's impulsive. He doesn't . . .* But now she paused, too, for the connective tissue of all these crimes had found its voice and was singing a beautiful song that he'd turned ugly, whose words still violated her ear.

Why else would he have chosen that song? And it would have been easy for anyone, even a thug, to make a copy of the disk while she slept. *The one you held up and waved to the crowd. The one you practically begged this psychopath to steal.*

"Suzanne!"

Ami's shaky finger pointed to her monitor. Her panicky voice barely rose above the hum of her computer.

"He wasn't kidding. Oh God, oh God"—Ami's eyes were skimming the story as she spoke—"what he did to her."

Suzanne sprung from her chair and rushed over. A Las Vegas newspaper account of Jesse's murder spared surprisingly few details, the most gruesome of which were contained in a graphic lead sentence:

> Homicide detectives are examining clues to the weekend rape and bizarre slaying of fifty-one-year-old Las Vegan Jessica Bonham, who was hung by the throat after every orifice in her body had been sewn shut with fishing line.

Every orifice? Could that really be? The ears? Lips? Eyes? Suzanne couldn't bear to consider the nether regions.

The next paragraph noted that Bonham's body had been found hanging from the neck with "hundred-pound-test fishing line" after an anonymous caller had tipped off police Saturday morning. The Clark County medical examiner was quoted as saying there were indications that she'd "struggled for hours" before dying, and that he'd found no trace of drugs in her body.

(No painkillers, was Suzanne's first thought.) Only evidence of ammonium carbonate—smelling salts—in the burns around her nostrils. A detective said this showed a "sick desire" on the part of the killer to keep her conscious.

"It's all related."

"That's what this creep says." Ami wiped her eyes with the back of her hand, a gesture that brought out the child in her as much as her tears did.

"I mean my rape, too—it's the same guy. It's got to be. That's how he got the disk. He made a copy before he raped me. And that's why he tracked me down in Florida."

"He tracked you down in Florida?"

"He sure did." Suzanne dug out the wrinkled message from her shoulder bag. "Take a look at this."

Ami read it.

"I can't believe you stayed there after getting this."

"I didn't. I checked out right away."

"But how did he know you were there?"

"All I can figure is he did a credit card trace. I don't see how else he could have done it. You didn't tell any—"

"No way! Anyone who called, I told them you were unavailable, and that's all. And I got all their names and numbers anyway."

"I'm sure it's nothing we did, Ami. It's him, the same guy."

"You really think the guy who raped you murdered them?"

"I really do. I think . . ." But Suzanne couldn't go on. Her stomach had seized up after her eyes had drifted back to the screen and spotted a photo captioned "Las Vegas police carrying the body of Jessica Bonham from her home."

"I'll be right back," she managed.

She grabbed her shoulder bag and hurried down the hall to the bathroom, lifted the toilet seat lid, and vomited, as if on command. This had happened before in moments of great stress, so a surging stomach didn't in and of itself alarm her unduly. No concerns about pregnancy, either: She'd taken the morning-after pill they'd given her at the hospital in Chicago.

Quickly, she rinsed her mouth and pulled out her cell phone. Before she talked to any cops or FBI agents, she wanted to sound out Terry Ramsey at the Bureau's National Center for the Analysis of Violent Crime in Quantico, Virginia. They'd met at an adoption conference, of all places, two years ago, and Terry, a strikingly attractive African American woman tall enough to look her right in the eye, had become a source of Suzanne's, willing to run down a name, license plate, address—the nuts and bolts of ID building. Nothing that had ever challenged the infinitely more sophisticated skills that had turned Terry into one of the Bureau's top research analysts.

Terry greeted her warmly, as if the sound of Suzanne's voice had cleared her desk of any other duties. Which could not possibly be true, but it prompted Suzanne to want to reciprocate by telling Terry everything as concisely as possible. Even so, she checked this impulse immediately: Terry was a confidential source, but she worked for the Bureau, had been sworn in by the director. If she told Terry too much, there would be no decision to make: The FBI would barge right in and take over the case. End of story.

Time to back up and reformulate and pare down the facts.

"I've got a client, a very good friend, who got a letter today from a . . . madman. I know that sounds over the top, but there's no other way to put it."

Terry listened without comment to Suzanne's select rendering of details: nothing about Karen and Jesse's murders, keeping the focus on the threat to her "client's" son, and finishing by noting his vow to slaughter the son, his wife, and his daughter if she went to law enforcement.

"'Madman' works for me. But let's go back a little. He said, 'because I am a son'? Is that right?"

Terry had homed in on one of the few lines Suzanne had remembered clearly enough to quote.

"That's right, 'because I am a son.' Those were his exact words."

"You still have that landline you use when you need it?" Terry meant the pay phone in the lobby of Suzanne's building.

"You want to call me back there?"

"In five."

Nothing unusual in Terry deciding to change phones if she planned to provide information sub rosa, so Suzanne had no way of anticipating the extremely painful nature of what she was about to learn.

The lobby phone was already ringing by the time she made it downstairs, and Terry wasted even less time bringing the facts back into focus:

"So your friend's got a threat to her son, whom she's never met. And a picture of him with a birthmark that's supposed to be the proof?"

"That's right. And—"

"He says he'll kill him and the family if she starts talking to the cops or us?"

"Exactly. So she's not sure what she should do."

Suzanne heard her voice break, not much, but she feared Terry had heard it, too, and would read the truth in that fragile fracture line.

"You see," Terry said, "what concerns me is the reference to being a son himself. In that context, he's clearly hinting that he's an adoptee."

Terry stopped talking right then, as if she'd muzzled herself. But there was more she wanted to say, Suzanne could feel it. Thousands of interviews over the phone, you get to know the hidden language of silence.

"What, Terry? Just tell me."

"This isn't about a 'friend,' is it?"

Now Suzanne paused. Tell her? *She already knows.*

"It's about my son. I just don't want the Bureau rushing in till I can think this through."

"I don't blame you, and I promise I'll keep it under my hat, but I'm going to tell you something you definitely need to know to make an educated decision. But it's tit-for-tat time, because you've got to promise me that it's not going to go any further than you."

Suzanne agreed, wondering—no, *worrying*—what Terry could tell her that would make this decision any easier, any more "educated."

"Remember when we met at the conference in St. Louis, and you asked me what I was doing there? I gave you some line about an investigation. That was true, but it wasn't the whole story, either. I was there because one of our research projects on violent crime has been looking at adoptees, and even though the numbers are small, the preliminary data are scary."

"What do you mean, 'scary'?"

"We've been going through old police records, archival stuff, and what we're finding is that adoptees are way overrepresented among killers who abduct and murder children."

Suzanne felt sick again, and not just over her son and his family.

"You there?"

"I'm here. How overrepresented?"

"I mean . . . adoptees abduct and murder children at a rate 200 to 300 percent higher than the rest of the population."

Suzanne stood at the pay phone staring at the cold hard numbers on each of the little silver squares. *Two hundred* to *300 percent higher?* This was horrible news for adoptees. It would make them all sound like killers, and not just killers, but the worst kind of all: murderers who would steal children from their parents and kill them, a crime perversely consistent with the view of a growing number of radical adoptees that they themselves had been stolen from their birth parents. This small but vocal minority had even started calling adoption "abduction."

But it's no coincidence, either, Suzanne recognized at once, that adoptees would stand out in this crime category: Their abduction and murder of children was the most transparent act of cruelty she'd ever heard of.

"I want to emphasize that it's preliminary data," Terry repeated, as if she might have lost Suzanne to the emptiness of the past few seconds, "but it worries us, and we're looking at it."

"And you wouldn't have mentioned it if—"

"It wasn't important? That's right. So I wouldn't take this threat to your granddaughter lightly. She needs to be protected. But so do you. There's even scarier stuff."

"There's more?" Suzanne felt her head fall forward, chin to chest, suddenly as sapped of strength as she was of spirit.

"A few years ago we had a comprehensive serial killer study underway, and one of the factors that intrigued us was adoption. There's anecdotal evidence to suggest that adoptees are more likely to become serial killers, so we wanted to see if the numbers supported the supposition. But then—boom!—9/11 hits and that study gets put on the 'back burner,' which is a bureaucratic way of saying that a different kind of terror had taken over."

"What was the anecdotal stuff?"

"Stuff you might have heard of. We've known for a long time that some of the most notorious serial killers were adoptees. Guys like David Berkowitz, the Son of Sam. Remember him?"

A rhetorical flourish: Who could forget him?

"What was interesting about Berkowitz was how directly his history supported the idea that adoption could be a factor. For one thing, he said he shot women to stop them from having bastards like him. The guy was so wigged out he was thinking of a bullet as a prophylactic. But that's not all. About six months before he went off on his killing spree, he looked up his birth mother and found out she was alive and had kept his sister. He'd been told by his adoptive parents that she'd died in childbirth. Or, to spin it another way, 'You were a killer right from the start, David.'"

"That's pretty common, telling adoptees that their mother died giving birth to them."

"I know, but not real good for your head, especially if you're a little unbalanced to begin with. Here are some of the others. And by the way, most of them went after women. You don't have to be Freud to read much into that."

Terry began to recite the names in the cool tone of someone deeply familiar with infamy: "Joel Rifkin, The Ripper; Kenneth Bianchi, The Hillside Strangler; Gerald Eugene Stano, The Italian Stallion, killed forty-two women; Steven David Catlin." And here she broke her monotone to say, "He was something else. He managed to combine serial killing with parricide by murdering his adoptive mother and his two wives."

"Oh God."

"Did this freak give any indication that he's killed anyone?"

"No," Suzanne lied, never pausing for the truth, instinctively backing away from the Bureau. It would prove wise.

"Read me the letter. The whole thing," Terry said.

"I can't. I left it in my office."

"Well, if he's not bragging about killing anyone, then maybe he's just talking trash. But this boy's got some very bad baggage. That's easy to see."

And you don't know the half of it. "So I guess I'm back to where we started: What should I do?"

"Everything you can to find your son as fast as you can. Once he's safe, and his family's safe, there's no credible threat."

"But I've looked for years. I can't believe I'm going to find him now."

Terry started to answer twice, three times—missteps that sounded as strangely staccato as static—before settling into her reply:

"I know. I'm sorry. I'd tell you to turn it over to us, but we're a leaky ship these days. We've got too many agents chasing headlines, and not enough of those good old boys chasing criminals. Some agent could get a look at this and say, 'Great story,' and earn a few chits with a reporter by leaking it. It happens. Happened just a couple of months ago in a ritual killing case down in Florida. If you really believe this guy's got a bead on your son, there's no easy answer."

"Terry, what if it was *your* son?" She had a four-year-old. She'd shown Suzanne a picture of him when they first met, when the boy was still a beaming, white-toothed toddler.

"My baby? Like I said, *I'd* find him as fast as I could."

"I think you just answered my question."

"I think you're right. I'm sorry I can't be more encouraging, or much help. But if I can run an address, or license plate numbers, phone numbers, anything like that, let me know. And that stuff about adoptees? Like I said, totally QT."

Suzanne headed back upstairs, horrified over what she'd just heard. It wasn't bad enough that for decades adoptees have had higher rates for all kinds of psychiatric problems—specialists even called this collection of symptoms Adopted Child Syndrome, or ACS—but for murder, too?

Ami turned from her computer as soon as Suzanne stepped back into the office.

"You okay? You look a little peaked."

Suzanne took a mint from a tin in her top desk drawer and popped it in her mouth. "I'm okay now."

"So you think he planned the whole thing?" Ami said. "The rape, getting the disk, everything?"

"Yeah, after I waved it in the air and practically said, 'Here it is, come and get it.'" Suzanne sat in her chair, eyes on the letter.

"Don't beat yourself up, Suz. What kind of a psycho comes up with something that sick? I mean, how totally tweaked do you have to be to say to yourself, 'I'm going to steal that disk, and then I'm going to rape and torture to death a bunch of birth mothers.'"

"He did."

"Yeah, well, if you're right, he was definitely attending the conference."

"Probably." This had also occurred to her. She might have even met him, shook his hand, one of the conferees who'd come up after the speech to congratulate her.

"Then we can check the registration list."

Suzanne shook her head. "I doubt he registered, but even if he did, that only narrows it down to a few hundred men."

"That's not so many."

"It's way too many without the help of the cops, and we can't bring them in. You read his letter. We're on our own. And I'll tell you, Ami, I don't want to find this freak anyway. I want to find my son, make sure he's safe, his family's safe. Then we can call the cops, the FBI, our birth mothers, everyone."

"But we've tried to find him."

"Look, if this creep can find him, then we can, too. But we've got to move fast."

"Point me. I'm ready."

"No, I've got to point myself downtown."

"Why? What's downtown?"

"Catholic Social Services."

"I thought you tried there a long time ago."

"I did, but I'm going to try again. Maybe this time they'll listen. And Ami?"
"Yes?"

"I don't care how much they plead with you, don't accept any more clients."

She felt terrible enough about the birth mothers who already had placed their trust in her, knowing she was betraying their safety with her silence. Even more appalling, the grinding understanding that her decision not to warn them had been engineered by The Searcher and now formed a key part of his savage plan.

Suzanne drove away from her office bolstered by little more than hope, and even its pitiful offerings were leavened by her experiences with the church.

When at fourteen she'd told her mother that she was pregnant, the woman who'd always treated her with kindness, love, and great patience grew flustered, then furious, and whisked her off to see Father Andrew, the youth counselor. Short, chubby, immensely popular with parents and children alike.

He welcomed them to the rectory living room on a frigid but sunny Saturday morning and asked if they'd like tea and hot cross buns.

Her mother thanked him profusely for his kindness, but declined. So did Suzanne. She was nauseated much of the time, and the thought of citron and cinnamon almost tripped her seething stomach.

An awkward silence ensued before her mother said, "Go on now. Tell him. Tell the father what you've gone and done to yourself."

But before Suzanne could gather her wits enough to speak, her mother burst into tears and blurted out the reason for their visit. The venom in her mother's usually gentle voice stunned her daughter.

"She let some boy get to her, she did. No child of Mary, this one."

Father Andrew smiled as gently as he had on all those Sundays from the pulpit and placed his hand on her mother's heaving shoulder.

"There, there now. We all make mistakes, dear."

After consoling her mother, he told her he needed to speak to Suzanne alone. She sniffed her understanding and let him direct her to a bench in the foyer.

Suzanne was grateful for his tact. After all her adoptive parents had done for her, she felt horrible knowing how much she'd disappointed them.

"What happened?" Father Andrew said sternly as he shut the door.

She told him in a sentence, but he waved off her explanation.

"Don't try to tell me that you went out with a boy, kissed him, and this . . ."—his hand now gestured at her groin—". . . happened. I didn't just fall off the turnip truck. You're lying, and I'd advise you not to compound your sins with insolence, girl. I will not tolerate it."

So she tried to sound like she was in a confessional, the same straightforward manner that she'd used to tick off the lies, deceits, anger, and petty thefts of her Catholic childhood. She assured herself that she'd soon know penance, and the blessed cleansing it would bring. But the details she so carefully provided about an older boy, a torn button, and a backseat reddened Father Andrew's pale face and left him shaking with rage. When his hands fisted, she flinched, fearing he'd strike her. He didn't. Not with his hands.

"There'll be no forgiveness, not now. Not till you have this baby, and you better pray this bastard baby of yours doesn't tear you apart from the inside out because it's your only hope of salvation. You have this baby, and you give it to a *good* family." His eyes shifted to the door, and his head moved back and forth in disgust. "Pray to Mary Magdalene. Not to the Virgin. Do you understand?"

Yes, she understood. She was a whore in the eyes of the church and needed to repent with the blood of her own being.

St. Mary's had been built in the late nineteenth century in the heart of Kansas City, Missouri. A large campus with brick buildings, and a brick drive lined with birch trees that blurred as the taxi sped the quarter mile to the front door.

She heard a Beach Boys song as they approached the gabled entrance and found comfort in the thought of sand and California sun as she stepped out into the frozen world that surrounded her. She struggled with her bags along a path that had been shoveled through two feet of snow. It would never melt entirely during her stay, only whiten and gray, whiten and gray, as winter storms held sway and hastened away.

The waiting had begun. Four months to her due date. She was assigned secretarial duties—typing, filing—and saw all the correspondence that flowed into St. Mary's from parishes across the country. So many bad girls having babies.

A TWA stewardess had befriended her, treated her like a little sister. The young woman had become pregnant at the end of an eight-month affair with a married pilot. Before coming to the home, she'd written a whole series of post-cards to her parents and arranged to have other stews mail them as they flew around the world. All this while she waited for the birth of her own child.

Suzanne's baby came after that brutal labor. When she awoke in the delivery room, she learned that they'd taken her son to the nursery.

"It's easier for you if you don't see him," the head maternity nurse told her. She could scarcely believe she'd carried a child for nine months and endured all the humiliation of hiding this fact from the world, only to be denied the right to see him. No, this couldn't be.

Every day she sneaked up to the nursery, which was on the third floor, and gazed at the infants, eight in all, though their number dwindled to three during her final two weeks at St. Mary's. The attrition came from the couples who marched in and out of the main building.

Suzanne or one of the other childless mothers would spot a car pulling up, and they'd pool by a beautiful stained-glass rose that looked out over the parking lot. While bathed in the flower's warm glow, they'd watch as a well-dressed couple disappeared through the entrance. An hour later they'd watch the same couple leave with a baby in their arms. Instant family. And why not? This was the age of instant everything—potatoes, juice, milk—so why not instant family?

But the wrenching fear was never knowing if it was your child who had been taken away forever. The brutal finality of the departure. Suzanne would find herself glancing at the others, hoping it was one of their babies, as they were glancing back, clearly hoping it was hers. None of them knew. None of them.

After five days of sneaking upstairs, a nurse spotted Suzanne and asked what she wanted.

"I want to see my baby. I don't know which one he is. It doesn't say."

The woman stared at her while Suzanne's eyes raced from infant to infant searching for a familiar feature.

"Come with me."

She thought the nurse was going to report her, but she led her to the third bassinet on the right.

"Is this my baby?"

"Yes, this is your baby."

"You're sure?"

"Can't you tell?"

When Suzanne stared blankly at the baby's face, the nurse added quickly, "Yes, I'm sure he's your baby. But he also looks just like you."

As Suzanne started to cry, the nurse picked her baby up, nested him neatly in a blue receiving blanket, and handed him to her.

Suzanne held him to her chest, felt the fluttery herald of his heart, and wondered how she could ever bear to live without his presence.

Fifteen minutes later the nurse, wet-eyed herself, said, "Come back at seven, after vespers, and you can give him his bottle."

Through the evening service she prayed to keep him, then swept back up to the nursery with great haste and none of her previous regard for secrecy.

This time the nurse encouraged Suzanne to pick up her tiny baby, and when she bent over the bassinet he clutched her finger for the first time. She fed him, burped him, and changed him.

He'd pooped, one of his first real poops, and she smiled as she cleaned him, overjoyed by the mundane maternal nature of the task. And then she'd wiped a little harder at a brown spot before seeing that it was a birthmark rising from his teeny bottom to his lower back.

Suzanne had always believed the birthmark was their secret, an intimate sign that no one else shared. But the secret didn't belong to them any longer. Someone else knew. Someone who called himself "The Searcher." Someone who already had committed a string of grisly crimes.

To stop him, she had to find her son and make sure he was safe. Nothing else could ever have driven her back into the clutches of Catholic Social Services.

CSS had their offices in a stately old high-rise that towered over the downtown. They'd been in the same location for five decades, but there was nothing musty or dusty about their headquarters. It had the crisp efficiency of the true believer who would never be muddled by the middle ground of second thoughts.

A receptionist escorted her down a wood-paneled hallway to the office of an outtake specialist, as they called themselves. Suzanne heard the introduction, but the woman's name—Paige Mertler—didn't register fully because Suzanne already had dubbed her "Stonewall."

From all appearances, she was born to the job. Her smile was broad, but as icy as a winter pond. Her eyes alert, as if to detect the slightest breach in the invisible walls that surrounded her. Her hands, soft and warm but already withdrawing.

"And you're?"

"Suzanne Trayle."

"I thought I recognized you; you're the search angel. And you're a birth mother, too, right?"

"That's right."

"Have a seat. How may I help you?"

Suzanne took a breath and began her plea.

"I'm not going to lie to you and tell you that I have a rare form of cancer and need a bone marrow transplant from my son."

The woman nodded with such sympathy that Suzanne found herself hoping that maybe, just maybe . . .

"And I'm not going to tell you that my son's grandmother is facing a quadruple bypass and wants to be able to meet him before she goes into the hospital."

Again, the sympathetic nod, but it was such a quick clone of its predecessor that Suzanne realized it was born not of feelings but of practice.

"All I'm going to tell you is that I'm an experienced searcher, which you must know if you already know who I am, and I can't find my son, and finding him really is a matter of life or death, as tired as that sounds."

As tired as you feel, she said to herself. She was so beaten from the prospect of coming here and begging that her words sounded weary even to her, shopworn, probably less sincere than the ready smile she still found herself facing.

"You feel like you're facing some real challenges, don't you, Ms. Trayle?"

Suzanne was stung by the practiced ease of Mertler's response, but forced herself to play along.

"Yes, I am. And I know you probably don't agree with what I do."

"You're right about that. We've made promises to birth mothers, and searchers like you violate them every day."

The comment was proffered without anger or urgency, which was more than Suzanne could say about her own snappishness.

"*I* never promised them anything. Every child has a right to know how she came into the world. It's as basic as the right to breathe. And it's no different for birth mothers. If they want to find their children, they should have that right, too."

Mertler shook her head and drummed her fingers on the table as she talked. "We promised *all* of these women that if they gave their babies a better life through adoption, we would give them the promise of secrecy. That wasn't for twenty or thirty years. That was for forever."

"I'm not here to try to change your mind, and if you know who I am, then you must know that you're not going to change mine. I just want you to look me in the eye for a minute and listen to me. Please, can you do that?"

"Of course."

Suzanne thought she detected a softening. She leaned forward and spoke deliberately.

"My son is going to die a terrible death. He's going to be murdered if I don't find him. This isn't melodrama. This isn't a movie. This is the truth. I'm not at liberty to tell you how or why I know this. If I was, I promise . . ." *Shit! She's looking away.* ". . . I promise you I would. But if I tell you why—*please* look at me—other people are going to die. Can you trust me enough to believe me? You say you know who I am. Then you must know my reputation for honesty, even if you don't agree with what I do."

Mertler blinked before breaking eye contact again.

The jury's out. Suzanne could read the woman's indecision. Should she say something more and risk this delicate balance? Or should she remain silent and risk refraining from the one additional plea that might succeed?

"Life is lived, *really* lived, in the exceptions," Suzanne said, wondering where those words had come from, wondering too if they held any wisdom at all.

Mertler trumped her plea by using it as an opening:

"But we can't make *any* exceptions." She locked eyes with Suzanne again, as if to say, *See, I can also make my claims without hesitation.*

But she *had* hesitated. Suzanne had felt it.

"No, please don't believe that . . . crap. I'm sorry. I shouldn't have said that. I'm—"

"No, you shouldn't have. That was very insulting."

"I'm sorry. I'm so sorry." *Oh, Christ, I've lost her.* "Listen, I need you to hear, really hear what I'm saying. I'm not exaggerating. I'm not lying. If you don't help me, my son will die, and birth mothers, these women you cherish so much, they're going to die, too."

"I can't really believe that."

"You have to!" Suzanne shouted, and quickly apologized again. "I'm sorry to sound like such a drama queen, but there's no other way to tell you but the truth."

"Why don't you tell me everything."

For seconds, precious seconds, Suzanne succumbed to the temptation. She thought of Karen and Jesse, murders Mertler could easily verify, and began to formulate her words. But before she could speak, she stopped herself, steadied her gaze, and said,

"Can you promise me that no matter what, you're going to keep everything I tell you to yourself?"

Mertler, Suzanne was shattered to see, proved a paragon of honesty. She shook her head.

"No, I could never promise you that. If you really think people are going to be killed, I think you should go to the police. We at Catholic Social Services maintain the interests of the birth mothers above all else. We made a promise . . ."

Her words stung Suzanne, though they were barely heard, as all words fail when they've grown overly familiar, when rote repetition has turned them to cant. And she had no need of their ill advisement anyway: Rejection was a tread worn deep in her path.

A moment later, as if on cue, they stood up together. Mertler handed her a business card and told her to call if she had any more questions.

But how can I have any more questions, Suzanne asked herself as she walked out the door, *when every answer is denied me?*

She stopped at a Starbucks and sipped her coffee on a bench in a nearby public square. She needed time to recover from Paige Mertler, a true believer if there ever was one.

But an innate sense of fairness forced Suzanne to recognize her own in-flexibility as well. Like two sides in the abortion debate, absolutes in action that never move.

Well, she'd tried. Brought her begging bowl and held it out and come away empty. *Maybe,* she thought, *you should be looking for answers not in the distant past, but in more recent—and violent—events.*

If The Searcher was the same man who'd raped her, and then murdered Karen and Jesse, why had he spared her life? To taunt her? What would make her so special to him? What would make him want to seek her out at a conference? To stalk her? Was he doing it even now?

She lowered her coffee cup and caught the eye of a homeless man in an oversize overcoat leaning against a bus stop shelter. He stared at her with the vacant intensity of the deeply psychotic.

She looked away. Her rapist had been so cunning, calm. He'd hummed that song to her. Had he hummed it to Karen and Jesse, too? And if he had, whom would he hum it to next?

Suzanne started striding to her car. This was no time to nurse a cup of coffee or ask questions for which there were no immediate answers. You've got to hurry up and find your son, or you're going to find pieces of him in the mail.

And then as she walked into the parking garage and spotted her hybrid car, an answer did come to her. An answer so devastating that it took the form of an insidious question, a "what if " question that had her squeezing her key fob and setting off the panic button by mistake. But even the insistent, drilling wail of the car alarm could not make her move because the question had paralyzed her. It was the one question no mother who's been raped would ever want to ask herself, and yet it was the one question she could no longer avoid:

What if The Searcher was her son?

8

I BLEND IN. SUZANNE Trayle definitely does not. She's too pretty, frankly, though I've noticed a distinct tiring in her appearance of late, an absence of regard for her appeal, and wondered if I should take credit for this, or if the downward slope of middle age has nudged her toward anonymity, as it does to so many women who find themselves withdrawing from the moist demands of sex.

But I am a perfect chameleon in my soiled rummage-sale overcoat. I blend in so well that only a minute ago I stared right into her eyes, and never once did she seem to suspect that I am the one person she fears most.

She's still sitting right there on a bench with a cup of coffee, not fifty feet away. It was a thrill to stare into her eyes. Firsts are always fun, and I didn't have this opportunity in Chicago. But I gave her my eyes today, opened them wide, and refused to blink for the duration. She looked, she stared, but she did not see. This happens all the time. People see so little of the world as it actually exists around them. They're too tied up with other concerns, which explains

Ms. Trayle's blinders. She'd just gone to Catholic Social Services. I watched her go in, and I watched her come out less than an hour later. I might ask Patsy to get a report from her counterpart up here. I'll be seeing Patsy tomorrow morning and will try to gauge her receptiveness to suggestion.

There goes Ms. Trayle. She's walking away, and quickly. A woman on a mission, I'd say. And I'm on one, too, that I'll make as memorable for her as that hotel room in Chicago, though I suspect the accommodations will be less plush here in Portland.

I keep my hood up and follow at a distance. Lots of people on the street, some so ragged that they make me appear almost princely. Not that I need worry. She's far too preoccupied. I could creep right up to her. I *will* creep right up to her.

As I'm closing the gap, feeling my pulse quicken, she grants me the greatest gift of all. She turns right into the parking garage where she left her car. This is not unexpected, but the delivery on the promise still thrills me. To those of us who prefer nonconsensual sex, a parking garage is paradise.

In anticipation, I casually open my coat and discreetly unzip my pants. She takes no more than half a dozen steps into the welcoming shadows (I'm almost upon her, my eagerness an erection) when a car alarm goes off, and she freezes not five feet in front of me. I could haul her down between cars (no one would hear her, and I have a strong track record for this kind of assignation), but heads are turning.

It takes me a few seconds to spot the key fob in her hand, and another second or two to figure out that she's tripped her car alarm. She looks as stunned as anyone else by the sounds now filling her ears. I realize that people might think (no, they *will* think) she set it off because of me, because of the hooded creature behind her. And I'm innocent. That's what really galls me. I haven't done a thing.

I should go up to her right now, take her hand, show her what she's done, earn her gratitude, turn all of this to my favor. She looks so confused. But if I try to help her there's a chance she'd recognize my voice, and a guy in a gray wool coat is already rushing toward her, throwing hard looks my way. His appearance gives her a start.

"Are you all right?" he shouts.

She stabs at the fob with her thumb, silencing the alarm.

"Yeah, I'm fine, thanks."

Her voice sounds shaky.

"Did you mean to set it off?" His eyes sweep to the sidewalk where I have moved. They linger on me for a second, no more, as if he doesn't want trouble, either, before returning to her.

"No. It was a mistake."

She says something else in a softer voice, perhaps an apology—it has that tone—but I'm already moving down the sidewalk.

This obsession with Ms. Trayle could have cost me dearly. That's what I tell myself as I drift farther down the street. But when I saw my opportunity, when she actually walked into that parking garage, I could no more resist taking her than I could have overlooked her sleepy vulnerability in Chicago.

The memory of her at the conference made me want to fly up here in the first place. I arranged a three-day weekend (a couple of cancellations and I was free) so I could pay my visit to Jesse B. and see the "Search Angel" when she wasn't basking in the attention of all her fans.

I arrived about seven on Saturday and went directly to her house. It looked like the lights were on in every room, but there was no coming or going. Same thing Sunday, except for her husband walking out to grab the paper off the porch.

This morning I thought I'd do better staking out her office. I was early enough to catch Ami opening up. She wore a trench coat, of all things, which looked ridiculous on her, like a kiddie detective in a school play. A fedora with the brim angled rakishly across her brow would have completed the ensemble. She's such a small girl, hardly a woman at all, and yet oddly appealing.

Ms. Trayle arrived about forty minutes later. Finally. She didn't look nearly so pleasing as her assistant, but as she climbed the stairs, offering a fine study of her bottom, I was all but overwhelmed with the urgency that first struck me in her hotel room in Chicago. I began to have visions of walking right into that office, of taking over up there; but then the UPS truck pulled up, and the letter it contained amused me even more. It took so little time for Ms. Trayle to respond; not more than an hour later she rushed out of there looking grim as a gargoyle.

Watching her this closely has been a desire of mine since I saw her on *Oprah* two years ago. This was the seminal moment I talked about before, when I was struck by the idea that she was hiding something. She was too obsessed with *The Search,* and I'd worked with enough birth mothers at that point to strongly suspect that her tears on that show were about a lot more than just being an adoptee. It's a given in my field that when a client goes over the top with her emotions, you start looking around for the real cause. With her, I thought it was a kid.

I was very confident I'd find her bastard quickly. After all, I was no slouch in this regard and had already enjoyed the rich pleasures of my own finds, though up to then the scattered offspring had interested me far less than their promiscuous mothers. And I suppose if I'm going to be completely honest, I'd have to say that it irritated me to no end that this poser was claiming attention that rightfully belonged to me. Here she was reaping public acclaim and admiration, while my considerably greater successes were by necessity confined to the private realm. But I knew that finding her kid, if she had one, would build an unbreakable link between the Search Angel and The Searcher. I would shine, if only by silent association.

So I started looking. I used the Internet with the full confidence that I would find the answer quickly (what I would do with a kid of hers was never in doubt). I then made trips to county courthouses and libraries in three states where I sought out dusty stacks of old newspapers, combing through the classifieds for those boldface legal pronouncements that disclose the most immoral acts in the most pedestrian prose.

But all of my work came to nothing, and I have to admit that I began to wonder if I was wrong. Maybe Ms. Trayle really was one of those people who get it into their head to do something like The Search and never quit. The Coon Dog Syndrome (a term of my own devising). I did come up with all kinds of scenarios to explain the absence of a child, the black hole through which he or she might have slipped. The most likely? Private adoption through a physician or lawyer to a family in a state where the secrecy of the act is held in the same awe as the Second Coming.

Months of raw frustration passed, and then my efforts turned up a footprint from the great Search Angel herself. I found it in a user file of birth dates of boys born thirty-two years ago. It was all the encouragement I needed. I was convinced that my own obsession had begun to bear the sweetest fruit. The metaphor, though overused, is not inappropriate because when I saw those dates in that file I sensed a cellular connection to her child, even though I'd yet to find him, a budding sense that more than her son would arise from the resolution of this mystery.

But even as my certainty of this grew, my frustration over not finding him became a fever, and I confess to having taken it out on others, finding brief satisfaction in the slow strangulation of a birth mother in Ottawa, who greeted my appearance without hesitation by throwing her arms around my neck and gushing "My son! My son!"

"Yes, Mama," I cooed in the cold Canadian air. "It's me. May I come in?"

Her warmth, her embrace would have been enough to convince even the prissiest critics of Genetic Sexual Attraction, that vaguely suggestive term for the swirl of incestuous feelings that accompanies the reunion of so many birth parents and their children. But GSA, as it's known to those of us who appreciate backhand sex, doesn't conform to our culture's rigidly rosy view of adoption, so you're less likely to hear it discussed in the public forums of an adoption conference than you are to find Mormon elders openly championing the polygamous behavior of their horny brethren.

The instant her lips found my cheek, I ripped off her blouse and bra, pummeled her face, and sliced off her pants without my usual regard for skin. What did I care of blood? It wasn't mine, and I intended to show her that it was no longer really hers either.

When I was nearly done, I decided to leave her gargling on a symbol of sorts: a broom I saw hiding in her hall closet. I found her throat more accepting than you might think, and thoroughly enjoyed the sight of the handle sticking out of her mouth, as if it not only belonged there but had finally found its proper home.

I might have remained a bitter man without Patsy's help, but when I studied Ms. Trayle's adoption records I discovered a fact so stunning that I had to take deep, *deep* breaths to recover from the shock. To tell you, I had discovered a jewel far richer than any I could have imagined.

Now that I had her son, I had all that I'd need to ensure Ms. Trayle's silence. But would the police spot a pattern on their own when birth mothers started dying? Would those puffed-up profilers at the FBI? Not a chance. We are, I'm thrilled to say, the most violent of the developed nations, number one in homicides in the Western world with upward of twenty thousand a year. By comparison, the Europeans are pikers, the Canadians not even players. The fact that a few victims here and there are birth mothers is, in the first instance, hardly worthy of the word *coincidence.* Statistically speaking, it is probable. And in the second instance, a birth mother's secrecy in life about her shameful past does a great job of concealing the most telling clue to her death. This amuses me immensely, knowing the way one secret keeps the other, like twins who can't stop holding hands, even in their dotage.

The age of terrorism, and they still have us deplaning on the tarmac in Phoenix. Where's the security in that? Where's the comfort? The desert heat blankets us the minute the attendant cracks the cabin door, and it doesn't look like I'm going to be getting out of here quickly. Right in front of me there's a fat woman in a loud dress clogging the aisle, and I have visions of having to put my foot to her enormous buns to push her off the plane.

I trudge through the airport parking garage savaged by the unseasonal heat and the awful associations that I'm now forced to make with these places. I used to love them, could draw on the finest of memories, but now all I can think about is her. What was Ms. Trayle thinking when she squeezed that panic button? She looked like she was in another world, standing there like she'd never move again. I was worried she'd seen me coming up on her, caught my reflection in a car window. But that wasn't it. She never turned and pointed to me when that man ran up. She never knew I was there. Whatever caused all that commotion was in her head.

My car is like an oven. The second I hit the a/c, a blast of hot, stale air hits me in the face. Dusk, autumn, and the heat's still enough to kill you.

I'm exhausted. All I want to do is sleep. Tomorrow morning I've got that appointment with Patsy. I'll see if she'll contact Catholic Social Services in Portland, find out what Ms. Trayle's been up to.

So far Patsy's been delightfully free with her favors, although I'm not sure I should be reminding myself of this. It only feeds my fantasies, which don't need any help these days: The boundaries of our therapeutic relationship have been dissolving faster than salt in the sea, and the diversionary games I've been playing with her of late are no longer satisfying my needs. I even avoided my archives before her last session on the theory, lame as it was, that abstaining might still my hands, but it only fired my desires more. It was as if a wild river had been suddenly dammed, and all that pooled, pent-up need was cracking apart a massive retention wall. You can't repress anything. Nothing. And you don't have to be a shrink to know this. It's as basic to life . . . and death . . . as blood.

Tomorrow morning I'll develop and print the first roll of Ms. Bonham's. I'd do it tonight, but I'm too fried. But I *must* see them soon. It's been three days since I looked her over for the last time. Three days of having to sustain myself with those memories because I've been on the road, and they're not the kind of pictures you drop off at a one-hour photo place. *Three days!* Abstinence is no cure. Abstinence is a curse.

So in the morning I'll indulge myself with Jesse Bonham, in the tangled pleasure I took with her, and then I'll try to control myself with Patsy. The tension will be sweet as syrup.

The freeway's crowded. The freeway's always crowded. This evening it's a van full of illegals. Guess they took a tumble. Ambulances everywhere. We have to edge past. Some of the bodies already have their faces covered. What a waste of death. What a waste of time. It takes me an hour to get home. It should have taken twenty minutes.

I do go right to bed, but the moment I close my eyes it's as if I've poured a pocketful of quarters into the dream jukebox. The worst part? I can't remember them. A night like that, and all I've got to show for it is an overwhelming feeling of dread. If I were one of my clients, I'd advise myself to look for the source of those shadowy dreams in the events of the day before, but I'm not one of my clients, so I don't have to put up with that crap. Instead, I try to take pleasure in the fact that it'll be a sunny day, even if that does mean more heat. A couple of days in Oregon is enough to make me appreciate the desert with its open, unabashed expanses, its naked willingness to be seen. I would not have wanted to awaken to a world of clouds; they would have looked too much like I feel.

The first roll develops nicely, and I make a contact sheet, pore over its damp surface with my magnifier.

These are good. These are very, very good.

I pick out the three that I'll print right away, including the one I'm drawn to the most. It shows Jesse's face when I first told her to smile.

She did a piss-poor job of it, but puncture wounds *are* painful, and the "thread" that I used was not what you'd call surgical quality. She lasted longer than Karen, so I trust my selections, not to mention my skills, are improving.

My memory of Jesse is sufficiently refreshed to get me through a short run, brief shower, breakfast, and the quick commute to my office, where I can now immerse myself fully in those photos. I know this is risky, getting myself all worked up before Patsy arrives, but doing without the pictures didn't help, either. And the truth is, I can't stop myself. The limits of control have stretched to the point where they have already begun to snap. Poor Patsy.

I keep picking up the picture of Jesse's face when I first told her to smile. It's tightly framed and in perfect focus. You can see every stitch, and if you study it closely, as I am, you can see how she tried, I mean *really* tried, to obey me. Her lips are straining so hard to smile that it looks like the seam is about to pop apart.

Patsy enters the outer office. It's amazing how attuned I've become to her movements, to the care she applies to the closing of a door, the moderation of her footsteps, the way she settles silently on the couch when those footsteps cease, as if her robust bottom floats above the cushion rather than sits on it.

I'm aroused by Jesse's pictures, but more by the roguish possibilities of adding Patsy to the archives. I've spent far too much energy restraining myself as it is, focusing on fantasies while she weeps about her lost baby. And I understand that even thinking of this is a way of giving myself license to do what means the most to me this morning, which is murdering Patsy.

It's the pressure in my pants that has me thinking such self-defeating thoughts. Lust, in whatever guise, is the body's simple greed, the organ's own ambition; and when it feels this powerful, it's as if it belongs to nobody, least of all me. And that's scary, because what would I do if it decided to truly take matters into its own hands?

As it appears to be doing now. I'm opening the door heedless of the photos that I've left shuffled together on the folder on my desk. The cabinet itself is cracked open.

The organ is taking titillation to an extreme that I never would have risked. I feel witness to my own weakness. As Patsy may be, too. Her glance has fallen to where my urges are most apparent. I didn't wear my jockstrap today. It's not that I forgot, it's that I didn't want to remember, teething even then on the possibilities of Patsy's skin.

Her eyes are alert with tension. Is this delight? Disgust? Or is she too distracted to notice what she is seeing, much like Ms. Trayle when she stared into my eyes?

My excitement recedes from view only when I sit, but its rich hunger devours Jesse's pictures, which lie before me.

As we climb out of the mire of greetings, I'm doing the calculations: Patsy lives alone. She has kept the secrecy of her motherhood to herself. She has but one friend, a female who sees her once or twice a month, a woman with many friends who coffees with Patsy only when it's convenient. (Patsy knows this. It breaks her heart.)

No boyfriend. Never a husband. Since the start of therapy, hasn't Patsy rued the absence of a lover? Blamed her physical "isolation" on her need for "true" intimacy before she can "get started"?

The calculations continue: This is a weekday. She's expected at Catholic Social Services this morning. If she doesn't show up, she'll be missed. Someone as reliable as Patsy doesn't blow off work. Someone as reliable as Patsy keeps a daybook or a Palm Pilot with her appointments listed clearly. Someone as reliable as Patsy might have e-mailed or called her boss to remind him she'd be late, leaving precious evidence of when she was last alive.

All of which intrigues me, makes the challenge of Patsy so much greater. Makes me ache for release.

"Patsy"—I hear my voice as if it, too, belongs to another—"take off your clothes."

My eyes fall to the folder. I watch my hands pick it up so I can look closely at Jesse again.

Smile!

Patsy does not see Jesse. Not yet. I'm still weighing showing her, knowing that with her first glimpse she'll condemn herself to death. I could never let her go then.

She's looking, but not at the folder. She's staring at me. I cannot help but notice that she's not running from my office. Not yet.

With effort, more than Patsy will ever know, I swing around in my chair, stand, and place the folder in the cabinet. I make sure I'm in profile, unmistakable in my intentions.

Patsy also stands. When she turns from me, when I'm certain she's refusing me, I could burst with joy because it means I can rape her. There's no willingness on her part, none at all, and if I'm going to destroy the dam that's been holding back my wildest impulses, then I want to make sure I drain it of every pleasure.

But just as I'm ready to leap after her and tear that cheap dress off her back, she lifts it up over her head. And there she is, facing away from me in her panty hose, underpants, and bra.

She's trimmer than I would have thought, been hiding herself in loose-fitting clothing. She looks like she exercises. Odd that she hasn't mentioned this. Not at all unpleasant to look at, to consider her flesh, taking hold of it, forcing her to contemplate her imminent mortality.

I sense she's taking pride in this, the way other women I've known will have sex just to show someone, anyone, the results of all those hours in the health club.

"Don't stop," I tell her, again in a voice that feels no more mine than the organ that drives me to do this.

Patsy still faces away from me. In shame, I now suspect. She does not move, and her head hangs down. But now she stands up straight, as if suddenly resolute, and her hand rises up her spine, fingers as nimble as cats as she unhooks her bra, which separates and falls to the sides like snakes from a tryst.

But then she surprises me by turning as she sheds the cups. Her willingness is robbing me of what I want most. She's stealing her greatest gift by giving up, thinks her consent is desired when it's roundly despised. It means only that for her my pleasure will have to come at a much higher price.

If you murder her here, you can never come back.

Everything I've achieved in this practice could slip away right now, the confidences of birth mothers, a steady income, flexible work schedule. And here's Patsy welcoming the lone act that could take all this away. Doesn't know what it is, but she's begging for it. *Begging.*

Without another word, she pulls down her panty hose and underpants, balls them up, and drops them on her dress, which she's draped across the chair she was sitting on.

She turns back to me again, and I see that she has surprisingly scant pubic hair, her sex almost as naked as a five-year-old's.

This does little for me. Only the immediacy of death drives my desire, which she's now confusing with ardor.

She kneels before me, and more than anything she's ever said, this act of humility and sexual hunger explains why she's here, why she works for Catholic Social Services. Why she's a lonely forty-year-old birth mother. She brought it on herself. All of it. This too. This most especially.

I take her head in my hands. I feel I could crush her skull as she opens my fly. I hear the sweet chatter of the zipper and feel her warm hand wresting free the object of her desire.

My hardness should not amaze me, but it does. She takes me in her mouth with none of the tepidness I would have expected minutes ago, not with obligation but with an enthusiasm that can be explained only by an obscene sexual drive. Right away she also starts touching herself, and looks as well practiced at onanism as she is in the oral arts.

I move my hands from her crown to her neck. I think of Claire in Ottawa, Jesse in Las Vegas, Karen in Denver, and the others whose names have faded, whose acute pleasures I can no longer feel. I try, I try mightily to imagine that I'm doing it to Claire again. If Patsy only knew how hard I'm working to save her life. But to no avail. I cannot substitute memory for murder, fantasy for fate, not with a desire to kill this powerful.

My fingers move closer and closer together, corralling her throat. Her noises grow louder. Struggle? Excitement? I have no idea.

In seconds, my organ flies from her mouth. She can no longer suck. Her head arches back. She goes limp. Collapses to the carpet. But it's not from lack of air. My God, she's had an orgasm, *le petite mort*, the little death, as the French call it.

Her eyes are rolled back, the lids open, revealing the whites and a slim crescent of iris in each. Seeing this triggers my own pleasure, and I stripe her chest with semen as I, too, drop to the carpet. My legs have turned to mush. Still, I reach up to my desk and grab it.

Her eyelids flutter. She's coming to.

I see red marks on her neck. I have bruised her badly. They will darken in the days to come. So might her memory of this moment. But for now she sees me and, yes, she smiles for the camera.

9

WIND AND RAIN scolded the windows, and weak light leaked through the curtains. Suzanne lay in bed staring at the ceiling, petrified by a plan that had come to her in the first moments of consciousness. A way to keep The Searcher from murdering again . . . if she could steel herself enough to follow through. A way to find her son, too, but only if he turned out to be the killer himself.

She'd gone to bed knowing she needed to come up with a means of stopping this beast, but its most crucial component felt no more bidden than disease.

After her panic attack in the parking garage yesterday, she'd called Ami and asked her to scour the Internet's most extensive databases. But when the rest of the day passed without a return call, she'd known that her assistant had not come up with any leads.

Then late yesterday, following a frustrating game of telephone tag, she'd managed to land an emergency appointment with Cara, the bulk of which she'd spent in tears grieving over the gruesome possibility that her son had raped her, and raped and murdered Karen and Jesse.

Cara had counseled the obvious, or what was obvious to Suzanne's cerebral side: Until she was certain The Searcher was her son, it was pointless to torture herself. A few moments later Cara buttressed this idea by nodding—always a sign of encouragement from a therapist—when Suzanne questioned the picture's authenticity: Maybe it had been doctored?

But Cara nodded just as readily when Suzanne's fears made her wonder aloud if The Searcher had found a cunning way to photograph himself. And if he had, were the woman and child his own family? Or had he hired them as unknowing extras for his horror show?

A period of silence followed before Cara said, "So what do you make of all this?"

"I think," Suzanne said miserably, "that it feels like a huge cobweb with a big black spider waiting in the wings, and until I can sweep it away, I'm not calling the police."

"Are you absolutely sure you don't want to involve them?"

"I'm not sure of anything anymore." Suzanne pointed to Cara, her hand shaking visibly. "Except that I don't want *you* calling them either."

"You know I wouldn't. I just want to make sure you're comfortable with your decision."

"Comfortable? I'm not comfortable. I could never be comfortable with this, but I feel even worse about what could happen to my son and his family."

As acute as these concerns were, they barely began to broach the two most excruciating—and inextricably linked—questions: How could she determine The Searcher's identity, and how many more birth mothers would die before he was unmasked?

No ready replies, and no balm for her curdled nerves until she'd stood at her easel and distracted herself well into the night with the lonely Japanese maple she was slowly bringing to life. She'd even managed to sleep peacefully until she'd awakened to this plan, as if to an alarm clock painted with the very face of fear.

You can't do it, and you know what? You don't have to. Nobody would ever expect you to take this kind of chance. With considerable relief, she finally threw the covers aside and got up, telling herself that it simply wasn't in her nature to take such a huge personal risk.

But she questioned what her nature was now. Could rape, murder, and the most brutal of all threats leave it essentially unchanged? That question needled her as she gently nudged Burton, who was still sleeping on the couch.

"Coffee?" Not that she really needed to ask, not after all these years.

He blinked and said yes, thanked her and sat up, looking as rumpled in his pajamas as he appeared starched and pressed when he presided over his hearing room.

She watched him make his way to the bathroom on legs stiffened by sleep and years of hiking and hunting. He'd grown up in rural Oregon, and until a few years ago had participated in the annual fall ritual of trampling through the forest to try to bag a buck. Alas (from Suzanne's point of view), he was more successful than not, and in the ensuing months she'd found herself eating more Bambi than beef.

Her husband's familiar gait warmed her, and she felt a genuine urge to hold him close. But it passed.

She fixed the coffee and was pouring out two cups when he walked into the kitchen, hair combed and face freshly shaved even though he hadn't sipped his first hit of caffeine, testament to his ongoing efforts to work his way back into her good graces. Every inch a mile, in his dreams.

"Appreciate it, hon." He helped himself to one of the cups.

She stroked his smooth chin. "Got a date?" She couldn't resist.

"I hope so," he said smiling. "With you," he added in a voice lynched by panic, as if she might have thought otherwise.

She patted him on the shoulder, and he settled at the table, hunkering over his coffee like he was worried about the thieving contractors whose excuses he had to listen to every day.

They breakfasted on cold cereal while she sorted through the mail that had accumulated over the past several days, his and hers, everybody seeking donations. And who could blame them? Hard times getting harder. The state had shredded social services, and had even slashed weeks from the school year. The parsimony had taken a personal turn when Burton and another administrative law judge had been urged to take their comp time before the end of the year, and he'd expressed more than a little worry over whether his promotion by the governor would ever take place.

She rued how little mail arrived that she actually wanted to read. Nobody wrote letters and mailed them. It's all e-mail, and she was as guilty as anyone.

No, that's not true, she remembered with a jolt. The Searcher wrote you a letter. A piece of mail she hadn't shared with Burton yet. She'd wanted to figure out how she'd handle its horrifying news and grisly threats before involving him. Burton could be impulsive, not only in his personal life—witness Gabriella—but also of late in his hearing room: He'd been reprimanded twice in the past two months for decisions he never would have made if he'd given himself even a moment's pause.

Now she had come up with a high-stakes strategy to snare The Searcher, but to make it work she'd definitely need Burton's help. Yet . . . she still didn't know if *she* had the stomach to carry it out, if her nature, so basically peaceful, could enforce the brutal imperatives that had darkened her first waking moments.

She headed back to the bathroom to get ready for work, tossing on clothes with little regard for style, rejecting its demands as reflexively as the lipstick and mascara with which she no longer bothered.

Burton was on his second cup when she stood beside him and rested her arm across his back.

"I want you to know how much I appreciate you staying with me."

He looked up, evidently surprised by her words. "Of course, I wouldn't think of not being here for you. Never."

She leaned over and kissed a bald spot on the top of his head. A year ago it had been the size of a nickel, six months ago a quarter. Now there wasn't a coin in the realm that could have covered it.

A gust of chilly damp air swept over her face as she walked to the garage, and the answer came to her, the one about whether the violence she'd known, and the recent threats, could alter her basic nature. After hearing what The Searcher had done, the details of his horrific crimes—and his promise to repeat them over and over—she could do anything to him. *Anything*. Not out of courage, out of fear. *Like a dog,* she thought bitterly, *that bites only with its back to a wall.*

Ami laid the photograph on her desk when Suzanne walked in.

"I couldn't come up with anything on the Net. Sorry. But I've been working on this." Ami pointed to the bench in the picture. "I got the manufacturer's name off it. It's Delton Designs of North Carolina. But I don't think it's going to do much good, either, 'cause they distribute to all fifty states, and Canada and Mexico." Ami peered at Suzanne, wrinkling her freckled forehead. "You okay?"

"I'm better. Is—"

"'Cause you look kind of pale."

"I always look pale. Is there anything in the photo that you think *will* help?"

Ami shook her head slowly. "No, to be honest, I don't think so."

As Suzanne hung up her coat, her assistant reported that Sun Systems, a company they'd used in the past, hadn't been able to do much with the angle of the shadows in the picture.

"They say it could have been taken pretty much anywhere in North America."

As for the tree branch in the background, Ami had determined that it was indeed a maple, but a species promiscuous in its profusion. The clothes, the baby carrier, and the baby herself had also yielded nothing. Not a clue, she reported.

"He's shrewd," Ami offered as consolation.

Until now, Suzanne hadn't given up entirely on the hope that her assistant would have news about her son. She was a whiz with computers, and if anyone could shake a leaf loose from the Net's towering tree of knowledge, it was Ami. A mere sliver of evidence would have been sufficient for Suzanne to shelve the plan, at least for a day or two. But there would be no postponing it now, even though she still searched for a reason to delay as she sat down at her desk. *There's got to be something else you can do.* But she understood as quickly that anyone who considers putting herself in serious danger probably engages in the same kind of desperate thinking. It's as predictable as pain: You stand at the edge of life's cliff saying to yourself, *No, I don't have to jump. I can't jump. The river's too narrow, the fall's too far.* But then you turn back to the hoary presence that chased you to the edge, and the drop looks less ghastly. How else can you explain the tortured souls who leaped from burning buildings, from certain pain to certain oblivion? How else can you explain yourself? she wondered.

She stared at the blank face of her computer and asked herself if that's what she was doing: getting ready to jump. *Then don't take Ami with you. Let go of her hand. She's got her whole life ahead of her.*

"Say it." Ami's voice jarred Suzanne.

"Say what?"

"Whatever's on your mind."

Suzanne looked at her. A kid, no matter her leggy outfits, heels, or the chic cut of her thick red hair. Still a kid.

"You've got to promise me something."

"What's that?"

"You've got to promise me you won't get involved."

"No way am I going to promise you that," Ami replied with such starch that she startled Suzanne. "I know you all too well. Tell me what you're thinking, and we'll work on it together."

"No," Suzanne insisted. "I need your total cooperation on this one. It's not like anything I've ever done before."

"Nothing you ever do is like anything you've ever done before. That's why you're so good, and that's why I'm here."

"No, trust me, Ami. This one's really different, it's very dangerous."

"Like Jesse Bonham dangerous? Karen Sephs dangerous?"

Suzanne nodded, rose and walked to the door, checked the lock.

"Okay, I hear you," Ami said, watching her. "Go ahead."

"Not until I hear you say that you'll agree to do what I say."

"Don't I always?"

"No, you don't. And you're still dancing around that promise."

"Okay, I agree. Now tell me."

"I'm going to pose as one of our birth moms. I'm thinking Laura Kessing, and I'll explain why in a moment. I'm going to go into the chat rooms, and I'll start running ads in the classifieds throughout the region. That's something you could help me with. In the ANN, too." The *Adoptees' Network Newsletter*. "I'm going to say I've got terminal uterine cancer, and I've got to find my son before I die. I'm going to make The Searcher come to me."

"That's insane!" Ami slapped her desk so hard her computer rattled. "What you're saying is you're going to turn yourself into bait and hope he bites."

"It's a sting operation. He says he likes to pose as missing sons. I'll draw him out." Suzanne sat back down.

"And then what?"

"Then I'll do what I have to do."

"You mean kill him. I think he's a little better at it than you are. The last time I heard he'd killed two of our birth moms. Who knows how many others he's murdered that we don't know about."

"I don't have any choice, Ami. I look at our list and wonder who he's going to torture to death next. Is it going to be Beth Saunders or Ginger Donahue? Kathy Biggs? Becky Margosian? It's a long list, lots of choices. Or is he going to go after my son? My son's wife and baby daughter."

"Maybe he is your son," Ami said in little more than a whisper. She looked away, too, and in the silence they heard the soft rain on the window, like the sound of rodents scampering along a floorboard. "I'm sorry. I shouldn't have—"

"I already thought of that. WCS, right?"

Worst case scenario. They'd trained themselves to envision the worst case scenario whenever they couldn't find a birth mother. Worst case scenario: The birth mom died in a fire, and all her identifying papers were burned up. Worst cast scenario: The grandmother had given birth to the baby that the mother had claimed as her own when she turned the infant over to the adoption agency. There were always worst case scenarios, but this was the worst of the worst.

"It *is* possible," Ami said.

"I know, and that's another reason to do this. If this guy's my son, then it's all the more reason for me to find him."

Not that she could really bring herself to believe that her own son was The Searcher. Not that she thought she'd actually have to kill the one person she'd spent most of her life looking for. But then she remembered the mothers she'd read about at murder trials, the ones who'd insisted on the innocence of their sons, even as their sons rose in court to offer surprise confessions.

"But if it's your son, it makes everything easy. You can go to the police, the FBI. What's he going to do, torture himself to death?"

"What you're saying is we make a guess. We *guess* it's him, and we go to the cops. But if we're wrong—and it seems just as possible that this theory is way off base—then we're setting him and his family up for horrible deaths."

"And if you're wrong about setting yourself up as a piece of bait, you're sentencing yourself to a death just as bad. You know that, don't you?"

"No, I don't know that. But I do know that I can't put myself before my son. I did that thirty-two years ago, and I'll *never* do that again. I'll draw this . . . this asshole out, and if I have to, I'll kill him."

Said so decisively, it forced her to weigh the means of delivery. Shoot him? That seemed most likely. In the head? The heart? *Just how* are *you going to kill him?* She found herself recoiling from these questions as readily as a gun after it's been fired. Safer, in these pressing seconds, to return to strategy.

"I'm going to have the element of surprise. He's never going to know what hit him. And I won't be doing this alone."

"I'm glad to hear that, but you just made me promise not to get involved."

"Not you, Ami. Burton."

"Burton?"

"I've been thinking this whole thing through. It's his son, too. He's just as responsible as I am, and he's a damned sight better with a gun."

Suzanne toyed with her mouse, knowing she'd overstated Burton's skills. True, he'd hunted most of his life and had been a grunt in Vietnam, a ground soldier who'd survived months of fierce combat in the aptly named Iron Triangle northwest of Saigon; but no matter how much she might wish otherwise, her estranged husband had settled into a creaky middle age in his hearing room, more gavel than grit these days.

"You really want to put your life in Burton's hands? I wouldn't exactly call him Mr. Reliable."

Ami caught her with that remark. She'd always refrained from commenting on her personal difficulties. Suzanne fiddled with her mouse for another second and looked up.

"He's been staying with me, sleeping on the couch. What I had in mind might even give us a chance to work a few things out. That's why I was thinking of Laura Kessing. She heads down to Costa Rica about this time every year. She lives near Cascadia, up in the hills—"

"Yeah, I know. I had to drive her daughter up there. It's in the middle of nowhere."

"It's not the middle of nowhere. The town's a half hour away. I could set up everything from her place."

"The town? The town's a gas station and a grocery store, and a couple of motels. That's it for twenty miles."

"Maybe that's good," Suzanne said. She clicked the mouse one more time and pushed it away.

"Good?"

"Be done with him, once and for all. No one's ever going to miss this creep."

Ami looped a length of hair around her finger. "Wow. When you said you had a plan, I had no idea. Would Laura let you? We never did find her son."

"But we found Cassie, and you know how grateful she was."

Laura Kessing had been one of the more unusual—and heartbreaking—cases: a birth mother who'd given up two babies in her teens, a boy, and sixteen months later the girl, Cassie. The son's case was still open.

"Let me make sure I've got this straight," Ami said. "You're going to lure The Searcher up there, and then you're going to kill him. You really think you can do that?"

"Do I really think I can do it? Of course I can do it. He's torturing and murdering our birth moms. He's *bragging* about it, and he's threatening to torture and kill my own son, my granddaughter, for God's sakes. I'll kill him on sight."

Now, fired by what he'd done and by what he'd promised to do, she *could* imagine his murder: a man sitting back on his heels, head hanging forward, blindfolded for an execution-style killing: a model for murder taken directly from the movies . . . and the mob. But curiously, there was no gun to his head, as if that element, the most critical, remained the one detail she couldn't conjure.

So she forced herself to see a pistol rising to his temple, and then *she* pulled the trigger. The sound seemed so real it startled her and jarred her into looking at herself anew. But that's what the murder of loved ones does to you. It makes you angry enough to kill. Nothing noble about it. Simple survival when the dregs of humankind come knocking on your door. She'd make certain The Searcher knocked on the wrong door at last.

Ami had walked across the room, stared out the window. She turned back to her now.

"Suzanne, are you really, really sure? You get upset if you see a dead cat by the side of the road."

"I don't have any choice. If I go to the police, he says he's going to kill my son and his family. Send me pieces of him!"

Her face fell to her palms, disappeared beneath their damp cover, though her words and anguish couldn't be muffled.

"I can't believe I could have ever given birth to this monster. I just can't." Her hands dropped away, lifeless as fallen leaves. "I've got to do something. I can't sit around. He's a killer, and he's promising to keep on killing. That's what he says, and that's what he's done."

Ami came over and put her arm around Suzanne's shoulder.

"Okay, then let me tell you about the hole in your donut."

"All right. What is it?"

"He keeps track of you. He knows you went to Florida, so he's either watching you or tracking you through your credit cards. You're not going to be able to skip town without him knowing. And what about Jesse's funeral? You going to skip that, too?"

"We're going to send flowers, and our deepest sympathies. I guarantee you that if Jesse were here, she'd say go after the guy who killed her, and don't worry about the good-byes. But you're right about him keeping track of me. That's a problem I've thought about a lot."

"And?"

"I think I can slip away, maybe take my car or leave it in the garage. And I won't dare use my cards."

"Not good enough." Ami stopped, forcing Suzanne to look directly at her.

"He's too smart. He'll notice that you're not using them, and if you leave your car in the garage, he could look in the window and see it. That's not going to work. There's only one real safe way to do this, and it's pretty simple actually. I'll take your car and credit cards, and take off. I'll even throw on a blonde wig and dress like you."

"Where would you go?"

"Anywhere but Laura Kessing's. I don't know, out to Fort Lauderdale. He tracked you there a couple of weeks ago. Let him do it again."

"But that turns *you* into bait, too. You'd be risking your life. I'm not going to let you do that."

"He didn't kill you when you went down there last time. He's not going to do it now. He just wants to know where you are."

"We don't know that. That's a huge assumption. Forget it, it's out of the question. I'm not turning you into a moving target."

Ami tugged gently on Suzanne's sleeve. "Just think about it. Sleep on it. We can talk about it tomorrow."

Suzanne paced as she spoke on the phone, frustrated that Laura Kessing didn't care to hear any of the details, not even after Suzanne warned her that she'd have to use her name, and that it could prove dangerous to turn her house over to them.

"I don't see how. I'm going to be gone."

"But it's still possible that—"

"And you say that it's going to help other birth mothers?"

"Yes, no question about it."

"Then that's all *moi* needs to know."

Suzanne pictured Laura making her big dramatic arm gestures as she swirled around in one of her muumuus, a style of dress she'd affected since her year in Tahiti with her third husband, a Parisian by birth.

To clear her conscience, which was heavily burdened with the murders of Karen and Jesse, Suzanne made one more attempt to warn Laura that turning over her house could pose a grave threat to her safety.

"I feel that I have to tell you *something* about what I'm doing."

"Yes, the devil's always in the details, isn't he?"

"Right, that's what I'm trying to tell you."

"Please don't. I don't like having all that bad energy in my life. I have faith in you, Suzanne. We all do. Do what you have to, and let me know when I can come back. I'll be gone till April anyway. Will that be long enough?"

"Plenty long enough."

Suzanne believed The Searcher would strike quickly, if he struck at all. Wasn't Cara always saying, "Past performance is the best predictor of future behavior"? Comforting to hear in her therapist's office, but frightening to consider its implications now: Only days had separated the murders of Karen and Jesse.

"Are you sure you're okay with this?" Suzanne tried one last time.

"*Certainment.* You say you need my help, so you've got it. Anyway, it sounds like you're the one who's going to have to be careful."

Suzanne paused in her pacing to perch on the edge of her desk. "Is tomorrow all right? To come up and see your house? Figure out what we'll need?" She felt extraordinarily pushy. She needn't have.

"It's not only all right, it's necessary: I'm leaving Thursday. The rain this year is unforgiving."

In less fanciful tones, Laura went on to say that torrential rains had been hammering the Washington Cascades for two weeks now. Flooding and mudslides had started at the lower elevations, and the mountains already had added more than five feet to their snowpack.

Suzanne turned to Ami next, digging through her wallet for her MasterCard and Visa.

"You're right, it would be a good idea to use these here tomorrow. Buy some gas for your car, and about forty dollars worth of groceries. I rarely spend more than that at a time."

"I'll pay you back."

That was *so* Ami, frugal to the point of despair. Forcing her to take pay raises had been a considerable challenge for Suzanne. The girl had grown up in lean circumstances, and to this day could match the vigilance of a banker with the money—hers or Suzanne's—that passed through her hands. Not an unattractive quality in an assistant, but Ami could take it to extremes.

"No, you won't. Consider it hazardous duty pay."

Ami crossed her eyes, a childish trick that *did* make her look about twelve. "I'm not the one taking chances."

"Then consider it a bonus; just use them."

Ami threw her a mock salute.

"Aye-aye, Captain."

Time to give Burton a heads-up. Suzanne reached him at his apartment, the one with the big sign always hanging above the entrance: "If you lived here, you'd be home by now." A few weeks ago she'd spotted him waiting below it, and had thought, *No, if I lived here, I'd have gone nuts by now.*

Burton seized the opportunity to make the four-hour drive with her. Hardly a surprise: She'd been avoiding his entreaties for months, and now was giving him the chance to move from the couch to the passenger seat for a one-day road trip.

Her hand clamped down on the alarm a beat before it sounded. The incipient, impatient buzzing tickled her fingertips as she slid the switch to "off." A good omen, she decided. A more gratifying one appeared in the guise of her husband, who'd already risen, performed his morning ablutions, brewed the coffee, and was ready to roll north. Unwilling to slow the momentum any more than necessary, she hurried through a shower and grabbed her travel mug.

She drove them through a series of downtown streets that outlined a broadly configured circle. Burton didn't notice their roundabout route until she turned into a parking garage, snapped a ticket from the automatic dispenser, and sped up the ramp.

He looked around, puzzled by the passage from Portland gray to parking garage gloom. "What are you doing?"

"I'll tell you in a sec."

She sped up to the fourth level, parked in an empty space, and stared at her rearview mirror. A minivan passed with a woman at the wheel, and an empty child seat in the row directly behind her. Nothing else.

"Say, what's—"

"Hold on."

She backed out, and started winding down to the street, braked to hand over her ticket, and watched confusion wrinkle the young attendant's face.

"I changed my mind."

"You gotta pay anyway."

"I know."

She merged into traffic and headed straight for the freeway, eyes still pin-balling from the road to the rearview. Raindrops began to pelt the car.

"It's about that stalker, isn't it?" Bad as "stalker" sounded, Burton apparently preferred it to "rapist."

"That and a whole lot more, I'm afraid. Karen Sephs was just the first."

"The first what? To be murdered?"

She nodded and told him all of it—everything.

Burton rested his travel mug on his thick thigh and shook his head, visibly stunned.

"He sent me this a few days ago." Without looking away from the road, she dug around in her shoulder bag and handed him the UPS envelope. He pulled out the letter and read it quickly.

"The Searcher? He really calls himself that?" But Burton never looked up, expressing his disbelief more to himself than to her. He raked his hair with his fingers, as oblivious to Suzanne's nod as he was to the rumpling of his crisp appearance.

Before she could tell him about the picture, he dug into the envelope and held it up. He stared at it, studied it for more than a minute. Suzanne wondered if he could see the resemblance, too, the narrow waist and broad back. But Burton's attention had been drawn to another physical feature.

"That's the birthmark you told me about, isn't it?"

"I think so."

Burton's head moved slowly from side to side. "Our boy," he said simply.

Suzanne watched him look away, try to dry his eyes by opening them wide. *Why can't he let me see his grief?* Then he had no choice and had to reach up and catch his tears before they spilled to his cheek.

"This is incredible, after all these years." His voice was husky and hollow at the same time, like a big rusty pipe gripped by the cold, whisked by the wind. "I know it's been a long, long time, but I guess I never pictured him all grown up."

"I just wish I'd found him first, assuming—"

"I wish you had, too!" he said, surprising her with his burst of vehemence. "This guy's . . ."—he finger-smacked the letter—". . . this guy's a sick miserable mother." But he spared her the obscenity, the one that would have wounded most of all, considering the rape and its possible perpetrator.

He shifted onto his hip to face her. "Have you called the police anyway?"

She told him she hadn't, wouldn't, as they escaped the commuter clutch by crossing the bridge from Portland to Vancouver, Washington. She set the cruise control at seventy, the state limit. Every vehicle on the interstate, including trucks with triple trailers, rocketed past her tiny car, spitting road gruel onto the windshield.

"We can't, Burton, not with this. A really good source of mine at the Bureau says they're such a mess right now that if it was her son, she wouldn't tell them because it might leak out. And I wouldn't trust that detective who came out to the house any farther than I could throw him. This guy'll kill our son. Look what he's already done."

"But you can't let him keep hunting your birth moms." The jurist speaking.

"I know." She stared straight ahead, thinking of her clients, the ones still alive, and winced, their names and faces a cruel tease in this ghastly context.

She forced herself to blink, to break this spell, and glanced at the photo in Burton's hand, trying to make the most of the little hope she had.

"Look at that," she said. "He's got a baby of his own. A little girl."

"We're grandparents," Burton said, as if he'd just realized this. "I really want to see him." His eyes were back on the picture, "The little one, too."

"Me too. The thing is, I can't get it out of my head that he might *not* be our son."

"What do you mean? Why would he go to all this trouble to send a picture if he wasn't our son? Unless . . ." He lifted his eyes from the photograph and looked at her.

"That's right, unless The Searcher is our son. That could even be a self-portrait of his back. Or Photoshop. Whatever."

Burton shook his head so abruptly it looked like a spasm. "Nope. No. I can't believe *our* son could—"

"It gets even uglier."

"How in God's name could it get uglier?"

"The guy who raped me? The stalker? He's the same one."

"No. No way."

"I'm sure of it."

"Our son!" Burton's voice was loud and shockingly defensive.

"Calm down." Her decision to drive had been wise. "And don't yell at me. I'm not saying it *is* our son. I'm saying it *could* be."

Burton sat back, stared out the window at the rain, and offered a perfunctory "Sorry." With noticeably more emotion, he said, "I just can't believe my son, *our* son, could rape his own mother."

"Imagine how I feel."

"I can't. I can't even begin to."

They drove for several minutes before Burton turned back to her. His eyes were wet again.

"I'm so sorry for everything, Suz. Sometimes I feel like I messed up your life right from the beginning, and then I kept right on messing it up."

She rested her hand on his, the one that held the picture.

"It's never that simple, Burton. You know that. We both made a lot of mistakes, and some of them we made together."

Another ten miles passed before Burton spoke again. After slipping the photo and letter back in the envelope, he asked her to spell out why she thought her rapist and The Searcher might be their son.

"I'm still kind of numb from all this, and I'd like to get it sorted out."

"I'll try. It might help me to think out loud." She used to do this all the time, before she'd grown so guarded with him. "Let's start with the birthmark. No one knows about it but me. Well, and you too."

Burton shook his head. "Wait, that's not true. Anyone who's seen him in swimming trunks would know about it. Like the . . ." Burton once more choked down a profanity. ". . . guy who sent this." He tapped the envelope.

"But how would he know to connect some guy with a birthmark to me? That's what is so creepy."

"Go on."

"Then there's the disk. The guy who raped me is probably the same one who killed Karen and Jesse because both of them were raped and murdered after someone got a copy of it. I don't think anyone's gotten into my house or office. And who else could have connected those murders?"

"You're right, what you're saying makes sense, except for one thing: He killed Karen and Jesse, but he didn't kill you. If it's the same guy, why not?"

"Why indeed? Maybe because I'm *special*." The word rolled off her tongue with a bitter tinge. "Maybe because I'm his mother."

Burton's hand rose to his mouth, as if to suppress another outburst.

"There's something else, too," Suzanne said.

"What's that?"

"He says he found our son, but how? I don't mean to sound immodest, but I'm the best in the business when it comes to finding birth mothers and their kids. No one finds more of them than I do, and I've done everything I possibly could to find our boy, but I haven't been able to."

"Except if he didn't find him, how would he know about the birthmark?"

"'Distinguishing Features.' It's a category I have for every file, including mine."

"And I guess if he found that in the file he could have used models and makeup. They wouldn't have known what he was up to."

"That's right, and that still leaves us not knowing the one thing we need to know, doesn't it?"

Burton looked away, then quickly back. "I think that's our son in that picture, I really do. It even kind of looks like me back in the day—"

So he had noticed.

"—but you want to know why he found him, and you didn't? Because you play by the rules, and he doesn't."

"That's true," she acknowledged, as much to herself as to him. Officials at state and private adoption agencies had been known to release adoption records for a sob story, or a satchel full of cash, though it was hard to imagine the Paige Mertlers of the world bending their principles at any price. Still, she could accept the possibility that The Searcher had paid off a source and learned the whereabouts of her son. She greeted this with relief because of its obvious implications, but she also found it deeply threatening because it meant her son was prey, and so was his family.

"I'm not playing by the rules anymore, not with this guy. What I have in mind doesn't even come close."

"What are you thinking of doing?"

She laid out the details of her plan and told him how he could help.

He stared out the window, and when he spoke his eyes never strayed from the passing farms.

"You're asking me to renounce the rule of law to try to trap—"

"A killer."

"To try to trap and kill him."

"We don't have to kill him." She hadn't thought of this till right now. "We could hold him at gunpoint and explain everything after the fact to the police. Nobody's going to take you to task for saving your wife and son, his family, *and* who knows how many birth mothers. People will love you for it."

"But once you start down this kind of path, there's no telling where you're going to end up." He was looking at her now.

"No, that's right. No guarantee at all. The only thing we know for sure is that he's killed at least two women and raped your wife. Don't go pulling a Dukakis on me."

A *Dukakis*? She watched his brow wrinkle.

"When he was running against Bush senior, remember? He was asked what he'd do if his wife was raped and murdered, and he gave some wishy-washy legalistic answer."

"That hurts," Burton said, clearly ruffled by the parallel. "And I don't think it's—"

"Fair?" She knew exactly what he was going to say. "No, it's not fair. I *was* raped. For us it's not some theoretical question."

Maybe it was the implied appeal to his ambition that finally proved persuasive; or maybe he simply understood, as Suzanne had before him, that their options had been narrowed to almost nothing.

"I don't want us killing him. *If*, and it's a huge if, we trap him, we call the nearest law enforcement agency. Don't go killing him, Suz. I don't care how angry you get."

"Is that the deal?"

"It is for me."

"I can live with that."

But even as she answered, she shuddered over her choice of words.

Burton reached over and touched her hand. "I do want to help you."

"I appreciate it, but I don't want you thinking it's only about helping me. It's also about saving a lot of birth mothers and our son, if he's not The Searcher. And if he is, it's about doing what has to be done."

Burton didn't disagree, but as Suzanne drove farther north, she knew it was more than those words allowed. If that was their son in the picture, and it wasn't The Searcher's self-portrait, then every step they'd take from now on was really about them as a family: the brief history they once shared, and the future that could bring them together again.

Laura Kessing's directions took them off the interstate and onto a two-lane road. Farm country. The town of Cascadia appeared in a blink and would have disappeared as quickly if Suzanne hadn't slowed down. The two-lane rambled on for another ten miles before the pavement turned to dirt and gravel, the farms to forest.

They bumped along for another fifteen minutes, gradually rising up a valley, and driving past several mailboxes along the road, but the houses themselves were hidden by a thick curtain of trees. Nor could they glimpse Laura's house when they came to a two-track driveway marked by a mailbox in the shape of a steeply spired Buddhist temple.

Mud season took on new meaning as the hybrid negotiated a half mile of ruts. Seconds later they drove up out of the trees and beheld Laura's beautiful log home.

She'd instructed Suzanne to pull into the open, attached garage; and with the rain thickening for most of the drive north, the promise of a dry landing was appealing.

As they climbed out of the car, Laura opened the door to the house. "Welcome, welcome," she chimed. "So good to see you." Three layers of gauzy green dress shifted in the stirred-up air. She squeezed Suzanne's cheeks with her warm hands and gave her a strong hug. Suzanne told her how thankful they were, but Laura dismissed this with a wave of her hand.

"It's nothing." Then, turning to Burton she said, "And you are?"

"Burton."

"My husband," Suzanne said, sounding far more decisive than she felt.

"My, what a hunk of a man," Laura said. She wagged her finger at Suzanne. "Way to go, gal."

If she only knew. Suzanne looked at her husband, who was beaming like a beacon, and thought, *You better not flirt,* Burt. He didn't. And Laura was just being Laura, which is to say flamboyant and impulsive. With four ex-husbands, both qualities had been surely stropped.

"This is too *too* much." Laura flicked her eyes at the downpour. "I can't stand another day of this rain. Give me some sun, *please.* Do you know they had another mudslide this morning, not fifteen miles from here? Another one! And Mount Baker's going to open before Thanksgiving. Great for the skiers, but it's driving me *crazy*! Come—come, I'll give you the tour."

She led them into the appropriately named mudroom, where they shed their jackets and shoes.

"Hooks, hangers, washer and dryer, as you can see. This way to the kitchen."

"It's beautiful," Suzanne said as she took in the granite counters, hickory cabinets, and concrete floor. *Warm* concrete.

"In-floor heating," Laura said when she spied Suzanne sliding her toes back and forth across the surface, which had been stained the mottled colors of autumn leaves.

"It feels so good. And I love what you've done in here. Did you pick all this out yourself?"

"Do I look like Martha Stewart?" Laura laughed. "I hired. I always hire. I'm good at marrying money. Everything else?" She cocked an eyebrow.

"So there's the range," Laura continued, "and the oven. A warming oven's over there. Oh, this is silly. You don't need me to tell you where the spoons are. Come, come."

They trailed her into the living room.

"Ta-da!" She pointed to the hearth.

"I love the rock," Burton said.

River rock—maybe a whole river's worth—had been used for the fireplace and the chimney, which rose more than twenty feet to a honey-stained plank ceiling.

"Recycled," Laura offered as she looked up, "from an old barn."

No mention of the log walls. Nothing recycled about them. They might, in fact, have been taken from a clear-cut hillside that towered over a thin row of trees behind the house.

"No, don't look there. You're forbidden ever to look out that window." Laura's eyes took in the stumps stippling the slope. "I should board it up. Can you believe they did that? Cut them *all* down."

"When did that happen?"

"Two years ago. Right after I bought the place. And then they left a row of trees by my property. They call them 'idiot strips.' For good reason, I should think. It's like I'm supposed to be so stupid that I'll see a long strip of trees back there and think the forest goes on and on.

"It used to be as lovely out back as it is out front. I've even got a four-season deck off the sleeping loft upstairs, but I never use it. It's too depressing. So you are commanded to just look thataway." Laura straightened her arm and pointed to the windows in front of them, which overlooked the gently rising slope they'd driven up to the house.

"That is nice," Suzanne said.

"Until you get up here. If I'd have known what they had in mind, I never would have bought this place. At this point, I wouldn't care if it burned down. At least I'd get the insurance money. Nobody's ever going to buy it with that view."

"Nothing's burning in this weather," Burton said.

"But the house is gorgeous, and this really is pretty," Suzanne added, looking out the double glass doors again.

"I know. I'm just bitter. I know what it was like before they went to work on it. Cassie loves it up here, so I guess that should be enough for me. She came up with my grandson, Raymond, for a week in June."

"How's it going with her?"

"It's going," Laura said in a voice suddenly weary. "Now that she knows I'm mortal, not the movie-star mother of her fantasies, she's been keeping her distance. She's only called twice since she left, and once was on my birthday. She mostly put Raymond on the phone. The honeymoon's over. We're adjusting."

"It sounds like you've got a good handle on things."

Laura shrugged, the first of her gestures that appeared genuine. "I'm not sure about that, but I can't be what I'm not. I think we're both making peace with reality right now. She was probably hoping her long-lost mother was Meryl Streep, and if I'm going to be honest I'd have to say that I probably had a little Julia Roberts in mind. Neither of us hit the jackpot."

Suzanne had seen this many times. Rare was the mother and child reunion that proved entirely satisfying: Too many years filled with too many fantasies almost always got in the way. But that was true for any family, even the ones without an adoption experience. Their reunions might be tempered by reality, but at heart were they any less fueled by illusion?

Laura took them upstairs to the sleeping loft and bath, pointedly ignoring the glassed-in deck, which did indeed reveal much more of the devastated hillside. Then she handed Suzanne a key and reminded them that she was leaving tomorrow morning.

Suzanne asked her one more time if she was absolutely certain that she wouldn't return until April.

"Not if I can help it."

"Because coming back early could be a problem. I want you to be safe."

"I'll be safe and I'll be warm, which is a lot more than it sounds like you're going to be."

"We'll be okay," Burton said.

"Whatever you're cooking up, don't worry about me. Whenever I talk to people about you"—she smiled at Suzanne—"I always tell them that whatever she's selling, I'm buying. Just tell me this much: Is my house still going to be here when I get back?"

"Yes, I promise."

"Darn! I really was hoping you'd burn it down."

On the soggy drive back to Portland, Suzanne used her cell to try to reach Ami. Almost dark, but she might be working. No answer, save the message machine. She was either gone for the day, or on another line. Suzanne hoped she'd headed home; Ami had been working overtime and deserved a break.

But after dropping Burton off at his apartment so he could round up his clothes and toiletries, she swung by the office and found her assistant still at her desk at eight-thirty.

"Shouldn't you have left a couple of hours ago?"

"I'm fine. Look at this. I got the classified ad done."

Suzanne pulled up a chair and looked over what Ami had written, specific where it could be, vague where it had to be, but the key words spoke loudly: ". . . so please help. So little time. Desperate. Call Laura Kessing, 360-662-2116, or laurakessing@emercee.com."

Desperation, that's the bait. *No,* Suzanne corrected herself: You *are the bait.* But she shelved her own concerns to compliment Ami.

"Perfect, I couldn't have done any better."

Ami smiled, clearly pleased with herself.

"I've identified the two most active chat rooms. If you want, I can send it out tonight."

"I think you should."

"I'm also going to send it off to a whole bunch of newspapers in Washington, Oregon, and Idaho, just in case he lives around here. And to the newsletter."

"Sounds like you've covered all the bases. Thanks."

"You don't think he's going to find this fishy?" She glanced at the ad on the screen.

"There are hundreds of them every year."

"From birth moms on your list?"

"I think it's very reasonable for a birth mom who's dying to do everything she can to try to find her child."

Ami turned back to her computer, then paused.

"How was Laura's place?"

"It's beautiful, but it's definitely out there. I think I counted a total of four mailboxes on the way up, including hers. And from what she says, the road stops not far from her place."

"I told you it was in the middle of nowhere. Have you thought about how you're going to keep him from tracking you?"

"We'll use Burton's credit cards. I won't be touching mine. Did you get gas and groceries?"

"Topped off my tank, and I've got dinner organized for the next few nights. But don't you think he's going to notice that you're not using your cards once you leave? Maybe I should take them and use them every day or so. I could keep the receipts and pay you back later."

"That's a good idea. But what if they check your signature?"

"I've got yours down to a T."

Suzanne nodded and started to lean back, drained by the long day of driving; but Ami caught her arm.

"You're still taking a huge risk, Suz."

"Burton's going to help me."

"That's not what I mean. What about your car? Are you taking it back up there?"

"No, it'll never make it in and out of there if the weather gets any worse. It's like a bog. We're going to take Burton's Land Cruiser, and we'll stick mine in the garage. It's not like I'm going to be leaving it in front of the house."

Ami shook her head as she put her computer in sleep mode.

"Not gonna work," she said in a whispery singsong. "He could still figure out that you're gone. Like I said yesterday, all he's got to do is look in the garage window and he'll see it. Or better yet, just hang out and see that you never leave the house or come to work."

"You're really good at seeing the holes in the donut."

"That's my job."

"But the risks you're talking about are very small for what could be a very big return."

"I beg to differ. I don't think this guy misses a thing."

"Ami, right now all he's thinking about is his next victim."

"Let's hope it's not you."

In the morning, Suzanne was surprised to find a note from Ami on her kitchen counter, shocked when she read it:

Dear Suz,

Don't freak when you read this. It's real early, and I just got the keys to your car. I'll reset the security system on my way out. What I'm about to do is the only way to make sure he doesn't catch on.

I'm going on the road for the next couple of weeks, heading to Florida, heading very slowly to Florida, I should say. I've set up the e-mail so now you have my address and I have yours. I'll be writing as if I were you, and

I'll be avoiding any specific location information. You write me as if you're
me. I'm not going to take any chances with cell calls or landlines. This is
the only way to make sure he doesn't catch on to what you're doing. If
you're in motion, it'll be hard as hell for him to actually eyeball you. You
know I'm right. What you're doing is really dangerous. I'm just going for a
drive.

You better be careful, and tell that husband of yours that if anything
happens to you, I'm going to be gunning for him.

Love,
Ami

As she laid the note back on the counter, Suzanne noticed that her hand
was shaking, the paper rustling like a leaf on the jade-colored tile. She looked
away quickly, as if to flee her fear, and found herself facing the window where
thick drops of rain pelted her reflection. She listened to the strangely percus-
sive rhythm of the weather and wondered what kind of madness she'd set in
motion.

10

When I was a kid—I couldn't have been any more than five—I believed that my whole life was a dream, and that at any moment I'd wake up to find myself in my real bed with my real family in my real world.

I'd go to my room and pinch myself as hard as I could (hard enough that I once drew blood on my arm), and when this didn't wake me up I even tried slapping myself in the face, though even then I had little faith in the animating qualities of a slap, having already experienced enough of them at my mother's hands to have lost any belief in their magical effect.

Still, I tried, maybe because I wanted to believe that the power of my own hand to change my world would be greater than the power of hers.

There was even a period of time when I tried squinting fiercely at the sun, under the inane impression that if the light hit me just the right way, the darkness of my sleep world would burn away.

I didn't stop trying to "wake up" until I was eight years old. That's how convinced I was that the life I was living was an illusion.

Other children looked at me strangely when I asked if they'd ever thought about this. None of them had. I found this extraordinary, that something so obvious to me should never have occurred to them. I told myself, *You're special. There's no one like you on this whole planet. No one has thoughts like you do. They make you what you are.*

But they became a puzzle to me. I wondered why I was having them. Why would I think things that no one else thought? What did these thoughts want of me anyway? What?

The answer came to me quickly, as it does to anyone who listens. They wanted me to take control of my world, and there was only one way to do this: I had to take control of others. Only as I grew older did I come to understand that few people ever realize this, the most basic of all truths. I was one of the lucky ones.

I began to enter new worlds every day by altering the lives of tiny creatures. I wouldn't pinch myself, I'd pinch them and wake them up to a world they'd only glimpsed till then: a parallel universe of pain.

Why, I found that when I pinched the wings off a beautiful butterfly, and its body squirmed like a worm on the hot pavement, I had done to the creature what I had tried to do to myself when I'd retreated to my room: I had awakened the butterfly to a new reality, one that I controlled.

Was it any different with the only kitten my hands ever claimed? She was offered to me by an old woman outside a grocery store. At her feet, several calicos crowded a cardboard box lined with shredded newspaper. They mewed piteously when I crouched down for a closer look. She told me to take one, it would make a great pet, and I did. I scooped up the runt, black and brown with an orange starburst between its velvety ears. I was so eager to get started that I can't even remember thanking her.

"What are you going to name her?" she asked, but I'd turned away already. I'd found my path and was hurrying down it.

Now don't go making any snap judgments here. Don't go saying, "He's one of them. He killed animals when he was a kid, so now he's killing people." That's not the case at all. In fact, after killing that kitten, I found that I had no taste for that kind of death. None. And I certainly killed her with a lot more regret than those farmers who toss them by the sackful into rivers and lakes.

The truth is, I was haunted by the experience. I didn't go on to kill puppies and rabbits and birds because I understood that killing that kitten had been a mistake. I didn't want to kill animals; I wanted to control people, one person in particular.

Still, I found out something very important when I killed that kitten. Very important. For the first time I understood that I'd been God to every creature I'd destroyed, and always would be. And that the God of church, any church, was no more alive than the lump of fur in my hand. I'd stopped believing in Santa Claus years before, and now I understood that God, capital G, was nothing more than the St. Nick of the creation myth. Those who controlled death, controlled life. And those with the courage to realize this possessed much greater gifts than the God of man.

Can you imagine the meaning of this when I got back to the house and saw my mother? I still remember it. It was the summer I turned fourteen, and my throat was so dry I'd headed straight for home. She walked into the kitchen while I was opening the refrigerator for a bottle of water. The cold air swept over my legs as I watched her stupid smile wrinkle up her face. It was like I was having a revelation standing there holding the water. The woman who'd controlled me would someday be controlled by me. My experiments with death would never be cheapened by another kitten, or any other creature with four legs and fur.

How I'd get started came to me the first time I seriously considered carbon monoxide. It was as if something clicked in my head, as if my subconscious had been working out the problem all along. *I* wouldn't kill her at all. She'd kill herself with car exhaust. It would be so simple. She'd passed out more than once after driving home. She'd even nicked the right side of the garage on one of her drunken attempts to park the Mercedes.

I gave a lot of thought to this. After checking her will and finding my name where I wanted it to be, I decided she would die as close to my eighteenth birthday as possible. I sure didn't want to go to another foster home. I'd spent six months in one after that fight at the middle-school art show, and that had cured me of any desire for another "family" or the meddling of any other adults.

The months and years passed slowly, as they do in an adolescence filled with longing. I spent a lot of time watching her closely, and what I learned served me well.

But killing a drunk is not as easy as you might think. Most of us keep a schedule, have a consistent course to our lives. The course of a drunk is to get drunk, and then they are not always predictable.

As my eighteenth birthday approached, I checked the liquor supply daily to make sure she maintained a healthy stock, and I saw very quickly that while my mother might have her lapses, keeping herself well supplied with liquor was not among them.

But no matter how much liquor was on hand, no matter how much she drank before going out for the evening, she didn't pass out in the car when she came home. Somehow she'd stagger in night after night, collapse on the couch, and work the remote. I realized that waiting for her to pass out again in the garage would age me much faster than it aged her.

This made me reconsider my plan, but not my goal. I'd still be my mother's God, but I'd have to use her beloved alcohol to fuel her demise in a more direct manner. And to do that I'd also have to violate one of my most deeply held promises and force myself to drink with her.

Days after my eighteenth birthday, which she remembered with a card (she'd forgotten my seventeenth) that said my "maturity" had arrived "at last," she rolled into the garage as I watched from the kitchen window. The car moved at an infant's crawl, a sure sign of a drunk hedging her hazy bets, figuring if she did strike something the damage might be minimized by a feathery foot.

The door to the house opened much more abruptly, perhaps on the theory that her body could neither deliver nor sustain much in the way of injury. Such are the assumptions we make, some fatal.

She appeared surprised to see me, but the only greeting I got was a barely sentient nod before she barreled into the living room.

From the look of her I'd say she'd been on the hunt, armed as she was in a short black skirt as tight as a sausage casing.

She flopped onto the couch and thumbed the remote. Leno came on. She was a great fan and made a feeble attempt to tuck her legs under her bottom to get settled.

Leno joked and mugged, but if any of his antics registered in her brain, she gave no sign of it. No smiles, no nothing.

This made me wonder if one drink might do it. Go for a double, I told myself. That ought to knock her out for sure. She was already propping up her head with her hand, eyes as droopy as dumbwaiters.

The liquor cabinet stood behind the bar. Right above it hung a tall mirror lined on both sides with glass shelves stacked with crystal ware. It was a real glittering altar to alcohol. I can't tell you how many times I'd wanted to destroy it, smash it to pieces with a hammer, or her head. Now I'd use it to destroy her.

I mixed a Manhattan and watched the cherry sink to the bottom of the tumbler. And then I downed it. I was drinking my courage and knew it even then. The alcohol burned all the way to my belly, but it was one of the few drinks I could stand. I upended the glass one more time to slide the cherry into my mouth. I crushed it with my molars and felt it explode with sugary juices.

In the mirror I saw her watching me. She looked puzzled, drunkenly so. She spoke, but I wasn't sure what she said. I thought it was, "You're drinking?"

"Yes, *Mother*," I said with the exaggerated emphasis that can come with a case of nerves, "now that I'm eighteen, I thought it would be nice to have a nightcap with you, to kind of celebrate."

She never noticed my unease, to judge by the way she mumbled on in the same spirit, gibberish that was all but unintelligible. I think I heard the word *drink,* but at that point I would have needed Tom Waits for a complete translation.

I did mix her a double, and she took it eagerly, downing it like water, and mashing the cherry as if it were an enemy of long standing.

"I'll fix you another," I told her, and she handed me the glass. It appeared that she was enjoying this turn of events, a son who could truly be of service.

But by the time I returned, she'd passed out. Leno was now joking with the stars of a situation comedy about a white midget doctor and his elderly black mother. Both of them were on the set, though the midget kept jumping off his chair to try to kick his host in the ankles, while his "mother," hair as white as her skin was black, was shouting, "Spank you a good one, that's what I a-gonna do, spank you a good one," a line that apparently provided the show with both its title and most enduring theme.

I squeezed *my* mother's knee just to make sure she was out, then hoisted her up by the armpits and backed out to the garage. I had to stop only once when her right shoe slipped off. I didn't want any abrasions on her heels or runs in her hose, nothing that would suggest her body had been tampered with.

With her shoe back on, I made it to the Mercedes, opened the door, and with more effort than I'd ever imagined necessary, managed to get her back behind the wheel.

"Don't forget your seat belt, Mom," I whispered to an ear as deaf as stone.

I clamped it shut and went back inside for her purse and keys, and a change of shoes. I didn't want any scuff marks on her shoe heels, either. I'd throw the ones she'd been wearing into a city garbage can before I ever called the police.

By the time I got back out there, her head had fallen forward, and she was supported solely by the shoulder strap.

Fine with me. She was as convincing a portrait of drunkenness as you're likely to see this side of a downtown mission.

But I wasn't about to leave the rest of her posture to chance. I climbed into the backseat, reached over, and grabbed the hem of her skirt. I wrestled it right up to her hips, and then stuck her hand down inside her panty hose. She offered no resistance and could have been dead already for all the awareness she showed. Then I reached up and unbuttoned her blouse until I could unhook the cups of her bra. She spilled out immediately, a flood of flesh. Not a pretty sight, but I assumed, correctly as it turned out, that the cops would find her autoerotic activities a potential source of mortal embarrassment to her son, and reason enough to protect him from the details of her death, not question him closely.

I said good-bye by raising my middle finger and placing it right in front of her sodden face. Then I wiped down the door and seat belt clamp, anything I might have touched. With the rag still in hand, I turned the ignition key. None of these precautions was necessary; the cops took one look at her and had their cause of death.

The Mercedes purred just like that kitten in the seconds before I killed her. It purred all night long, and in the morning I awoke to a whole new world, just like I'd dreamed I would so long ago.

Patsy paid for her session promptly. Which is only fair. I did, after all, extend myself for her. I took a huge risk for her, a much bigger one than I ever had for any other client. What if she'd died having her precious orgasm? What then? I should have billed her for a double session.

The check arrived with the morning mail. Patsy never makes me wait, and she rescheduled faithfully. I'll see her again next week. That's if I don't have to cancel. I might. I've been cruising the chat rooms again. Old habits do die hard. Even after getting Ms. Trayle's disk, I can't keep myself from checking out the other possibilities out there. In this regard only, I'm no better than some of my birth mothers who claim to be happily married but can never bring themselves to flip past the personal ads in the local paper. You just never know what you might find, right? It's a good thing I checked, too, because I found the most interesting ad I'd seen in a long time. It's the name that grabbed my attention. I knew I'd seen it before.

I mulled over the birth mothers I'd met at conferences, past and current clients, and all sorts of other mental clutter before I thought to check the obvious: Suzanne Trayle's list. And there it was. "Laura Kessing." Bingo. Bingo. Bingo.

Uterine cancer. How terribly ironic, isn't it? Your womb is taking your life, Laura. And why shouldn't it, since you gave up the only life it ever bore. And here you were, depending on the great search angel herself to find your boy. Couldn't do it, could she? But I'll bet I could. Maybe after I'm done with you, I will. Just for sport.

I'm already thinking of what would be a suitable and slow way of killing her. What household tool am I going to come across in Laura Kessing's home that will find its most exquisite—and unusual—application in her final moments? What would be appropriate for a birth mother with uterine cancer?

The really good answers are always slow in coming, and sometimes don't greet me till I'm in the door.

Laura. I roll the word around in my mouth as I might have enjoyed doing with wine, if my mother hadn't turned drinking into an obscenity.

Laura. It's in the same vocal family as "mother." Laura. Mother. There's a sweetness in their affinity. A melding of their sounds. Already I can feel one morphing into the other.

Laur-a. Moth-er.

Moth-er.

Mother.

Yes, *Mother*, you'll see your son before you die. More of him than you ever dreamed.

11

THE FINAL STRETCH of rutted driveway up to Laura's house looked no worse than it had two days ago, but in Burton's old Land Cruiser they felt every bump. It had the suspension of a tank, but Suzanne was glad they'd taken the beast because several inches of muddy water were racing down the twin gullies, striating the two-track as if the rain were the sky's own claws. Stark impressions unmollified by the sudden appearance of the house, which seemed far less inviting without Laura to greet them.

Burton had to unlock and open the garage door, and as Suzanne sat there reviewing the grisly circumstances that had brought them here, she found herself in the unprecedented position of trying to take comfort in the guns he'd brought along. They were packed in a black canvas bag in the cargo area in the rear. As she glanced back, a chill made her shiver visibly. It's the weather, she reassured herself, not the guns. This did make sense. When they'd made their last stop at a rest area, several fat drops cold as refrigerator water had struck her bare neck.

She tried to imagine what it would be like when the rain changed to snow. Would they make it out of here? Burton had brought chains, and the Land Cruiser had a winch mounted on the front bumper, making it the total back country bully, but they really were in the "middle of nowhere," as Ami had put it.

Burton hustled back to the car, throwing himself into the driver's seat and slamming the door on the storm. His jacket was soaked, and the rain had flattened his hair and spilled down his face. He looked wild, and Suzanne was surprised to find that he looked good.

Within twenty minutes of toting their bags into the house and putting away the groceries they'd stocked up on, Burton had worked the woodstove in the fireplace into a blazing frenzy and parked himself on the couch a few feet away with his caseload, files that fanned out before him.

He'd taken the comp time urged on him by his boss at the contractors board, but his calendar was still crowded with claims and counterclaims that would come his way after the first of the year, when emergency funds promised by the legislature might restore the board to its normal schedule.

As he settled in with his work, Suzanne climbed the stairs and took in the disturbing view from the glassed-in deck. The clear-cut hillside appeared barren and broken above the top of the "idiot strip," as Laura had called the stand of giant pines marking the periphery of her property.

Suzanne watched a thick rolling fog descend the hill until it swallowed all the stumps. A half hour later, as the last of the light drained from the sky, she happened to catch the fog lifting like a theater curtain, revealing the same cast of dim orange circles. *Be interesting to paint,* she said to herself.

For dinner they polished off the sandwich makings they'd grazed on during the long drive up here, a fitting enough conclusion, in her view, to the slapdash schedule of the past forty-eight hours. Suzanne's most frantic efforts had been directed at trying to contact her itinerant assistant. After reading Ami's note, she'd rushed from the kitchen to her home office to dash off an imperative e-mail, before remembering that she had to write elliptically, in code and in character. Thankfully, she caught herself, so she'd begun all over again with a softer tone, and a salutation that seemed very strange ("Dear Suzanne") before urging Ami (as herself) to return.

Until she hit "send" the whole exercise felt silly, like a game of pretend that children would play. But as soon as she launched those words into cyberspace, an unmistakable eeriness crept up her spine, as if The Searcher really were looking over her shoulder. Creepy enough that she'd walked to the front door of her house to check the lock and security system.

Another concern both more imminent and intimate occupied her now: sleeping arrangements. She and Burton hadn't discussed them. Maybe they should have. He was about to join her in Laura's king-size bed.

"What are you doing?" she said, making little attempt to hide her alarm.

"I thought I'd come to bed. This thing is big enough for both of us."

"I'm not sure it's big enough for both of us *and* all of our baggage."

"Let's try," he said. "I mean just sleeping together. I mean that, too, just sleeping," he repeated, as if she could possibly have failed to grasp his point. "I miss you, Suzanne. I've been missing you for a long time."

His need sounded so genuine that she went from wanting to physically repel him to settling back on her side without speaking another word. Not an invitation, but neither did she object when the mattress surrendered to the length of him. They shared the bed but not their touch, an awkward occupation that made her feel as if she were falling asleep in a foreign land.

The territory felt far more familiar when she awoke in the morning: Burton's arm was wrapped around her, and his body pressed against her back. The air in the house felt chilly, and the great radiator of his weight was more welcome than she might have imagined had she pictured this cozy scene eight hours ago.

Rather than slough off the only physical intimacy she'd known with her husband in months, she remained as still as sleep itself while her eyes adjusted to the gray light. But as quickly her thoughts came alive with The Searcher. Her message to the chat rooms had been out for three days. The classifieds for the newspapers would start running today. She figured he could show up at any time. Speed was part of his pattern. He had names, addresses, phone numbers, e-mail—all of it—because he had her list.

But surely a killer with his concern for detail and secrecy wouldn't move too precipitously. What did that give them? A day, maybe two before they'd have to be on constant alert? *Guesswork,* she told herself. *Pure guesswork. You'd better keep your eyes peeled now, and you'd better get moving. Him, too.*

She shrugged off Burton's arm, waking him to the torpor of his mornings. "Come on, Burty boy, wake-up time."

Burty boy? She hadn't offered that endearment since Gabriella had snaked into their lives.

Burton sat up in bed as she hurried to the bathroom for her morning routine, hair, teeth . . . lipstick? Why not? No sense letting herself totally go, though lately she'd been pondering that phrase—*letting yourself go*—and had decided that it wasn't about dishabille, not really. It was about freedom from the expectations of others, from the demands of their desire.

No doubt, but her own desire had been stirred—not sparked, nothing so incandescent—by Burton, so after another moment of debate she compromised with a subtle shade that drew scant attention to her lips as she headed downstairs.

She found Laura's coffeepot in the shuttered appliance garage, the French roast beans they'd brought in the fridge where she'd stashed them, and the brew as appealing as ever when it began to sow its welcome scent.

Burton appeared in the doorway, washed and shaved and showered—still *trying*—and managed a clear-throated "Good morning" as he poured himself a cup.

But neither of them offered more in the way of conversation until the caffeine fanned their brain cells. Then, a good five minutes after he'd seated himself across from her at the heavy pine table he blinked quickly, as if to unshutter his thoughts, and said, "Now that wasn't so bad, was it?"

"What wasn't so bad?" An old gambit: Throw the question back when you know the subject but need an extra second or two to cobble together an answer.

"Sleeping together like that."

She hesitated before she spoke, buying time more blatantly now. "No, not too bad."

"You think we have a chance?"

She nodded. "I wouldn't be up here with you otherwise."

"Not even to have me ride shotgun?"

"Not even for that."

"You look great, Suz. You really do."

"It's the lipstick."

"It's a lot more than lipstick."

She looked him in the eye, an intimacy that held them both, but then he blinked; and while moments before the flutter of his eyelids had provided an opening, the movement now held little that appeared gentle or vulnerable. It was as if his eyes were signaling a hardness as necessary to the morning's agenda as ammo.

"I'll go get the guns. You never know." He glanced at the front door.

He'd get no argument from her, though she had little enthusiasm for the weapons she was about to handle. It had been years since Burton had cajoled her into joining him at a pistol range. She'd failed to score even a single "body shot" and had been deeply uncomfortable aiming at the outline of a black figure on a white background. Why not a white figure on a black background?

She heard him trudging back down the stairs, the heavy tread of his weight, and watched him haul the black canvas bag over to the table, careful to put aside his coffee mug. As soon as he unzipped it, she smelled the gun oil, the rich industrial scent of so many finely honed machines.

He peeled back the Velcro strip that cinched the handgun's thickly padded Cordura case, revealing a Sig Sauer nine-millimeter, and a smile of clear admiration.

"This gun's perfect for you. You remember it, don't you?"

She did. It's not easy to forget the only pistol you've ever fired, but he didn't wait for an answer or even an acknowledgment.

"A lot of people think of it as a woman's gun because it's on the smaller side, but I always liked the weight of it myself. It feels like a toy."

He checked the butt of the semiautomatic to make sure the clip wasn't in, then eyed the chamber in another act of acute caution.

"Here," he said as he handed it to her. "See what I mean?"

It felt heavy to her, but she wasn't accustomed to handling these finely calibrated cousins of crime.

He pulled out the twelve-gauge shotgun. She'd fired his bird gun several times at a skeet-shooting contest Burton had competed in long ago. The recoil had left her shoulder feeling bruised for days.

"I remember this one," she said as she put aside the Sig Sauer. "But what about your deer rifle? I thought you said you were going to bring that, too."

"I'd planned to." He broke open the twelve-gauge and eyed it closely. "But then I realized there was no point in bringing it. We're not hunting this guy. We're trying to bring him to us. We want weapons that'll work in tight spaces, not out in an open field. You get too many guns around and you end up grabbing the wrong one at the wrong time."

She couldn't believe she was having this conversation, seeing this side of Burton. Or that he was seeing this side of her. That *she* was seeing this side of herself. The last few days had been a revelation. God only knew what the next few would bring. There had been one new development after another in the past two weeks, and each of them had triggered reactions she'd never known. But what else could she expect after she'd been raped, and her clients had been raped and tortured to death? And then in the wake of these ruthless murders, explicit threats to her son and his family had shown up, along with what could be a photograph of them. *So go on, Burton, show me what you've got.*

He snapped the stock and barrel back together.

"I don't know if you remember, but this has a really nice wide pattern. Let's say he's fifteen feet away." Burton pointed it toward the living room, talking now over his shoulder. "If you shoot with the barrel pointed anywhere near him, you got him."

"It's that simple?"

"It sure is." Burton lowered the shotgun with an entirely pleased look, which prompted Suzanne to wonder if men like her husband could revert to their hunter killer status in an instant.

He'd never talked much about the war, and he'd never made much of the medals he'd won. Her own feelings about Vietnam had been equivocal enough to make any conversation dangerous ground, and by the time their lives had converged again, what he'd done in some distant delta was of less concern to her than what he'd become in the years since his return.

But it all comes back into play now, doesn't it? Everything he once was is what you want. Your son's father and a former soldier. But he's also a man of limited loyalty, she reminded herself uneasily, limits she was about to test all over again.

He pointed to the Sig Sauer pistol, which still lay before her on the table. "Why don't you go ahead and grab that."

She picked up the handgun again and thought the stock felt funny. "What's it made of, plastic?"

"Parts of it, that's right. I want to show you how to load it."

"I don't even know where I load it."

"Hand it over and I'll show you. You start with this." He retrieved an empty clip from the handgun case. "This goes up inside the butt like this." He used the heel of his hand to snap it into place, then popped it out. "You try it. There's the release."

She jammed the clip back in with no difficulty and popped it out as easily. "Pretty smooth there, Suz. Let's go ahead and get it loaded."

He opened a box of shells and inserted one into the top of the clip, compressing the spring that would eventually drive the bullet up into the chamber of the pistol.

"It's no more complicated than that. Your turn."

"Can the bullets go off accidentally, if I drop them?"

"That's highly unlikely. They'd have to land on an extremely sharp point at exactly the right angle, and then they'd also have to hit with enough force to set off the cap, so I wouldn't worry. But in general it's not a good idea to go dropping live ammunition."

She didn't need the added admonition, and though irritated by his patronizing tone, she did her best to remain unrankled. Anger and ammo and all that.

The last two bullets were the most challenging to load because the spring was almost completely compressed.

"Glad that's done." She flexed her fingers.

"Now you can slide the loaded clip into the gun."

She drove it back up into the handle in one smooth motion.

"Okay," he said, "it's loaded, but it's still not ready to fire." He put out his hand for the gun. "Let me show you why."

He pointed the muzzle at the living room wall twenty feet away and tried to squeeze the trigger. Nothing.

"Because the safety's on?" she volunteered.

He shook his head. "It doesn't have one. What it has is this thing." He tapped the housing on the top of the barrel. "All semiautomatics have them. You've got to slide it back before you can shoot it. Why don't you give it a try."

"That's right, I remember now."

Sliding back the housing was harder than it looked. She had to exert serious effort, and without realizing it, caused the pistol to rise. Burton fended it off, and she apologized.

"Don't worry. I was ready for that. It happens all the time at first. Try it again."

Her second attempt proved more successful, though it still took a surprising amount of strength.

"Now it's ready to shoot."

Hearing this prompted the most disturbing thought. She wouldn't have called it an urge, not precisely, not even an impulse, but more than just a fleeting image made her understand that she could turn the gun on Burton and kill him, be done with all the anger and angst that he'd burdened her with these past eight months.

The image of shooting him right there at the kitchen table appalled her, but there was no avoiding its animal appeal. And now, as if feeding on this grim momentum, it *did* begin to feel like an urge.

"Let's put it in here." He gestured to the cabinet closest to the front door. "I'm thinking we want to keep it where we can grab it in a hurry. I know you fired it years ago, but I want to remind you that you've really got to hold it with both hands in front of you and aim when you shoot."

He took the gun back—she was relieved to hand it over—and demonstrated, saying, "I just wish we'd had some time to practice before we got up here. It's not easy hitting a target with one of these. Remember that story on the news? The one with the two guys shooting at each other from across a car?"

How could she forget? Two enraged morons emptying their guns at each other from a distance of no more than eight feet, and never finding their targets.

"Wasn't that on *America's Funniest Home Videos?*"

Burton laughed appreciatively. "It should have been."

He parked the Sig Sauer in the cabinet before turning his attention back to the twelve-gauge.

"This is a whole different story. Like I said, just aim and shoot, and it's hard to miss. You point it even close to him and he'll be dancing."

"I don't want him dancing, I want him dead."

Burton paused. "No, we don't want him dead, remember? That's our deal. These things are our last resort. But it's probably not going to matter much with this"—he eyed the shotgun—"because unless you score a direct hit from just a few feet away, he'll survive. He'll be a real mess, and he'll probably be screaming and crawling around like a baby, but he'll be alive."

"I don't want him crawling, either!" A dreadful thought: a serial rapist murderer bleeding and crawling toward her with a huge dose of vengeance to fuel his glutted reserves of rage . . . while she tries to reload? No thanks.

"Don't worry, you hit him with this and it's going to take all the fight right out of him, believe me. Now, I think we should keep it upstairs, like I did last night. If we wake up in the middle of the night, we're going to want a scatter-shot approach."

"Sounds good. Actually, it sounds strange to be even talking about this."

"It does, especially with you."

He made it to the stairs before shouting back to her, "Are we ever going to talk about the real issue?"

She stepped out from the kitchen and caught his eye. "Let's put the guns away first." Anger and ammo and all that.

But the morning passed without any discussion of their marriage, or the means by which they might recapture everything they'd lost. Burton grew distracted with his upcoming cases, or used them to avoid delving into their problems, and Suzanne found herself happy to explore Laura's house, taking in the elegant flourishes, like a hand-carved footstool in the downstairs bathroom, and the oils and watercolors she'd hung on the walls.

When she wandered back up to the glassed-in deck, her own artistic impulses were once again stirred by the sight of the clear-cut hillside. Its barrenness and devastation hovered over the unseemly beauty of the idiot strip, and led her to set up her tripod by the double doors leading to the deck. Though enclosed in glass, it felt far too chilly to work out there. And she didn't want to expose herself to an element far colder than the weather: The Searcher.

She slipped on her overalls and an old woolen sweater. To keep her fingers nimble, she set up a space heater a few feet from the tripod. Not a perfect view of her subject, but the muddy hill and the idiot strip were still visible enough to paint.

When she opened her portfolio for a fresh sheet of rag paper, she saw the Japanese maple she'd worked on at home. Her judgment came quickly and harshly: terrible. She had all she could do to restrain herself from tearing it up and tossing it onto the brightly stained redwood deck.

But she saw almost immediately that it might prove useful in the new work she planned, as a model of an urban tree as stark and sad in its solitude as those stumps appeared in their abundance.

The relationship grew on paper, and by lunchtime she'd planted the image of the maple amid the ragged remains of the hillside. Its fragile limbs grew wild as ivy, weaving the stumps together in a macramé of ghost trees, unhinging botany from reality. Nature could inspire her, but she had no interest in simply reproducing it on paper. She liked to make sly allusions to the natural world, and with this image she felt she was making real progress at last.

As she stood back to appraise her progress, deeming it "progress" indeed, she felt the familiar tug of her e-mail, a need only sharpened by Ami's absence.

She kept her laptop on a bedside table where she could tell at a glance if she'd received mail. She hadn't. Not a word from the young woman since she'd found her haunting note in the kitchen.

"Come on, Ami," she said softly, "play fair. Answer me. Let me know you're alive."

12

AFTER DRIVING ALL day, Ami pulled into a two-story motel on the outskirts of Salt Lake City. She told herself she should turn right around and head downtown, stay somewhere more upscale, more secure, as Suzanne would have, but couldn't bring herself to spend the extra money. It wasn't hers, and she felt she'd tapped all of her boldness in absconding with her boss's car and credit cards.

The motel sat off the freeway in a cluster of gas stations, minimarts, and a sprawling outlet mall.

She checked in, signed Suzanne's name to the credit card slip with less self-consciousness than she had the day before, and noticed once again that desk clerks and gas station attendants rarely check signatures. When they had, it was with no more thought than they'd give to a yawn. But she still signed the slip carefully, executing the loopy *S* that began Suzanne's signature, and the flamboyant *e* with which it ended. A second look, though, revealed an overriding flaw—the uncertain line quality of an unsure hand—and she worried that The Searcher would find a way to screen the credit card slips.

Could he? Ami shook her head. She knew a lot about what you could get through computer records, and an actual copy of her signature on a credit card slip was a stretch. *Not impossible, not at all, but highly unlikely. You're just getting paranoid.*

No, she corrected herself, *it's not paranoid to look closely at every detail when a serial rapist murderer has threatened your boss, and you're traveling under her name.*

But he never said anything about killing *her*. He raped her, if Suzanne's right about that, but the killing stuff, that's what he's been doing to the *other* birth mothers. Cruel consolation, and Ami squirmed when she realized she was taking comfort in it.

She dragged her bags up to the second-floor room and glanced furtively down the balcony hallway before closing the door behind her.

Immediately, she threw the bolt and slipped the chain into place, though in these anxious moments the latter appeared to have the tensile strength of a tissue.

She pulled off her blonde wig and shook out her own red hair, fluffing it with her fingers, trying to give it some life after having smothered and smushed it all day. A knock on the door stilled her hands.

Oh, shit. This wasn't the kind of place with room service or bellmen. She took pains to steady her voice.

"Who is it?"

"The guy from the front desk. You forgot your copy of the bill."

"Can you slip it under the door?"

Silence. Then, "No, I can't. It's getting bunched up."

"Hold on."

She saw the wig and thought she should throw it on. She saw the door and thought she should keep it closed. But instead she moved closer to the voice.

"I'm coming."

But as she neared the door her stomach went wild, as if she could feel The Searcher's presence on the other side. *Don't open it. Don't!*

What are you talking about, she berated herself. *It's the desk clerk. A receipt. What's the big deal?*

Her hand went up to the chain, slid it free. But as she moved to turn the bolt lock, she paused. "Just keep it in the office. I'll pick it up later."

He said nothing, but she could hear him walking away.

She washed up, put the wig back on, and assured herself as she went out for dinner that she'd been overreacting.

When she entered the office, the young sandy-haired clerk glanced up from a small, desk-mounted TV.

"I'll take that copy of the bill now."

He furrowed his brow and turned down the sound. "Yeah, sure, if that's what you want—I can give it to you, but if you're gonna make any calls or have any other charges, we're just gonna have to give you another one when you check out."

She stood still as rubble, as if to defy the movement of thought, of the pressing threat unleashed by his unguarded words.

"Didn't you just come to my room a few minutes ago to tell me that you had a copy of the bill?" Her right hand tugged nervously at a stray strand of blonde hair.

"No. Why would I do that? The bill's not ready until you check out. If you want—"

"Wait! Wait! You're saying *you* didn't knock on my door?"

"No." He shook his head emphatically.

"Who checked in after me?"

"No one. We've got you and one other check-in, and they've been here since about four."

"A man?"

"A whole family with a bunch of kids. They took two rooms on the far end."

"And that's it?" Her voice scaled the peak of panic.

"Yeah, that's it."

"Because someone knocked on my door and said he was from the front desk."

"He did?" The clerk looked at her closely for the first time. "Are you sure? Because there's this guy—"

"A guy! What kind of guy?" A full rush of adrenaline weakened her, made her whole body feel as wobbly as a stick in a storm. She gripped the hard edge of the narrow counter, not only to steady herself, but to keep her rubbery legs from racing to the safety of her car, locking all the doors, turning it into a cell. One that *moves.*

"A guy who's been"—the clerk's voice lowered noticeably—"raping girls in motels around here. The police—"

"Call them!" Ami shrieked. "Right now!"

When he paused, evidently stunned by her outburst, she lunged over the counter and grabbed the phone.

He protested—"I wish you'd let me . . ."—but she'd already punched up a line and was dialing 911.

The Salt Lake City police responded remarkably fast. A stocky white guy not much older than Ami arrived with an African American partner in her thirties. The woman took notes in the tight lobby of the motel and nodded when Ami finished telling them what had happened.

"You did exactly the right thing," the female officer said. "We've got a guy we've been looking for for three weeks now. He waits for a single woman to check in, and then he does his trick with the bill. No one gets a motel bill when they check in, but they don't think about it when he knocks and says he's got it. Then they open the door and he forces his way in and rapes them. He leaves them tied up. Two of his victims weren't found until the maids came around in the morning."

"That's what I told her when she came down here." The desk clerk spoke from behind the counter.

"But did you tell her when she checked in?" the female officer snapped.

"You tell her that we've got some creep going after women traveling alone? That she should be extra careful?"

The clerk didn't respond. Ami shook her head.

The officer turned back to her. "See, that's the problem. We've been asking the 'hospitality industry'"—she used her fingers to make the marks—"to post warning signs and call us, but they don't want to scare away business."

"My boss said there's no reason to because we hadn't had any problems."

"He give you a DNA kit, too? Since when are you guys cops? That's ridiculous. You put those signs up, or you at least tell a woman who's checking in alone about what's going on." The officer shook her head. "We'll be talking to your boss, don't you worry."

"How many rapes have there been?" Ami said.

"Six that we know of."

"Count yourself lucky," the younger officer said.

"No, she's smart." The African American officer closed her notebook.

"Should I get out of here?" Ami asked, looking around.

"My guess," the female officer said, "is that you're safer up there in your room than anywhere else but home. He tried, but he didn't get what he wanted. Now the bad news is that he's probably moved on to somebody else by now. We're going to have a special unit out here tonight looking for him. Just stay inside and keep the door locked. And do what you did earlier if there's a knock; don't open it, but this time call us right away. Now, if it's okay with you, we'd like to walk you up there and look around your room."

"Totally. Are you kidding? I'd really appreciate it."

The officer turned to the clerk. "I'll be coming back down here to talk to you. And I want your boss's numbers. I mean *all* of them. I don't want to be talking to no message machine, you hear me? I want his cell, home, business, if he's got anything besides this place"—she cast a disapproving glance at the motel sign on the wall—"all of them."

She and her partner checked Ami's room thoroughly—under the bed, shower stall, closets—before testing the window latches and door locks.

"You'll be fine," the female officer said to her. "You did the right thing and saved yourself a whole lot of heartache. Trust your gut, girl. You got yourself a good one."

Ami thanked her profusely, locked the door when they left, and fired off an e-mail to Suzanne describing the events of the evening.

"I think you should get out," Suzanne wrote back, "first thing in the morning. Please come home. This is too weird."

Suzanne was right; it did feel weird, no question; but Ami was now convinced that it hadn't been The Searcher. Another serial rapist was operating on the outskirts of this city. He'd gone after her as he'd gone after other women. No more complicated than that.

As for leaving, she needed no urging from Suzanne. She'd already made her decision to move on at first light. The hybrid, tiny as a tuna can, still felt safer than a locked room.

Just keep moving, Ami told herself, *and when Suzanne nails The Searcher you can turn around and head home.*

It all seemed so simple as she checked the locks one more time, and the windows too, testing them as the police had to make sure they wouldn't slide open, and hurrying-hurrying-hurrying so she wouldn't have to think even one extra second about the glass shattering, and the furious hands that could reach in and grab her.

She retreated to the bed, pulled the covers up to her neck, and stared at the teeny green light peering out of the smoke detector.

"Go, girl, go," she whispered.

But her words weren't filled with bravado, they felt forced and filled with fear—of the day, of the night, and of the morning to come.

13

I'M ON THE road again. And it's not just me. Ms. Trayle is on the road again, too. How do I know? My retired detective. He sends me e-mail alerts when she's in motion. Idaho Falls, Salt Lake City, hideous places, really. And heading farther south. What's next? Albuquerque? Now there's a burg for you.

Money must be tight because she's been staying in some real dives, even a Motel 6, which is a big step below her normal digs. They're the "We'll leave the light on" folks. How considerate, though personally if I had to stay in one of those dumps I'd prefer the dark.

Maybe Ms. Trayle's failure to find Laura Kessing's son is catching. Maybe she's suffering other failures, too, ones I don't know about yet, and they're forcing her to become more budget-minded than she's had to be in the past. I can't imagine she's recruiting new clients, and thanks to Laura Kessing's ads the word's out about her less than stellar performance. I was thrilled to find Kessing in the chat rooms pleading for her son. She might as well have taken out a big bold ad saying, "Suzanne Trayle Sucks." When a birth mother pleads for help, it's another way of saying her search angel's a dud.

So Ms. Trayle's heading south and staying in cheap motels. Lovely image, isn't it? Suz the sleaze lying on a cheap mattress. Maybe she's thinking about the company she kept thirty-two years ago when she was on her back, and the uninvited guest who showed up nine months later. Maybe she's haunted by the memory. She should be. She *will* be.

Soothing thoughts, and why not? While Ms. Trayle heads south, I'm going north to stay with Laura for a spell. See how long she lasts, what with the uterine cancer and the cure that I offer.

I like a good road trip. I flew back into Portland for the second time in a week so I could enjoy several hours of driving, although there was also the business of not wanting to arrive at an airport too close to my destination. Distance not only makes the heart grow fonder (or so the dewy-eyed romantics would have us believe), it also shreds the paper trail in the unlikely event that an enterprising cop ever decides to chase it.

But the immediate payoff for my caution is the open road. It gives me all this time to think, and my mind has certainly been busy. As soon as we landed, I found my thoughts traveling to Ms. Trayle's office not twenty miles away. I was even tempted to drive into the city, knock on the door, and pay a visit because who would be there all by herself? Why, little Miss Ami, clueless as the child she appears to be. Did she wear her trench coat today?

But I have other plans. Planning is what it's all about. I packed my binoculars, day pack, rain poncho, hiking boots, energy bars, and water bottle. *And* my camera. I wouldn't think of leaving home without it.

From everything I can gather, Laura lives alone; but she's dying so there's no telling if she's got a caregiver up there, some do-gooder hospice type. That would kill my interest immediately, and it would be back to Portland International empty-handed. Wouldn't be the first time I've had to back away. Three's a crowd, and don't I know it.

But if she's decided to spend her final weeks, months, whatever her diseased uterus is granting her, in quiet contemplation, then I will soon be by her side, coaxing her toward her only true terminus by slowly cutting the rich red cord that connects her to life.

Cascadia is too small for me. Motels, a gas station, market, that's about it; but even if it had a shopping center with a twelve-plex theater I'd get out of here. This time of year I'd be remembered far too easily. The summer crowds are gone, and only masochists would choose to visit in all this rain.

Laura's a grandmother. It's all right there in her file. Isn't that *sweet*? Laura's daughter kept her boy, unlike her whore mother.

Thinking of her waiting for me up there makes me feel so good I almost start singing my favorite song. Paul Simon would be proud. I plan on meeting him some day, letting him know in no uncertain terms how much "Mother and Child Reunion" means to me.

The road to Laura's is climbing through a dense forest. Gorgeous. The scent of the pine trees is subtle, but it seeps through the Subaru's ventilation system. I rented an all-wheel drive for exactly the kinds of conditions I may be facing.

I'm always prepared, which is a damn sight more than you can say about certain women down in Galveston, Texas. I had a good long laugh reading about them. A serial killer's been terrorizing them. (There's a lot of competition out there: the FBI says thirty-five to forty of us are "operating" nationwide. A few more and we could have a convention.) He's murdered three of them and left no clues for the cops. But what's really befuddling the flatfoots was how he got into their homes in the first place, because it appeared that he'd gained access without a "forced entry."

Don't these cops know that getting into a woman's house is the easiest part of all? All you have to do is give them a good story, and there's a story for every occasion.

I've got the best one going, if you know for certain that she's a birth mother. Once you know that, you not only have the key to her heart, you have the key to her house.

Laura has neighbors. Not many, but I've counted three mailboxes at the end of driveways heading off into the trees.

That's good. If she's got neighbors, even a mile or so apart, then she's not going to be alarmed by every vehicle that goes by. Lucky me, though I have yet to pass anyone driving in, not even hunters, and it's deer season.

The driveway to Laura's place comes up so fast I almost shoot past it. Looks like a long one. What an odd mailbox she's got. Shaped like a pagoda. This'll be fun. She's eccentric. I can feel it already. A woman with a mini-pagoda for a mailbox will by all means open the door. She'll be *open* to life, consider it her mission to embrace life fully in all of its dimensions. And to embrace the death "experience" as well. The one she thinks she's going to have.

Now I do drive past it. I'm in the neighborhood, but I'm hardly ready to introduce myself. Time to reconnoiter, get some of those surveillance shots.

The road's getting worse. Hard to believe, but true. And now it looks like it's ending. I'm not a half mile past her driveway, and there's nothing but forest. For the last hour the whole drive's been thick with trees, but this is really thick. This is impenetrable. I'm just going to have to park it, but I want to get it off the road far enough that you can't see it.

There's a spot between a couple of trees on my right that I could maybe slip into, but I'm going to have to get out of the car and make sure I won't get stuck.

It's firm enough, probably from the roots that are snaking along the ground. Deciduous trees of some kind. Maybe oak. I can't really tell without the leaves.

I back in carefully, and I keep backing in until I'm at least thirty feet off the road. I plan on being here a few days, and I don't want her—or anyone else, for that matter—wandering up and finding a strange car.

This is good; the few tire tracks I left are already getting beaten down by the rain.

It looks like my best bet is to hike in a direction roughly parallel to her driveway, as much as I can place it from here.

I'm glad I came equipped for all this rain because it's really coming down, even under the cover of these trees. There's a boatload of underbrush, too, and tramping through it is a pain in the ass. Vines and bushes and saplings. But it looks like I'm getting a break. I'm not two hundred feet from the car, and I see a cleared-out section. Get this, it's a logging road, and it's curving in a direction that I think will take me toward Laura's place.

No, I'm wrong. It's taking me to the ugliest mountain I've ever seen. I guess you'd call it a mountain, maybe it's a hill. It definitely looks like it's been butchered. Every inch of it's been logged. All I can think of is some bullet-headed guy with a buzz cut.

There's also a row of trees standing off to my right. Peculiar as all get out, if you ask me. It's like they're guarding the front of the hill. But if I climb this huge mound of mud, I might be able to get a bead on Laura's house.

To be safe, I stay low and work my way around to the far side. Somebody did a real number on this hill. Looks like they went insane with a bulldozer. A bunch of stumps have been ripped right out of the ground, roots and all; and there are dozens of smaller holes, and gouges deep as graves. Rain's collecting everywhere. I'd hate to step in one of these puddles, I might disappear. It looks as beat up as a battlefield. But as bad as this is, it still feels good to get out and move around after a day of travel. I don't even mind the climbing part. A few more feet and I should be able to see over the tops of those trees.

There it is, Laura's house. It's got to be. It's directly across from me. Instinctively, I duck down. If I can see her house, she can see me. I'm looking around for a place a little higher on the hill that'll give me some cover, and I see it. Another one of those huge uprooted stumps. I can set up surveillance there. I'll have to go down and work my way up from the back of this mud pile again, but I'll be able to hide behind the stump, which looks like an octopus with its arms twisted out in every imaginable direction.

It takes me about fifteen minutes, but here I am kneeling in the mud, the smell as strong as a shovelful of fresh dirt. I get out the binoculars and focus on the house. If it were sunny, I'd have to worry about light reflecting off the lenses, but the sun is not a factor today. It's rainy season, and the mountains have started to move. I read that it happens every year, mudslides wiping out roads and parks and cars and people. So I'm not worried about the sun. I'm only worried about getting a good view of her house and some good pictures of Laura Kessing.

But in this weather, the camera's not coming out of its case till I see her. So I keep watch on the windows. The minutes feel like hours, and then I see something that absolutely staggers me. I mean, what's *he* doing here? Fornicating with Laura's diseased privates? Wouldn't surprise me. Good old Burton, up to his old tricks again. He's slipping out the back door looking around like a guilty husband, which is a part he plays so well. Look at this, he's grubbing for wood.

Wait a second. If he's here, it could be that *she's* up here, too; and if that's the case, then both of them could be up here keeping Laura company, a happy threesome (another sick possibility that no doubt crossed *his* mind) in the forest—what's left of it anyway.

Burton's ducking back into the house with the wood, still looking around as he closes the door. I catch some movement at the very rear of the second-story deck. From where I am, I'm slightly above it. There's someone, I can't see who it is, bending over to pick something up. A woman, I can tell that much. It must be Laura. She halfway straightens, and then bends over again, as if whatever she's trying to grab keeps rolling away from her. I keep the binoculars right on her because if she stands up facing me I should be able to get a good look at her.

Oh, this is too rich. It's Ms. Trayle. What's she doing? Taking care of the dying, now that she can't find the living?

My hands are starting to shake from holding up the binoculars for so long, and I can see I'm going to have to do some serious surveillance to figure out what's going on here, so I look around for a place to steady myself. It takes only a few seconds to see that I can lean my shoulder against the stump and rest my hands on a naked root sticking out to my left; but by the time I've moved Ms. Trayle has turned and walked back to an . . . easel? She's painting? Suzanne Trayle is at Laura Kessing's, and she's painting? With her husband? Since when are they getting along? And where the hell is Laura anyway?

A lot of questions, and I can't keep myself from asking them over and over. At least it's starting to get dark. Lights are going on, and that's making it easier to see inside. But I'll be damned if I can find anyone other than Ms. Trayle and her husband. And just about the time I'm thinking Laura must be confined to her bed, another thought occurs to me, and I finally realize that I could sit here for days and days and never see her. Why?

Because she's not here!

I think I've been set up. Call me thick, but it's taken me a while to get it. Laura's not in the house any more than Ms. Trayle's in her car. But somebody's buying gas and staying in motels. Somebody's doing it under her name. Somebody named Laura, maybe?

And then I realize it could be anybody. But here's what's absolutely certain: Somebody's acting as a decoy. Somebody's been told something about what's going on. And that somebody's got to be stopped.

As angry as I am at Suzanne Trayle for thinking she could trap me, as much as it makes me want to punish her severely and immediately, I see that I've got to deal with the decoy first, and fast. If anything happens to Ms. Trayle, the decoy has every incentive to go straight to the police. But if the decoy goes silent, nothing changes for Suzanne. She still knows her son is finished if she goes to the cops, and she'll have another striking example of what happens to anyone who violates my rules. Of course, she's the biggest violator of all, so as soon as I dispense with the decoy, I'm coming after her. Quickly. I'm not wasting any time. Once someone like Suzanne Trayle starts talking, even to one person, she might not shut up.

This could explain the cheap motels, too. Laura, or whoever's the decoy, isn't accustomed to Suzanne's standards, or else they're too self-conscious about spending her money.

And then I'm gripped by another possibility, one that has my head turning in all directions at once: What if she's working with the cops? What if they have this place staked out?

A sick feeling, like gravity suddenly sucking all the blood out of my gut. If she's shown that letter to the authorities, there's no way they're going to let me walk out of here. But then I notice again how much light has faded, and I breathe in the darkness with a great sense of relief. No self-respecting cop would ever let an *alleged* killer take cover in the night, especially in a wide open place like this. The chance for escape would be too great. No, if they were here, I'd have heard from them by now. Their absence is testament to the strength of my strategy, and to the power of that photograph. Nothing like knowing a killer has crept close to your kid to make you behave.

I don't think Laura's here, either. I'm actually hoping that I don't see some sick, haggard face in that house, not with those two around. Better she's out on a highway, or in a motel, thinking she's safe, playing her game with Ms. Trayle.

I have to give the devil her due. Ms. Trayle's clever. But her trick has turned into the sweetest twist of all. Here's what I'm talking about. When I find the decoy and work my wonders, I'm not even going to have to worry about my private detective linking me to the murder, should he run across the odd news item. Thanks to Ms. Trayle's simpleminded machinations, the woman he's tracking for me, the decoy with the credit cards and car, is not the person who will appear to have been killed. There'll be no connection to me. No clues and no concerns. When the cops find the body, that's if they do find the body, there'll be no ID, either; and if forensics ever figures out who it is, it won't be Ms. Trayle.

She's going to disappear in Washington, a long way from the last place her credit cards were used. It's possible that my private detective could link me to her at that point, *if* he happens to hear that people are looking for her; but a link is not conclusive, and it'll be a confusing link at best. And if there's one thing you want hovering like a cloud over every crime, it's confusion. It obscures facts, raises questions, and makes a final proof an almost impossible goal.

I must confess I'm anticipating the murder of this decoy with the most intense longing, bringing as it will another smear of blood to Ms. Trayle's conscience. *She'll* hear about it. When the time comes, I'll whisper the details in her ear.

So go on, Ms. Trayle, paint all you want. You're not going anywhere, and I've got some business to attend to first. Ms. or Mr. Decoy can't be that far away. Maybe a couple of hours by air.

I give them long enough to fix dinner . . . all by themselves. Eat dinner . . . all by themselves. No lights going on in other rooms. No bedside service for the sick. Just the two of them.

It's time to tell my retired detective to e-mail me updates as soon as they become available. I don't want to be more than a few minutes behind the decoy.

When I catch up to the decoy, I'll simply watch and wait and take the person apart. And if it turns out to be Laura Kessing, I'll do what every other self-respecting male does when he releases himself from the obscene social constraints that bind him: I'll indulge myself. I'll help myself to her just as I've planned to all along. I'm not going to alter my plans because Ms. Trayle thinks she can stop me. All the more reason to concede nothing to the Search Angel. Nothing.

All the more reason to make it the most memorable murder yet.

14

THE WOODSTOVE CRACKLED and popped as Burton fed it one of the damp logs he'd hauled in from the deck. He'd been keeping it going all day, had even joked about being a "fire provider" as he'd loaded the first of the logs into the stove this morning. Suzanne had allowed herself a smile at the primitive role he'd assigned himself, remembering in the days before they'd married how he'd walked her up to his house and grunted, "Cave provider," a line so incongruous, coming as it did from a young lawyer with a starchy streak, that she'd convulsed with laughter. She couldn't help but wonder if he'd been trying to hearken back to their happier times with that fire provider business.

Or had he summoned a lighter mood to gently remind her of his most serious role—provider of protection—as a man sometimes will if he's smart enough to see that modesty can italicize courage?

This wasn't a question she felt comfortable asking, wasn't even sure Burton would be mindful of his motives; but she understood in an instant that his willingness to help with such a risky plan had warmed her—if not as much as the flames themselves, then enough to shift her from the aspish anger she'd known only a few weeks ago to an edgy form of ambivalence, though even this uneasy acceptance of his presence was tempered by the terror she'd experienced in the immediate past. No part of her, for example, wanted to encourage his increasing physical intimacy, which was no longer confined to wrapping his arm around her, as it had been on their first night; this morning she'd wakened to feel his sleepy, half-erect excitement pressing into her bottom, which had left her frozen for several minutes with an underlying fear that had almost as much to do with his betrayal as it did with The Searcher's brutality. She'd fled quickly to the bathroom, and Burton, still soggy with sleep, hadn't appeared to notice.

Once she washed up and was fully awake, the morning—and now the bud of the afternoon—had passed more easily for her.

"Wait'll you hear this." He looked up from a magazine and she lifted her eyes from a popular biography of John Adams.

"What is it?"

"Story about a civil suit. Guy's family in Portland claims that he willed his body to UCLA, and then they started selling off his parts to private researchers. Kidneys, frontal lobe." Burton peered at the magazine. "'Everything from his spleen to his spine.'"

"It says that?"

"Right here."

"Wait till the *National Enquirer* gets ahold of it."

"I'd hate to see the headline."

"I'd hate to see the photos."

They both moaned, a response that fostered Suzanne's smile.

"I'm going to check to see if she's e-mailed me."

She scaled the stairs two at a time to the large sleeping loft and hurried over to her laptop, which she'd left on the bureau next to her easel. She'd spent the morning working with her pastels, and periodically checking to see if anything new had arrived in her in-box. Nothing earlier, but now the annoying time icon twirled and twirled, and then spit out a passel of new messages, including one from Ami.

Yes!

"Dear Ami," Ami had written, continuing the online impersonation:

> I'm out of Utah and headed down into Colorado. I stopped at a
> truck stop near the border where I found this Internet cafe.
>   I'm just checking in to let you know everything's going well. It's
> quite beautiful out here. I can see the Rockies, and there's snow
> all the way down to the foothills. But it's very cold, daytime
> temperatures already in the twenties, and it's only November.
>   Love,
>   Suz

She's safe, the sole message of import to Suzanne as she leafed electronically through the remaining e-mails, almost all of them from birth mother clients, or birth mothers who wanted to become clients.

For the latter, she composed a standard rejection letter. She tried to write a similarly standardized response to the women who were asking about the status of her efforts on their behalf but found it impossible to consider anything but her own guilt.

Tears splashed on the laptop before she realized she was crying. They shone on the very letters that could save her birth mothers: A few lines of truth and a single keystroke and they'd all be safe.

And he'd be dead: your son and his daughter and his wife. Innocent of everything but lineage.

But *all* of them were innocent: her birth mothers, her boy, his family. Everyone but her. That's what The Searcher had done to her. Turned her silence into a weapon, her kindness into a killer.

Burton rested his hand on her shoulder. She hadn't heard him climbing the stairs. When she looked up, he saw her tears and softly massaged the back of her neck.

"I don't know how long I can stand this," she said in a voice choking on itself. "I feel like this . . . *animal* has made me God over all these lives, and I don't want to be."

Burton sat beside her and took her in his arms. She buried her face in his chest and sobbed as hard as she had in memory.

He rocked her and knew better than to repeat the stingy platitudes of hope. And when her tears no longer soaked his shirt, he looked over at the painting on her easel and said, "I like it, Suz."

He's redirecting me, she thought. Like you'd do to a child; but she believed him, too, thought the work was perhaps her best.

When he reached for her overalls and handed them to her, she nodded: He did know her better than anyone else. Since she was fourteen, and he was all of eighteen, a lifetime had passed: young soldier to middle-age judge. Young girl to search angel. The two of them always linked by their son, whom they did not know and could not find.

"It really is very good." His eyes had remained on her painting, studying it.

She slipped on the overalls as he slipped away. Yes, he knew her well: when to stay and when to leave. More important than it might seem.

The Japanese maple had grown under her touch to fill most of the painting. She appreciated the irony of this, the way such a humble urban tree stood supreme over the ravaged landscape of a remote hill. And she'd studied enough psychology to know that it represented more than arboreal life, that it spoke forcefully of the emotional isolation she'd experienced during the past eight months, and of the shattering physical violence of the past two weeks, as if all she'd known of marriage and mayhem could be captured in a single penetrating image.

She used a gray pastel to fill in the sun-speckled shadows, then slipped the box cutter from her pocket and studied the trees that formed the idiot strip. They looked as unsuspecting as stones before a mob.

Carefully, she scraped the razor across the bottom of the painting, then worked brown pigment into the roughed-up fibers. She repeated this process until the paper in the foreground furred with dark colors. Stepping back to study it, she could almost feel the coarse bark of one of her downed conifers rising from the easel. It unsettled her with stark imaginings of all the trees on the hillside that had been snapped and splintered and smashed to earth.

Her eyes rose to their remains, mottled by the rainy windows but clear enough to let her study the scars left by the bulldozers, skidders, and chain saws that had savaged the trees, the underbrush, life itself, and left behind huge gashes and gaping holes, angry craters on the face of this stricken moon.

Rain collected in these crudely formed basins and dimpled their dark surfaces. She couldn't see the individual drops at this distance, only the dim pointillism of their depressions. The perception sent an eerie sensation down her back and arms, goose pimples roused not to snap at the icy air, but to send their roots into the chilly cover of blood.

Sundown in the Rockies, and Ami's favorite REM song of all time on the radio.

Considering her scare twenty-four hours ago, she felt pretty good. A great song helps, but so does having a handsome guy hold the door for you at a gas station. Happened at her last stop. He'd smiled at her, too. Not like a wolf, like a guy. A *normal* guy. About the only normal thing she'd known for a while.

So what if he'd been a little older? He was cute, and interested, too. You can see it in their eyes. Like the UPS guy, except he's so shy. Shows up every day, sometimes twice a day, always tries to make conversation, and still can't say, "Want to go out?" Four words: "Want to go out?" No big deal. What was she going to have to do? Jump his bones? Which she'd never do, but it could be *so* frustrating dealing with the shy ones. She'd been ready for a guy to hold the door for her and try to strike up a friendship by the gas pump. Good line, too. Not the usual stuff. He'd said, "It's funny how even the sun can look lonely at the end of the day."

She'd looked up at the last sliver of sun slipping behind the mountains and known exactly what he meant. It *did* look lonely. How's that for getting your point across without coming on like a geek?

So she'd given him her best smile and a winsome good-bye and drove away.

"*Can* look lonely." *That's nice,* she said to herself as she passed a rest stop. Not the typical guy thing of going, "*Sure* looks lonely . . ." Being way too obvious, a sandwich board for sex.

Colorado plates. She'd checked the rearview mirror as she pulled away. Tan sedan. A no-personality car. Kind of thing you get as a rental, or as a graduation gift from a rich aunt, if you have one. She sure didn't.

But now as she spotted a Holiday Inn on the east side of Denver—no more totally cheap motels for her—she had a queasy feeling about the whole thing. Yesterday a rapist had tried to get into her room, and today a guy had come on to her. And The Searcher's still out there somewhere, maybe even zeroing in on Suzanne.

Hey, it's not like guys haven't tried to pick you up before, she reasoned with herself. *It's happened a lot, so don't go getting* totally *paranoid. It's not like you're going out with him for a drink or dinner. You're way too smart for that. All you did was smile back and say good-bye.*

Feeling better, she checked in, and damn if the desk clerk wasn't giving her the eye, too. Twice in one afternoon. Now that's unusual. Not unprecedented, but odd enough to make her wonder what was going on.

She hurried to her room to check the mirror, pausing only long enough to throw the bolt lock and hitch the chain before rushing to the bathroom. Not even taking her coat off, not wanting to change a single thing about herself.

The wig! The blonde hair. That's it. That's what it's all about. Not me.

It was a letdown, but it was also comforting, once she thought about it.

The guy at the gas station wasn't some weirdo freak out to get her. He was into blondes, like the desk clerk.

But you're faking it. She ripped the wig right off, told herself she'd go to the restaurant as Ami Mathison for a change, see if maybe there was some magic in *her* tonight. See if any guys noticed anything about her besides some phony blonde hair.

But as she flipped the wig onto the top of the toilet tank, she knew she couldn't do anything of the sort. Instead, she grabbed a tissue and blew her nose. Saw her nose was red, almost as red as her real hair. Cheeks, too, from the cold. Then she reminded herself to call her mother, who scolded her gently for having been out of touch.

"I'm sorry, Mom. I had to take off quickly. It's research for Suz."

Her mom forgave easily, especially when she heard it was for Suzanne.

They chatted about her mother's job at a cosmetics counter, and at the end of the fifteen-minute call Ami told her she loved her. Then she listened to her mother struggling to reciprocate, half-formed words hanging limp as linen in the dead air between them. Last month she'd admitted to Ami that the reason she found it so hard to say "I love you" was rooted in the shame she felt for having given her up for adoption "because if I really did love you, and I know I do, but if I really did, how could I have ever done that?"

"Mom," Ami had said, "you've got to forgive yourself. Don't be judging who you were then by who you are now. That's not fair."

Her mom had cried and hugged her and whispered that no one had ever had a better daughter. Ami had smiled into her shoulder, happy that after all the empty years they could share such closeness.

As they said good-bye on the phone, Ami heard her squeak out those treasured words and offer a favorite mandate of mothers everywhere: "You be careful out there."

"I will, Mom. You too."

Ami rested the receiver in its cradle and walked back in the bathroom. She stood before the mirror and began to put on the wig, tucking away stray strands of red hair as thoroughly as she did the knowledge that the wig, along with the credit cards and car, was part of the bait, and that to re-create herself in front of the mirror was to impale herself on the sharpest of hooks.

But none of that seemed to matter as she entered the softly lit restaurant and heard the symphony of hushed voices and shifting utensils.

The hostess asked if she'd be dining alone and led her to a padded booth. After sitting down and taking the proffered menu, she looked at the car lights flashing by on the freeway. *He's out there,* she told herself, *the guy in the tan car.* And while this sparked a moment of regret, it also left her feeling safer for having moved on without flirting back. For not taking any chances at all. *When this is over, there'll be plenty of time for guys,* she assured herself. *All the time in the world.*

15

I KNOW A LOT about Laura Kessing. I'm a quick study, and I do my homework.

I know, for instance, that Laura Kessing is one of those cranks who writes letters to the editor extolling the virtues of nature, decrying the cutting of trees (despite living in a log house), and proclaiming the greatness of "nature's cathedrals," by which I believe she means all the ancient trees that have yet to be pounded into toilet paper for her pampered bottom.

I know not only her age (fifty-four), but the color of her hair in its natural state (gray), and in the way she presents it to the world (bittersweet chocolate brown). Ms. Trayle's files are a trove of such details.

There's nothing *blonde* about Laura Kessing.

There's nothing *young* about Laura Kessing.

There's nothing *Ami* about Laura Kessing.

A shell game's going on, except the pea of all things has gone missing. And what Laura Kessing knows about me is a major concern. But I'm not about to overlook the consolation prize, Ms. Trayle's very own assistant, the little office girl, Ami.

The moment I caught her eye at the gas station, I wanted to rip that wig right off her head and sink my fingers into all that thick red hair she was hiding. I wanted to yank tangled fistfuls of it to my face so I could see the blushing refusal of her pale scalp when I played my tug 'n' tease game (I do take great sport in the resistance of skin and skull). I wanted this as much as I wanted to see what lay beneath her soft sweater, her deliciously short skirt, her underthings. Her skin. What lies *under* her skin, below the blushing pores. Yes, that too.

So I gave my Little Red Riding Hood three carefully timed minutes after she pulled out of that Texaco. That's plenty, about a three-mile head start on an interstate. It took me twenty minutes to catch up and sneak into line two cars back. Ten minutes more and it would have been so dark it would have been tough to pick her out.

Keeping her in sight wasn't hard after that. She's the kind of driver who settles into the middle lane, sets the cruise control slightly above the speed limit, and doesn't brake or accelerate unless she has to.

But when she signaled for the exit, I had to fall in right behind her. These were anxious moments, and when we stopped at the end of the exit ramp, I hunched down and waited to see if she'd check her rearview mirror. Not that she would have been able to see me in the dark, not easily anyway, but I didn't want any slipups at all. It wasn't a problem, though, because she was trying to make a right, and traffic kept coming at her from the left, leaving her little time to worry about who was looking over her shoulder.

After she made that right, I let several cars go by before following her. And when she pulled into the Holiday Inn, I sped by and didn't turn into the lot until I reached the far end.

I have to say I was surprised at how appealing she was when I met her face-to-face at the gas station. She's small-breasted with a really tight little bottom and narrow hips, and even with that wig on she looked more like an effeminate boy than a girl. But I like that. I like boy-girls a lot. I even have a formative history here, which I'll get to in a second, and which comes into play as I sit here in the car considering Ami's androgynous appeal. If I didn't see a lot of potential in her, I wouldn't have stayed out here with my binoculars watching her eat her dinner in a window booth. (Personally, I don't have much of an appetite. Not for food. I'm always this way before a new event. An energy bar's all I need.) I would have simply come up with a plan to kill her after I'd tailed her to her room.

It wouldn't be that difficult. A push-in when she turns in for the night, which is part of my plan in any case, is a quick example. And that'll be easy. She's on the ground floor right by some ice and Coke machines. But if that doesn't work out for some reason, I can always give one of her tires a slow leak and wait until she has to pull over to the side of the road tomorrow. Then I'll surprise her by stopping. Look, that's weird, she'll probably think, it's the guy I met yesterday. But not nearly as weird or surprising as everything that'll follow: the abduction at gunpoint, the vigorous interrogation on a less traveled route, where the trees in their thick solicitude will provide cover, and the sound of a single shot will be swallowed by the distances that'll surround us.

Regardless whether it's tonight, tomorrow, or even the next day, she dies. She's taking part in Ms. Trayle's vicious little sting; and if she knows enough to wear a wig, drive her car, and use her credit cards, then she knows too much. Once I have her, I'll make sure she shares all the details, everything I'll need for my return trip to the great north woods.

For now I take pleasure in the surveillance itself, the power in being the watcher, and in knowing that those ice and Coke machines can't be more than ten feet from the door to her room. A man could be dwarfed by machines of that size. A man could disappear beside them . . . for a few critical seconds. A man absolutely will.

I've got the engine going, heater on. She's sipping her wine now. I wish she didn't drink; it reminds me too much of Mother. I hate alcohol on their breath, but in size and shape she reminds me much more of Marty, my first boy-girl. As I said, I have a formative history here, and I wasn't overstating the case in the least.

Marty picked me up at a game park a month before my eighteenth birthday, which would turn out to be so liberating, thanks to Mom's gratifying demise.

She was a year older than me, with brown hair even shorter than mine. Her chest wasn't much bigger than my own either, as I discovered in her bedroom moments after her roommate took off for work, leaving us alone in the small house they shared.

"What are you doing!" she said as I lifted her top off to find large erect nipples, with little cushion to support them, poking the eyes out of the air.

"I'm taking your shirt off."

"But . . . I don't want you to."

But . . . her arms had risen to accommodate me, and then settled by her sides as I unbuckled her belt.

"Stop!" she said, all smiles and excitement. "Don't you dare . . . *rape* me."

A game for her, I could see that right away: the alert, playful smile, alacritous eyes. The edge she needed before she could succumb, but the word *rape* wasn't a game for me; it was a gate that opened to a whole new world. For the first time I sensed the brooding, blooded, smutty indignity of that single sharp syllable. I swear, it was like hearing a bell, so clear was its call, so distinct its tidings.

Until then I'd thought little of rape, or of the men who practice it so enthusiastically that they're willing to risk death, prison (and their own rape) to engage in it. But when Marty sat there naked from the waist up, pleading with me not to *rape* her, I felt a rush so hot, so thick, so undeniably real that it was as if every cell in my body had found its Eden at last.

The next time she said the word she laughed, and I said, "Don't laugh."

She caught on and struck a frightened pose, curling her spine and shoulders forward, and then (she was good, she was very, very good) she began to whisper her pleas in a terrified voice.

"Don't rape me. Please! I don't want to be raped."

She struggled so hard I could barely get her pants off, and I had to take a break before going to work on her panties. When I did grab them, I couldn't resist an overwhelming urge to put my hand over her mouth, to mug the screams that would have come from the much more serious threats I was already starting to envision. She was great. She played along some more, moving her lips frantically against my fingers until I felt like a blind man reading the Braille of her body.

Her panties came off with a lot more squirming, and my jeans came down and all of our clothing took flight. I paused only to take out my knife.

Yes, my *knife*. She'd played her game, and now it was time for mine.

Who did she think she was, *pretending* to be scared?

"What are you doing?" she said as she had at the very start, but now her voice shook with real fear. The effect on my erection was a surge so great that I thought it would explode. But it didn't, and when I survived that luscious threat I knew there would be time to savor every second.

I didn't respond to her, not with words, and she grew silent, too. Sweat trickled down her brow, nose, cheeks, and chin, and puddled in the hollow at the base of her neck.

She covered herself with her hands, a blanket of fingers over her dark triangle (as if that could stop me), and shook. Her nipples quivered, and a tremble took hold of her thighs.

"Move your hands."

Now her head shook, too: No.

I pulled the knife away, and then she did unveil the flurry of tight dark curls flattened against her skin, every strand soaked and shimmery from the moisture I'd wrung first from her desire, and now from her fear. I was so aroused I ached. But when I moved the knife close again, she covered herself back up.

This happened each time I appeared ready to prick her sex. It was no longer a knife, but a conductor's baton directing, or should I said *dictating*, every movement in the orchestral pit of her body.

"Put it away," she pleaded. "Please."

"If that's what you want," I said. "But are you sure you want me to *put it away?*"

She hesitated. Who could blame her? Her eyes widened and went wild as she cried out in what I can honestly describe only as agony; and then, brave girl, she nodded.

"You're sure?" I repeated.

Again, her head moved up and down, but slower.

"Okay, then, here goes." I was hardly aware myself of what I would do next.

Seconds no more alive than a freeze frame held us both before I pressed the dull edge of the blade between her tiny breasts, heard the bleatings of her panicked breath, and folded the five inches of beautiful shiny steel back into the handle.

When it snapped into place, I let it lie by those soft dark dots, rising and falling with the bellows of her fear.

"Feel safer now?"

She didn't seem to know how to answer, or if she should grab it, and I was on unsteady ground myself. I had no idea what to make of my first foray into the demimonde of my mind. She'd opened the door, and both of us had raced down those stairs under the incantatory spell of "rape." For her it had been a game that had turned all too real, while for me that single ringing syllable had become in those fervent minutes, and in the fevered ones that followed, the Spanish fly of physical persuasion.

After waiting until she could bear it no longer, she brushed the knife from her chest in a fury, as she might have a spider or snake. It hit the floor and sprang back open, as if it would not be denied, either.

She smiled through her tears and drew me to her, and we had fierce sex on her bed, the floor, and finally against her bedroom door, the hinges screaming and the wood jamb pounding in the great distance beyond our bodies.

Marty called for weeks afterward. "Come see me," her messages always said. Finally, in what could only have been desperation speaking, she added, "And bring your knife."

Eventually, I did, and Marty never called again.

I don't expect nearly as much sport from Ami the androgyne, but I do expect the peculiarly potent frisson that comes from the carnality of gender confusion. I wouldn't be much of a psychologist if I failed to see how appropriate this is for an adoptee. At its core, our identity is always in flux, as elusive as the wind, the rain, or any other element of passage.

She's paying for her meal with a credit card. No surprise there. These imprints led me to her, and I'm sure that in a very short time there will be an e-mail alert about the card's use at a Holiday Inn on the east side of Denver.

As soon as she gets up from the table, I shut off the engine, get out of the car, grab my garment bag, and go.

I see her by the door, coming out, and hoist the bag up over my shoulder so it casually covers up most of my face.

As she turns a corner of the building, blind to me now, I rush to the ice and Coke machines. I don't want to arrive too soon, but I definitely don't want to arrive too late and have her catch me using them for cover. There's a fine line between loitering and being late, and a little luck in hitting it just right.

No one else is around as I slip beside the machines and bend over, as if I'm chasing a coin that's rolled over here. I take the opportunity to look around one more time. It's clear. The parking lot and building lights are on, but that's not bad. Lights give everyone a false sense of security. Let's hope they do the same—

Footsteps. Here she comes. It must be her. The steps are light, a woman's, and if they stop by that door, then—

They've stopped.

The sound of a key. A jingle. Or did I imagine that? No, it's real. Metal finding metal, the key going in the door. A handle's getting turned. I look around the Coke machine to confirm that it's Ami. It is. She's working the handle. The key's holding her attention.

No one's coming. Give me a few seconds. That's all. No one's coming (I keep checking). Come on, get that thing open. Just a few more seconds, that's all I need. Open it!

The door does crack open, but then she surprises me by looking around, *checking*. That's smart, but not smart enough because the door *is* open. She looks me right in the eye, shakes her head, first in obvious confusion and then in panic over my strange and sudden reappearance; but instead of pulling the door shut to keep our confrontation public, she tries to get inside.

I blitz her so hard she butts the door all the way open with her head and crashes onto her side in the room, a near-fetal position from which she tries to launch a scream; but the sound that comes out is a squeak. I've knocked the wind right out of her.

Now I swing the door shut, careful not to slam it, not to draw any attention to this room, and take a second to listen for the sound of frightened voices, hurried footsteps, any sense of urgency out there. What I hear is a scream. Somehow, Ami's found the strength.

When I turn on her, she's crab-walking backward, legs open, all panties and gulping air, working up another shriek. I throw myself and my garment bag on her, smothering and flattening her tiny body, muffling the sound she makes. In less than two seconds I find her mouth and cap it shut. My other hand grabs her throat hard enough to cut off her air. She struggles, kicks, and tries to claw me, but she's not finding any flesh.

The waiting begins as I hold her tightly. Did anyone hear her? And if they have, are they assuming it's from a television, or the hysterical squeals that occasionally erupt from a motel room, the drunken, sexual blathering of a stolen night?

She stops fighting me. It's the lack of air that's slowing her down. I feel the delightful twisting of her body that comes from slow strangulation. I'm not going to kill her, not yet. There really is too much that I need to find out, and even more that I hope to enjoy. But she doesn't know any of this yet, so I expect she's all ears as I start to talk.

"One more scream and you're dead."

I ease up just enough to let her gasp for breath. Her chest fills. It's against mine, and I can feel it rise. With my hand still on her mouth, and my forearm crushing her tiny breast, I can also feel her heart beating madly.

"Ami," I tell her, "you're mine. Do you understand that?"

She doesn't answer. Doesn't even try to nod. But she will. She'll answer *all* my questions, and do everything I say. She'll have no choice.

16

BURTON HAD COOKED dinner, a western omelette, one of the few culinary offerings he prepared with any consistency. Then he'd earned real points by insisting on cleaning up, slipping on one of Laura's full-length aprons, an ugly affair featuring the most garish sunflowers Suzanne had ever seen, as he shoo-shooed her from the kitchen.

She'd returned to the plum-colored couch by the woodstove and the John Adams biography, spending the past two hours immersed in the details of eighteenth-century farm and family life, wondering every few pages if Abigail's peripatetic, presidential-bound husband had cheated on her during his many absences. Probably, she'd concluded at once (he's a man, isn't he?). But after reading through much of their correspondence, she'd decided that maybe, just possibly, he'd been faithful.

Now she and Burton were reclining on the bed, shotgun leaning against the wall beside them, watching the opening credits of a movie he'd brought along. It was the most recent film mailed to him by an online video club he'd joined. In a matter of minutes, Suzanne realized the entire plot ran on the dreadful fuel of infidelity. She would have moaned aloud if it wouldn't have drawn greater attention to how deeply uncomfortable she felt. Burton sat stiffly beside her, apparently as skewered by self-consciousness as she. Awkward marital moment? None the more so. Here they were tentatively talking about patching up their problems, and Laura's little TV screen could have been a mirror of their past eight months. *Thanks,* Burt, *for bringing this along. Don't you ever read the plot summaries? Or do you just click on whatever busty movie poster grabs your gonads?*

The story was as contrived as it made her feel: A couple on the verge of divorce (his faithlessness, *of course*) were trying to explain to their two adorable daughters that their marriage was coming to an end. They reassured the girls of their love for them and for each other (Crock. *Crock!*), but each time one of the parents attempted to explain the future configuration of the family, the other one would interrupt to try to soften the worst news a young child is likely to hear.

Meantime, the two girls sat so pie-eyed from shock that Suzanne could hear their poignant pleas for reconciliation long before the kids ever had a chance to croak their lachrymose lines.

So after having read more than a couple of hundred pages before deciding that John Adams might not have violated his vows—and finding genuine hope in such a cautious conclusion—Suzanne now found herself enduring a cinematic echo of her own tacky betrayal.

Uncanny how the hangdog expression of the adulterous dad bore a rough resemblance to her own guilty spouse. Unbearable how the slump-shouldered daughters resurrected the barren facts of her infertility.

She and Burton had tried for years to have another child. They'd gone the whole route—fertility testing, sperm analysis, hormone treatments—before finally spending inordinate sums on in vitro fertilization. After the fourth go-round, she'd had to reconcile herself to the infertility that plagued so many other birth mothers, a condition so prevalent that it bulked up the considerable body of literature about women who had given up their children for adoption.

Better than 30 percent of them never got pregnant again, and while that number undoubtedly included women so traumatized by the adoption experience that they never wanted another child, she was certain it also included many thousands of women like herself whose bodies refused, at a deep undiagnosable level, to bear a child after suffering the primal wound of separation.

She and Burton had never stopped trying, but at forty-six she'd been stripped of the hope that had sustained her for years. Now when her period was late, she didn't brim with joy at the prospect of a baby, she became moody and depressed with thoughts of menopause.

On screen the rapprochement telegraphed from the first few frames began to take place, thanks to the subterfuge and shenanigans of those incredibly cute girls.

Burton laid his hand on hers, and she wrapped her fingers around his; but rather than dissolve the awkwardness that festered between them, it made it worse. Then his body stirred, and she felt his approach before he shifted onto his side, much as she had the movie's long-anticipated climactic clinch, a group grope with squashed cheeks, squeals, and kisses.

For the first time in many months, her husband leaned his face toward hers.

"No, Burton, I can't."

She turned from him, from the film, and caught the flickering glow of the screen on the window to her side. For a few brief moments it covered up the darkness with a family's jubilant reunion. But then Burton shut off the TV, and as the screen went blank, the world outside turned black.

He'd duct-taped her mouth shut, wrapping it around and around her head until the pressure numbed her lips and cheeks. In those first few terrifying seconds, when he'd pulled the tape out of his pocket and forced her head to the carpet with his gun, Ami had worried about the pain she'd endure when the tape was finally torn from her face.

Now she knew better, and feared the worst: The tape wasn't coming off. He'd let her see him, had never tried to hide, and that couldn't be good.

Even so, she'd studied him closely as he taped her hands together, memorized his features so she'd never forget his face.

His skin was smooth with the poreless appeal of a mannequin whose eyes are carefully balanced and even in size, and whose nose is no more prominent than its mouth. Perfectly proportioned, except for the cheekbones. They jutted out directly below the corners of his eyes, enough that had he been carved from stone the sculptor could have been faulted for failing to chip away at a most obvious flaw. A nick here, a nick there, and they'd have been gone, unable to chafe the view.

His chin stuck out, too, making him appear strongly masculine, but those cheekbones lent him a peculiarity she hadn't noticed during their brief encounter at the gas station. Willem Dafoe came to mind. Not that he resembled the actor, but she thought he possessed the same eerie blend of handsomeness and horror that can be gleaned in a single glance.

His eyes bored into her. Cobalt blue. She'd always found blue eyes in darkhaired men unsettling. They looked suspicious to her, cunning and out of place, as if they should belong strictly to blondes. Or wolves. Ridiculous, but never more true than at this moment; they held her with an unnerving intensity.

She was sitting on the floor with her back to the bed, hands on her belly. He stared at her from a few feet away, kneeling beside her suitcase. It had opened when he'd flung it aside, spewing her tropical-colored underwear across the dark carpet. It seemed a horrible provocation, for this was rape. She had no doubt. And it might be worse, much worse. Who was he? The Searcher? The answer seemed as unavoidable as the question.

He upended her purse, scattering its contents as well.

"Look at that, a closet smoker." His voice was muffled by the tape over her ears, but she could still understand him.

He picked up the Winstons and held them before her face, thumbing a book of matches nesting under the cellophane.

"I've always liked the smell of tobacco before it starts to burn. It's a wonderful . . . fragrance. But once you light it up, it smells terrible. It stinks. It's kind of like a woman with a great perfume. It just fills your head with the most incredible scent. But when you put a match to her skin"—he raised his hands as if to say, What can you do?—"it stinks, too. Don't you think?" He smiled and sniffed the cigarettes. "This is very nice. Fresh. You must have just opened them today. Every time I smell it, I'll think of you. How much do you smoke?"

She shook her head, wanted to deny smoking entirely and every horror those cigarettes and matches might now portend; but he grabbed her chin and spoke calmly, cruelly.

"Fingers, show me with your fingers how many you smoke a day?" His demand as clear as the packaging he continued to molest.

She held up her arms, wrists pinned tightly together, and separated the index and middle fingers of her right hand, thoughts so hazed by the final depravity of all that he'd hinted that she never noticed the flimsy peace sign she'd made.

"Two a day? Not much of a habit, now is it, Ami?"

She turned from him, as terrified by his sudden use of her name as she was by his attention to the matches. Even with the tape over her ears, the crackling cellophane sounded like a blaze starting to build.

Her eyes settled on her laptop. It sat on a small table by the window, which was covered by thick drapes. A telephone cord hung from the back of the computer.

Instinctively, she turned back to him, as if she knew her fate lay in that deceptively simple cord and everything it could communicate.

But his eyes had tracked hers.

"You're in touch with her, aren't you?"

She raised her eyebrows and shrugged, like she had no idea whom he was talking about; but his question frightened her more than anything that had transpired since his initial assault. He had to be The Searcher. No one else would have asked that question.

"Get over there and sit down." He directed her to the computer with his gun.

She hobbled to the chair she'd used earlier, limping from the impact of his body landing on hers after she'd screamed, the throbbing she still felt in the small of her back.

"Bring up your e-mail."

She double-clicked the icon, but with the tape around her wrists her hands felt as clumsy as clubs.

"Hit that." He pointed to "Send and Receive." "Then go to your in-box."

Most of the older e-mails were from Suzanne, but in Ami's name. A new one quickly appeared in boldface.

"Open it."

He read over her shoulder. Nothing important, but Suzanne's elliptical language did little to disguise her identity with the supposed author sitting right there.

He had her open all the old e-mails from her boss.

"Go to 'Sent Items.'"

She swore to herself. If he hadn't figured it out by now, he was about to.

"Open the first one."

He read it, along with the others she'd sent to Suzanne.

She chanced a glance. He was smiling. No different from the first smile he'd given her back at the Texaco, but what had appeared warm and friendly then looked plainly demonic now.

"You overestimated me. I like that. You thought I'd get your e-mail, didn't you?"

She didn't nod, shrug, move at all. She was too consumed with trying to find a way out of there. She considered hurling herself at the drapes to try to crash through the window, but knew this wasn't Hollywood where breakaway glass made the most spectacular escapes possible. This was the real world, where glass breaks you.

He nudged her neck with the gun, the muzzle chilly as mint. "You did, didn't you?"

Now she did nod, gave him what he wanted.

"You know who I am, don't you?"

Another nod, reluctant as twilight.

"And you know what? You were right. I have intercepted your mail. I just did it. And it's given me the most fantastic idea. You're an inspiration, Ami."

He let the gun graze on her neck, up and down, then up until he found her ear, or where her ear would have been if most of it hadn't been covered up by the duct tape.

"Mon Ami, I'm going to become you, the way you became Suzanne. Why not? We're all adoptees. That's the thing about us, our identities are constantly changing. They're as fluid as spit. Or maybe I should say . . . semen? Why shouldn't I become you? You became Suzanne. Fair is fair."

He pulled out a knife and traced the air along the side of her head. She closed her eyes, shaking so badly he laughed.

"I'll bet she has a red wig so the two of you can play dress up. I'll have to look for it when I see her." He leaned closer. "I won't cut you if you don't move."

She opened her eyes and tried mightily to remain still as he incised the tape where it held down the wig on both sides of her face, leaving her mouth and cheeks still covered. Then he pocketed the knife and began to lift it off her head. She felt the release of the elastic, and the slow separation of the dry synthetic strands from her own hair. Her skull crackled with static electricity. It sizzled across her scalp, every pop distinct as a pinprick. He must have heard it, too, because he paused before proceeding at an excruciating pace, letting every tiny explosion snap until her head felt as if it had been plugged into a light socket.

When she couldn't stand it any longer, when she thought she'd have to jump out of her chair to end this torment, he lifted the wig all the way off and draped it across his head.

"What do you think? Do I look like Ami trying to look like Suzanne?"

He curtsied, and let the wig fall to the carpet where it lay like a dead animal. Once more he leaned close to her. "You know what else, Ami? When I start e-mailing her, she'll be e-mailing me as you. What do you think of that?"

He pushed her head aside, as if joshing with her, the cruelty of the tease all the more evident for the tape and gun.

In truth, she didn't know what to think, but knew she had plenty to fear because there were only two seats on the carousel of impersonation he'd described.

The cold barrel pressed against her neck again as he picked up the remote. He used it like a weapon, aiming and firing at the TV, flipping through channels rapidly, stopping only when he heard rough commands. She couldn't see the television, but figured out that he'd found a war movie. Wars meant gunfire, and gunfire would cover the sound of the real weapon he was holding next to her head.

I'm dead, she thought. *He's killing me no matter what.*

Moving only her eyes, she checked the position of the gun. Still pointing at her neck. She looked up at him, again without moving her head. Still pointing the remote at the TV, pumping up the volume.

She drew in a long fortifying breath, and spun in the seat, pushing the barrel away. Her heart pounded so hard it physically ached as she sprang from the chair and tried to force her way past him.

He punched her in the face so fast that she never saw his fist. She flailed her arms for protection and to try to get away, but he brought the butt of the gun down on her shoulder with such shattering force that it drove her to her knees and left her swaying side to side, dizzy with convulsive pain.

For a second she clutched at the air for balance, then clawed at the tape, muffled screams emerging before she could tear it from her mouth.

He seized her throat and shoved her on to her back, pressing the gun into her face. Blood seeped along the edges of the tape.

"Worse things than death, Ami."

He drew the gun from her face to her chest, chest to her belly, and when the hard line of his threat stopped, she understood what he meant. He'd set fire to all her fears, and now they were burning down every barrier she'd ever known.

She hadn't cried till now, till the end. With tears shining on her cheeks, she began to say her good-byes. To her mother especially. *Poor Bunny*, she thought, *it's going to be so hard on her.* And then she wished she'd never found her, that her mother would never have to know the grisly death of the only child she'd ever borne.

He jarred her from her mourning by wrapping fresh tape around her head, heedless of the long strands of hair caught across her face.

"This'll be a lot more fun than I imagined." Another show of calm as he led her back to the chair at gunpoint. "I'm going to get to be you pretending to be Suzanne. I can lead her on, set her up. I can tell her what I want her to know. Think about the fun I'll have when I can tell her *everything* about you."

He stood and edged behind her. She watched his reflection on the screen, expecting at any second to be strangled; but his hands never landed on her neck, they yanked down her top, exposing her bra.

She sat stiffly, frozen, afraid to feel, yet wishing every sensation she'd ever known would wash through her now and cleanse all that he would claim. She felt her life could be measured in minutes, and that she'd already begun to pay dearly for every second.

"I trust that you and Ms. Trayle are calling me The Searcher," he murmured near her ear, drawing his moist lips over the stiff folds of sensitive skin just above the tape, "because I really do deserve the name. I've earned it by doing a lot of searching. I'm always searching. I'm going to do some searching now, Ami, my friend. I'm going to search for the real you. I know it's hiding in there somewhere. It's deep inside, isn't it? *Deep.*"

His fingers crept down her back and unhooked her bra. The straps fell limply to her sides. The sudden loss of tension across her chest left her feeling weightless, oddly marooned, and more scared than ever.

"It's just crying to come out, isn't it? The real you."

Hearing him say "crying" made her want to stop her tears, but maddeningly they wouldn't stop, and she began to sob as he peeled away the cups and exposed her.

Her head hung down, and she saw her tiny breasts, her tiny nipples, as she had seen them all her life. They never seemed to have grown at all. Years ago she'd forced herself to stop staring at them, in the vain hope that they'd blossom through indifference. Now they looked so sad, so helpless, so tender and drawn and lost. Petals from a fallen flower.

He gripped the shoulder he'd smashed with the gun, triggering sharp spasms. Her pain only appeared to encourage him; he drilled the barrel into her neck.

"Stand up and take off everything."

It's not about rape, she said to herself, *and it never was.* This was about a darkness that even the worst sexual violence couldn't claim.

As she fumbled her way out of her skirt, and bent over to push her hose down around her ankles, the barrel of the gun moved with her, scratching her temple, bumping her cheekbone, always a reminder of the blank moment that lay beyond the present.

She began to pray, a mumbling beneath the tape. She didn't care if he heard, if he figured out what she was doing. He'd seen her tears, and the bald language they spoke was much louder than any prayer she could say. So she wept anew, and implored the unseen, and received no answer save those of his hands.

Within an hour she'd become godless. He'd driven faith from her as surely as death drives life from the flesh.

She lay bound and twisted on the bed, alive only in seizure and twitch. He'd used the matches, cigarettes too, then found her toiletries and made them his tools, the sharp point of the eyeliner and the stiff bristles of her toothbrush, the one so inky black, and the other white as bond.

He'd written indelibly on her body. Not his name. Not even The Searcher. But his mood of the moment, and every moment had dimmed and darkened, as day does when night begins its crawl.

17

AMI'S LAPTOP IS the Holy Grail, and I didn't even know I was looking for it till her eyes led me to that telephone cord. I now have a direct line to Ms. Trayle's PowerBook, which I know so well. It's fun to think of my messages popping up on her screen. Now I can tell her what I want, when I want. It'll bring me as close to her as I was in Chicago.

When Ami opened up those e-mails, I realized immediately what I could do. I was so happy I could have strangled her with joy. I had all their seedy secrets *and* the identities they'd built their entire scam on.

Now every one of those identities is up in the air, no weightier than helium. Ms. Trayle thought she could set up a sting using a dying birth mother looking for her long-lost son, but what we've got now is something even deadlier. And it's going to get *frenzied*!

It's hard to believe that they actually thought they could pull this one off on me. If they were my clients, I'd consider them delusional. Right, Ami?

I turn to check on her. She's lying on the bed. I'd hate to have her suddenly rear up while I'm writing my first e-mail, like one of those monsters that keeps rising from the dead, the *Fatal Attraction* of the recently subdued set.

Not that she's dead yet. She's resting. Just lying there taking a breather. I can't afford to have them finding her body in this room. I can't even afford to have them find a single drop of her blood. That's why a tarp is such an essential part of my garment bag.

In a little bit here, I'm going to drive out to the Denver airport. It's not that far away. But what a monstrosity. I've used it once since they redid it. Ugly as a prairie dog, which is a line that could die from overuse in this city.

Ami's car—or Ms. Trayle's, I should say—will be heading straight for long-term parking out there. It'll be weeks before anyone notices it, and by that time I'll be long gone. So will Ami. So, for that matter, will Ms. Trayle.

But first I hit "Reply," and remind myself that I'm posing as Ami posing as Ms. Trayle. And that I'm writing Ms. Trayle posing as Ami. Got it.

"Dear Ami," I begin, "I just had a great dinner with the nicest man. His name's Marty, and he's an African American man from Chicago."

Marty? For a black guy? Sounds more like a ranch hand in a Disney movie. But I can't resist paying homage to my first boy-girl. And it's not the name that's going to snag her attention anyway; it's the African American angle.

I'm pretty sure she'd say "African American." "Black" would be too blunt for her. It also sets the bait for the donut dunkers. The cops will take a huge bite as soon as they hear that Ami was last seen with a black guy. And the media will love it! A petite redhead do-gooder disappears after having dinner with a *big black man*.

We like to think we've come a long way, but we haven't, not in our core beliefs, and every year or so another Susan Smith comes along to remind us of this. It might be a cliché to blame it on a black man, but I'd be a fool not to lead them there. People love familiarity. It's comforting to them, and that goes double for the really juicy crimes.

I proceed with a note about dinner that's vague enough to keep the cops busy, should these e-mails ever fall into their hands. I'll do my best to make sure that never happens, but you can't be too careful. That's why I build rings around my identity, why for the purpose of this e-mail Marty's ancestors came from Africa. And it does make me laugh to imagine Ms. Trayle's reaction: dinner with a man she's just met? A *black* man? She'll hate herself for thinking it, but she will, and the distraction will help.

I finish the e-mail on a cheerful note, à la Ami as Ms. Trayle. I've studied the ones she's sent, and this keeps it consistent with them. I might let myself get a little cuter as I get closer, but there's no point in pushing it right now. I have way too much to take care of.

Look at her eyes, open as sores. Stark terror, I think they call it.

It's time to make sure she's tied down as tight as possible. The duct tape and rope are going to have to hold her while I'm gone.

There we go, a couple more times around the head, avoiding her ears as much as I can; I want her to be able to hear me, but at the same time I want to make sure it's nice and tight on her mouth. You see people on TV all the time slapping a piece of duct tape over someone's mouth, like it's actually going to stick. No way. If they're scared, and they're always scared, they're sweaty; and if they're sweaty, they've got damp, oily skin, and there's no sticking to that. There aren't any shortcuts to success.

I came close to violating my own rules when I cut the tape right by her ears so I could have a little fun with her wig. She almost managed to pull the rest of it off when she tried to get away. I lost my temper at that point. I'm not proud of that one bit. What a waste of energy. But I still had a lot of tape on her face, though not like now. Except for her nose, she's going to be sealed up like a coffin. Got to do it. If they can cry for help and get away, you don't get a second chance. You know why? Because they've just stolen it. They're all thieves, every last one of them.

Mon Ami had the nicest cheeks. I loved those freckles, I really did, but

I've got to stop distracting myself; I'm getting away from the real job at hand, which is putting the tape over her eyes. It's messing up her hair, a bunch of it's getting pasted across her face, but as long as it sticks I don't really care.

Some extra for her hands and feet, too. Even though she's naked, this isn't as exciting as you might think.

I peel off another yard or so to keep her tied tightly to the bed frame. The last thing I need is to leave her enough slack to start banging around, though I seriously doubt she has enough energy left for that, pain being the valve that bleeds the body most quickly of resistance.

But as I've said before, you can't be too careful. With that in mind, I jerk the entire bed a few inches from the wall, just in case she tries to knock the headboard around. No sense rattling the neighbors, in any sense of the word.

Before I say good-bye, I slip the matches out of the cigarette pack. The second she hears the cellophane, she starts to stiffen. This isn't the first time she's heard that sound tonight. She knows what it means. I tear off a match and pass it under her nose. The citrus smell of the unburned sulfur makes her shake and sets off more squirming and moans.

"Settle down," I say in my best counselor's voice. "I mean it. I just want you to know what's going to happen if I come back and find you chewing your leg off or something to try to get away. You hear me? You hear what I'm saying?"

She tries to nod, but she's hurting and her head hardly moves.

"Okay, I understand. Take it easy. I'll be back in a bit."

That brings on the biggest moan of all, which pisses me off. Here I've been holding back, and she does that to me.

I strike the match close to her nose. She freezes so fast and so perfectly she could already be dead. Possum time? We'll see. I let it burn all the way down, almost to my finger, before I blow it out. Then I carefully lay it on her taped-up mouth, right below her nose so it can fill her up with stinky smoke.

She knows what it means. She's smoldering with memories right now. It's the smell of hell.

The match is still giving off smoke as I grab her car keys and room key and head for the door. She's coughing and trying to shake it off her face.

With the "Do Not Disturb" sign in hand, I look around the room one more time, double-checking myself. Nope, I've thought of everything. I could teach a course in this.

I close the door, test the lock, and hang the sign. Her car's a few feet away, exactly where she said it would be. I already knew this, but it's good to test them. I found her honesty directly proportional to my means of persuasion. I'm sure she didn't want to be asked again.

Unfortunately, her car's so tiny I can barely fold myself into the front seat. I hate these things.

The radio blasts as soon as I start the car. It takes me a few seconds to find the dial to shut it off. Now I know what she listens to—the hard stuff. Much harder than she turned out to be.

I can't stand that kind of music. Almost as bad as the garbage "Mother" used to listen to. I'm not that much older than Ami, but I can't take hard rock. It's been one thing or another all night, and I need a break. Some quiet. Besides, I've really got to concentrate on driving. I can't afford to be stopped and checked for registration. I don't want anything that'll create a record of my being back in Denver. I've paid for everything with cash. I don't want some enterprising detective at a computer finding it more than coincidental that one woman was raped and murdered, and another one disappeared, on the two occasions when Harold Brantley was in town. Highly unlikely, I know; but things are considered "highly unlikely," as opposed to purely impossible, precisely because every once in a while they do, in fact, happen.

My caution is more than warranted when I spot a traffic cop lurking by the airport exit; but I'm no more suspicious than a sparrow passing through, and in this tiny piece of crap I'm not much bigger, either.

I turn into the long-term lot and park next to a Dodge three-quarter ton with a camper the size of a South American village.

Then I take the shuttle to the terminal, grab a cab, and head back to the Holiday Inn.

I trust she's been a good girl. No chewing on her leg, nothing like that.

18

THE NIGHTLY ROUTINE in Laura's house had established itself quickly, and from Suzanne's point of view included a most unsettling kink. She recognized this as Burton retrieved the shotgun from the closet, broke open the action, checked the twin barrels for shells, and snapped it back together. Reassured, he threw the safety off, and rested the twelve-gauge against the wall next to his side of the bed.

Armed and ready for battle, thought Suzanne, as the thick smell of gun oil drifted over to her, hardly aromatherapy for sleep. Generally, she found her own habit of propping herself up against a pillow and checking e-mail much more soothing, but not tonight.

"What's wrong?" Burton asked. "You look like something bit you."

He slid under the covers as she stared at the computer on her lap and nervously—uselessly—clicked the cursor.

"I just got an e-mail from Ami, and she says she had dinner tonight with some guy she met at a motel. What's she doing having dinner with a stranger?"

"Living to tell about it, I suppose."

"But what's she thinking?"

Burton folded his hands behind his head and lay back on the bed. "She's not thinking, Suz. She's twenty-four and her hormones are cooking."

"You should know. That's about how old Gabriella was, right?"

Wrong. And Suzanne knew it, too. "Shabby Gabby," as she had once referred to her, was thirty-three. But true enough to make Burton wince. Suzanne, too, over the spite that could still slip out eight months after learning of the affair.

Burton sat up, but before he could respond, Suzanne apologized. "That was a cheap shot. I shouldn't have."

"I had it coming. That and a lot more, I know."

He sounded tired, a little old for a nighttime routine that included a weapons check *and* a bill of particulars.

"But I want us to move on, and that kind of stuff doesn't get us anywhere."

"We are getting somewhere, Suz. We're back under one roof—"

"More like Fort Apache." She grimaced at the shotgun.

"I know it's not exactly our house, but it's a start, and I never expected everything to get better overnight."

She nodded before turning back to the screen.

"I have to tell you, this thing with Ami really bothers me."

"She say anything about him?"

"Yes," Suzanne suddenly sounded emptied of air. "She says he's smart and good-looking."

"Sounds like she's interested. She mention his name, or anything else about him?"

"Marty," she said without looking up. "And he's African American. From Chicago."

"Marty? That's a name for a black guy from Chicago?"

"That is kind of weird, isn't it?" She frowned, turned back to Burton. "The only Marty I ever knew was that Mouseketeer kid on the 'Spin and Marty' episodes."

"You knew that little cowpoke?"

"No, I mean I knew who he was. Actually"—she tapped his arm—"I had a terrible crush on him when I was a kid."

"Maybe this Marty's mother did, too. Anyway, I don't see the problem. She had dinner, and sent you an e-mail. End of story. She's okay. In fact—"

"I know, but she's not being supercareful." She held the screen between her hands, as if admonishing Ami herself.

"I think you're being superparanoid. What I was trying to say was that you ought to be glad he's black because—"

"I don't care that he's black."

"—*because* you know The Searcher isn't black. If he were black, he never could have passed himself off as Karen's or Jesse's son. I'd say Ami is a helluva lot safer with this Marty from the old cattle yards of Chicago than she might be with some white guy she doesn't know."

Despite herself, Suzanne smiled and looked past her easel to the empty deck, listening to the cavernous sound of rain drumming the many windows.

She spoke more evenly now. "I just want her to be careful. It's hard to tell, reading between the lines, but I'm assuming she didn't sleep with him."

"They don't sleep at that age, hon. They just hop into bed and—"

"Stop making light of this!" Equanimity eclipsed by exasperation. "You *know* what I mean."

"Seriously? She's not the type. Ami? With some guy she's just met?" Burton shook his head with such authority that she felt the motion in the mattress and had to stifle the urge to ask him how he could be so sure. Had he come on to her too? Did he know from personal experience that Ami wouldn't treat sex casually?

Months ago Suzanne had realized that after the first wave of shock settled, the worst part of your spouse's infidelity was seeing how suspicion subverted your entire world—your most important expectations—by making you question not only the man who'd cheated on you, but all the others in your orbit who might have rolled around with him, too.

"No," Suzanne said flatly, "I don't think she's the type either." Whatever that "type" was. God knows, as a young woman she'd had a few itchy, impetuous moments of her own.

She started poking the keyboard.

"What are you going to say?"

"Same old, same old: Be careful."

A few minutes later she hit "Send" and rose from the bed to put her laptop aside. She paused at the easel to look at her painting. Burton was right. It was good. Not pretty, but beautiful in raw, ravaged terms. It depicted the affinity she felt for the brown landscape of the barren hill, for the ruin of a land that had lost all that it had ever held dear.

"You're going for a ride, Mon Ami."

Until The Searcher spoke those words, Ami believed he'd finish murdering her right here in the room.

Now her great hope lay in the few moments when he'd have to carry her to the car. There was no way she could walk. She felt so battered she could barely breathe.

Even in her muddled state, she knew he couldn't leave her here. He needed other guests to use the room, to shed their own stray hairs and clothing fibers, and he needed housekeeping staff to run vacuums and wipe down counters and muddle whatever evidence there might be to this crime.

These calculations, the rude algebra of survival, helped clarify her thoughts as he rummaged through the room.

She sought clarity wherever she could because her eyes were taped shut, and her sense of time had been obscured by far more brutal means: She'd passed out repeatedly from pain. Day? Night? She had no idea, but in the midst of her literal darkness came a glimmer of hope: Maybe he didn't plan to murder her at all. He could have carried her out of here dead as easily as he could have carried her out alive, right? Maybe someone will see them. Nothing could look more shocking than her savaged appearance, and wrapping her body up in the tarp would look no less suspicious.

But she couldn't have anticipated his omnivorous appetite for cruelty, nor the cheer with which he provided the answer to the questions she'd posed to herself. After rolling her up in the tarp, and slinging her over his shoulder fireman-style, he paused—she guessed at the door—then took four swift steps and dumped her in a trunk. At the very moment she expected to hear the cover slam down, she heard his voice instead:

"You're wondering why I let you live. I know you are. You wouldn't be *normal* if you didn't. There's a simple answer. I didn't want you messing your pants, little girl. Leaving behind any DNA. See, if you had, there's no telling what I might have missed, what might have dripped off. But I'm not missing anything now."

Nausea turned her thick and weightless. Sensations so patently at odds found an uneasy alliance in the stormy embrace of her stomach. It surged once, twice, three times, launching a fiery spurt of bile up to the back of her gagged mouth. Its vile metallic taste seeped forward, and she panicked as she fought the urge to vomit. She knew that if she failed to settle her system, she'd choke to death on her own sickness. She struggled to control her belly as she had struggled to control her bowels, her bladder, to hold on to the little dignity he hadn't claimed. Through the worst of it she'd been steadfast about not shaming herself, only to learn with his last few horrid words that he'd spared her life to prevent the leakage of clues.

The road moved beneath her, and as she imagined the swift retreat of signs and mile markers, the taste of the bile thinned, the nausea passed. Her attention gradually shifted to the cold creeping up through the bristly carpet, the slow but welcome numbing of her limbs. She willed the iciness to her belly, her breasts, to all the other places he'd touched, first with his hands, and then with the flame, private places that were no longer hers; for if ownership were a function of will, of prerogative, of the wherewithal to do what you wanted with your body—to sit, stand, scream, have sex—if it came down to such bare essentials, then she'd become a slave to his sadism. She acknowledged this at last in the flood that spilled from her. What shame now?

As urine soaked her legs and belly, and burned her cuts and sores, she filled with a frightening sense that pain now fused every notion of life and death that she'd ever known, and that her willingness to survive had been furiously diminished by what she'd been forced to endure.

How do you end up like this, she asked herself. *Aching from his touch, his savage attention, from what he'd done with such horrifying delight?* But she quickly abandoned these questions for an unmitigated desire for death. She wanted it more than anything she'd ever known, more than the desire she'd felt for finding her mother.

Then for a second or two she'd experience a respite from the pain of the burns and puncture wounds. It would vanish as if weary of its work, and in those briefest of windows she'd find inalienable hope. It made her think of a weed that's pulled and stomped and wrenched from its roots, yet refuses somehow to surrender its crack in the pavement.

She also found that the body prioritizes pain as effectively as a trauma unit triages its patients, and that if she focused on what he'd done to her left pinkie, she could go for entire seconds without feeling the other agonies he'd inflicted on her.

His heated breath had poured into her ear as consciousness had passed seamlessly into unconsciousness, until the latter—and the relief it had brought—had been abruptly severed by the smelling salts he'd used, their sharp scent every bit as pointed as the eyeliner. Her reluctance to awaken, to rejoin the world of the living, had been her first intimation of death, of its blessed beneficence.

She felt nothing of the leg cramps that might have afflicted her in a more durable state, and nothing of the claustrophobia that lying locked in a trunk would have induced under any other circumstance. Claustrophobia seemed a luxury now, ensuring as it did a barrier between herself and the man who had done this to her.

The motion of the car provided distance, too, if not in space then in time: As long as they moved, he couldn't touch her. He couldn't hurt her. She never wanted anyone to hurt her again, though she knew that no one could ever hurt her as he had.

And curled up in the trunk, she discovered that by concentrating on her breath she could experience the wondrously pain-free sensation of drawing air over the crusted hairs of her nostrils. She focused intensely on the way they quickened with each inhalation and settled as it passed back out.

This was how she kept her sanity. Kept alive. *And where there's life,* she reminded herself, *there's hope.* But he'd told her she'd die, had been uncompromising in his assurance.

"You're a dead girl," he'd said. "Like all the others. No one will ever find you, Mon Ami. No one. Know why?"

She hadn't been able to answer. He hadn't cared.

"Because I don't dig shallow graves."

The car thumped down a bumpy road. Maybe a logging road. Somewhere in the forest. They didn't have roads like this through wide open land, none that she'd ever seen, unless the land had been forest that had been clear-cut; and then there was nothing but rough roads ridden by the sun and rain and snow, eroded as much by the ravening elements as by the thick-tired trucks that tore them apart.

Time still felt as elastic as hope, and as full of contractions. She couldn't have guessed within an hour how long they'd been driving.

She allowed herself the relief of knowing it was coming to an end. No man drives this far after promising to bury you without fulfilling his pledge. But then the reality of death, of her life actually ending, terrified her, and she prayed that her mother would learn that she'd died. As fragile as her mom was, it would be easier than having her daughter disappear, never to show up again. For so many years, that's how Ami had lived, with the twin burdens of disappearance and absence. They had formed the bleak pillars of her earliest pain.

The car stopped, but the trunk didn't open for the longest time, and when he finally unlocked it, she learned that her imagination of her worst possible fate could not compete with his plans.

He dragged her out of the car, shoved her against a tall mound of freshly dug earth, and ripped the tape from her head, rudely unveiling her mouth and eyes.

Her vision, blurred by the sudden sting of daylight, landed first on the pit he'd dug. It looked about six feet deep, and long enough to accommodate her short body. As she stared at it, she felt the rain. Drops as thick as ice chips, and almost as cold, pocked the loose earth and snapped at her bare skin like rubber bands.

She raised her eyes and saw that he'd stopped in a pine forest. But the trees looked odd: denuded, no needles. Gray as charcoal. Diseased.

A clear-cut huddled in the near distance, maybe the one they'd driven through, and she wondered why this sickly stand had been spared, found dim hope in this. But then she knew the answer, and understood the incurable kinship she shared with these dying trees: They had become useless to their masters, so they had been left to rot. As she would be. Before he ever spoke, she knew that he'd bury her alive. He'd driven her to her grave, and now he would fill it.

His hands, filthy from their toil, unzipped his pants and pulled out his penis. From his pocket he retrieved the eyeliner, flicking its point.

"Get down on your knees. See if you can save your life."

She stared at his sex, swallowed, tasted her own blood. Her last seconds on earth. She looked at the pit and knew with a sickening certainty that she would not survive. Nothing, no one—least of all she—could stop this now.

Without another glance at the grim figure before her, she hurled herself into the hole, landing on her side. A bone cracked in her shoulder, but she felt no pain, only an odd electric shudder that streaked up the back of her neck.

He towered over her, wiping his face, stuffing himself back into his fly.

The rain formed a brown stream that spilled from the dirt mound into the pit. She lay propped on her elbow, her shoulder and neck now throbbing, as the murky water inched around her body, an enclosure as cold and dark as the walls that surrounded her.

Another stream formed, and another, spattering her face and chest. She heard him swear at her for the first time, then calm his voice immediately.

"Look at me. Come on," he urged almost gently. "Look at me."

Her frantic eyes did look up, blinking from the ceaseless splatter.

"I know who your mother is, Mon Ami. Bunny, right? And because you did this, because you *chose* to do this"—he nodded at the pit, his eyes raking her pale nakedness and the darkness into which she'd fled—"I'm going after her, too."

She screamed, tried to use the brute force of breath to tear the forest down, to topple trees and forge a raging, harrowing bedlam; but her voice could no more summon miracles than it could the love of the living, and she knew only the damp earth pouring down, shovelfuls that darkened the sky and blanketed her in death and silenced the last of her cries.

19

IT'S BEEN TWELVE hours since I buried Ami, and I've used the time well. I've relived the burial and all the moments that preceded it while driving along, passing very pleasurable miles rekindling those memories and fiddling with myself.

The miles have added up, too. A long time ago I passed the Holiday Inn where I caught up with little Miss Ami for the last time. And now I'm back over the Rockies on my way to catching up with Ms. Trayle and her husband again. I plan to teach them a lesson or two about how you really run a sting.

I'm staying in touch. I wouldn't want Ms. Trayle to start worrying about Ami. A few hours ago I sent her another e-mail with more kind words about Ami's new *black* friend. It'll resurrect whatever latent racism she's got. She'll see a whole line of black men from the likes of Will Smith to Tupac Shakur, and she'll hope for the whitest one imaginable, whether she can admit it or not.

But that reaction's not going to be anything compared to the way she'll light up over my next one. I'll send it out at my next stop. It'll get her going like nothing she's heard in years. It'll be the key to her heart, and as I always say, that's the key to their door. It opens in, but it also opens out. They don't know that yet, but they will.

I'll bet the two of them think they're ready for anything. I'll bet they have guns and plans and all kinds of dark ideas. But the one thing they don't have is the one thing they want the most. It's their son, their precious boy. He's my secret. My sting. My *key*. They'll see.

There's a truck stop up ahead. The sign said fifteen miles. I'll get some gas on Ms. Trayle's card and take a room. That's what I like about a lot of these truck stops, especially the older ones. You can be as anonymous as you want to be. You pay for a room, and they give you a cubicle not much bigger than the bed. Sheets, pillow, blanket, phone, that's all. They'll take cash. You don't need a credit card because there's no room service or any other way to run up charges. And if you do want to use the phone, better have a phone card handy. I always do.

It's one thing to stick Ms. Trayle's MasterCard into the gas pump and hit "credit," but it'd be crazy to stand at a desk and try to pay for a motel room with her card. I just don't look like a Suzanne. Crazier still to use my own card and create a paper trail alongside hers.

I'd like to push on, drive another hundred miles, but I need sleep, and enough time to let my sting get moving. Like I say, the first truly tricky e-mail's about to go out.

There's the truck stop. I pull off and see a Colorado State Highway patrolman driving by. Am I imagining things, or did he stare at me?

I run my hand over my chin, feel the stubble. I probably look like a homeless person in a stolen car.

Not for long.

I gas up and park in the lot behind the truck stop. Then I pay for a room and a shower that is down the hall. They hand me a towel that's not much thicker than a piece of cardboard, and not much softer either, and I head for the lockers, stopping at my room to drop off my stuff. But the second I put Ami's laptop on the bed I know I can't wait any longer to get started.

Those first two e-mails just showed that Ami was alive, and suggested in a sly way that she might also be falling in love. But this is where the sting really gets going.

First, I hook up the jack and check for messages. Isn't that nice? She's urging me to be careful. Don't you worry, Ms. Trayle. I'll be very careful. I always am.

My new message is all but written in my head. I've had hours to think about it, but after hitting "Reply" I force myself to review Ami's other e-mails for style. They all sound the same, so it's critical to get the tone just right.

After rereading the last half dozen, I see once again that it's actually very straightforward, like she's trying hard to be Suzanne but can't quite get it down. But I've got it. I learned a long time ago how to be someone else, and do a good job of it.

> Dear Ami,
> I have the most incredible news!

Yes, Ami used exclamation points, far too many for my taste, but my taste isn't on trial here.

> My son was adopted in Tennessee. Can you believe it? This is
> just the best news ever.

A bit of that girlish enthusiasm that Ami let slip out when she wasn't being careful.

> I found out by calling Children and Family Services in Portland.
> I got a case worker on the phone who recognized my name.

She wanted to know if it was really Suzanne Trayle she was talking to. When I told her it was, she said she'd seen me on *Oprah* and was an adoptee herself. She said she really liked everything I was doing for adoptees and birth mothers. So I took a huge chance and asked her for help in finding my son. For a while she didn't say anything, and then she told me to hang on.

I'm in the flow now. I can practically hear Ami's e-mails in my head.

A few minutes later she got back on and said she shouldn't be doing this because she could get fired, but my son was adopted by a couple from Tennessee. She said that's all she could find in the records there.

I didn't believe that for a second . . .

(and I don't because Patsy showed me what's in those records)

. . . but I thanked her anyway and told her she's one of my heroes.

So you can probably guess where I'm going. The capital is in Nashville, and I'm going to go through all the public records I can find. I know the date he was adopted and the day he was born, so I've got something to work with, and a great lead. It's not like Tennessee's a big state like New York or California. There's only going to be so many boys born on that day.

I'll keep you posted, don't worry.

Love,

Suzanne

Tennessee. Country music and the Great Smoky Mountains. Shotgun shacks and small-town sheriffs. I could wax eloquent about all this and more to her, but it's still too early because if Ami were really going there, she'd have at least two days of driving ahead of her.

I'm proud of myself, though. Telling her it was Tennessee was a stroke of pure genius, as she'll find out soon enough.

Before I click "Send," I make myself stop. *You're tired, and you're rushing this out. You're totally fried from all that driving, not to mention Ami. You had a great time with her, but it was also a lot of work digging that grave and burying her.*

So I force myself to hold off. A few hours isn't going to make any difference. *Get some sleep and look it over one more time before you send it out. You're baiting the hook here, and you want to make sure that worm really squirms.*

I'm groaning as I grab the towel. It's hard to hold back, but I head for the showers. They're not bad, and the warm water feels good. Lots of road jam running off me. Ami jam too. All going down the drain.

After drying off, I decide to shave after I sleep. I'm just going to have to do it again later anyway.

Truckers are slouched over the video games along the wall going to my room. Great, I get to listen to pings and pops and other sounds of idiocy as I try to get some sleep. Every one of these guys is facing down intergalactic enemies and terrorists, and firing away for all they're worth. Get a life, guys.

As soon as I get back inside my room, I grab Ami's cigarettes and matches and lie down. I've only got two matches left, but plenty of cigarettes. You get a lot more out of them because they burn so slowly.

Sniffing them brings back more of those memories. The matches do, too. Such a nice girl, so willing to cling to . . . life, to everything she professed to . . . love.

Ami, my friend. She was, too. Right to the end. Behaved as I wanted her to with one painful exception. I couldn't believe she'd draw the line there. She'd done everything else, but when it came to satisfying such a routine demand, she refused. Then, before I could encourage her, she threw herself into that grave. I hadn't figured on that, that she'd actually rather die than pleasure me with her mouth. And I've got way too much pride than to go climbing down into a hole to get her to do it.

So I let her steal her one little crumb of freedom. Didn't she know it wouldn't make a bit of difference in the end, that her adoptee depravity would still be stamped on her skin like a stain?

It'll be necessary, I can see this already, to point out Ami's failure to Ms. Trayle. And then I'll explain that reparations are in order. She trained her, right? There'll be no shirking of that responsibility. There's way too much of that nowadays, people refusing to face up to their obligations.

I squeeze out much more intensely pleasurable memories of Ami than her final refusal and clean up after myself with the tissues I took from the bathroom. They don't give you any extras in these rooms. And then I lie back down, completely enervated by the events of the day, but excited by the prospects of the ones soon to come.

When I wake up I can hardly believe almost eight hours have gone by. When I'm moving in on a new mother, I rarely sleep more than four or five hours. I must have really needed it.

Four o'clock in the morning, and there are still pings and pops coming from those video games in the hallway. On my way to the bathroom, I walk past several truckers staring at the screens. I think I even recognize one of them from earlier.

It feels good to have my body back at square one. That's how I think of it when I'm shaved and showered, and I've had enough rest to replenish all of my energy.

I grab the laptop and a booth across from the area roped off for truckers. They get all this "King of the Road" crap in places like this. Real royalty.

It's time for another look at that e-mail. I flip open the computer as a waitress comes over.

"Coffee?" She's got the pot in her hand.

"Sure," I tell her. "Sounds good. Could I get some cream, too?"

She has a vicious tic that seizes up the left side of her face and makes both eyes blink. It's hard not to stare. No wonder she's working graveyard. I promise myself right then that I'll leave her a good tip. When I was a kid, a friend of mine's mother had a tic like that. She was a waitress, too, in a diner. People were awful to her. They'd say things like, "You want a tip? Try relaxing." And then they'd expect her to laugh, too, like she hadn't heard that one before.

"What'll ya have?"

"The eggs," I tell her. "Number five," I add after a quick look at the place mat, which doubles as the menu. "Over hard, all right? I don't like them runny."

She walks away, and I go right to "Drafts." That's when I spot my mistake. It's a little one, but it's the little things that'll trip you up every time. I'm just glad I didn't send it out, "Love, Suzanne," because it's "Love, Suz," in all of Ami's e-mails.

Then I get a real start when I think I might have sent the other two out with the same mistake.

I can't hit "Sent Items" fast enough and take such a deep breath when I see that I signed them "Suz" that the waitress asks if I'm okay. She's back with the cream.

"I'm fine. I just got some great news, is all."

"Lucky you," she says as she leaves. I can't tell if she means it, or if she's just so sick of her job that she can't stand to see anyone else who's happy.

I must have been exhausted last night. That's the only explanation for that screwup with the name. But it reminds me all over again that I can't be too careful.

The sun's melting the darkness as I pull back on the interstate. It feels great to have a whole new day ahead of me. That e-mail's waiting for Ms. Trayle's hungry eyes, and I'll bet she just gobbles it right up.

20

S UZANNE ROLLED OVER and flopped her arm out of the bed, groping the nightstand for her laptop. She flipped it open, mostly by feel. At 6:35, the day was still frugal with light; but her fingers worked their gentle magic, and the screen came alive quickly, beaming with a fresh message from Ami. As she read it, her eyes swelled from slits to circles; she grabbed the computer and pulled the screen closer for a second, slower go-round. A minute passed in stunned silence before she rallied enough to shake Burton.

"Wake up. Wake up!"

He stirred, sat up suddenly. "What? What is it?" he blurted as he reached for the shotgun.

She grabbed his arm.

"Not that. It's this, Burton." She tugged him toward her. "Look at this."

"News? What?" He looked around wildly, sleep crusting an eye. He swiped at it as he might a fly.

"It's Ami. She's just e-mailed me that she found out that our son was adopted by a couple from Tennessee. She's heading there now."

"Tennessee? She's driving there?"

Still half asleep, from the sound of him.

"Right, right."

"How'd she find that out?"

He leaned over and looked closely at the e-mail for the first time.

"She got a caseworker at Children and Family Services in Portland to help her."

"She *did*? She cracked Fort Knox? How'd she manage that?" His incredulity was the most obvious sign of his awakening.

"She says right here that she told the woman she was me, and the woman had seen me on *Oprah* and knew all about my work, so she helped her out. Not completely. She could have told her a lot more, but at least she told her that."

Burton swung his legs out of the bed and reached for his robe, which lay draped over a chair next to the bed. He cleared his throat before pausing to look back at her.

"You think Ami might be carrying this impersonation business a little too far? It's one thing to pretend to be you in an e-mail, but it's another thing to do it to government officials."

He raised himself up slowly and carried the shotgun over to the closet as Suzanne tried to swallow her impatience.

"I don't have a problem with it," she called after him a little more loudly than she needed to. "She just got the first real news of our son in thirty-two years. Don't be such a stickler for rules all the time, *Judge* Trayle."

He closed the closet door, turned to speak, but she interrupted him.

"If *I'm* not complaining, I don't see why you should. You'd think you'd be happy about this." Now her impatience had slipped out in force, along with anger and umbrage and a good billet of her *own* incredulity.

"I am. Don't get me wrong, I'm very happy. And I'm sorry if I sounded like I was more concerned with her impersonating you than I was with the news. It's just that I've never been comfortable with the way she just took off. I know you two have a method to your madness, but sometimes it makes me uneasy is all."

He sat on the bed by her feet and gave one of them a squeeze. "But you're right, this is great news. It really is. What do you know about Tennessee?"

"I'm not sure. I'm going to have to get an update on what's been going on there." Her hesitation came from having seen adoption rights groups successfully back legislation in a few states that had opened thousands of birth records virtually overnight. "I haven't had a client with any connection to Tennessee for at least a couple of years."

"The Volunteer State, that's all I know. And Nashville, the Grand Ole Opry."

Burton stood, more easily this time. "I'll get the coffee and breakfast going. Why don't you hook that thing up in the kitchen?"

They descended into the downstairs gloom, the early hints of daylight blocked by the blinds, which they kept closed all the time now, even the ones in the rear of the house. Both of them had become uneasy with the idea that The Searcher could watch them from a distance.

For the first couple of days, they'd tried to strike a balance between the appearance of normalcy and the need for security. They'd lowered the front blinds a foot from the top and left the ones in the rear drawn fully open. But by the end of their second day, their sense of breathing room had vanished. The classifieds had started to run, and when they realized that he could show up at any time, they closed all the blinds, deciding it was far better to have him think Laura was a privacy bug than to expose themselves and the sting.

The only daylight now entering the house leaked through a pair of skylights and the glassed-in deck. They didn't feature him scaling the house without their notice, and the deck created a broad buffer between the window and the sleeping loft.

Burton threw on lights and opened the kitchen cabinet to check on the nine-millimeter.

As she plugged a telephone line into the laptop, he put on the water and ground the beans before turning his attention to Laura's impressive sound system.

"You mind?"

She looked up. "No, that's okay."

A little early for this, she thought, but after denying him the greater pleasures, she felt stingy denying him the smaller ones, too.

Though he was just a few years older, it was enough time to bridge him to a musical era as foreign and grating to her ears as Farsi: doo-wop. She loathed the saccharine lyrics and syrupy strings—songs so sweet they could give concrete a cavity—and he never left home without them.

"Oh, for the love of God, not this one again," she muttered as Burton tweaked the volume on a song about fools falling in love, a sentiment that in recent months had struck her as being as redundant as it was maudlin.

"What's that, hon?"

"Nothing."

She clicked e-mail again to see if Ami had an update. No message from her, but two from birth mothers.

"Could you turn that down a *tad*?"

Burton poured her coffee before reaching over to the receiver. Whether he actually turned down the sound, though, remained questionable.

She Googled Tennessee and clicked for a map. Start with the big picture. Several cities, none of them huge: Memphis, Chattanooga, Knoxville, and Nashville, of course. She wondered if he was a country western musician.

Wondered if he was a country western *star*, then stopped herself from falling into the most common of all birth mother fantasies: that her child had been crowned by the heavens for a royal existence.

But as soon as she tried to search online records, she was reminded that Tennessee, like Oregon, provided access to original birth certificates only to adoptees, not to their birth mothers.

She could have wept. They'd narrowed it down to a single state, a relatively small one at that, and now this. It was like learning the needle you'd lost on the farm had ended up in the haystack.

No, it's not that bad, she insisted to herself. *Ami's right. You've got dates of birth and adoption to work with.* But after no more than ten minutes of searching, she saw that most of the documents she needed were not online, and the bulk of the research would have to take place in Tennessee itself, the same conclusion Ami had apparently reached, given her destination.

Now that her initial excitement had subsided, she remembered to thank her assistant:

Dear Suz,

she quickly wrote.

Thank you so much for sharing such great news! I'm so happy. You must be ecstatic.

She wanted her gratitude on bold display, a whole string of uppercase appreciation for a start, but recognized the need to remain as careful as Ami had been.

I thought I could help you from here, but there's not a lot in Tennessee that I can access online, which I'm guessing you already

know. But please e-mail me right away if there's anything I can do to
speed things up on this end.

    Good luck!

Love,

Ami

As she sent off the e-mail, she felt a powerful desire to leave for Tennessee
herself. Every day left her more and more anxious. She'd nervously check
the blinds and peer outside, or open the cabinet, as Burton had just done, to
make sure the gun hadn't moved, as if it could march off on its own and leave
them defenseless.

Obsessive-compulsive behavior, and she knew it. Even now, as she looked
up at Burton mixing batter by the stove, she found her eyes drawn past him to
the front door. Oak, two inches thick. A solid slab with only a rectangle of
glass the size of a postcard to violate their privacy. Bolt lock never opened,
though her nervousness had her testing it several times a day just to be sure, as
she did the one to the deck that Burton used to bring in wood for the stove.

They were in lock-down mode, armed, fully prepared, but her uneasiness
had intensified to the point where abandoning the sting and putting all of her
energy into finding her son was immensely appealing. That would be the safest
way to stop The Searcher, after all. Then they could call in the cavalry, the
cops, Terry Ramsey, and the rest of the FBI. Everyone. They could finally end
this sting and the constant . . . waiting.

But knowing your child had been adopted by a couple from a particular
state hardly ensured finding him. His adoptive parents might have moved to
five other states by now. Eight, ten. More if they were military. Or overseas.
Most times she could find an adoptee or birth mother quickly, sometimes in
hours (if all the stars were aligned). But searches could also take weeks,
months. Some—her son's was a good example—never ended and became irri-
tants that chafed until she could find the time to review them again, to see if

laws had changed in the relevant states or if a grandmother or uncle had stepped forward.

You're going to find him, she assured herself. She could feel her son's presence almost as clearly as she could feel her fear. He wasn't going to remain lost to her. She refused to believe that. Not after this, not after getting so close. *We'll find him. But when, and will he still be alive?*

All these worries brought her back to the question of how long they should stay in Laura's house behind a barricade of locked doors, twelve-inch logs, and shuttered blinds.

"What do you think, Burton?"

He was singing along with The Spaniels—"Goodnight, Sweetheart, Goodnight"—and dripping the last of the batter into the frying pan.

"About what?"

"I'm sorry." Had she been doing that a lot lately, assuming people had been privy to her thoughts? She'd been preoccupied enough. "About how long we should stay here."

"Didn't you say his pattern was to move fast?"

"It was with Karen and Jesse." Even saying their names still hurt.

"Then I'd say if he doesn't get here in another week, ten days tops, we should get out of here. See what Ami turns up in the meantime."

"But then if he comes and the house is empty, he might wonder what's really going on."

"Maybe he'll think Laura's given up and had the presence of mind to head somewhere warm. You notice those snowflakes out there?"

"Really?"

She hurried to the little window in the front door and peered out at big fat flakes that melted as soon as they touched the ground.

"It's getting colder." She'd worried about this.

"A little bit. Few degrees." He flipped the pancake. "But it's like the snow we get down in Portland. Melts right away."

"You think we'll be able to get out of here if we stay?"

"If it really starts to come down, we'll have to leave. But I don't think that's even going to be an issue for a few weeks yet. I caught the weather last night on the radio, and they're not calling for anything like that."

"Did they call for this?" She took one last look out the window before returning to the breakfast bar.

"No, they didn't, but I don't think this is anything to worry about. We're not that high up in the mountains here. I got a look at the peaks yesterday, and there's plenty of snow, but it's got a ways to go before it gets down here."

"It sure looks like it's trying." Her attention had landed back on the white specks falling past the tiny window.

"It'll be gone by lunchtime. You find anything interesting on the Net?"

He put a plate of buckwheat pancakes down in front of her.

"Thanks for cooking. No, not much, and there's not a lot I can do from here." She passed on the butter and used the syrup sparingly. With her free hand, she checked messages again. The laptop made a series of soft clicking sounds that sent her stomach into a swirl of anticipation. But no new messages appeared.

Better get used to it, she cautioned herself. You've waited thirty-two years to find him, and there could be a lot more false alarms coming your way.

Those she could deal with. It was the prospect of The Searcher's arrival that spread fear to the whole of her body and left her mind to wander the chilly ruins of courage.

21

M Y LAST DAY in this dump. This is the dirtiest motel I've ever stayed in. There's paint flaking off the walls, grime on the counters, and rust stains on the bathroom floor. But they take cash and they don't pay any more attention to me than they do to their kid. He can't be any older than three, and he's out there all by himself playing in the rain in the parking lot. If they're not careful, he's going to get run over, which would be horrible. There'd be cops all over this place knocking on doors, asking if we'd seen anything, taking names. I'd have to bag all my plans. You'd think they'd keep an eye on that kid, if not for his sake, then for the sake of their guests.

Well, tomorrow I'll be gone. I can't wait to get going. I've got everything I'll need spread out on the bed. My gun, a .38, fully loaded, though I doubt I'll need more than one bullet. That'll be for him. I'm not going to need any for her. Never do. It's a point of pride with me. I use the gun only to get them where I want them.

Next to my gun is my knife, binoculars, and energy bars, enough to keep me going for a couple of days. Her, too, if she tries to fade too fast. There's not going to be any of that, not after all the work I've put into this.

Let's see, what else? Plain blue Gore-Tex jacket. Just picked it up at an REI outlet on the way here. Rain repellent and drab enough, no offset colors. A rain hat to match. Rain pants, too.

Water bottle. With weather like this, it feels like bringing coal to Newcastle, but then again you've got to take care of the basics when you're going into battle.

Wireless e-mail. Picked that up too. That's going to be essential from now on.

Everything's in order, everything's in place. All I have to do is hit "Send," and we're really in motion.

I wrote it earlier today, and I've checked it several times since, but I want to read it over one more time before I send it out. It's the trump card in the game we're playing, and I want to make sure I use it wisely because I can use it only once.

It comes after two days of keeping Ms. Trayle up-to-date on all of my efforts to find information on her son in the courthouses in and around Nashville. With each e-mail I've hinted that we're almost there, almost have his name. In reality, I'm no more than two hours from Laura's house, but I've been keeping "Suz" right on the edge of her seat with the news from Nashville, and that's right where I want her, all pumped up and ready to jump at just about anything.

Yesterday, I made sure to give her enough to leave her salivating. It's right here in "Sent Items."

> Dear Ami,
> I think I'm right on the verge of finding my son!

(Those exclamation marks again. Can't forget them. They always remind me of high school cheerleaders bouncing around.)

234 · *Mark Nykanen*

Can you believe it? After all these years of searching I'm almost there. I came across some incredible records in the courthouse in downtown Nashville. They showed that a social worker was sent to look into the suitability of a house for a baby boy. They were inspecting the actual house, as the parents were prime candidates to adopt. My sense is that they were already approved. This was only a month or so before my son's records were transferred to Tennessee.

But the real find here is the name of the social worker, because she did a lot of these inspections. She retired six years ago, and I'm pretty sure I've got her address. I'll know for sure tomorrow.

I can hardly wait.

Love,

Suz

I put the new message in "Drafts," and now I'm going to give it that final read. Dot the *i*'s, cross the *t*'s.

Dear Ami,

We are so close I can hardly stand it. I found the social worker. Her name is Rose, and she says she definitely knows my son's name, and the names of his adoptive parents. She says they're still living in the Nashville area, to the best of her knowledge, but she won't release their names to me until I get Burton's notarized signature attesting to his paternity, and to his desire to have his son's name released. She even printed out a form for this that she says is just like the one they used to use in her old department for documenting paternity. She says she totally supports opening up records, and is willing to do it "under the table," but only if it's going to reunite the entire family, not divide them. It's a religious thing with her (we're in the Bible Belt here), but this delay is killing me!

She's really fussy about details (she and Burton would get along great), and wouldn't budge on this, so I sent the form by overnight mail to Burton's temporary address in Washington. Please make sure he knows that he's got to sign it right away with a notary, and then send it back to me by overnight mail. I don't want to give her any time to change her mind. The address is inside with the form.

If we can get this turned around right away, I'll have my son's name in 48 hours.

Tell Burton I love him, and that we'll be together soon as a family.

Love,

Suz

P.S. Please confirm that you've received this e-mail. You can just hit "Reply," and I'll know.

Overnight mail always gets immediate delivery. We of the rural Postal Service wouldn't think of making our most valued customers wait for a delivery to their mailbox, not when they've paid such a premium for speedy service. No need to trek out to that pagoda-shaped monstrosity when I'm more than willing to drive it right up to your door.

You've seen us before, right, Ms. Trayle? We drive our own cars with our own little signs propped up on the dash or taped to our flipped-down sun visors, the signs that say "U.S. Postal Service." Most of them don't look as official as the one I made. That one, right over there by the pillow.

The all-wheel-drive Subaru is a favorite of the letter carriers in rural areas. Mine fits the profile perfectly. So does my dull blue jacket and pants. I look just like the pictures of letter carriers that you see hanging in post offices all around the country: neat, courteous, kind.

Neither rain nor sleet nor snow is going to stop this one.

I hit "Send."

There's nothing I can do to make it better. It's perfect. Every word carefully weighed and measured. I'll bet she reads it within minutes, and I'll bet she's not going to sleep all that well tonight, either, with that much anticipation bubbling up inside. That's okay, too. I want her jumpier than a rabbit in a snake pit. The same goes for him. He has no idea what's coming, but he's got plenty to worry about now.

I love thinking of the two of them reading it, each of them twisting inside over what it means, each for their own reasons.

22

11:17. ALL MORNING SUZANNE had been eyeing her watch. She hadn't been able to stop even after she'd started painting, what, an hour ago? Who knows? She couldn't keep track of anything except when the overnight mail was supposed to arrive. "By noon, one at the latest," the postal worker had assured her on the phone. "Pretty standard delivery times," the woman added in a sleepy voice.

Suzanne felt tired, too. A restless night. This morning her brain felt as fuzzy as felter's wool, yet her energy had been coming in frantic spurts that had her painting feverishly one minute, and . . . checking her watch the next.

So much at stake. All they needed was her son's name, and in another twenty-four hours they'd have it. Then they could leave all this wretched anxiety behind and call in the cops, FBI, everyone.

The moment she read Ami's e-mail yesterday, she wrote back a full and grateful response. "Just hit 'Reply'" after the girl had come up with that kind of info? *I don't think so.* Better a bouquet of roses. Better still, a bouquet and the biggest bonus of her life. *Make* her take it (Suzanne could already hear her refusal). She's earned it.

Burton sure had been acting strange, though. A few minutes ago he trudged back up the stairs asking about paternity forms again.

"I told you," she'd said as patiently as she could, "some states use them, or have in the past, and some never did have a specific form."

He'd plopped down on the bed looking morose. Morose! At a time like this? So she'd just come out with it:

"What's the problem, Burton? An elderly social worker wants your signature on a form, by God you give it to her. What's the big deal? He's your son. All you have to do is say so."

"I know, but what if they confuse me with another Burton Trayle?"

"Confuse you?" Had she heard him right? "What are you talking about?"

"It wouldn't be the first time, you've told me so yourself. I've had cases too where the names were—"

"I don't know about you, Burton, but I've never had a case where the circumstances were this spelled out and there was any kind of mistake. We've got a boy born on a specific date thirty-two years ago in Kansas City, Missouri. Mother's Suzanne Wendt. Father's Burton Trayle. Not a lot of room for confusion there."

"I guess not." But he said it forlornly, as if he were disappointed.

Was it his professional ambitions? Was he worried the governor wouldn't promote him to the circuit court if this came out? She refused to go there, couldn't stomach the thought that he'd put anything in front of finding their son.

So she'd stayed at her easel as he went back downstairs and put on his damned doo-wop.

She didn't have the energy to carp about the music, and the familiarity of this particular complaint felt almost soothing compared to her anger at him for appearing so unhappy about Ami's success.

But then she told herself to cut him some slack. It's a momentous time for him, too. The fact is, some birth parents *do* react strangely when they're about to find their kid. *You of all people should know this,* she told herself. *Burton's probably wigged out over feelings he repressed decades ago.*

She returned to shading a dense cloud in her painting of the clear-cut hill, pressing a black pastel over the gray lines she'd drawn earlier this morning. Day after day she'd studied that hill, had sketched every snag and stump, and watched the crudely formed ponds that pocked its face fill until they were now overflowing. As she stood there, she found herself wondering what kind of machine had ravaged it, had been so hugely hungry for roots and limbs and trunks that it could leave the soil scarred beyond recognition. It was as if a raw randomness had ruled the hill, ruled it still, and had ripped the nubs of trees from the rigid grip of the earth and left other stumps to stand and rot and gray with no regard for reason.

The hill, hanging wasted and dying from a darkening sky, could have been Christ on the cross. *The bastard God of the Christian faith.* A disturbing idea, but she wasn't the first adoptee to recognize its harsh truth or personal significance.

Burton had just lugged himself back up the stairs with that same gloomy expression when the doorbell sounded above the sirens of puppy love in four-part harmony.

She rushed the window overlooking the front door, and shouted, "It's here," passing Burton at the head of the stairs in her hurry to get the door. He followed right behind.

Her hands fumbled with the bolt lock before she could spin it around and pull the heavy door open.

The letter carrier smiled. He held the large overnight envelope and a black shoulder bag. He also looked familiar, strikingly so, but this didn't register consciously with Suzanne, who was reaching for the envelope and thanking him profusely.

"Special delivery."

He didn't use this stale line to refer to the mail, but to the gun in his hand, revealed as she took the envelope from him.

It pointed right at her, then moved to include Burton as he backed them into the house and closed the door, throwing the bolt lock without taking his eyes from them.

"You're . . ."

He nodded before she could finish, and then said, "I am. We've met before. I know you," speaking as casually as he might to a colleague he'd met at a conference.

She clutched herself as Burton wrapped her in his arms.

"I'd advise both of you to listen very carefully to what I'm about to say. I have no qualms about killing you if you don't do exactly what I want. But if you follow my instructions, one of you gets to live. Understand?"

Then it struck her. "Where's Ami?" If he were The Searcher, he'd stashed her somewhere, forced her to send those e-mails.

This was Suzanne's blind side, the part of her always loath to admit the cruelest possibility; but it came to her in his smile, as if he wanted her to answer her own question.

"What did you do to her!" A cry of grief.

"She's fine," he said. "Safe and sound. Cozy as can be. Hasn't she been sending you e-mails? I told her to. Don't tell me you haven't gotten them." Smiling the whole time, joking around. "Ami and I have had a lot of fun together."

"You've been doing it. You must have sent them."

"No," he shook his head, good-natured as a greengrocer. "No more than you've been you or I've been me when we've been sending messages. The judge here is the only one who's who he's supposed to be. Right, Judge? You never change."

Burton didn't respond, his eyes on the gun.

"Let's go see if there are any more e-mails from Ami. She's a busy girl. Where are you keeping your computer?"

"Up there. But I checked a little while ago." She didn't want to go to the sleeping loft, she wanted to go back to the instant before she opened the door. Make herself stop.

"Is that right? She's got wireless e-mail now, so she might have sent you something in just the last few minutes." That smile again. She wanted to tear it from his face.

Burton squeezed her. A warning? Had he sensed her fury? She wondered which of them would go for a gun first.

"I suggest we take a look just to make sure you haven't missed something important, something life-changing, but before we do let me explain something to you. If either one of you doesn't do exactly what I tell you to do, I'm going to shoot the other one in the spine. Shatter it like glass. And then I'm going to do the same thing to you. Believe me, I'll be close enough to do it. So unless there's some real hate between the two of you, and we're not there yet," he added with a wink, "I'd suggest you do precisely what I tell you to do, and when I tell you to do it.

"Now I want you to turn around slowly and go up the stairs to your computer. When we get there, I'll tell you what to do next."

They walked toward the stairs, Suzanne acutely aware that they were leaving the nine-millimeter behind in the kitchen cabinet. But the shotgun was in the closet. If she could come up with an excuse to go—

"Move a little faster. I didn't mean this slow. This'll take all day. And quit holding on to each other."

He shoved the barrel into her spine, and she jumped.

"Come on, hon." Burton took her arm again.

"No, Judge. You don't want me repeating myself. Hands to your side."

In this manner they ascended the stairs, the barrel brushing against her back every few seconds.

She pointed to the computer sitting on the nightstand next to the bed. "There it is."

The Searcher looked around, sized up the situation.

"Okay, I want both of you sitting on that side of the bed facing the computer, but I want you to move as slowly as you were when you first started up the stairs."

Once he had them in place, he told Suzanne to pick up the laptop. Then he circled tightly around them until she felt him on the bed and the gun at her back again.

She and Burton were sitting hip to hip, close enough that she could take his hand and whisper, "I love you." But not so close that The Searcher didn't hear her.

He cocked the trigger and pressed it harder into her spine.

"Check your e-mail, Ms. Trayle," his voice as relaxed now as it was when she took the envelope from him at the door.

Her in-box showed a message from Ami.

"Now open it and read it out loud. Every word. I think Ami has some things she wants you to know."

She swallowed as the screen filled.

"Dear Ami,

"I found him! His name is Robert Byers. He's an electrician in Nashville. He's married, and he's got a fourteen-month-old daughter. My granddaughter! I have his address and everything, but first I have to tell you why this search has been so complicated. I'm sorry to say it's really awful news . . ."

Her voice faltered in the lee of her eyes, and despite The Searcher's warning, she read the most devastating sentence of her life in numbed silence:

Burton fathered another boy who was born two weeks before your son.

Suzanne was so stunned she couldn't read on.

"I said read it out loud, and I meant out loud." Each of The Searcher's words punctuated with the barrel of his gun.

She forced herself to reread that last sentence aloud, sensed Burton collapsing beside her, even though he hadn't moved, and continued with the e-mail.

"I'm sorry to have to tell you this,"

tears striped Suzanne's cheeks, and the suppression of sobs haunted her voice,

"but I thought you ought to know that your son has a half brother. His name is Harold Brantley, and he's a psychologist in Tempe, Arizona, who specializes in the emotional problems of birth mothers.

"When he was twenty-one, he was arrested for malicious mischief after a fraternity party turned into a riot. The worst part was a local girl got raped. He was named as a suspect, but never charged. I dug up his mug shot. It's attached as a JPEG."

When she paused the cursor, he said, "Go ahead, open it up."

She clicked on the attachment, which slowly revealed the police photo from the top of the head down.

When the face finally appeared in full, her heart sounded so loudly she could hear it thumping: She was staring at a picture of the dark-haired man behind her.

"What do you think, Ms. Trayle?" He leaned forward until his lips paused right at the back of her neck. She felt his breath when he spoke again, as she had when he'd sung to her on that awful night in Chicago. "Do you think I raped that girl? Do you think I'm capable of that?"

She wouldn't respond, not to that, but he didn't care. He leaned back and said, "There he is, your other boy, Judge Trayle. You got a kid in Nashville, and you got me right here. Aren't you the lucky dad."

"So the electrician, Robert Byers, he's really my son?" She tried to keep her voice flat, to strip it of all hope and love and meaning, believing he'd try to turn her words on her.

But The Searcher chuckled. It sounded genuine, and when he answered, his mirth was still apparent.

"Some things are just too good to make up. He's as real as I am. I've got some other stuff I want you to see, too. It's more reading material, but it's not from anyone going under the name Ami."

He eased himself off the bed and walked around until he faced them. Using his free hand, he dug into his shoulder bag and pulled out a fistful of letters.

"Burton sent dozens of these to my mother when she was sitting around waiting to have me, and for the first few months after I was born, but these are the best." He flipped them onto the laptop, which Suzanne still held.

She looked at the yellowed envelopes, exactly like the ones Burton had sent her thirty-two years ago: same return address in Vietnam, same sloppy handwriting, same postmarks. But the recipient's name was as unknown to her as the ruthless manner in which her own life was unraveling.

Her hands didn't move until The Searcher pressed the barrel of his gun to her brow.

"They're worth reading."

He'd highlighted the first letter with a red felt-tip pen. Burton had referred to Suzanne as "trouble" and had promised to marry the mother of his other son "soon."

Burton's eyes also ran down the crinkled page, and he began apologizing right away.

"I couldn't bring myself to tell you about him." His eyes darted nervously to his son. "I never even met him," he added defensively. "I loved *you*, Suz. I came back for you. Remember? I came for *you*."

"He's not telling the truth. He's lying again. Here's the truth. He was all set to marry my mother—it's right there in the letters—when he found out you were pregnant. So suddenly his eighteen-year-old girlfriend, my mother, could go fuck herself. She couldn't hold anything over him, except for having his kid, and what's that compared to the statutory rape of a fourteen-year-old?"

The Searcher never lost his smile. Even his lone expletive sounded kind, almost sugary on his breath, less an act of the driven flesh than of whimsy with its unbroken prerogatives.

"I never held that over him," Suzanne said softly.

"You didn't have to, not with a guy like him. You knew what was at stake, didn't you?" He looked at Burton, but only briefly. "He couldn't go marrying my mother after knocking up a fourteen-year-old. He had to keep my mother on the line the whole time. Back then he might have ended up in prison. So I lost my mother *and* my father because you"—he tapped Suzanne again with the barrel—"had to drag him off on some bone-down safari."

Only with those last few words did he give evidence of anger: the vernacular as venom.

"I never did that. I never did anything like that. It wasn't like that at all." *He was the one. He pulled me into the backseat.*

But she'd never say this to a stranger, could barely admit it to herself, though the memories spoke with unflinching force: Burton tearing open her pants, popping the button off the top of her fly; the threads lying as limp and defeated as she felt after he yanked her pants down; and when he finished, when he lay above her with his body still heaving, the vinegar of his breath pouring out "I'm sorry." She'd turned her face away only to smell the sour scent of the black upholstery, never wondering, as she should have, whom else he'd had to apologize to.

These memories, smells, still reigned thirty-two years on. Her stomach roiled because she knew without question what Burton had spawned: a rapist, as he himself had been on the night he'd forced her into the backseat. But she'd been too young and too naive to know the name, too young to do anything but accept the blame. Raped first by the father, and then by his son, for there was no doubting who stood before her with a gun.

"Where is she?" Burton asked.

"Where's who?" The Searcher said, poking the gun at Burton before returning his attention to Suzanne. She stared at the dark, round opening, dimly aware of another doo-wop song rising in the background.

"Your mother. Where is she?"

To Suzanne, Burton sounded remarkably calm, as if he were in his element.

"She's dead. I killed her. I found her and ripped her apart." He spoke with the same casual disregard that another young man might use to describe a date, a nice though not particularly memorable one. "I took out all of the kitchen knives and made her play with them. She was my first."

He lifted the gun to Suzanne's brow once more. The steel smelled like a dentist's drill, the same cold indifference to pain.

"Ami was my last." That smile again.

Suzanne's eyes squeezed shut, and when they opened they released a fresh rush of tears.

He tapped her head with the muzzle. Just as she assured herself that she could accept a quick death, he offered a ghastly vow that made her recognize the savage consequences of surrender.

"After you two, I'm going to work on your son. He really does live in Nashville, and he's really got a daughter, too. Her name's June. They call her Juney. They don't know a thing, the three of them. Living their lives like they don't have a care in the world. That's the way it is when you first have a baby, isn't it? Some people just couldn't be happier. But they're never going to know what hit them. And then I'm going to hunt down every one of your birth mothers. All of them. Hit 'Delete.'"

She sat there, trying to sort out what he'd said.

"Hit 'Delete.' I want that e-mail out of there."

She hit the key, and the younger face of The Searcher dissolved in an instant.

"Your computer's going with us, too. We're not leaving that behind."

"What's the point?" Suzanne heard Burton mutter.

The Searcher must have heard him, too, because he looked over and pointed the gun at him. "What'd you say?"

"I said I can see your point."

The Searcher shook his head, apparently in disgust. The instant his eyes glided away from them, Burton seized the barrel. The gun went off in a deafening roar.

Suzanne jumped back, eyes widening as her ears closed down from the explosion. She saw her husband's hand still on the barrel, but his face was pinched.

Another gunshot—this one sounded distant and hollow—made him jerk his hand away, and she spotted blood spilling from his thigh and belly as he rolled off the mattress to the floor. He heaved and moaned and started to convulse on the carpet. Suzanne sprang toward him. The Searcher shouted "Stop!" with such effect that it was as if her body understood far better than she that survival lay in absolute stillness.

Burton stared up at her, shaking horribly, one hand gripping his gut, powerless to stanch the blood.

The Searcher turned his unhinged anger on him. "You're making a mess, *Dad.* You're bleeding all over the fucking floor, *Dad.* Next you'll be pissing your goddamn fucking pants, *Dad*!"

A rumble rose above his fury, and the doo-wop still playing insipidly on the sound system. Suzanne and The Searcher both looked from Burton to the clear-cut hill that loomed beyond the glassed-in deck. It had calved a massive wall of mud and stumps, like a glacier shearing off its outer edge. The brown mass, weighted by weeks of rain no longer absorbed by thirsty trees, was sliding toward them, its fragile stability shattered by The Searcher's gunshots as surely as avalanches are triggered by the rifles of hunters.

"Oh God," Suzanne said, bending down for Burton.

"Forget him."

"I can't . . ."

But terror choked her voice as she peered past The Searcher to the wall of mud advancing on the house, moving at the pace of a brisk walk. She watched in horror as it began to crush the idiot strip at the back of Laura's property. Trees snapped with piercing claps, and with no more resistance than an infant could offer a steamroller. The tops of the trees, unmoving moments ago, shook violently, like dust mops raised in anger, and then they succumbed. The viscous mass ripped entire root systems from the earth. They rose with a great crackle, and the evergreens toppled slowly into one another.

"No, no," she whispered, not to The Searcher but to the expanding horizon of destruction. The trees will stop it. They have to. But trees sixty, seventy feet tall simply snapped and fell and were sucked into the slowly moving mud. Crushing sounds, ominously soft and brutally hard, clashed in the air and rose to her ears. A gaily skirted fir, as big as the Christmas tree that stands outside the White House every December, pitched toward the house. Soon a second tree smashed down, and a third. Nothing, she now realized, would stop the mudslide. Nothing.

Great lengths of mangled trees, split and splintering, stuck out of the brown pile like spines from sea urchins. A huge uprooted pine, its taproot obscenely long and pale and exposed, aimed straight for the house like a battering ram. The tip couldn't have been more than eighty feet away.

Suzanne yanked on Burton's arm, trying to drag him to his feet. He whispered to her, "The gun, the gun!"

She moved him no more than inches when The Searcher shoved her away. She spun to the side, lost her balance, and fell. When she recovered, she saw that he'd put his gun to the back of Burton's head. Without warning, he smashed the butt down on her husband's skull, driving Burton's chin to the floor with an audible thud.

"I'm not wasting another bullet on you. The mud can have you."

He snapped her computer shut and advanced on Suzanne, grabbing the straps of her painting overalls and hauling her to her feet.

As he pushed her toward the stairs, Burton screamed for help and reached out. She hesitated, then started back, managing only three steps before The Searcher smashed her in the face with the laptop. The pain proved so paralyzing that she could only yelp and cover her mouth. He forced her back to the staircase, and when she didn't start right down, he kicked her. She crashed to her elbows and slid down headfirst. Her right arm jammed against a banister, and she tumbled twice before she hit the hardwood floor—knees, head, and back battered by the brutal passage.

Stunned and bleeding, she staggered to her feet, dizzy, off balance, trying to get her bearings, thinking, *The cabinet, the cabinet.*

Through a glaze of tears she saw it, tottered toward the kitchen as The Searcher bounded down the last of the stairs and kicked her wobbly legs out from under her. She fell to the hardwood floor with a crack she felt in her chin.

Before she could start to pull herself up, he dragged her to her feet and shoved her bleeding face against the glass rectangle in the oak door. Rain pelted the surface millimeters from her swelling eye.

"He might as well have announced it to the world. Where is it?"

"Upstairs. Closet." Wanting desperately to see him run back up there, seeing herself grabbing the gun from the cabinet and racing insanely down the road. But he wasn't stupid.

"Any others?"

"No."

"Didn't have the guts to go for it, did you?"

He jerked her from the door. Her face left a red smear as large as an apple on the glass. He threw open the lock, and with a furious shove drove her out into the rain.

"Get in that car." A white Subaru sedan sat before her. No, she wouldn't do that. That's death. She knew it even then.

A powerful tremor gripped the ground, and when he glanced over to see the house shuddering, she ran toward the garage, Burton's Land Cruiser. A key under the seat. *Get it, get the thing going.*

She expected to hear the gun at any second, to be shot on the run, but he never fired and she made it around the house to the side door, lunging for the handle. Locked.

The Searcher cleared the corner as she wrestled with the door, weeping loudly in frustration.

She spotted him, and her breath seized up so suddenly that her chest felt banded by steel staves. She turned to bolt, only to face a massive wall of mud no more than forty feet from the rear of the house. It crept steadily toward her, more breakage alive in the air. The plowed-up earth reeked of must and mold, of everything dead that had risen.

His hand clamped down on the back of her neck, and he jammed the gun into the small of her back.

He dragged her to the front of the house as another tremor rose from the ground to her feet, compounding her fear.

Three painful steps later, the double-wide garage door was shaken from its frame and crashed to the ground directly in front of them.

The Land Cruiser was vibrating on the concrete floor, which started to crack as they stood there. Then the far wall began to blur.

He pulled her to the Subaru, opened the passenger door, and forced her into the seat.

"You move, I'll shoot you in the belly. You won't die, but you'll wish you had."

The look on his face was terrible, as twisted as hemp rope. When he slammed the door, she clasped her belly without realizing it and watched filthy water surge around the tires of Burton's car. A sharp crackling, like a giant bonfire, penetrated the Subaru when he climbed into the driver's seat, and she pictured the risen taproot ramming the rear of the house, collapsing the second-story deck, the imminent submission of walls and floors and glass to countless tons of mud. Most horrifying of all, she imagined Burton's hand still reaching out for her as the mudslide swallowed him whole.

The walls of the house now shook so violently that it was as if an earthquake had struck. With a tightening panic she understood that it could collapse on top of them, and in those steeply pressing seconds her most overwhelming fear was that she'd be buried alive with this man.

"It's going to kill us," she screamed, wanting nothing more than to sprint to the life-giving sanctuary of open space.

He started the car as the rear wall of the garage seamed in scores of places. The splits oozed dark, crooked lines before the wall burst apart, spewing an ugly mix of mud and drywall, two-by-fours and logs onto the hood of the Land Cruiser.

"Go!" Suzanne pleaded. "Go!" though the trade-off felt no less frightening, only less immediate.

Then she froze as the roof of the garage smashed down on Burton's car, showering the windshield with more drywall, more two-by-fours, and a six-foot length of pink insulation. The garage light dangled on a long cord and sparked crazily a foot above the hood. Her panic proved so complete that she could not breathe in the frantic seconds that followed, yet a foul chemical odor infected her nose. She guessed it rose from the house itself, those crushing sounds that would not stop.

The Subaru roared out of reach of the house, but The Searcher kept his gun trained on her. He braked and stared back at the spectacle.

She wiped blood from her face and made herself look up, and that's when she saw what held his attention. The wall of mud was forcing the entire house forward, as if the leading edge of the slide were the blade of a giant bulldozer. The front of the house split open, and the log wall crumbled and pitched forward, exposing both floors, leaving Suzanne with the surreal sense that she was staring at a dollhouse.

A gasp singed her throat when she spied Burton's arm rising from the mud oozing across the crumbling loft. It held what appeared to be the shotgun. In the next instant a red flare issued from the muddy barrel, and they heard the shocking report in the car, one concussion followed quickly by another. And then the weapon and his arm were sucked back down, like a man drowning in the surf.

The Searcher said nothing, Suzanne shocked into silence by the image of her wounded husband crawling to the closet and trying to crawl after them.

The churning mass pushed Laura's king-size bed over the edge. It fell awkwardly, like a big bird with a broken wing. The frame smashed into ungainly lengths, and the mattress bounced on end before flopping lifelessly to the sodden ground. An antique pine armoire fractured beside it.

Suzanne's clothing followed, heaps that fell in clumps, but also a white nightgown that billowed and floated with the grace of a ghost. She spotted her painting, too, the last few feet of its flight as it seesawed in the air like a leaf. It settled near the broken bed.

The Searcher hit the accelerator hard, and as they sped down the long driveway she gripped the armrest, her body as rigid as ice or steel or stone.

But as they approached the first curve, she looked back to see if Burton had somehow escaped. What she saw made this appear as unlikely as her own survival: the house had been leveled, and the remains resembled flotsam on a swirling sea.

The Searcher stuck the gun in her side and told her to turn around.

"Do what I say or you get it just like him."

She straightened in her seat and felt the muzzle press deeper into her skin.

Her eyes closed, and a prayer came to her unmoving lips. She had no firm faith in God, nor did she seek the deliverance of the devout. She asked only for stillness, for all of this to end.

23

THAT MUDSLIDE WAS magnificent. I've never seen anything like it, not on television or in the movies or anywhere. It wasn't like an avalanche, which comes on so fast it's over before you really have a chance to figure out what you're seeing. This thing took its time, gave me a chance to really enjoy it. It was nature's slow-motion riot. It destroyed everything. I watched that thing creep right toward the house and had all I could do not to bow, throw out a welcome mat, and toss her into it. But I need her more than she realizes. I went to great lengths to keep her alive, and that's not going to change until she tells me everything I need to know.

She's still sniveling, blood still dripping from her nose and mouth, and she's got herself all backed up against the door. She looks like one of those butterflies whose wings have been pinned to a corkboard. I can see her shooting looks at me. She senses it's the end. An act of kindness is called for.

"Here." I hand her a box of tissues. "Clean up your face. It's disgusting. And do a good job. I don't want to see any more blood on it."

I mostly don't want anyone else to see it. We'll be off this muddy strip soon enough, and I'd rather we didn't look like a horror movie when we hit the paved road. Just a normal couple out for a drive, now that we've left *Dad* behind.

To even think of calling him that feels strange, I mean really bizarre. Dad? For *him*?

But now that I've met him it feels even stranger to call him Burton. So Dad it'll be until I can come up with something better. One of the more common expletives comes to mind for reasons that should be obvious to even the dimmest bulb; but nothing, *nothing* is as profane as calling him "Dad."

Everything was going along so smoothly. I got in the door as easily as I'd thought I would. No problems there. And they both cooperated going up the stairs to her laptop. I loved hearing her read that e-mail out loud, the way her voice cracked when she got to that business about my half brother. There aren't too many moments like that in life. It's like actually seeing an accident happen, as opposed to coming on the scene later.

To that point it couldn't have gone better, but then he had to go hero on me and grab the gun. Now that was shocking. I've never had that happen before. I fired without thinking, and then I got so angry that I really got obscene with my language. I usually don't have any patience for that, or for the imbeciles who use four-letter words, but that grabbing the gun really set me off. I'd wanted to take them away cleanly, make it look like they left on their own. But as soon as I pulled the trigger and he started bleeding, I knew I could forget all about that. We all know about the best-laid plans and what happens to them.

I couldn't kid myself about the blood. Once it started flowing, there was a river of evidence in that house. But then that magnificent mudslide started, and I knew that as much as I'd created a problem by shooting him, I'd solved it by setting off that slide.

One second you think you're finished, or at least that your life has become infinitely more complicated, and the next you've got this huge hill of opportunity rolling right at you. Obstacles really can become opportunities. I was so thankful I could have raised a toast to that insatiable sky.

It meant that I could leave him there. Let nature have its way with him. We're talking tons and tons of mud, as wide as a football field and at least twenty feet high. It wasn't leaving anything behind, least of all *Dad.* I figured his friends would end up holding a memorial service on the muddy remains.

But I had to be sure. That's why I waited until I saw that house smothered. A death and burial have rarely gone faster.

Even if they eventually bring out the sniffer dogs and probe poles to see if there were any fatalities, *and* they find him somehow buried under all that mud and hundreds of logs and assorted rubble, she's going to be the only real suspect. Nobody knows about me, and the two of them had been separated. That was common knowledge, in *People,* no less. It'll play out like this: The two of them went off on a country retreat to try to patch things up. Instead, they got into a violent argument, probably over his affairs. He hadn't changed in all those years, and I'll bet he'd had a string of them.

Anyway, there they were, just the two of them alone in the country when their marriage finally fell prey to the twin fiends of rage and hate.

Not the first time that scenario's played out. It's older than gunpowder. The only unusual twist is the mudslide, but it's not going to take much of a detective to put two and two together.

Her disappearance will reek of panic and only heighten suspicions about her. It's great to see how easily all of this comes together. There's only one possible problem: Laura Kessing.

I need to find a place where Ms. Trayle and I can spend some quality time together. I need to know exactly what she told Kessing to get her house. I've never failed to extract the truth from my mothers, and I'm not going to fail now, not when the truth means more to me than it ever has before.

Finding a place shouldn't be an insurmountable problem. From what I could gather from the tourist brochures I picked up at that dump of a motel, lots of people have summer homes around here. As soon as we get out of the immediate vicinity, in another thirty miles or so, I'll look for an empty house. A nice place where we can regroup, recoup, and replenish ourselves.

She's got her face cleaned up, but what a slob. She dropped the balled-up tissues on the floor. They look like her eyeballs, red on white. Is she crying? She will be. As soon as we can find a place, I'll make her cry till she talks, and then I'll take the measure of what she says about Laura Kessing. If it doesn't feel right, if I sense the least little insincerity, then she'll just have to cry some more.

I'm very good at reading my birth mothers. I've made a practice of it. I'll just have to make sure to keep my excitement under control. I can feel my hormones on a rolling boil, and it's given me an insight . . . no, I'd have to say a *theory* of God that's as fresh and welcome to my way of thinking as an October frost.

It's doubly strange that it should come to me, because as I've said before I've never considered *God* as anything more than the St. Nick of the creation myth.

Here's what I'm thinking. Maybe eons ago God looked down on the damp, dreary certitude of earth and decided to break His unending boredom by giving man the option to murder. Not a mandate, but an option.

He understood that all other choices would follow, and that the world could go up in flames of grief from this one little spark.

There was no apple, no Adam and Eve, no loss of innocence. One second there was peace on earth, and the next there was the harrowing sense of living on a precipice.

Now for the first time He could sit and watch as a random element, *the* random element, the most primary of all, far outpacing the procreative urge (though in its origins and outcomes murder and mating are as close as blood and bone), began to mingle among men and women.

There was no predicting, not even for Him, when murder would become manifest, or how wild the permutations might become. And it was the very fact of not knowing that gave this most interesting God a game to amuse Him, to lift Him from His infinite ennui.

Why not, if you're God, provide the itch to kill, and enjoy the spectacle of every scratch?

Now here's the most intriguing part of my theory. Those who kill, it naturally follows, form a logical kinship with He who creates, because He provides us with the means to achieve His ends. In this single and most critical sense, you could say we are divinely inspired. You could even call us search angels on a mission of murder.

We worship. You bleed.

Right, Ms. Trayle?

"Pick up those tissues. Don't be such a slob."

She does as I ask.

You always begin with the simple requests.

$$\boxed{24}$$

THE SEARCHER RARELY braked, not for the gentle curves that climbed higher into these hills, not for the rain that battered the windshield.

After leaving Laura's, he'd turned the Subaru onto a back road and had stayed on it, a narrow paved strip bordered on both sides by thickly flanked conifers, stately trees so tall that they obliterated all but a slender strip of the sky.

A hallway to heaven, Suzanne thought without understanding why. But she had only to look at the bloody tissues to make the connection between her present condition and her snap conception of the afterlife.

She shivered as the forest flew by. The only openings in the woods came when they passed huge, gaudy, gated estates, McMansions surrounded by tall stone walls. These were the rural retreats of the newly rich, refugees from the Silicon Forest that stretched from Seattle to Portland, multimillionaires in their twenties and thirties who'd been smart enough to cash in their stock options before all that techno-tinsel turned to trash.

He slowed as they approached a driveway, peered closely at a distant house, and drove on. He did this three more times in the next few minutes. She panicked at what he'd do when he finally stopped, and wondered if she could throw open the door and survive a high-speed jump. She glanced at the speedometer. The needle hovered near fifty. No way.

She also thought about grabbing the gun still pointing at her belly, but after what he'd done to Burton, this felt like suicide, an especially painful form of it.

The openings in the forest wall disappeared, and once more they raced through a seamless corridor. But the appearance of the trees had changed, and when she looked closely she saw that it was no longer a forest, but a facade, another idiot strip like the one back at Laura's, another thin curtain that opened only to the blunt emptiness of the clear-cuts beyond.

A mile, then two, passed in absent horror before she spotted the fires. They appeared as one huge orange glow, but as they drove closer each one resolved into distinction, like a camera lens finding its focus: slash fires, maybe twenty in all. Burn season had begun. Loggers had bulldozed countless boughs, "limbed" from the firs and pines and cedars, into piles eight, ten, even twelve feet high. Then they'd soaked them with diesel and set them ablaze. The final plunder.

She watched the flames rise as if in a rage against the rain, spewing smoke and cinders. The orange embers zigzagged crazily, sparks alive one moment and snuffed to death the next, darkening the air with ash as the sun smothered helplessly in the steely embrace of the sky.

"Take off your clothes."

Suzanne didn't move. He looked over, and before she could blink he backhanded her with the gun. The barrel struck her face, and her eyes pooled from the sharp pain.

"When I tell you to take off your clothes, you take them off."

Still, she held firm. Not out of courage, out of numb fear of another rape. The only part of her that moved was the blood spilling from her nose and lips.

He buried the gun between his legs and grabbed her hair, shook her head. Shook it hard enough to make the roots scream.

"Take them off or I'll rip your eyeballs out."

She squeezed them shut and raked the straps of her overalls off her shoulders.

"Faster." He raised the gun, but she never saw the threat. Her eyes opened only when a button on her blouse troubled her. She drew her arms from the sleeves, revealing a white bra. He yanked the front of it down.

"Come on," he said in a voice sickened by a strange sweetness.

She undid the buttons on the sides of her overalls and pushed them over her hips.

He kept glancing over. Driving carefully, but taking in her white underpants, her pale thighs.

When her overalls were down to her knees, she stopped, hoping that would be enough.

"All the way."

She slipped them down to her ankles, but before she could remove her shoes, he smacked her head with the butt of the gun. A stinging pain, like he'd gashed her skull.

"I told you to move fast."

Even now his voice sounded unreal in its restraint, meaning and tone at such obvious odds, like a recording from a machine, not the words of a man.

She wrenched her shoes off and kicked her overalls to the floor, then lifted her knees to her chest and clasped them with her arms. She caught him eyeing the very bottom of her buttocks.

"Please don't," she said. She hadn't planned to plead but it had arisen from her like all hope, all life, with an irrepressible urge.

His response was to tell her to sit up straight. "I want to be able to see you."

She released her legs, and her feet settled on the overalls now lying rumpled on the floor. She stared at them, the simple decency they'd provided. Then she looked at her underpants, sickened at the thought of exposing herself to him. But she knew this wasn't about her body, and it wouldn't end with rape. She knew this with a terrifying certainty. This was about something else, a conclusion she could not calculate with the crude equations of flesh.

"Get them off."

Her hands slipped inside the waistband, and she took a measured breath. She lifted up to inch her underpants down and caught the reflection of a car in the side-view mirror. It was so far back that she wouldn't have noticed it at all if its lights hadn't been on. She settled back in the seat without removing her underclothes.

"I feel sick," she said.

"I'm sick, too. I'm getting sick of you." He shoved the gun into her belly and caught the waistband with the sight. He paused and pulled it back, as if lured by the way he could look inside her panties. "Do it," he spoke in a voice gone soft, and more frightening for the change. "Do it or we're going to get blood all over the place."

The barrel so close to her sex, so insistent and prodding. Her stomach swirled as she revealed the dark border of pubic hair.

He started humming "Mother and Child Reunion."

Don't sing, don't sing, she pleaded silently. But he did sing, and those few words in his off-key voice brought back all of the rape, and the rape brought back all of the violence that had followed: Karen and Jesse's savage murders. Ami's. Burton's. His promise to kill even more birth mothers.

I'm really sick, she thought. Really sick. She cupped her mouth, but admitting this made her even more nauseous, the weight thought can give to sensations, to the dizziness rolling through her torso, that was expanding from her stomach like a sour balloon. He must have noticed.

"Don't puke in this car. Don't you dare."

She gagged and heaved her body forward, gathering her overalls tightly to her chest, as if worried that she'd soil them.

"Don't do it!" His self-control had slipped away as fast as her sickness had appeared.

He jammed the gun back between his legs and grabbed her hair again, holding her at arm's length, as if he didn't know what to do with her. Then he yanked her head up. She offered no resistance, appeared to have none to offer, until she leaned into him and vomited a yellowish, curdled liquid in his face.

His hand ripped away from her head as cloudy lumps dripped from his nose and cheeks to his jacket. They beaded and squiggled down the smooth surface until slowed by a sudden friction, only to tumble again, as if urgent for his lap. He wiped madly at his features, and brushed chunks from his pants, holding his hand far from his body after each swipe, as if the heat of her insides had scalded him with disgust. He sputtered and swore fiercely that he'd kill her, and did exactly what she'd hoped: He slowed down to pull over.

She bent forward, as if to vomit again, and while choking loudly clawed the door, pulled the handle, and hurled herself onto the pebbly surface by the side of the road.

Her body bounced twice, skinning her knees and elbows and hammering the side of her head; but terror inured her to the pain and made little of the added blood and bruises.

His car skidded to a stop as she rose unsteadily to her feet, shaking viciously from the fall, the startling cold, and unrelenting fear. With her overalls still clutched to her chest, and her underpants still rumpled around her crotch, she staggered through a ditch flowing with icy water. As she scrambled into the forest, the car with the headlights pulled up, an old Buick 88 with body cancer and a hood that was cinched to the grille with a bungee cord.

The Searcher threw open his door and looked toward the woods, eyes moving wildly over the trees and the path she'd taken.

A heavily built man with a long, scraggly beard climbed out of the Buick.

"What the hell's going on? I saw a—"

The Searcher trained his gun on him. Suzanne pulled up her bra, under-pants, and overalls and backed away as the man began to beg The Searcher to let him go. In seconds, she heard him begging for his life. She couldn't see them anymore—she'd retreated into the trees—but still she backpedaled, too fearful to turn away.

"Move! Move! There!" The Searcher screamed.

Where? What's he going to . . . But before she could ask herself the question, the answer rang out in a brutal roar. Her throat tightened, and her pulse felt as fast as the bullet that had just been fired.

25

WHEN I FIND her I'm going to have to get a lot firmer. No more of her dirty little sex games in the car. I'm just going to grab her by the neck and lead her straight out of here before a cop or someone else stops to find out why two cars are sitting by the side of the road in the middle of nowhere. They're not going to have to scratch around long to come across the guy I shot. I did what I could in the time that I had, but he's still going to be hard to miss in that ditch.

When he hit the ground, he was already halfway in the water. One good shove and I had him all the way in, belly-up. I didn't want to look at him a second longer than I had to to make sure he was dead, but I can't wait to get ahold of her.

Puking on me! I can still smell it. I washed off as much as I could with the ditch water. I didn't want to lose time, but I couldn't bear the smell. It still stinks, the sour guts of her.

For the first few minutes, I ran as hard as I ever have. I thought I'd catch her quickly, but I haven't seen any sign of her. I know where she went into the forest, but there's so much brush, and it's so thick with pine needles, that I haven't seen a single footprint. What are you supposed to look for then? Broken branches. *Disturbed* leaves? What am I, Grizzly Adams? My only consolation is that from the look of her, she's no nature girl either. And she's going to freeze out here. All she had were those overalls, and the temperature's got to be in the low thirties. I'm worried about that. I've got to find her before she dies. I've got questions that still need to be answered. I want to know what Laura Kessing knows. That's critical. So I can't have Ms. Trayle dying on me out here. She doesn't know it yet, but we're interested in the same thing: keeping her alive. At least for a while.

I try calling her name. I hate the sound of my voice. It sounds hollow. I've never liked my voice. Even when I was a kid playing around with a tape recorder, I thought it sounded weak. I don't want it sounding weak right now, but it does. Almost like I'm asking her for a favor, *begging* for one like that yahoo begged for his life, instead of making it clear that it's going to get a lot worse for her if she doesn't come out from wherever she's hiding.

It drives me crazy to think she could be ten feet away, and I wouldn't know it. Who would? There are trees everywhere.

"I see you." Okay, here we go. "You're right there behind the tree. Come on out. Don't make me go in there after you or I'll shoot you on the spot."

Nothing moves, not even a squirrel. She's not buying my bluff, that's assuming she can even hear it.

The forest drip-drip-drips. I can feel cold rain falling through the trees, these endless trees. I really can't see ten feet without having another one in the way.

I'm already so far from the road that there's no way I could hear a cop pulling up. I know that's unlikely. Why would a cop be out here? But it's possible, and it's this possibility that eats at me. All I need is one person to drive by with a cell phone, one person curious enough to stop and walk around, and that's it. They'll find his body in that ditch, and the woods will be crawling with cops and dogs.

This has got to stop. I'm getting paranoid. If I saw two cars by the side of the road, I'd notice. Sure I would, but I'd drive on. I'd never stop. I'd figure a couple of friends had pulled over for some unfathomable and equally uninteresting reason.

I feel better when I remind myself of this. I've got some time to work with still. As soon as I get her back to the car, we'll take off and find a place to settle in. Somewhere warm with a fireplace.

"Ms. Trayle, come on out. Let's go back. We're wasting time out here. You must be freezing. It's warm back in the car. You hear me? Warm."

My voice sounds calmer now. I like it so much better. I sound *so* understanding. I *am* understanding. She should take advantage of this while she can. But the fool doesn't respond. All I hear is the incessant patter of raindrops on pine needles and my jacket. It's annoying to listen to, but what I really hate is the sound it makes when it drips on my hood. *Pock. Pock. Pock.* It's the kind of hood that unfurls from the collar. But I can't stand that sound, so I try slipping it off. The rain is even worse. It runs down my back and feels like icy fingers on my skin, so I pull the hood back on. It's infuriating to have to put up with all this, but my voice betrays nothing. Not even a hint of my frustration. I'm the picture of equanimity. The perfect therapist.

"It's not going well for you, Ms. Trayle. Not well at all. You want to know why? You want to know why this is getting worse for you every single second? Because I'm getting really angry. I know I don't sound like it, but I am. And it's *your* fault."

I've given her all the restraint I can bear. Now I've even warned her about my anger. That's more than any of my other birth mothers got, but she's still not listening. That's not right, so why should I hold back? What's the point? I'm going to lay it right on the line.

"Think about my anger when you look around. Think real hard when you see a pointy stick or a rock."

I must be screaming. My chest is compressed with fury, but she hasn't listened to reason. Maybe she'll listen to fear.

"Think about what I can do to you with a stick or a rock. And then think . . . *think,* Ms. Trayle, about how angry I'm going to be if I have to keep looking for you."

I let several empty seconds fall between us, then bring in the good cop.

"Do you really want me to be angry when I find you? We both know the answer to that one. It's time to go back with me. If you stay out here, you're going to die. It's that simple. I really don't want you to die. I mean that. If you come with me, we can talk. This is your last chance."

There's still no answer, just that incredibly irritating *pock . . . pock . . . pock.*

I beat my way through the brush, tear wet branches and tree limbs from my face. I know she's here. I can't see her, hear her, smell her, but she's here. Same as the trees are standing, same as the rain is falling, she's here: wooden and wet with fear, and waiting for me.

26

SUZANNE RACED THROUGH the thickening forest as gun-spooked as any October deer. No idiot strips here, no trails to follow either, nothing to smooth her passage through the dense conifers and prickly underbrush, the burgeoning boreal world that fought her flight with cold, with rain, with the fingernails of evergreens that scratched her naked shoulders, and with the sharp needles of berry bushes that clawed her shoeless feet and lacerated her bare back and upper body. The straps of her overalls kept slipping, and she had to withdraw a hand from these raw encounters to hold them up as she straight-armed her way through the tangle of trees.

She knew she was making far too much noise, a racket of snapping branches and crackling twigs that haunted her reckless plunge through the woods. Her own breath rose loudly too, ventilating her fear with hard gasps and cloudy puffs quickly parted by the forward rush of her body. And yet despite extraordinary efforts to inhale, she felt as if she hadn't taken in any air at all. It was as if the entire forest had turned to white water and foam.

Every time she looked back a shadow shifted and drove her onward. Christ, how she wished she'd been a runner, a hiker, anything that would have made her fit. She was in lousy shape, and she could feel it now. Her lungs, her heart, her legs all rubbery. Fatigue slowing her down, fear forcing her forward.

Her hands battled a web of brittle branches that popped and crackled with startling clarity as she recalled the pressure of his gun on her belly. *He'd said he'd kill you. That asshole wanted you naked and dead.* He'd just about succeeded on both counts.

She clutched her overalls and leaned her whipped shoulder into a series of overlapping boughs, a forceful move that showered her with biting-cold water. She shivered violently. Her hair hung lank and soaked, and she didn't have a dry spot left on her body. What hadn't been drenched by rain had been dampened by terror.

A stabbing pain flashed through her knees, and she looked around, dazed, wondering how she had fallen, how she could be upright one moment and slammed to the ground the next. She spotted a jumble of roots, but a burning feeling forced her attention to her elbow, where blood ran off the crook of her arm. Still bewildered by the fall, she probed the cut gently, a superficial wound, and tried to stand, stymied by a grotesque pain that sliced through her left kneecap.

She winced as she rose all the way to her feet, and she risked a moment to glance back. Nothing but trees, the countless overlapping boughs. She looked at herself too. Brown pine needles clung to her overalls, and her white socks had turned the color of mud. She took a step, relieved that her knee no longer ached so badly, and tried to control her breathing long enough to listen to the sounds that drifted through the woods. But she heard so little, the rain, the constant drone of rain, and then, as she turned to move, her name, "Ms. Trayle," reaching through the trees like long frightening arms. She also heard the unmistakable noise of a furious man forcing his way through the forest.

A measure of terror, distinct and desperate, throbbed in her chest as she realized he was closing in on her. He had not abandoned the chase, and he was not that far away. Not that far at all. Each understanding proved brief. *Move. Move. Now!*

She darted into a small clearing, cleansed of all pain but panic. She had no idea where to turn, yet knew she'd be doomed if she hesitated much longer. He'd find her. He'd kill her. She spun around, eyes burning—*there, there, there*—but each impulse died of indecision, falling like dominoes that spelled defeat.

The dull thunder of his feet traveled through the trees on the heels of her name. He kept repeating it as if it were a sounding device, and another wave of fear rocked her body. She backed up, unwilling to look away from the gathering sounds, from the threat that edged closer and closer. A pine branch stopped her retreat, and she brushed it aside irritably. The branch snapped back, smacking her head, and she turned toward it angrily. *Climb, climb.* The words arose in a misting madness, and she tore at the branches, rough uneven rungs, hurling herself upward with no understanding that to be treed was to be trapped.

Bark scraped her toes right through her socks, and her arches settled on twisted boughs for the briefest of seconds. Every step and handhold was slick and wet, as if snail spoor had been spread over the intimidating length of the tree. Her foot slipped, and she felt one of her socks inching off, a distant sensation that quickly passed into the fear of a treacherous foothold. Seconds later a six-inch snag snapped off in her right hand. It exploded like a gunshot and her feet gave way. In a ghastly instant she found herself hanging with all of her weight on her left arm, legs dangling fifteen feet above the ground.

The branch bowed precipitously, its surface wet and slippery. She begged herself to hold on, even as the ache in her hand began to pry her fingers apart. The force of the brief fall left her body twisting from side to side, loosening her grip still further. She wiggled her feet, searching frantically for purchase, and found a knot that allowed her inches more reach. Her right hand strained and stretched for a branch, and caught it as her afflicted grip failed. She found secure footing, too, and knew she would not fall, would not lie broken on the ground for this animal to devour at will.

She listened again, to see if he'd reacted to the exploding snag. She heard him. God, how she heard him, the dumb thud of his feet pounding through the forest. Not that far. Not that far. Simple words came back to her. *Move, move. Now!*

Her hands negotiated the web of branches. She was frantic for cover, and didn't care that the straps had fallen from her shoulders, leaving her bra and back exposed. She struggled, hands and feet pushing, grabbing, grappling, recalling the words of a rock climber who'd said you saved your arms with the power of your legs. But goddamn it, her feet kept slipping; and as she swore again in silence, her right foot grazed a branch and her sock came off completely, glancing off several boughs, taunting her with the hope that it would not fall all the way to the ground.

It didn't. It caught on the second to last branch; and that's where it hung, size 8, dirt brown, at eye level.

And there he stood in his jacket. He'd just walked into the narrow clearing in which she'd spun around, indecisive for unending moments. She feared traces of herself lay on the damp surface.

Her eyes lifted off him long enough to look up, and she wondered if she could outclimb him, scurry like a squirrel onto the lighter branches where he would never dare to go. But she knew immediately that these were absurd and pathetic calculations, that he'd climb after her and shake the tree like a furious bear, or more likely just shoot her down.

When she looked back at him, he'd paused to study the earth for tracks. She couldn't see any, but she was farther away. Mostly she worried about her sock, hanging like a soiled "welcome" sign.

She could just make it out from this height. It shared the colors of the muddy earth, the bark, the branches, the autumnal hues dark and damp. But the artist in Suzanne, so attuned to shape, to form, knew that what could prove most arresting was the incongruity of its lines, for if this were a giant painting the sock would be the one element that would capture the eyes and hold them fast. It lacked the husky angularity of the forest. It belonged to the vegetable or fruit kingdoms, to aubergines and squash, peppers or pears, not to the hard lines of branches and trunks. Dangling there. *Dangling*.

He turned his head, but not his body. His eyes traveled left, then right.

"Suzanne. Ms. Trayle."

He spoke her name softly, intimately, as if she were by his side. Then he walked toward the tree, as if he had indeed found the source of his words, but his pace proved slow and lacked the spark of discovery.

Still, she held her breath. A pinecone broke from high above her, as if his footsteps had cast a gravitational spell. It bounced from branch to branch, and as it passed the direct line of her vision her stomach took a plunge of its own. The cone landed at his side. His head snapped around. Then he looked up, eyes rising slowly, as if to retrace the cone's flight, to see the source of this sudden insult. She pressed herself into the tree as closely as she could, daring no other response. Her arms shook, her body too, and she tried mightily to still them as she choked down the cries that agitated her throat. Shivers of fear riddled her skin, shivers from the carnivorous cold, too. She'd been out in the rain for what? Half an hour? An hour? No telling. She couldn't even hazard a guess. Fear addled time, toyed with its staid standing no less than working at her easel turned hours into minutes and minutes into seconds, the shrinkage that comes from the hot wash of creation. But time now mushroomed, as if the prospect of pain, of death itself, could only prolong the most primitive moment.

He studied the tree inch by inch. His head rose as slowly as the moon on a winter night. She felt his focus on the trunk to her right. It could not have been millimeters from the tips of her filthy fingers, so close she could feel the chilly shadow of his sight. She saw that she was off center to him, but very much on the margin of discovery. Then his eyes inched higher, past her to the tree's crown. He had missed her altogether. A look of recognition had never filled his face, which she glimpsed now, the smooth features, and the narrow band of dark hair poking out from the hood of his jacket.

She felt a spy's satisfied certitude as he turned away, the disembodied eye that takes great pleasure in quiet observation, even as she felt a scorching desire for a quick, even clamorous retreat.

But she must grant him time, lots and lots of time. She must not move, not even now as he rushed on. She would wait . . . and wait . . . and work up the nerve to head back to the road.

As the first of these swollen minutes passed, she saw that her overalls had fallen all the way to her hips, and that if she moved at all she might find them around her knees. *You're quite a sight, girl.* No shoes, no shirt—and because she'd grown giddy from the near miss of his eyes, and because the rhythm of the line had embedded itself in her brain from a thousand signs, she whispered—"no service." But the saying, foreshadowed as it had been with humor, came now as a dry recitation, rote and unfunny. With renewed fear she risked just enough movement to slip her right hand under the strap and slide it up over her shoulder. Then the left.

Decent again, but cold. Real cold. And stupid. Logy. Juvenile expressions began to play in her head. Expressions she would never use. *Cold as a witch's titty. Cold as a witch's titty.* She hugged herself with one arm and noticed that her own nipples had turned numb, like her face and hands and feet. Clinging to the tree had left her frozen. She climbed a few more feet to a branch on which she could sit. Taking weight off her legs proved far more pleasurable than she would ever have thought possible. The relief supplanted the discomfort of the cold and the cruel constant of rain. She perched as an untroubled child might have, looking at the overlapping branches of trees that crowded the distance before her, and spied an owl peering back. Its sudden appearance startled her. It looked away, as if bored, its head swiveling with singular grace before turning back to her. She wished she knew her owls. Was it a spotted owl? How they hated them here. Even now. That a small stately bird could still the chain saws and the metal claws of the huge log loaders remained a wonderment to her. But then she remembered that many Native Americans believed that if an owl visited you, death was imminent.

When she feared her body's numbness would soon make it impossible to move, she began to climb down. She snatched her sock off the branch and lowered herself to the wet ground. She looked around and listened closely. Only the rain. She pulled on the sock. Scant protection, but perhaps better than none.

Doubling back seemed the best plan, but her sense of direction proved sketchy. She recognized this as soon as she passed through the last of the boughs that had soaked her earlier. She thought to continue straight ahead, but faced a broad thicket of impenetrable-looking berry bushes, and could not believe she'd ever plowed through them. She pivoted around and saw that she could go left or right, hard left or soft.

She stood unmoving, a mouse in a maze, before heading right. At the very least it would take her farther from him. Was he lost, too? He must be. But maybe not. He hadn't run like a panicked animal into the woods. He'd moved like a hunter and had stalked her with care. He was The Searcher, and he'd almost found her. He'd done a good job, she thought. *But you've done better,* she assured herself. *You got away.*

The forest thickened, and she had to bushwhack until she came upon hoofprints four to six inches deep, large enough to have been left by elk. She followed them to a stream, where she paused and stared at the ice on the rocky bank, wholly transparent layers that had just formed, or so she assumed. But the appearance, so crystalline and pure that it might have delighted her at any other time, left her with an overwhelming dread because she understood in a dim, distant manner that she had succumbed to the first stages of hypothermia. You begin to freeze, and your IQ falls as fast as the rain. Except the stream's surface no longer dimpled from raindrops, but melted the nickel-sized snowflakes that fell so gently. That death could arrive so quietly, so unceremoniously, seemed an insidious deception, warped in its cunning coldness. She reached out a hand, so bone-chilled it felt unmoved, and watched wet flakes fall to her palm. They melted and dribbled away, and she never felt their presence, the niggardliness of their weight, only the visible drain of death, its clarity, its quiet, its eternal emptiness, like the mind itself when life suddenly ceases.

She studied the snowflakes touching down on the stream, picked out one and then another and another and watched them all dissolve and disappear. She saw in their brief unrankled beauty her own demise. *They'll kill you. Not him.* She placed her tongue on her lips but felt neither. She looked to the sky. *What time is it?* She saw no sun, just autumn's gray ceiling. It could have been two o'clock or late afternoon. She lowered her eyes to the stream again. Maybe six feet across, a foot or two deep. So clear. So very very clear. How should she do this? Should she do this?

> *Little Ducky Duddle*
> *went wading in a puddle.*
> *He said, "Quack-quack. It really doesn't matter*
> *how much I splash and splatter,*
> *I'm just a little ducky, after all."*

The song came to her as clearly as the bottom moss streaming brightly in the current. One verse. That's all she'd ever known. Her adoptive mother had urged her to sing it at a party that her older sister had thrown. Suzanne was seven.

"Go ahead, Suz, the ducky song. You know it."

Her mother's hands had guided her gently to the center of the finished basement, encouragement for a shy girl. Suzanne wore a special party dress with a ruffled collar and matching hem, white tights, and black shoes that she'd shined the night before. She looked around, almost dizzy from all the attention, and began to sing "Little Ducky Duddle" with her hands on her hips, fingers flared outward for a ducklike profile. She bobbed up and down as she sang, flexing her knees and leaning her upper body from side to side, trying gamely to amuse. But she saw her sister's quick disdain and the way she began to laugh, her sister's friends, too. By the time she finished those few lines her voice softened to a whisper, and her body grew damp with embarrassment. Her mother clapped, and so did a few of the older girls, but Suzanne wanted to slink away. She'd never fit in. Not in that family. Never.

She stepped into the stream for want of any direction at all, or maybe to chill the sting of remembrance that burned like a wire brush on her back. But the stream tricked her with its clarity, and a foot of water turned into three, and she plunged to her hips. Gasping, she lunged toward the opposite bank, numb momentum carrying her forward. Three steps along she lost her footing on the mossy bottom and fell to the side. She thrust out her hand to break her fall, but her fingers slid on the slick rocks that lined the bed. She tumbled all the way in, managing to keep only her head above the surface. She rose in a spasm of shivers. Her arms clutched her naked chest, and her fingers burned as if she'd touched an electric range. For seconds she could not move. Then she slogged forward and climbed from the icy water into the frozen air.

Now she knew she'd die. She had no strength to go on. For what? The onslaught of snow?

She staggered from the bank and stepped through a thin layer of ice that covered a small puddle. She heard the frozen surface crack, but felt nothing, just the stumps she had for feet.

After edging past the broken ice, she felt herself crumple to the whitening ground. She hugged her belly and thought of her baby from so long ago. Had The Searcher really found him, or was that a hoax, too? How could she have let so many years go by without finding her son? But she told herself that she'd tried, really tried, and that she'd promised herself to try again. There had been so much time then, but life's most generous allowance had dwindled to these final moments.

Her frozen fingers slipped inside her overalls and cupped her belly, the memory of her son still so near. She spoke his name, the one she'd given him, though back then she hadn't believed she had the right to do anything more than give him away. But she had named him Wells, taken delight in knowing it meant "from the springs." Recalled too how she'd spent hours poring over a book of names she'd discovered hidden under her bed at the home, left in shame and secrecy by another unwed mother.

She tried to stand but couldn't, and she returned to the ground that had received her so well. The flakes fell faster now, paling her skin. She moved beyond cold, beyond the platitudes of hope, grateful for the snug peacefulness she'd finally found lying on the earth itself. Her death would not be bad, not like with him. The end didn't promise pain. It promised nothing worse than a wistful longing for what might have been: finding her son; putting her fractured family together; and going on with her work, taking part in a cause so much greater than herself.

But you're not going to die, she told herself dully. *You're just taking a break. That's all. See, your eyes are open. As long as they're open you're just resting, not dying.* She blinked away the snowflakes alighting on her lashes and tightened her fetal position. *Maybe you'll be rescued.* This became a cozy glow amid the cold, an ember of longing for someone to show up and take care of her, make a fire and brew some tea.

Fire. She thought she smelled smoke but it disappeared in the next breath, a succulent tease that left her dreamy for chamomile or English Breakfast, licorice or peppermint, raspberry, ginger. . . . Teas tantalized her, and in the drift of possibilities she saw herbs boiling in a kettle over an open flame, and steam rising as lazily as a sun-drunk cat. She tried to smell the spicy scents and imagined the taste of warm scones with strawberry jam. Just as quickly her head filled with a tangy cloud of wood smoke, and this made her think of oranges in the middle of winter, bright colors on a Sunday table, and meats roasting in a pan with peeled potatoes browning beside them, onions limp in a bubbling stew of buttery drippings. Carrots too, sweet and crunchy with brown sugar crusted on their candied backs. Meat, oh yes, juices still crackling from the heat of the oven. Hunger made her dizzy with desire. In her excitement this morning she'd managed no more than a light breakfast, and whatever had remained of its weak sustenance had been lost to her sickness in the car.

Her eyes closed in concentration, and the flakes fell on her unmoistened lids. She felt their frail weight, the hypnotic rhythm of their soft teeming. She nested in these comforts and inhaled sensuously, seeking the wanton evocations of scent: teas and meats and oranges. Smoke. Smoke. *Smoke.*

She lifted her head, driven by the stupefied belief that if she could only open her eyes one more time she would see, actually see gray currents drifting by. Her eyes parted the thin veil of snow that had formed on her lids, but no, no smoke greeted her, only the world turning white by degrees. She blinked and settled back down, but the smell, now vaguely pungent, nagged her. Groggy, as if drugged by the opulence of dreams, she rose onto her bloody elbow and sniffed curiously. No, wait, that's smoke. *Absolutely.* Smoke!

The odor rallied her, and she sat all the way up, a spectral figure dressed in white. There was no mistaking it now. She'd smelled it when they'd driven by the slash fires, and surely she smelled it now. *Fire.* She imagined the heat radiating from those huge piles, rising wastefully into the chill air, heat that could dry her out and save her life. How far? How far? Or maybe it's coming from a house, a chimney in the forest.

The smoke drew Suzanne to her feet with the promise of warmth, a lure as powerful as food to the starving, or water to those who are dying of thirst.

27

IT'S MISERABLY COLD, the kind of cold that really does cut to your core. I've got a chill running deep into my chest, and it's going to take hours to get this icy feeling out of me.

How many times have we heard that desperate times call for desperate murders? I mean *measures*. Freudian slip there—I'm so cold I can't even think straight. Everybody thinks they live in desperate times, especially nowadays; but they have no idea, do they? No idea how truly desperate it can get.

I do. After I finally realized I wasn't going to find her, I had to take a desperate measure of my own. It sounds like I made a decision, but it wasn't a decision. It was the very definition of desperation.

The night overcame me and left me with no choice. It descended so slowly, I hardly noticed. It was like a candle out of string, sputtering in a buttery pool of wax. One minute the light was weak, fragile as a baby's skull, and the next it was gone, and the daytime shadows had dissolved into darkness.

I knew better than to try to find my way out of here at night. That'd be a good way to die. I'm going to have to wait for morning, and then I don't think it'll be a problem. But for the next twelve hours, I'm stuck. That's how long I'm guessing the nights are up here. Six hours of this would be long. Twelve hours will be an eternity.

It's enough to make me think that the biggest mistake I ever made was leaving the desert behind. I'm out of my element, and now I'm facing the night, all this cold and ice and snow.

But so is she, and if I'm cold, she's frozen; and if she's frozen, she's even more desperate than I am.

I've given up calling her name. Given up on any of that. If I'd had the chance to train her, she'd have come when I called. All the others did. All the others except Ami did exactly what I wanted them to do exactly when I wanted them to do it. But I won't have time to train Ms. Trayle. I'll consider it good if I have five minutes with her, and if I do, I want my questions answered, questions about Laura Kissing and anyone else she might have told about her stupid sting.

If I don't find her, all's not lost. It's the beginning of winter, the first of the snows. If she ends up collapsing from the cold, the most likely scenario, her body will stay buried for months. So if I don't find her by the time I head out, I'll make sure I drop my gun in a creek before I get back to the road. And I'll make sure I have a story ready, in case there are cops waiting. I have a long night to come up with a story.

But chances are I'm not going to need one. I'll step over that ditch and leave all of this behind. And if at that point I haven't found Ms. Trayle, if I haven't had a chance to pry a few answers out of her, then I'll start looking for Laura Kessing, and hope like hell I get to her before she finds out that the cops are looking for her search angel.

Not that I've given up on Ms. Trayle, not by any means. It's just that in these frigid conditions, I've begun to see that patience can be much more rewarding than even the most vigorous pursuit.

28

T HE SMOKE DISAPPEARED, and Suzanne worried that she'd never really smelled it. She trudged on feeling stupid, numb, hopeless, longing for the smell of smoke so deeply that she wept.

Her overalls had frozen, and the bib and straps, stiff and abrasive as sandpaper, had chafed her shoulders, back, and breasts. Movement had not brought her feet to life, and her hands were almost useless from the first stages of frostbite.

But the smoke came back to her, delicious, delirium-inducing smoke, the last breath of the dying forest. Its elusive trailings strengthened her as she slogged up a hill steep enough to make her slip and fall back to the snowy earth.

The smoke filled her with the heady glories of heat, like a great white cloud of opium had swirled through her brain. The swift abundance made her stagger with anticipation, and she looked for the house from which it might have arisen, the well-lit windows that would reveal a hearth with a wall of warm stones, and a fireplace or woodstove alive with logs that burned and glowed and sizzled with life-giving heat. The smoke smelled so rich that she knew she must be close, but no matter where her eyes strained she saw no house, no sweetly lambent windows, just the anguished frozen forest, pale and icy and hunkered down for the long night.

Snow rose over her ankles, and the temperature dropped as she climbed higher and higher. She turned to see the path she'd trod, but the night was now as dark as the holes she'd left behind.

A fresh taste of smoke righted her course and reminded her of the duty she had to her life, and to the lives of all The Searcher would kill. She made herself savor each strand of scent, and her flesh responded with a primitive longing. She saw all the hot coals that had ever warmed her, in woodstoves, in campgrounds, in the autumnal fires of childhood when red and yellow and orange leaves curled and crinkled and blackened in burn barrels and rose in gray formless shapes to the empty, expectant sky.

The acrid scents followed one upon the other quickly now, like footprints on a trail. The intervals of untouched air withered, and she felt herself drawing nearer and nearer, though the glow had not appeared, but that's . . . that's because the forest is so thick. *Thick,* she said to herself, *thick.* Like her brain, her tongue, those parts of her that could no longer think or speak clearly.

Now the smoke burned her nose. But why couldn't she see the house, the flames?

Because . . . because there was no house. No windows alive with light, no break in the trees, no dark rooflines. She stopped, and her body swayed inside her frozen overalls. No, no house.

But fire. She saw its glow, barely perceptible through more than a hundred yards of forest. She tried to run, but stumbled and had to grapple with the trees to find her balance. Then she pitched herself forward with visions of standing over the flames, embracing the air above the coals until her body ran sweet with sweat, and her overalls slumped from the heat.

She tripped and fell, mishaps that slowed her but never calmed her enthusiasm. She clambered to her feet, smacked her numb hands together to knock off the snow, and drove herself on. The fire now burned brightly. She believed she could actually feel its heat. She smiled. A slash fire. Enough wood to burn all night. To save her. She could have laughed out loud for all the simple joy she felt.

Smoke burned her eyes, she didn't care. Twenty feet, yes, ten. And then a whole wall of heat greeted her, and she dropped to her knees, lacking the strength to stand over the flames as she had envisioned. She hovered covetously close to the fire. Heat tingled her flesh, and she raised her frozen hands and put them out. *Be careful,* she warned herself, *you're so cold you could burn them.*

She was enormously pleased to find herself thinking clearly, even to feel the ringing ache in her hands as their numbness melted away. Heat enveloped her, and she experienced a bright infusion of clarity and common sense.

Rejoicing, she drew her fingers to her cheeks. A dim sensation penetrated her skin, and slowly she felt the pressure of her hands and their warmth. It was as if a mask had been lifted from her undying flesh, and now she could know her own true face. Then she asked herself another question: *Why? Why a bonfire out here?* This wasn't a slash fire. She could see that now. It didn't stand eight or ten feet high. It was big, six, seven feet across, up to her waist when she'd been standing, but nothing compared to what the loggers burned.

Warily, she looked at the trees that surrounded her, the skeletal shadows of trunks and limbs flinching in the amber light. *This doesn't make any sense.* And then a horrifying thought violated her, an insane thought really: She had died in the stream. She'd drowned in the frigid water and left her body on the mossy rocks that lined the bottom. It had been her spirit that had shivered as she rose not from the stream, but from her own flesh, and if she were to return to the snow-covered bank she would see herself as she had seen others who had died, with eyes open and empty and staring into an unblinking universe. She realized that every step she'd taken on her numb journey into the night had been part of her penance. Heaven, she understood finally, was this fire in the forest. That's what God had granted her because that's what she'd sought most dearly at the moment of death. She fixed on this thought so thoroughly that she saw herself from a distance, as she had seen the fire itself minutes ago. It was clear to her now why she knelt before the flames: She was a worshiper who had found her final salvation in the sacred heart of heat.

She reached down and clutched a handful of snow, gazed at the ice crystals and discovered a single ponderosa pine needle buried in their midst, tawny colored and long as her finger. She broke it in two just to see it snap. *No*, she told herself, *this is real*, real. *Why would God bother to build a fire for me? For Suzanne Trayle?*

The broken pine needle fell from her hand, and she stared at it lying in the snow. Then she looked up and saw him on the far side of the fire, his face glowing red above the flames, and knew without question that it was not her heaven that she had found.

29

I T T O O K H E R almost ten minutes to see me. Ten minutes of staggering up to this fire and kneeling down, raising her hands like she was in church. *Glory be to God.* Easy to see the good Catholic girl she used to be.

I let her warm up. I sat on a rock in the shadows and let her soak up the flames. *That's it,* I said to myself, *get nice and warm. Fire is your friend.*

She has Ami to thank for the flames. A secret smoker. She was ashamed of her filthy habit; and when I held them up, she turned away, as if even then she didn't want me to know. Or perhaps she had sensed for the very first time the intimate, inner life of a flame, the one I was about to reveal to her. No telling now.

I kept the cigarettes and matches, sniffed them several times during the past week. Olfactory memories are among the strongest, and tobacco smells especially sweet when it's mixed with the sulfur of an unburnt match. Strike the match and light the cigarette, and it stinks; but before they burn the odor can be intoxicating.

But I didn't spend any time playing scratch-and-sniff games tonight. What I did do was work like a hound to find dry pine needles and branches. I had to dig under clumps of fallen boughs to come up with enough of the dry stuff to make a fire.

Then I used the cigarettes, not just the matches, to get it going. The tobacco companies have always denied putting gunpowder in their cigarettes to keep them burning; but anyone who's ever smoked knows that they must use some kind of accelerant because if they didn't, all but the driest, harshest tobacco would snuff itself out.

Winstons do not snuff themselves out, I'm here to say (Ms. Trayle will attest to that soon enough). No, Winstons will burn until they leave behind a gray caterpillar of ash, or until they start a fire. I made four of those caterpillars before I succeeded.

When those flames started to rise, I'm not ashamed to say that I almost cried out with joy. I needed a fire to survive, but it was also my only hope of finding her. Once I'd lost her, I said to myself, *you're never going to hunt her down in the dark. You've got to make her come to you.*

I knew we couldn't have been too far apart, and the wind would help me. It had been an insatiable, invisible beast all afternoon and night, racing through the trees, rising up the hills, dropping into gullies, bouncing off boulders. And as the first puffs of smoke rose from the fire and were swept away, I saw that I was right, that the smoke would travel over greater and greater distances.

One good sting deserves another. What was she going to need more than anything else in the middle of this black, frozen forest but heat and light, those sweet providers of life? I gave her what she thought she wanted, and now I'm going to take it away.

30

Suzanne jumped to her feet, losing the strap of her overalls to her elbow. She yanked it back up, covering the bra so briefly exposed.

She'd moved no more than a few feet before he shouted, "You leave here, you're going to die."

The truth of it stunned her. *But I'm dead if I stay.* She stared into the darkness and wondered how far she could run before he chased her down and murdered her in the brutal frozen blackness of the night. As horrifying as she found this, it was the bite of the cold that turned her back to the fire.

He pulled a branch from the flames and waved it at the shadows surrounding them. The red tip flared in the wind, and she saw the damage it could do.

"You're dead if you leave here. Do you have *any* idea where you are?" He tossed the branch back into the fire.

No, she didn't. She'd been lost, and now she was found. One as bad as the other. Each promised death. She recognized this as clearly as she saw the snowflakes falling into the flames and heard their helpless sizzle.

He sat on a rock, as if to invite her closer, then reached into his jacket and pulled out an energy bar. He made a show of unwrapping it, biting into it.

She was starving, and the cold began to creep over her again. A sudden spasm shook her. She simply could not outrun him. He was younger, faster, warmer. And she needed heat. She'd die without it.

He continued to sit and eat, as if he had no fear of her escape.

"Do you have any more?" She needed calories to fight the cold, to stay alive. To fight him.

He laughed. "Of course. I've got them in banana and chocolate." He reached back into his jacket and held one up. "Come and get it."

She approached the fire, and a wave of heat broke over her. She would move no closer. He dangled the bar. She didn't even know she was shaking her head no until he said, "You don't want it, fine. I'll save it for later, for when I work up a really good appetite."

She looked at the branch he'd waved around and wondered if she could pull one out fast enough. But then what?

"You really bought the bait," he said.

"The bait?" He wants to talk, make him talk. "What bait?"

"This." He nudged the fire with his boot. A flame shot up. "You lose someone in the great outdoors, you start a fire. They'll come around. Especially when it's this cold. *Brrrr.*" He gripped himself and laughed. Then his face straightened and he pointed to her.

"Once you got away, I knew I'd never find you, but I came close, didn't I?" She nodded.

"I can't hear you."

"Yes, you did."

"Where?"

"In the clearing. I saw you stop and look around." *Keep him talking. Oh God, for what? For hours if you have to.* "Do you remember?"

"The clearing? No kidding. Where were you?"

"In a tree."

"A tree!" He slapped his leg.

"How'd you do it?"

"How'd I do what?"

"Get the fire going?"

"You think I'm stupid, don't you?"

"What?" She faked indignation.

"You think you're going to keep me talking all night, and what? I'll fall asleep or something?" He pointed to her. "We're talking right now because I want to. I'm getting my strength up. And besides, I like looking at you."

It was enough to make her turn away, and she did, but the fear that came from not seeing his every move spun her back around. She was perspiring profusely. Fire and fear. Snow spattered on the coals, the sloppy kiss of steam.

He unwrapped the rest of the bar, put it in his mouth, and reached down to a pile of branches to feed the flames.

Her body was so alive from the heat that she could feel every snowflake on her skin, icy sprinkles that stung, and she wondered if she'd made a terrible mistake standing so close to the fire: If she were numb, she'd feel so much less when he started.

She heard the sizzle of snowflakes again, and the spitting and popping of green wood, all that sap boiling alive. Her time was up. She knew it, could feel it in the way he looked at her.

He took his first step toward her. His second and third were lost in the blur of his advance. She turned, as much to protect herself as to flee, but felt hopeless on both counts. He grabbed her from behind and wrapped a powerful arm around her neck. The back of her head pressed against his jacket. She smelled vomit, and then smoke drifted over them and burned her nostrils.

"We should finish what we started . . ." He thrust his hand under the loose-fitting bib, seizing her breast. She gasped, but he paid her no mind, ending his sentence in a whisper, ". . . don't you think? Take them off."

She tried to nod, to let him know she'd cooperate, but any attempt to move her head was mugged by the arm that crushed her neck. She reached down and slapped her overalls, like a woman trying to find loose change in her pockets. Then she squeezed fistfuls of fabric, found the metal buttons on the right side, and undid the first of them by feel.

Do what he says, she told herself. *Do it. Appease him.*

Her fingers found the second button as the pressure on her throat increased. She stabbed spastically at the third.

"You're too slow. Faster, faster."

His lips brushed her ear, and his hot spit made her shake. Her breast throbbed from his fierce grip, and her fingers ached before she could free the third button.

"Ami was a lousy lay. You know that?" His words quickened, as if he'd grown excited. "She wouldn't even take me in her mouth. But you're making up for all that."

She squirmed, seeking a weakness, a way out of his arms. He responded by biting her ear so savagely she could feel him crushing the cartilage. She cried out and froze, fearing any movement at all, and then she felt his breath, amplified by intimacy, his nostrils pumping out hot, moist air.

He ground the gristly flesh with his front teeth, but it was she who tasted salt, the brooding advance of blood that came from chewing her own lip.

In a muffled voice, he said, "Maybe I should bite it off. What do you think?"

She couldn't talk, she could barely breathe. All she felt were his teeth, and the hurricane of breath in her ear.

He ran his hand down to the waistband of her underpants and yanked them up so hard her body lifted. He released her ear and spit on the side of her face. "I want you to tell me something. And don't lie. If you lie, it'll get worse. I want you to tell me what Laura Kessing knows."

"She doesn't know anything."

His arm tightened around her throat, and his voice deepened. "You're lying, Ms. Trayle. You had to tell her something to get her house."

"Please," she gagged, "I can't talk."

"You better talk fast."

He ended his choke hold, and her lungs expanded rapidly in relief.

"I told her Burton and I needed a place to get away. We'd been having problems. Separated. That's all."

"You lie. You *lie*. You told her all about your stupid little sting. I know you did, didn't you?"

"No, I swear. I didn't want to put her in danger."

In his pause, she sensed a smile.

"We know each other so well, don't we? And now I'm going to get to know you even better. I'm going to get to know you inside and out, face-to-face. Now get them off."

She felt empty, soulless, sinking like a ghost ship.

He tightened his grip again, and she choked and fumbled as she undid the buttons on the left side of her overalls. Her mind darkened from lack of air, and she feared she'd black out. Once more his arm relaxed, but just enough to let her fill her lungs with a labored wheeze.

"Where is she? Tell me now, or tell me later after I hurt you really bad."

"Tahiti."

"I like that. It's warm there. Where in Tahiti?"

"I don't know."

"That's too bad, because if you knew you could help yourself. Where's her kid live?"

"What kid?"

She felt him shake his head, as if he felt sorry for her. His hand still clutched her waistband, and his knuckles dug into her belly. She thought that would be it, what more could he do? His right arm ended the choke hold, and she breathed deeply, gratefully. But then his fingers crawled over her face and pressed against her eyes, and he spoke in a voice that scarcely rose above the sound of the fire.

"You're trying to keep me from seeing the truth, so I'm going to tell you about rattlesnakes. You know about them?"

She started to shake her head no, but couldn't: those fingers on her eyes.

"Then you better listen carefully."

He pushed down sharply. The pressure lit up her lids with ghastly flashes of yellow and red and purple, explosions of color and piercing pain.

"Rattlesnakes lose their skin. You know about that, right? All snakes do."

He released her waistband to shake his hand in front of her face, the tail of a rattler. A hissing sound filled her ear. As quickly, he stilled his voice.

She took a deep breath and shifted slightly, anything to ease the pressure on her eyes. But he pressed down harder, punishing even the smallest insurrection. She cried out, only to be shushed with a laugh, as if her suffering were a trifle.

"When a rattlesnake loses its skin, it can't see a thing. For a whole day or two, it can't see a single thing. It's blind!"

His fingers drilled her eyes. She thought they'd explode. Pain so migrainous she couldn't move, and terrified that if she did his fingers would slip to the side and plunge into her skull. Seconds passed like this. An eternity. Her breath pulsed sharply, a woman giving birth to agony, splitting her apart with a ragged torn life of its own. A scream pealed from her lips. For three or four seconds it rent the night, then ceased with a speed that could have come from a bullet or a blade. Her breath pulsed in its wake, as it had before. He continued to talk without easing the pressure, as if he'd never been interrupted.

"The skin's like a hood over the eyes. The snake senses anything, anything at all, it strikes. It has to. It doesn't have any choice because it can't see what's out there. It could be something bad. You get it, don't you? *I'm* like that snake. I can't see what I've got to see, so I'm striking out at *you*. You tell me where she is, then I can see again, and I'll feel a whole lot better. So will you. That's a promise. But if you lie to me one more time, I'm going to rip out your eyes. Then I'll hand them to you and make you stuff them back into your head. I've done it before, and I'll do it to you. You better think about that. There's not going to be any looking for birth mothers, I can tell you that much. The great Search Angel's not going to be searching anymore."

She screamed as he began to crush her eyes.

"Please-please-please-plea—"

"Where . . . is . . . she?"

"The Royal Tahitian Resort."

He pushed her forward, and she put out her arms to catch herself. The pain rushed from her eyes, and she wept as her hands sank into the snow. She'd saved Laura, Laura's children, too. But there was no saving herself. She'd never believed he'd spare her, not even now that he let her go.

She groped in the snow, saw only blurry shapes, trees and shadows, before he yanked her overalls down to her knees. She hadn't realized she was on all fours. She tried to crawl, but he'd already grasped her underpants.

"Where are you going, *Ms. Trayle*? It's time for you to make amends." He tensed the waistband as he had minutes ago. "Do what I say or I'll grab your eyes and rip them out right now."

As her vision began to clear, he jerked her underpants down to her knees. She turned her head to look back at him and met his fist. A quick, horrible hurt. Her eyes flooded, and the blurriness returned.

He saw what he'd accomplished and stared at her.

Her hand rose to her cheek. So clearly dazed. She hardly had time to sit before he dragged her to the fire and unzipped his pants. When she looked up she saw his uncircumcised penis in the flickering light, thickening, lengthening, as if hungry for more of what it had tasted.

"Put . . . it . . . in . . . your . . . mouth." Words as sharp as stones on snow.

She would have wept, but he'd kill her. She was sure of it. She pulled her overalls up around her waist.

"Do it!"

She jerked away without thinking, not of life or death. He grabbed her hair and forced her forward. "You do it, or you're going to die like Ami."

The sight of him revolted her. She worked to swallow saliva, as if her own juices might settle her roiling stomach. She reached for his penis, but he slapped her hand.

"No," he hissed. "Don't touch it. Use your mouth. That's all."

He yanked her head up, saw her face bruised and bloody, and squeezed her jaw, forcing the oval of her lips.

Her stomach rolled, as it had in the car, but now she sickened without any effort. She fought the spasm, believing that if she vomited on him again, he'd murder her immediately. Or worse: He'd murder her slowly. She closed her eyes as she opened her mouth, then told herself, *No, no, keep them open.* So she saw when she touched the tip.

She tried to bury her tongue in the back of her mouth, had accepted no more than an inch when the gag reflex arose. She tried mightily to think of ice, of snow, the frozen world that surrounded her. Anything but this. Times when she was so cold she couldn't feel, times when she couldn't feel and didn't care.

He leaned over. "You better get moving." He ran his fingers over her eyes again, pausing to press each of them.

She buried her hands in the fabric of her overalls, her fingers clenching and unclenching, as if steeling herself to keep going.

He grabbed the hair on the back of her head and forced her to take all of him. She couldn't bear the taste, or the feel of the thick vein violating her lower lip. But she made herself perform the act. His hand fell away, as if it had done its duty. Seconds later she saw it flexing by his side, all of him stiffening.

She tensed, too, then feared he'd sense her resolve and all it now harbored; but when she looked up his eyes were accepting, as if the pleasure were his due, and she a lover of long standing. Her right hand rose quickly from her pocket, and his eyes widened as he saw what it held. She hacked him with the box cutter, and then again even more deeply.

He squealed and stumbled back. She threw herself to the side, pulling up her overalls so they wouldn't bind her, but her legs were tangled in her underpants. She struggled with them without looking down, too horrified to take her eyes off him. He stood stunned, blood washing down his pants, as she scurried backward on the ground, retreating like a crab.

His hands seized his penis, as if to stop the flow. She cursed when she saw it still hanging there. His eyes looked up, and he lunged for her.

She scrambled to her feet, legs still caught in her underwear. He reached out and grabbed the bib hanging from her waist. She tried to back right out of her clothes, and hacked wildly at him with the box cutter. But in the confusion of his advance and her retreat, she couldn't tell if she'd sliced through his jacket to his skin.

His face, wrenched in pain, closed within inches of hers. She continued to stagger backward, hands and arms tangled in his, hoping he'd collapse from loss of blood, that it would drain away his murderous hate and every last ounce of his life. But he moved with her, matching her step for step. They covered ten feet in two or three seconds. She backed right into the trunk of a giant fir. His body slammed into her, pinning the hand with the box cutter next to his thigh.

"You're fucking dead." Spittle sprayed her as he screamed.

But even in his fury, he never moved the hand that clutched his penis, as if deathly fearful of a loss of blood. Neither did he ease the pressure that kept her weapon in check. A standoff that lasted for several seconds while they stared at each other, so close she could smell his breath, almost taste his hate.

He tried shifting his free hand upward, and she knew instinctively that he wanted to tear at her face, her eyes. The move covered only a few inches, but it freed her enough to twist the point of the box cutter into his leg. She felt the resistance of taut muscle and spotted a tremor in his cheek. Incited, she dug the razor deeper into his flesh, desperate for the scrape of bone.

"Drop it." A deep, guttural utterance.

She'd never give it up, he'd have to tear it from her fist; but she nodded and said, "All right." Made to let it go.

He lunged for her throat, and as his hand closed on her skin she brought the blade straight up, slicing him open all the way from his thigh to his chest, scoring him like an orange.

He inhaled sharply, as if shocked, and glanced down. She spotted his weakness and whipped the box cutter across his eyes, forward and back, slashing both of them on the return motion.

His hands flew to his face, and she bolted to the side. He tore at his eyes as if to eviscerate the pain. She backed up, legs churning as she reached down to pull up her underpants and overalls. His head whirled from side to side, and when he rushed into a branch, she knew she'd blinded him.

A howl, slow and gruesome, rose from his bent form.

She could leave now, race into the forest and let him die his own slow death. She had done what she had to do to survive. She spit at the memory of his taste and turned to the fire. But an understanding came to her reluctantly, as if she'd already fought too many battles at once: fatigue, fear, and the undying desire for flight. She stared at the flames and accepted that if she left, she would return to a world where her body had been battered by the cold, and her thoughts had grown slow and stupid.

You can't go. Out there, her eyes traveled the darkness, there's snow and ice and death. But here, she looked back at the bent figure hunched over in pain, you've got a wounded blinded beast of a man. She sickened again when she realized that she would not only have to stay, but somehow, some way, she would have to kill him.

BLOOD STREAMED DOWN his face, torso, pants. Suzanne backed away, her own face slick with thick red smears. He must have heard her move because he stepped forward, carefully this time, with one hand still on his crotch, the other leading his way.

Kill him.

Hatred mauled whatever pity she might have mustered. It made her world no different from his.

Kill him.

He reached into his jacket and pulled out his gun, shocking her less with the weapon than with the certain knowledge that he'd never feared her, never believed she could fight back.

But as she studied him, the gun became less a curiosity than a deadly obstacle to her desire to murder him. It would complicate her chore, and if it kept her from the fire, it would freeze her to death.

He leveled the barrel and pointed it a few feet to her left, head high, then swiveled his arm like a tank turret. She ducked, and watched as he stabbed the darkness to her right. He didn't appear to know where she was, but she drew little consolation from this observation: The fire held them both in its orbit, and he had to be aware that even now she wouldn't veer from its warm promise of life.

She stilled her breath and tried to will away a spell of shivers, fearful that he'd sense even the smallest movements of the flesh. The only sounds that punctuated the silence arose from the fire, the snowflakes that fell on the coals, and the green wood that still spit and popped, though less frequently now that the flames had begun to surrender. Neither she nor the fire could remain untended for long. She saw a pile of branches stacked near the large rock where he'd been sitting, but they lay a good twenty feet from where she now stood.

The gun passed over her two more times. Then he jabbed it forward, as if to fire, and she inhaled. Her hand flew to her mouth when she understood that he might have flushed her out. The gun came back toward her, the barrel an eye, uncannily sentient as it looked for her. She crouched down quickly and stepped aside as a bullet ripped the air a foot above her head, and a few feet to her left. It would have missed even if she hadn't moved. She took another step as he inched forward with the gun in one hand, the other still on his crotch. His eyes were clenched shut, as hers had been when she'd been in his grip. But she saw in his agony not the edge she had gained, but the violent depth of his revenge. She had to make him use those bullets, and then she had to find a way to kill him.

Carefully she picked up a rock and lobbed it over his head. It landed with a moist thud, and he swung toward the sound. Then he whipped back around, as if he'd figured out what she'd done. She retreated three strides toward the fire before she saw the pistol moving toward her. She lost her nerve and stopped abruptly, hoping his arm would sweep past. But it didn't, and his aim landed squarely on her face, though he gave no indication of knowing this, for he shifted it left and right, inches at first, then a foot or two at a time, passing it back over her every few seconds. When he finally steadied the muzzle, it pointed directly at her again.

Less than ten feet separated them. The heat washed over her. Smoke too, thick dark drapes that threatened to choke her, but she didn't dare move. Her eyes teared ferociously, tortured by the fumes. She squeezed them shut, as blind in these moments as he. Breathing no better. She felt like she was swallowing fire, each searing second a conflagration in her nose and throat that kindled a cough in her chest. She was seized by the need to expel the noxious air. Her upper body shook, and she held her hand over her face like a mask. Pure illusion. It filtered nothing, least of all her fear. Still, she clenched her mouth and nose and suffered the wrenching revolt of her lungs as quietly as she could, silence her only shield.

He grunted, and she dropped her hand and opened her watery eyes, unsure if the sound had come from pain, frustration, or fury. But not a clue creased his face, not even now. All that pain, and he appeared no less intent than any other predator ready to pounce.

They remained like this, both of them motionless, both of them quiet, for a full minute, then two. Agony as eternity, breath its unstinting second hand. The fire made the only noise as snowflakes continued to eat the flames. She knew without having to think that she had to reach the pile of branches or she'd suffer a slow death, and whether he lived or died would matter less and less as the night wore on; but she also worried that her legs, deadened by cold and wind, would refuse to move.

He stepped forward, stumbled, and she raced on her naked numb feet to a tree near the large rock and the fire, coughing wildly at last, gulping fresh air, and rubbing her eyes, blinking them fiercely.

Looking out, always wary, she saw him halt, as if he now understood that so little had stood between them. She reached for a branch, slipped it from the pile, and tossed it into the flames. His head turned toward the sound, not toward her, so she did it again. He never pointed the gun, and it occurred to her that he might want her to do this. The wet branches smoked, but within a minute the needles began to burn.

She carefully retrieved two more branches, tossing them into the fire as well. One rolled almost all the way out. Only its tip lay smoking on the coals. *The hell with it,* she thought. *That'll do for now.*

He turned his head, as if to lead with his ears, and approached her slowly, shuffling, probably to keep from tripping again. She picked up a fist-sized rock, and when he moved closer, she threw it, spinning back behind the trunk as it left her hand. She heard it hit a tree and swore to herself.

Even then, when he must have known how close she was, he didn't shoot, a reluctance that made her realize that he was saving bullets. He'd already fired once at her, and there was that shot back at the road, which she assumed had killed the man who'd stopped. He'd also used two bullets on Burt. So that was four in all. He had a revolver. Six shots total, so that left him with two more, if he hadn't reloaded. Then what? She had no idea.

The gun hung by his side, reflecting the light of the fire, while he soaked up the intense heat that she desired so dearly.

He raised the gun until it pointed straight ahead, as if she might have been right there, an easy target for his unseeing eyes. His words came back to her, the taunts and mockery when he'd tortured her. Those goddamn words. She threw them back at him now.

"We're going to have to finish what we started. We're going to have to cut your penis *all* the way off."

He stared in her direction, perhaps stunned by the viciousness of her voice, the words and tone she'd stolen from him. He raised the gun, then lowered it quickly. But then he brought it back up in an instant, pointed and fired. The bullet tore away a fist-sized chunk of bark and would have hit her if the tree hadn't stood between them. But she'd squeezed another round from the chamber. He was spending the only currency he had, wasting it on impulse; and she had discovered a high-stakes strategy: Goad the bastard to death.

"You're shooting blind, but I guess that's the way you're going to be from now on. The *Searcher's* going to be *blind*. Imagine that, a Searcher who can't search."

The taunting felt so juvenile, and yet . . . she began to relish her revenge, to enjoy the strange echo game she was playing with him. And if her words were virulent, her tease perhaps even more venomous, it was only because the voice she'd adopted embraced both his hatred and hers.

He moved toward the tree that protected her, and ran right into a branch on the other side. He pushed it away angrily. She laughed.

"You're such a stupid blind *bastard*. That's all you are now."

She'd willed her voice to the distance, as she thought a ventriloquist would. But he wasn't fooled, and his arms waved wildly as he gained momentum and fended off the branches blocking his way.

Be careful, she warned herself. *Be very careful.* But as soon as she thought of the song, she couldn't stop herself from "Mother and Child Reunion."

As she sang, she circled the tree, always keeping the trunk between them. She could recall so little of the lyrics and had to stop. In the lull came the chilling sound of him struggling with the branches. She wanted to break away, but she needed a better gauge of exactly where he was and where he might appear. Right then he reached around the trunk and clawed the bark inches from her knee. She backed up, terrified that he'd almost touched her, and sprinted to another tree about fifteen feet away.

She turned back as he crawled out from under the lowest bough and stood where she'd been seconds ago. She hadn't anticipated how fast he could move.

He didn't even raise the gun, and she thought he appeared lost, unsure of where she was. But he had the fire in his favor.

She reminded herself that he'd shot again. Five down, one to go. She felt around in the dark for a rock, scooped up two and stepped quietly from behind the cover. But there he was, almost upon her.

The rocks spilled from her hand as she backpedaled behind the tree, then raced away, leaving him clearly befuddled, head twisting left and right. She took shelter behind a smaller tree that stood halfway back to the fire.

She hummed the song now, and he pivoted toward her, tripped, and fell.

"You're a lousy lay, you know that? Your penis is so tiny, no one's going to miss it."

She stepped out from behind the tree to grab a rock the size of a baseball. He regained his feet and inched forward. She could almost feel his concentration. She did not pull back. She kept telling herself he's blind, *blind,* as she waited for him to ease into her line of fire. He cooperated, but slowly.

The angle of his approach was leading him almost directly to her, but his gun still pointed to the ground. She took a long slow breath, drew back her arm, and threw the rock as hard as she could. It struck his mouth with a sickening sound, teeth cracking, maybe bone too.

She ran behind the tree as he weaved sideways, moaning loudly, head low, gun waving madly, as if he expected an onslaught of rocks.

He was in such obvious pain that she expected tears, for the boy to appear in the man. But all she heard were those moans, and they stopped as suddenly as they had begun.

She kept her eyes on him and felt around for another rock. She found one and stood back up. He looked so pathetic. His moans prompted her pity, not much but enough to give her pause.

"We don't have to do this. Put the gun down and back away. Let me have it, and we can share the fire, you on one side, me on the other. I'll keep it going, and we can leave in the morning."

"Fuck you! You think—" He hacked up a tooth and spit it out. His mouth was a bloody, gaping hole. "You think you're getting away with this?"

"Don't be an idiot. You're blind and you're probably bleeding to death. What the hell do you think your chances are?"

He pointed the gun, though not accurately. It shook with his anger. "I've got a good chance of shooting you, and if I do and I'm lucky, you won't die un-til I get my hands on you."

"You have no chance of that. None. You're going to die out here if you don't put that gun down. You're going to bleed to death or freeze to death. You're going to die. That's what you're going to do, die! Now put that gun down and back away."

He bulled his way forward and ran into the tree. She skipped away easily as he fought with the branches. She moved to the fire once more, taking the precious heat while she could.

As he untangled himself, she completed a rough circle by retreating to the fir that she'd hid behind less than ten minutes ago. The heat of the flames rose to her, and she saw that the branches she'd thrown in had caught fire. The blaze now burned as brightly as it had when she'd first glimpsed it through the trees. She added the last of the branches from the pile. A thick pillow of smoke drifted over him. He coughed and tried to cover his face.

"You're pathetic. Drop the gun and back away."

His head turned at the sound of her voice. He raised his weapon defiantly, but it pointed nowhere near her.

She stepped out with the rock she'd picked up moments ago and threw it, striking his shoulder. He dropped his arm and gripped himself, then the gun came right back up and he shot, missing her by a wide margin.

"That's it. You don't have any bullets left. Or can't you count either?"

She prayed she was right, that *she* had counted correctly and that he hadn't reloaded.

He looked in her direction and aimed again. She ducked, so she only heard the empty snap of the trigger, the sound of him squeezing it repeatedly. She was about to plead with him again when he charged her.

She thought immediately of racing back behind the tree, hesitated for a shattering second, then ran several steps into the open and screamed. Terrified?

Yes, but also calculating, deliberately inciting his rage with the scent of fear. He bought the bait. He ran right into the fire.

The flames roared halfway up his body as she grabbed the branch that had all but rolled out of the blaze the first time she'd fed it. She rammed its fiery tip into his gut. He screamed and pushed it aside, but the impact slowed him, and when he tried to force himself forward she jammed it between his legs and tripped him. He fell face-first into the flames.

He shrieked insanely. His hands had plunged into the bed of red coals, and they must have burned to the bone in the seconds it took him to stand. The fire raced up his jacket to his head. The air thickened with the bitter smells of burning skin and hair and melting synthetics.

She raised the branch and screamed as she tomahawked him. The tip flared like a torch on the downswing; then cinders exploded off his scalp and showered his smoking body. The blow didn't drive him back down to the coals, but it did stun him.

When she failed to pull it away quickly enough, he grabbed the end, burning himself on the glowing tip. He pushed it aside and stumbled forward as she cocked it like a baseball bat and swung. All she hit was air, and the momentum spilled her toward him.

He staggered from the flames with a hideous groan as she toppled into him. She recoiled from the collision, but not before he grabbed her arm. She jerked it violently, but he held on. In a seizure of terror, she jammed the smoking end of the branch right into his face. His head snapped away like the head of a snake after it strikes. She backed up, raised the branch, and slammed it down on his head a second time. He collapsed to his knees before pitching forward onto his face.

Her hands stung, as if she'd struck a steel plate on a cold day. She stared at his burned, unmoving body, and began to shake. Frenzy surged through her system, and she pounded his head again and again, until her hands no longer rang from the impact with his skull, which had grown moist and accepting.

She stopped only after she could no longer stand without leaning on her weapon. The bloody tip smoldered in the snow as her eyes traveled to the damage she had done. She'd shattered his cranium, and spotted a length of bone expressed through ragged skin and wet hair. Lines of blood ran down his face and clasped his features like claws. And then, before she could turn away, she also saw the expression of fury she'd frozen on his face.

Trembling, she grew daunted by what she had done and unsure of who she had become. Or what.

But you're alive, she whispered. *You're alive.*

32

ALL THROUGH THE long night she watched him, never once growing sleepy. Fear burdened every moment. When daybreak finally came, she gathered more branches, but she moved cautiously, stiffly, and never so far that she couldn't see him.

She fed the fire, and black smoke fouled the sleepy morning sky. Someone's going to come, she told herself. Two cars by the side of the road. A dead body. Smoke in the air. Someone will come.

At ten after ten two sheriff's deputies and a German shepherd hiked up. The fur on the dog's back rose when it spotted the man lying in the snow, his bloody privates baldly displayed. Both officers drew their weapons. Then they spotted the woman sitting by the fire. She looked at them and blinked tears.

$$\boxed{33}$$

A SINGLE EMPTY ACRE in the middle of Suzanne's neighborhood. Never built on. Never used. And not exactly empty either. For decades garbage had collected beneath its few paltry pines. It wasn't as if her neighbors had turned it into a dump, but assorted urban flotsam—plastic grocery bags, candy wrappers, bottles and cans and the like—had collected in the overgrown grass and thistly bushes.

It had suffered its neglect for as long as Suzanne could remember, almost as if it had been waiting all these years for the teams of people who were claiming it for a children's park.

The call for help had gone out a month ago, about the same time that Suzanne had learned that her final HIV test was negative. A sign-up sheet had been posted on a jerry-built bulletin board set up on the corner of the lot. Suzanne had volunteered to work for two days.

"Bring work gloves, wheelbarrows, rakes, shovels, and hand tools, if you're handy," the flyer advised.

She wasn't particularly handy, but she did own a wheelbarrow, which had been filled since she left her house with the most animated cargo.

"Suz, may I have a treat when we get there?"

Kids and sugar. Over the past four months Suzanne had been getting a quick introduction to a child's appetite for sweets. Darlene Sephs agitated at every opportunity for candy, cookies, and cake. The Three Cs, as Suzanne had come to think of them.

Not that the girl looked like she lived on junk food, or behaved as if she had the sugar "crazies," but she did have a hunger for all things sweet.

"Yes, you may have a treat. I packed one with your lunch."

"What kind?"

"A chocolate graham."

"Thank you."

Comfort food, Suzanne had concluded, for a six-year-old who dearly needed comfort, who had a hole in her soul that would never heal. Darlene's mother had been the first of her birth moms murdered, and providing the details of the death, which the child had demanded, had been a heartbreaking challenge for Suzanne.

How *do* you tell a six-year-old about the murder of her mother?

No easy answers, Suzanne had concluded. No formulas, no reliable guides, so she'd resorted to the most general principle of parents everywhere when they've been asked an awkward question: Answer with no more details than necessary.

And then there were Darlene's questions about the killer: Was he still around? And now that he'd murdered her mom, would he look for her?

It had been far easier to assure Darlene of her safety than for Suzanne to reveal that she herself had slain the man who'd murdered her mother. She'd feared the girl would see her as the same kind of killer and wonder if she'd be the next to die.

But children, she'd learned quickly, have a fierce sense of justice.

"You're saying you killed him?"

"That's right," Suzanne said.

This uncomfortable exchange had taken place only a week after Suzanne had begun adoption proceedings, which was a few days after she'd learned that Darlene's half brother in Fort Lauderdale wouldn't be able to take her: He was undergoing a divorce, an unpleasant possibility for most married couples, but a statistical likelihood for adoptees, many of whom suffered from attachment disorders.

"How?"

Another challenge, that one. Suzanne told her that she'd killed him defending herself on a snowy night in the woods, though in truth Harold Brantley's death had not been as quick as she suggested. The medical examiner determined that she'd beaten him into a coma, and that in the long night that followed he'd died from a combination of head injuries and loss of blood.

That he was, in fact, dead was all that mattered to Suzanne. Not surprisingly, the same held true for her charge, who insisted on seeing his grave. Suzanne had understood immediately that words alone could never reassure Darlene as much as the burial ground itself.

The trip to the municipal cemetery in Washington State produced one final—and dismal—surprise for Suzanne, and a baffling experience for the six-year-old. The Searcher's grave had been festooned with flowers. Several offerings had been left in front of the modest headstone, including a garland of white roses that had been draped across the top of it, and a bouquet of orange tulips whose petals had peeled all the way open, whose pistils protruded brazenly. There had been massive media coverage of his crimes, and these flowers, in all their lurid simplicity, were the harvest.

Worshipful notes, smeared by rain, or perhaps by tears, had been left, too, as if a great personage had died. Darlene asked Suzanne to read them to her, and she pretended to, lying to the girl, and wishing the lie could hold for herself as well, that you really could transform adulation into condemnation so readily.

"You're a horrible man, and you should never have done those terrible things."

But even as Suzanne turned the meaning of these missives upside down, her stomach began to spin, and she wondered what we had become. She'd just read that the creators of a serial killer calendar had announced plans to feature The Searcher next year, marking the dates of his murders with the tools he'd used to commit his crimes: a steam iron, sewing needle, broomstick, all the household items he'd turned into weapons. Symbols of traditional motherhood.

Suzanne's sweetly gentle lies did little to comfort Darlene, who began to cry as she stood before the grave of her mother's murderer. Suzanne put aside her most unsettling thoughts, the notes too, and took the girl in her arms and loved her. There was no other response.

On a wondrous day like this, with Darlene bubbling over at the prospect of a new park, it was easy to forget that adoption could prove difficult, but Suzanne knew too much to kid herself for long. She was as prepared for the pitfalls as anyone, and she remained painfully aware of the burden the girl would always carry. But she also knew it was precisely people like herself who needed to take on the task of raising a child whose mother had been murdered, and whose father had long ago disappeared, for she understood the complexity of adoption and brooked no illusions about its stark demands.

Adopting Darlene had also helped her understand the loss sustained by her own son, whom she'd given up. Or had she? She'd wondered about that. What *do* you call it when babies weren't pried from their mothers' arms so much as from their hearts? From women like herself who'd been persuaded to hand over their infants to strangers so their babies could have "a better life."

Suzanne had accepted this lie and had been duped into believing that once the adoption was completed, she'd be free to live the rest of her life.

Free?

There had been nothing free about it. The price had been the deepest longing she'd ever known, a gritty realization that resonated again when her own son had refused to see her.

Two months passed before he finally consented to talk on the phone, and then only to ask, "Why'd you give me away?"

Suzanne spent many hours in the ensuing weeks trying to explain her life as a pregnant fourteen-year-old in 1972. She told him she'd had no choice: She had been a child herself, and her parents had insisted she give up her baby; the nuns at St. Mary's had never offered her any other option either.

But all he'd said in response was that he'd sooner die than give up his own baby girl.

She wept in frustration and had to fight a powerful impulse to say, "Don't you realize what I did for you? That I almost died trying to save you? That your father did die?" But she wouldn't burden him with guilt, not with her own conscience still muddied by what she'd done to him thirty-two years ago. She also knew the poignant irony of birth mothers who'd spent decades finding their children, only to face an agonizing inability to reach them.

There were no breakthroughs for Suzanne until a wrenching insight left her clutching her stomach. It came in the midst of writing yet another late-night letter to him. In that grievous moment, she understood that giving up her son had been the biggest, most tragic mistake of her life, and that she'd sacrifice everything she'd ever had and everything she'd ever become just to re-call that decision.

She knew that for many birth mothers adoption had been a blessed, if bittersweet experience; but as her letter dampened with regret, Suzanne saw that her adulthood, like the adulthood of so many of the women she'd worked with, had been one long struggle to find what had been taken from her as a child: the only baby she'd ever borne.

Her honesty with herself and with him had provided an opening, and they met for the first time last week when she flew to Nashville.

She spotted the resemblance to Burton as soon as he greeted her in the downtown restaurant where they'd arranged to meet. He had the same light wavy hair and strong build, the same eyes and smile, too. But after all the simplistic and sensationalistic news stories purporting to link blood ties to bloodletting, she felt an anguished need to point out the obvious differences between Robert Byers and his infamous half brother.

"You've got a family, a child, a life that's so much bigger than anything he ever had. Harold Brantley was—"

"A nothing," he finished for her. "I don't care what the papers and TV say, he was never a brother to me, and he never will be."

He needed little coaxing to turn the subject to his daughter. She was twenty-one months old now, and he spoke of her with such obvious warmth that Suzanne wasn't at all surprised when he said that he and his wife planned to have at least one more child. In his earnestness, she sensed the softness that would make him a marvelous father. Clearly, he'd been raised with love, care, and great kindness. She could have asked no more of the world that had taken him away, except to have given him back a long time ago.

When she'd arrived at that restaurant, he'd greeted her by himself with an obligatory handshake. When she departed Nashville two days later, he brought her granddaughter to the terminal. Suzanne cried at her first sight of the toddler. In Juney she saw her own oval face and fair complexion, blonde hair, and—if she could allow herself an immodest moment—the same beauty that she glimpsed in her own childhood photos.

Suzanne kneeled and the girl looked up into her eyes.

"Juney," her dad said, "this is Grandma Suzanne. She's your granny, too."

Suzanne hugged the girl and then hugged her son, and had never felt a greater love. It was as if the very cells of her body were reclaiming their own, a depth of feeling she'd known only once before, and that had been thirty-two years ago in Kansas City, Missouri, in a home for unwed mothers.

Suzanne had her sorrows, too, and they all had names. Henrik Johansson was the man who'd stopped to see why a nearly naked woman had fallen out of a car on a lonely road.

"A Good Samaritan, that's what he always was," his widow said.

The news that he'd helped save Suzanne's life came as little solace to his wife, and Suzanne understood why: She herself was a widow, too, and knowing that her husband had also died trying to save her sometimes made the burden of surviving twice as hard to bear.

And then there was Ami, whose body had never been found. Suzanne harbored no hope that the girl was alive, knew with the grimmest certainty that The Searcher had spoken the truth when he'd bragged that he'd killed her.

She remembered Ami every day and prayed that wherever she lay, her repose was easy, her rest never disturbed.

The ground was still damp from a spring shower that had passed in the early morning hours, and the sun now raised the moist mushroom scent of the needle duff beneath Suzanne's work boots. She smelled it when she paused to check on Darlene, who was busy with her new friends on the far side of the lot, running and laughing under the eyes of the young man who was handling child care.

"Hurry, Suz. We want to play in the park," Darlene shouted.

Suzanne waved back and started loading cedar-stained four-by-fours into the wheelbarrow. She rolled it over to the volunteers building stairs near one of the three slides. Other men and women were placing truck tires in the ground to form a step bridge.

After she unloaded the wood, Suzanne paused again, this time to look around and smile at what she saw. The children's park, with its sandbox and slides, swings and monkey bars, was rising from an empty lot.

ACKNOWLEDGMENTS

I have a number of people I'd like to thank, beginning with my old friend, Judie Hanel, who revealed to me many years ago that in her youth she'd given up her son for adoption and had begun to search for him. She found him, and her story and the story of other birth mothers who refused to take no for an answer informed the emotional makeup of this novel.

I also feel a deep debt to the adoptees who were willing to tell me their stories. I admire the courage they've shown in searching for their birth parents. They, too, have refused to take no for an answer.

A book on this subject should not end without acknowledging the incalculable contribution of adoptive parents who did their very best to provide wonderful lives to their children. By emphasizing "The Search," I am by no means minimizing the role of these mothers and fathers. They are honored every day by the lives they did so much to enrich.

I spoke with a number of search angels in researching this novel. Darlene Wilson was marvelous. She spent time with me on the phone and in person, and to her I owe a great thanks. As well, I'd like to thank search angels Donna Wells and Carole Vandenbos for their time.

I read many books in preparing to write *Search Angel*, along with numerous academic papers. In particular, I'd like to acknowledge Nancy Verrier's book, *The Primal Wound*, for helping me to understand many of the emotional challenges faced by adoptees.

Others I want to thank for help along the way include Lucinda Taylor, John Laptad, Chris Van Tilburg, Dave Betz, Tim Burton, Claudia Burton, Gary Young, Peggy Dills Kelter, Rose Marie Kolman-Stich, and Steve Comba.

Many thanks, too, to Leigh Haber for very helpful input in the manuscript's formative stages.

I have a long-standing circle of readers whose encouragement and criticisms have helped me greatly over the years. As I did with my last book, I want to offer a special thanks to Ed Stackler, with whom I shared my earliest thoughts about *Search Angel*, and who read various drafts along the way. His editorial insights proved, once again, invaluable.

Lars Topelmann, Mark Feldstein, Catherine Zangar Arp, Elizabeth Mead, and Steve Comba also read the manuscript at various stages and provided needed insights and encouragement.

I'm fortunate in having a wonderfully energetic and talented agent in Luke Janklow. He and his assistant, Claire Dippel, are a terrific team.

Finally, I want to thank the staff at Hyperion, especially my editor, Peternelle van Arsdale. She has a keen eye and a kind manner. What a persuasive combination. Her suggestions, and those made by Will Schwalbe, helped shape this book. Thank you.